A Sense of Loyalty

By

Craig McCabe

Happy Reading

Craig
x

Craig McCabe has asserted his right under the Copyright, Designs and Patents Act, 1988 to be identified as the author of this work

All the characters in this book have no existence outside the imagination of the author, and have no relation whatsoever to anyone bearing the same name or names. They are not known or unknown individuals to the author, and all the incidents are pure invention.

Acknowledgements: - Thanks to Ralphie Smith, Ryan Wiseman, Joe Hepburn, Van Keith and Davie Kerwin ...for being themselves.

Cover artwork by Frankie Kent.

Prologue

The two barmaids in the Stobswell Bar had been busy serving united supporters since lunchtime. This was a regular occurrence when the team had a home game, as the pub is less than a mile from their stadium. The payphone had been ringing for a little while before one of them picked it up. The caller, who had a vaguely familiar voice, had politely asked for Ginge. At first glance, she could not see him, but she knew that he was on the premises. He had entered not long ago, accompanied by several known troublesome faces and they had all blended into the crowd beyond the bar. The barmaid stood on an empty beer crate and scanned over the faces amid the sea of Black and Tangerine colours. They were hiding in plain sight, like a group inside a group, and were part of a larger crew called The Utility, a title that had been doing the rounds since the mid-eighties when football violence was at its peak. With the exception of the select few, who occasionally joined up with other football firms to take on England, their national team rivals, the Utility had all but died down by the mid-nineties. The revival, some years later, had been down to one man, Rodney McNaughton, mostly known as Ginge, but occasionally as a derogatory term, 'Trotter.'

The barmaid had managed to gain eye contact with one of his crew and mouthed the words 'Ginge' while holding up the receiver. Ginge had purposely sat in the corner of the pub, out of the way of any of the regular punters, but still in full view of both doorways for any unsuspecting visitors. While those around him had been downing the pints and shots as fast as they could, Ginge had been slowly sipping a large coke. He never drank alcohol when there was business to attend to, and today was all business. He had been sitting quietly listening to his crew talk themselves up, he didn't mind all the bullshit, whatever they had to do to hype themselves up was fine by him. He stood up and pushed his long thick red hair back from his face. He could feel the eyes on him as he squeezed through the crowd towards the payphone.

"This is he" Ginge said down the receiver.

"They are on Victoria Road now, full mob, coppers up either side."

Joe the Bull heard the receiver clicking and then a silence on the end of his mobile. Joe is the leader of the young team and has been a trusted acquaintance of Ginge for many years. He is only eighteen years old and is appropriately nicknamed 'The Bull' due to his appearance. He is fifteen stone and most of that weight looks as though it has gathered around his neck and shoulders. He is as ruthless and as hard as they come, and his fighting ability has been on par with any grown man since he was a young teenager.

Ginge smiled at the thought of what lay ahead. He knew the Hibs crew would bring through a large mob. They would not let him down. A quick call to their top boys guaranteed this. Their size of mob did not faze him though, the Utility might have fewer numbers but that suited him, as he did not want anyone that was there to make up the numbers. He knew each face that was with him and they were all game. If he had pulled in a bigger mob, it would end up looking more like a standoff or a running battle, but by keeping it tight, the Hibs crew would think they had the upper hand and come straight for them. Ginge downed the rest of his coke and gave Ritchie, his younger brother, a wink. This was a signal to send a text to Ryan, their eldest brother.

The Wise Man had been sitting in the back of a stolen van with new plates, not far from where the Hibs casuals had first set foot off the train. There had hardly been a word said between the other men in the van for over half an hour. Each one had checked their weapon several times, going over the roles in their heads obsessively. This was the big one. Each of them had done petty crimes in the past but this job had the expectancy of ten years to life, so they were not taking it lightly. They had all spent time with The Wise Man in prison at one time or another and he had chosen each one of them for specific reasons. Neither of them had come from the Dundee area and neither of them knew each other outside of prison, but all were trusted. Just like his father, he could always tell the difference between the rats, the mice and the loyal dogs. The only thing that ever came above the loyal dogs was family. His father, Buster, and his brother Ginge were one hundred percent straight down the line, no question. With Ritchie, it would all depend on what mood he was in, but The Wise Man knew he could keep him in line. His half-brother Brody was still to be tested. If the test never came, that was fine by him.

The text came through 'Ready for kick off.'

Ginge wrapped his scarf around the bottom half of his face and pulled his hood tight over his head so that only his eyes were visible. He pushed open the side door of the pub and his crew followed. He knew the CCTV on the corner of each building were watching his every move, and even with his face covered, the police could still point him out from a distance due to his bouncing walk and swagger. It was only a five-minute walk along Dura Street to the junction with Dens Road where they planned to cut off the Hibs crew's path to the game. On the way, they passed two more pubs that were bursting at the seams with utility. Ginge had planned it out like terrorist cells. They all knew the procedure, if the police closed off one pub, the next one would take the lead. If they had all gathered in the same place, the police could have easily kept them contained until the opposition reached the stadium. On appearance, each pub looked to be full of Scarfer's, the regular supporters. This was another ploy by Ginge so as not to arouse suspicion, as the police are not concerned with genuine football fans. Minutes later as they walked passed the Balmore Bar, the pub emptied and the mob expanded. By the time they reached the last pub in the street, Ferraris, the rest of their crew were waiting outside. This pushed their numbers to almost eighty. They could hear the Hibs crew chanting as they marched up Dens Road towards Tannadice stadium and they could see the blue flashing lights in the distance. Ginge turned to face his crew and absorb the adrenaline that was flowing through each one of them.

"Let's do them" He shouted.

The Utility mob moved forward and spread wide across the road. Joe the Bull joined them with several of his young team and this stretched their mob to almost a hundred. With Ginge at the front, they turned the corner to encounter over a hundred and fifty Hibs casuals and nearly fifty police. Ginge turned to face his own mob with his hands in his pockets. When he pulled them out, he clenched his fists and raised them high above his head to reveal a knuckleduster on each hand. A loud cheer was heard from his mob and Ginge smiled proudly at them from behind his scarf before turning back to face the Hibs crew.

"Come on" He shouted while charging forward with wide eyes and clenched teeth.

The minutes ticked by after the first text had come through and The Wise Man had started to get impatient, but he knew he had to wait, the walk from the pub to the planned meet had been timed to perfection, any hold-ups and the call would have come in. The timer beeped and a slight panic came over the men. It was time. The Wise Man pulled his ski mask down over his face and pumped the sawn-off shotgun. The first man burst open the back door of the van and they all followed him out onto the street. They entered the building society and shouted for everyone to get on the floor. There was a slight hesitation by some customers, which suited The Wise Man as this gave him an excuse to blast the shotgun. The noise was deafening and the hole it left in the ceiling was enough to convince the staff and customers of exactly what size of wound they would receive if they didn't do as they were told. The Wise Man stood by the doorway in silence and let the other men shout the orders, with their various accents from different parts of the country it was highly unlikely that they would be looking for local men. One of the men ordered the manager to open the door to the back room that contained the large money. There was a slight hesitation, but another blast from the shotgun and the door soon opened. It was all over in less than two minutes and the men walked out the door with sacks stuffed full of unmarked, untraceable notes. The Wise Man stood by the back door of the van until all the men had entered.

"Wait here, I'll be ten seconds" He said before taking off across the road.

"Where the fuck are you going? We've got to move."

The Wise Man ran towards the jewellery shop that was parallel with the bank and before he reached it, he blasted the shotgun at the window. It was the one containing the display of Rolex and Cartier watches. He grabbed the whole display and laughed to himself as he ran back to the van. The streets were busy with afternoon shoppers and the traffic was tight but they had planned this well. The van had been fitted with a blue flashing light and as they raced through the streets, the traffic, in both directions, pulled in to the side to let them pass.

There were bodies lying on the road from both mobs including some brave police officers who had attempted to intervene. The other officers had little option but to stand back and wait for the riot squad to arrive due to the fierce battle that was happening before them. As soon as it had kicked off, Ginge had gone out of his way to make sure that one of the officers went down. He knew that as soon as one of their own was in trouble, the call would go through and reinforcements sent from every scheme in the city. He went a bit over the top once the officer hit the deck, but he knew an opportunity like that would not come along too often. Flashing blue lights started appearing from nearly every direction and Ginge knew it was time for his mob to disperse. Both mobs began to scatter and the police officers that had arrived late on the scene started to grab and cuff anyone that was within their reach. Ginge knew he was their main target and with Ritchie by his side, they sprinted off. Two officers were immediately on their tail. Ritchie's breathing was heavy and he was slowing down very quickly. When two of the officers caught up with him, Ginge turned and nutted one of them in the face, knocking him clean out. Ritchie and Ginge were both struggling with the other officer when two more appeared. Ginge stood toe to toe with one of them for a few seconds but the other sneaked behind and placed him in an arm lock. They wrestled to the ground and the two officers were on top of him, when Ginge looked up, he saw Ritchie face down, with his wrists cuffed behind his back. Ginge struggled violently as they tried to put the cuffs on him and this turned into a wild rage. He looked up to see more officers running in their direction and he knew things were about to turn bad. Then, out of nowhere, Joe the Bull appeared and Ginge felt the weight lifted from him. Joe had lived up to his nickname by shoulder charging the two officers and forcing them to fall over like bowling pins. Joe pulled Ginge to his feet and he turned to run at the officer holding Ritchie.

"Come on, we'll have to leave him, or we'll all get jailed" Joe pulled on Ginge's arm and they both started running.

Ginge glanced back to see one of the officers lifting Ritchie to his feet, while the other picked up his mobile that had fallen to the ground during the struggle.

PART 1 - BRODY

Chapter 1

The journey from Edinburgh to Dundee is close to an hour's drive, but for me, it would usually feel a lot longer, this was because I used to hate coming here. I had loved it as a kid though and for many years it still held a certain fondness for me, but that was now long gone. My dislike for the city had started when I was a teenager, as I grew accustomed to my families embarrassing way of life. My three half-brothers, Ryan, Rodney and Ritchie and also my father Buster, are what society would term as 'career criminals' and each one of them has spent time in prison. My father has spent the most time behind bars but my oldest brother Ryan is destined to overtake his record sometime soon. I have distanced myself from them for years, but now, with my own new chosen profession, I am about to embrace it.

Ever since I was a young boy, sitting with my brothers watching reruns of old undercover police shows like Starsky and Hutch or Miami Vice, I wanted to join the police force. I can remember way back when I was only knee high, running around with my toy gun pretending to be Bodie, a character from a T.V. show The Professionals, after miss hearing his name and thinking it was Brody. We would watch films like Dirty Harry and they would always root for the hero cop to blow the bad guys away. This always confused me when he was growing up as they had so much hatred for the police. In fact, they had hatred for any kind of authority. All I ever dreamed about was being a detective, but due to my upbringing, I never dared mention this in front of my family.

I grew up in Edinburgh with my mother after her brief relationship with Buster. His first wife had upped and left him due to his lifestyle of being in and out of prison and not long after I was born, Buster was locked up once again. My mother, having been left with four young boys to bring up on her own, three of them not even hers, she also upped and left, taking me with her. Each time Buster had his release from prison it would not take long until someone else was playing mum to my three older brothers and once things settled with them, my mother would allow me to visit. It was usually every second weekend and some school holidays. I had grown up in two completely different environments, from my quiet neighbourhood in Edinburgh to the rough and ready scheme in Dundee. My mother knew that as I grew up in my father's household the criminal activity and violence would not be far from my surroundings, but she insisted on my visits as she thought it was more important for me to get to know my father and brothers. Her way of thinking was that if she brought me up properly and instilled in me right from wrong, that as I grew older, I would make the correct choices in my life.

With so many things going through my mind, not least of all that I am now an undercover police officer, my journey to Dundee passes quickly. I arrive at my father's house just in time to catch Ginge slamming the door.

"I popped over to see Buster, is he in?"

Ginge does not answer. After fixing his jacket, he pulls his hair to one side to reveal a raging look on his face.

"Are you okay, what's happened?"

"Armed police have surrounded Ryan's house, he's refusing to come out."

"Why, what has he done now?"

"I don't know. Buster called me and said there were coppers blocking his whole street. Come on, you can drive me around there."

"Is Buster already there?"

"No, he's in hiding, he can't get too close, he has a warrant out."

"I see nothing's changed since I've been away"

I can see the anxiety in Ginge's face that he wants me to hurry up. I put the foot down and drive fast through the streets until I see the roadblock at the start of Ryan's street, which forces me to screech to a halt. I am about to manoeuvre into a vacant space when Ginge opens the car door.

"Fucking Pricks" He shouts while bolting out of the car and running up the street.

I watch from the car as he pushes through a group of spectators, most are neighbours from the surrounding area. There is a police tape tied from the railings on one side of the road to the other. As he reaches over and snaps the tape, several officers run towards him and put their hands out to grab him.

"Get to fuck away from me. I want to see my brother."

He pushes them back and more officers approach and stand like a wall in front of him.

"Get to fuck out of my way you bunch of pricks."

I rush out of the car and stand near the edge of the crowd but have stopped short of actually going past the police line. An inspector who looks as though he is in charge of the operation has witnessed the clash with his officers and hurries over to diffuse the situation. If Ryan is watching, this could possibly be enough to set him off and if he does have some sort of firearm in there with him, it will not be a good outcome.

"Rodney, Rodney." The Inspector says walking towards him with his arms outstretched and his palms facing down in a sort of pleading manner. This is probably the first time he has ever called Ginge by his first name and I cringe as it shows on the inspectors face that he is uncomfortable even saying it. I can understand though, it is to get his attention to stop him from kicking off due to the delicate situation. The inspector tells his officers to back off and nods at Ginge to follow him. They take a couple of steps away from the group of angry officers.

"Rodney, look I'll be straight with you. Your brother is about to be arrested on suspicion of armed robbery. We have reason to believe he has firearms in his house. He says he's not, but he's refusing to come out because he thinks they'll take a pot shot at him."

"For fuck sake, do you blame him, you bastards give him nothing but grief, he has his wife and kids in there with him, no fucking wonder he doesn't want to come out."

I knew exactly why Ryan was refusing to come out, I could actually picture him sitting behind his curtains and peeking out with his kids and laughing. He would be milking the situation for every bit of attention it had created.

"Rodney come-on, we need him out of there, you know this could turn bad."

The inspector was looking at him with his fake pleading eyes, knowing that it would not put him up or down if a stray round from one of the sharpshooters' weapons were to find its way to Ryan's head. If another one happened to stray even further and hit Ginge, this would be like icing on a cake. The only thing that would bother the inspector would be the lengthy report he would have to write up afterwards.

"And what if I persuade him to come out and one of those arseholes takes a shot. Then I will have talked my brother into getting himself killed. I don't fucking think so."

"Rodney, come on, see sense."

"I'll tell you what, why don't you come with me and we'll both go and bring him out."

"What do you mean?"

"You know exactly what I mean,"

The inspector hesitates. He knows Ginge is testing him. He turns to his officers and then faces some of the crowd who are in earshot. They are all staring back at him awaiting his reaction.

"Okay, let's do it."

Ginge smiles to himself, turns to me and gives me a sly wink. The inspector picks up the police radio and announces that he is going in and for the sharpshooters to be on standby. As Ginge walks in front of the inspector, I am scanning the different positions where I see the sharpshooters positioned. I feel that Ryan was right to keep himself holed up, if he had walked out of his house and made any sudden movement, it would only take one of those sharpshooters to have a slight twitchy finger and he would have had no chance of surviving. They walk straight up towards his house and when they are within a few meters from his front door, it opens slowly. Ryan appears in the doorway and although he is only slightly taller than Ginge, his presence is much more intimidating.

"Turn around and keep your hands in the air" Shouts the Inspector

Ryan smiles and stands back from the doorway. He puts his hands in the air and shakes his head at all the commotion going on around him. The inspector steps forward and quickly places the handcuffs onto Ryan's wrists. He radios in for the sharpshooters to stand down and then quickly walks Ryan out to a waiting meat wagon. Davie, Ryan's oldest kid, is peering out from behind the living room door. Ginge signals for them to come out and while he walks Nikki, Ryan's wife, and his two kids from the house, a team of officers rush passed them to begin their extensive search for firearms. I am still looking on from the edge of the crowd, rooted to the spot and shaking my head in disbelief at the scene before me. My job has now moved to a completely new level.

Chapter 2

It was only days after completing my extensive training course to become a full-time police officer that my superiors had called me into a meeting. I was confident that I had passed all the tests, academically and physically I knew that I was above average. I never fucked around when I was at school and I left with top grades in every subject. I think my family thought I was going to be a lawyer or a doctor or something, which I felt put more pressure on me in telling them I wanted to be a police officer. In a spur of the moment decision, I signed up for the army. I did my first three years of fighting on the front line and after showing potential as a boxer, I served my last few years training in a gym. In all that time, the urge to join the police was still there.

    I sat in the waiting area outside the offices of the Police Headquarters waiting for them to call my name. I entered the room to smiles and handshakes from two senior detectives from the Lothian Police Force. After congratulating me on my first class result, they then introduced me to The Director of the Scottish Crime and Drug Enforcement Agency. The three of them sat in front of me at a large desk as the Director went on to explain what the agency was about and a little of their recent history. I listened intently and was intrigued as to where this meeting was going until he placed a large folder in front of me. It was two inches thick and I could see that it contained several slimmer folders inside. I looked at the name on the cover of the folder and the smile suddenly dropped from my face. It had 'McNaughton' my father's surname, in bold letters. I glanced up and stern looks had replaced the smiles on my superior's faces. One of them nodded at the folder and gestured for me to pick it up. I was not shocked or surprised, as I knew that the file existed. The large folder contained a file on each member of my family including their prison records and surveillance photos, some of which I was present. I placed the folder back on the desk in front of me and slouched back in my chair. The 'making a good first impression thing' had gone right out of the window. They sat in silence looking at me for a reaction but I had nothing. I had more or less cut that side of my family out of my life. I had grown up with my mother's maiden name Thomson and then changed it to many years ago when she remarried to Buchanan. I had been confident enough throughout the whole entry process that my tracks were covered. I felt defeated. The only thing going through my head at that moment was 'How long had they known? In addition, if they had known since I applied, why did they still let me continue with the training and complete all those tests?

As I take a slow walk back to the car, I try to work out how to explain this to my bosses, they will no doubt know of this situation before I contact them. Then Ginge catches up with me.

"So where will I drop you off?"

"What do you mean; I thought you had come through to see Buster?"

"Yeah I did but I thought you said he was in hiding because he had a warrant out?"

Ginge smiles "He is, but he hasn't exactly left the country"

"So what's he done this time?"

"He smashed somebody last week, apparently."

This news does not faze me as I am well used to my father having a warrant out for something or other. I am more concerned that my bosses had failed to mention it. It is my first day on the job and of the two main targets that I am investigating; one of them is in custody for armed robbery and the other is in hiding due to having a warrant out.

"Why is he in hiding?"

"What? He was a beast; Buster found out he had been touching up some young girl. Well, you know what Busters like, instead of setting the beast up to get him on his own, he came across him in a local pub and thought nothing of giving him a beating in front of everyone in the place. The guys on a life support machine so they want him for attempted murder."

"Is that the third time?"

"Fourth. He has had a not proven on two of them and the third was reduced to serious assault."

Oh, I feel so proud.

"I take it he's not going to walk away from this one?"

"You would think."

"What do you mean?"

"Well, it was a pub full of people but only one witness..."

What he really means is that there was only one person who was brave or stupid enough to give evidence.

"It's was the victims son" He adds.

"So I guess he's pretty much fucked then?"

"Well we'll see, you know our line of work Brody, nobody grasses, no matter what."

Oh, I know the scenario all too well. How could I forget one of the many lines drilled into me from a very young age? The only difference now is that I am not in their line of work and I certainly do not intend to be anytime soon.

"Buster has the address, I'm going to have a word with the son and ask him to drop the charges."

I hate to think of the outcome if the 'have a word' does not work.

We arrive outside the Claverhouse Pub and the sight of the place immediately brings back memories of my childhood. Apart from prison, this was my father's second home. I grew up visiting this place regularly and for as much as my father tried to guard me against his criminal activities, what I did not pick up at home I learned in here. It was and still is a dark violent pub and every face in it is a hardened criminal, even the women in here are hard, some even harder than the men are, and they look it. There has rarely been a criminal activity not been planned or discussed in this pub. Ginge opens the door and as forever showing his manners, he holds it back to allow me to walk in first. Nothing has changed; it is the same hard-worn faces staring back at me. If anything the smell of the place has gotten worse, but like most pubs in Scotland the smell has always been there, disguised over the years by stale smoke. The introduction of the governments smoking ban took care of that. Now the smell of piss from both the men and women's toilets floats passed the bar towards the door each time it opens. The snide looks I encounter as I step forward soon change to a glint of smiles when Ginge appears behind me. Ginge guides me through to the back of the pub, where behind a partition wall sits my father Davie, also known as Buster, a nickname he acquired since before I was born. I pop my head around the partition wall to see Buster sitting with a mobile phone stuck to his ear in 'mid-rant' at someone. He spots me and ditches the phone on the table, no 'goodbye' or 'see you later' just throws the phone and stands up to greet me. I have not seen him in over two years and it shows as he reaches out with one of his massive arms and grabs me to pull me close in a bear hug.

"Soldier boy, how's it going?"

"Fine, how are you? I take it I've caught you at a bad time."

"Don't be stupid." He shakes his head then looks over at the barman and gives him a nod.

"A top up and a couple of pints for my boys"

I thought it was a bit early in the day to be drinking especially as I have the car outside, I am about to refuse but as I have not seen my father in a long time, I decide not to be impolite and just go with the flow.

"Did you get that address for me?" Ginge asks.

Buster stares at him and then at me.

"It's cool. I filled him in on what happened" Ginge says, before giving him a sly wink.

"He's out of the coma. It's now dropped to serious assault" Buster says before pulling out a folded piece of paper and handing it to Ginge, who slips it into his pocket without even reading it.

"So what brings you up here, I thought you'd had enough of the jungle?"

"I'm struggling to get a job."

"How long have you been out?"

"A few months"

"A few months and you are only coming to see me now."

"Well I wanted to get settled and that, I thought with my record in the army I would've found work easily. I've had a few odd jobs, nothing great, I was doing the doors for a bit but that wasn't really my thing."

"Are you still boxing?"

"Yeah I have a fight next week, it's in Edinburgh. I could get you tickets if you want to come and watch."

"Oh I don't know son, you know how it is."

I shake my head. "Buster, you're in your sixties now, you can't keep living like this" I blurt out in a rare moment of genuine concern.

He smiles back at me. "I hope you're not going to start waving your finger at me."

"He's right though Buster, you'd better watch out, some of these young wide fuckers can be right sneaky little bastards."

"Like you, you mean?"

"That's my point. You might come across somebody just like me."

"Even if you ever manage to dig up all your weapons, you would still need half your Utility to match me." Buster winks. "This brother of yours had a good friend of his bury some weapons for him, but what happens, the fucking cunt dies of a heart attack and never bothered to tell him where he'd buried them."

"I know where he's buried them. I just don't know the exact spot" Ginge smirks

Buster turns and looks at me. "Seriously son, drive up Templeton Woods one night and you'll see Ginger here and his sidekick Joe the Bull with a halogen lamp, a metal detector and a shovel. The number of hours these two idiots spends digging they'd be easier off buying new ones."

I am laughing along with them but am waiting for the wink because I cannot tell if this is an on-going piss take.

"So come on then, what happened with Ryan?"

"Nothing really, it was the usual coppers heavy handed scenario. Would you believe it? They actually had fucking sharp-shooters on the roof."

Buster laughs. "What the fuck did they think he was going to do? Come out swinging like something out of the Wild West?"

"Well knowing Ryan, if he did have a shooter on him the thought would probably cross his mind."

They both laugh and I find myself laughing along with them but taken back at their attitude. It was just over an hour ago that Ryan had several armed police pointing guns at his house waiting for a command to take him out, and here is his father and brother making jokes about it.

"So what is he actually being charged with?"

"Armed robbery, I told him last week they were coming for him."

"How did you know?"

"Well I got pulled the other week about the Hibs game from a few months ago when Ritchie got arrested, so I kind of knew they were onto something. They are trying to fit him up with some conspiracy charge; they are saying that the battle with the Hibs that day was set up as a diversion for an armed robbery. This is all from a text message on his phone that he sent minutes before the robbery happened. They tried to nail it on me, they grilled me about knowing the Hibs boys and arranging the whole meet up but they have fuck all. They have CCTV of somebody with my description walking out of the Stoby bar and heading towards the meet with the Hibs. My face is covered; my phones are clean, so fuck them. There's apparently a witness saying she recognised Ryan either coming out of or going into the getaway van, which is bizarre because they all had balaclavas on."

"So what'll happen now?"

"Well, he'll definitely be remanded, possibly until it goes to trial if it ever reaches that."

"Exactly" Buster adds.

"So three months after an armed robbery they charge someone and all the evidence they have is a text message?" I put it across as though it sounds far-fetched, but I have read the file and including a few other bits and pieces, that really is all the evidence they have. I could sit here and ask them if the Hibs meet really had anything to do with it, and there is a possibility that they would blatantly tell me, but I think it probably best if I pick my moment to question these things.

"Look you know how it is Brody, it's like with Buster here, they can't get anything on him so the judge looks at his record and on the recommendations of the coppers, and he is remanded. It doesn't matter if the charge is murder or pissing against a wall."

"It's political" Buster adds.

"In their mind, it's their only way of keeping people like us off the street. You know, dangerous people like us" He grins.

Although I sit and nod in agreement, to what they are saying, I know fine well how the system works and if all it takes is a nod to a judge by a top cop to deny a person of their criminal level to get bail, then that is fine by me. After another couple of drinks, which I try unsuccessfully to refuse, there is more banter and sly comments with added winks between Ginge and Buster, and for as much as I try to keep up; most of it goes above my head. We both say our goodbyes to Buster and walk off leaving him to blend into the back of the pub as we had found him.

Chapter 3

I am not much of a drinker so when I step out of the pub into the fresh air I feel light headed due to the many beers that I have consumed. I get into the car but I know I should not be driving. Ginge sits down next to me and pulls out the piece of paper that Buster had given him. He does not read it out but he tells me to drive towards the Hilltown.

"Which part of the Hilltown?"

"Well it's nearer Dens and Tannadice but the cunts from the Hilltown. Do you know Sandeman Street?"

"Yeah"

"Well, that's where we're heading."

"I thought you were banned from the surrounding streets of both stadiums?"

"Yeah, on match day" Ginge smirks.

"Oh yeah" I mumble to myself as I drive on feeling slightly stupid.

I reach the start of Sandeman Street.

"Right, go slow so that I can see the numbers."

I drive slowly and out of the corner of my eye, I can see Ginge pulling out one of his knuckle-dusters and slide it over his fingers. I start to feel anxious as Ginge begins counting down aloud the numbers on the tenement doors. Less than a minute passes when Ginge shouts. "Pull over, quick. That's him there."

I slam on the brakes and stop the car in the middle of the road.

"Wait here," Ginge shouts as he opens the door and walks fast towards three people that have stepped out of a tenement block doorway. As Ginge reaches them, he pulls a cosh from the sleeve of his jacket and smashes one of the people over the head with it. The person goes down and Ginge hovers over the top of him and continually punches him in the face with the knuckle-duster. As the other two people try to pull him off and start laying into him, I am out of the car and running towards them. Ginge looks up and smiles as they turn their attention to me. I now find myself involved in a street battle. One of them catches me with a punch to the side of the head and a rage takes over as I let loose with punches and kicks knocking both of them clean out. I turn to Ginge who is standing back with his face and jacket sprayed with spots of blood.

"Get in the fucking car" I shout at him.

Ginge casually walks over to the car as I stand by the driver's door looking at the three bodies lying on the road. I want to rush back and put them in the recovery position or at the very least, check if they are still breathing. Ginge is in the passenger seat and I hear him shouting at me to drive. I can see a few people at their windows watching what is going on and I have no doubt the police will be on their way. I put my foot down and we speed off down the street. I stop back at Buster's house; the same place where I arrived this morning full of high hopes for my new job, things could not have gone any worse for my first day.

"Wait here" Ginge shouts as he gets out of the car and slams the door. He is in and out of the house in under a minute with a bag over his shoulder.

"You've not locked the door."

"I never lock it. It saves me from buying a new one when the coppers come with their warrant. If it's not locked they won't have to smash it down."

"Where am I going now?"

"Just drive, I'll show you."

"What's in the bag?"

"Clothes, I'll have to bin the ones I'm wearing, I suggest you do the same."

I let out a sigh. "I can't believe you've got me into this."

"Wait a fucking minute, I told you to wait in the car. I never said anything about you getting out and jumping about like fucking Van Damme, did I?"

"Oh right, because I'm just going to sit in the car and watch three guys kick the shit out of you."

"They couldn't fight sleep. I would've got up and smashed both of them. But it was good to see that you had my back though" Ginge smiles but I do not have the same enthusiasm.

I drive along the street and after a few lefts and rights, Ginge tells me to pull over.

"This is me here. Go and get yourself cleaned up as they'll come for you."

"Who will? Those guys"

"No, the coppers"

"Oh right."

"They'll trace your car and if they're not at your door by tonight, then expect the early morning knock, they're good at that."

My first thought is my bosses. How the fuck do I explain this to them? Apart from the fact the undercover operation could be at risk, my whole integrity is now in question.

"By the way, I know it's not really your thing but with Ryan possibly gone for the next few months I could do with some help."

"What do mean? Are you offering me a job?"

Is he actually serious? The fucking lunatic

"Yeah, sort of, It's mostly driving and looking tough and I think you've proved that you can handle yourself" Ginge smirks.

"I'll have a think about it."

Ginge shuts the car door and I drive off.

The Scottish Crime and Drug Enforcement Agency (SCDEA) is a special police force in Scotland. It is solely responsible for the disruption and dismantling of any seriously organised crime groups. The Director of the agency is responsible to Scottish Ministers and the Scottish Parliament for financial and administrative matters. The agency also works alongside other Scottish police forces and is part of The Scottish Organised Crime Task Force. They share some of these functions with the UK National Serious Organised Crime Agency. During my initial meeting with the Director of the agency, he informed me that they had watched me closely from the minute my application was processed for joining the police, and while they let me continue with the training, they were digging into my background. Once they were convinced that I was genuine and my initial training was completed, they decided to pull me in. On my application, I had explained that my main goal in the Police was to become a Detective, which in any department of the force; you have to complete a minimum of two years uniform service before you can even apply to be a Detective. They laid out an offer for me to join their small team and go undercover in an operation to gain Buster and Ryan's contacts. If I accepted their offer, I would be fast-tracked to a

Detective Constable and once the operation was completed, a transfer to a department of my choosing. Detective Inspector Whyte and Detective Sergeant Drummond would become my immediate bosses. They, along with the Director and the two other senior detectives from Lothian police force were the only people that knew I was undercover and everything from then on, was to go through them. I accepted their offer without a second thought and they wasted no time in explaining the situation of my family.

My father, although imprisoned many times for assault and serious assault, had been under surveillance for a series of other crimes but they could never gather enough evidence to proceed with an arrest. It was not until 'The Task Force' was formed in 2006 that he, along with my brother Ryan, had come to their attention for a long list of crimes including money laundering, extortion, drugs, dealing in counterfeit money and also illegal arms. I disliked Drummond from that first meeting, his attitude towards me was disrespectful considering the position I was putting myself in. Whyte was more suave and I could tell from that first meeting that he was the more diplomatic of the two

"Through our intelligence, we know your family are one of the main suppliers of illegal drugs in Dundee. All we are asking of you is to go undercover and find out their contacts."

I was about to speak when Drummond cut me off.

"We are not meaning for you to get all zealous and arrest them...well not yet anyway." He smiled but it was one of those fake smiles. He appeared to be the type who had intentionally perfected this to come across as a sneer.

"All we are asking you to do at this moment is gather information. We need the name or names of their suppliers, where and when or even how they contact them, how they bring it in, their delivery route, their drop-offs and if possible, each other drop off, by this, we mean their dealer's dealers. They will have certain drop-offs for their larger amounts, this will be cut into several smaller amounts and given to the smaller dealers, and we need the names of them all."

My head was starting to spin as they talked like a tag team.

"Another thing" Drummond added. "The Donaldson's, you've no doubt heard of them?"

I nodded "Of course. There have about fifty relatives and they all swagger about thinking they are gangsters."

"Gangsters, I've yet to ever hear of a gangster that does time for housebreaking or shoplifting. Anyway, the Donaldson's are also heavily involved in the drugs trade, and through our intelligence and surveillance, we have managed to intercept many of their deals. We also know that their main supplier is a hard-core firm from Glasgow"

"Intelligence and surveillance, you mean the hard-core firm from Glasgow is not as tight as they would like as they clearly have a grass."

"The Glasgow firm have a grass? Brody, we are talking about the Donaldson's here. The person who started the old saying 'no honour among thieves' probably said it with them in mind...oh and do not think for one minute the McNaughton's are immune from grasses."

Drummond gave White a look and he cut in and took over. "Brody we know your families rivalry with the Donaldson's has gone back for many years, but one of our problems is that we don't know why the Glasgow firm won't back them up when it comes to your family."

"Could it not be that my family are also involved with the Glasgow firm?"

"It's possible, but we have no record of any contact between them. We think it is because your family are connected with a bigger firm."

"Basically, this is where you come in. This will be your main objective, to observe and obtain information." Whyte stressed.

As soon as I arrive back home in Edinburgh I leave a message for Whyte to get in touch immediately, I am hoping to get my side of the story over before they hear it from some other source. He does not get back to me straight away and the next few days are stressful as I am constantly on edge waiting for the knock on the door from Tayside Police, but it does not come. The inevitable phone call from my bosses, however, does come; and by the time my meeting with them comes around, I am ready for the outcome of looking for a new career.

"Well you were a busy lad on your first day at work weren't you?" Drummond says smugly.

I go to speak and plead my case but Drummond cuts me off with a quick wave of the hand.

"Before you say anything, I'd just like to let you know, we've had word that your brother Ryan is going to be fully committed until he goes to trial, so your little street battle is probably going to work in your favour."

I look at them confused.

"Well, that is unless you're not keen on spending a little time behind bars."

"What do you mean?" I am still confused.

Drummond and Whyte both look at each other and realise that I am obviously not catching on to their train of thought.

"Brody, why don't you explain what happened?" Whyte says.

"Well when I arrived in Dundee, I had been informed that my father had beaten up some guy that had been touching up some little girl and the guy's son was a witness. Later that day I was giving Ginge...sorry, I mean Rodney a lift and he got out of the car to talk to..."

"Talk to!" Drummond does his typical sneer and raises his eyebrows.

"...before I knew it he was on top of one guy and the other two were attacking him. I got out of the car and they started on me."

"Brody I think you better take a seat" Whyte says.

"You were set up to get involved in that assault" Drummond says.

"How do you work that out?"

"Brody they were testing you," Whyte says. "The guy that Buster attacked never touched up any little girl, he had run up some debts with Ryan, your father ran into him and took it upon himself to pull him up about it, he got lippy so Buster put him in a coma."

"That's how your family works" Drummond adds.

"I lived with them. I know how my family works." I snap.

"He touched up some little girl. What a load of crap" He sneers at me.

I stand up and force my seat back.

"Brody calm down."

"Calm down! He's talking to me like I'm the criminal."

"Hey, you better get used to it because from now on that's the way everyone is going to treat you."

Whyte gives him a look and he backs off. "Look, Brody, I know this is your family but just remember what you're getting involved with. You have read the files. You know exactly the type of people you are dealing with."

I take a deep breath and sit back down in the chair. Whyte goes on to explain to me that with Ryan remanded and charges on me now pending, it is the perfect opportunity for me to get close and get him talking.

"Is this a wind-up? What am I supposed to do? Plead guilty to assault and hope that I end up in a cell alongside him?"

"Assault, oh it's a bit more serious than that. You are about to be charged with serious assault and tampering with a witness. We put them on hold until we spoke to you. Tampering with a witness is a pretty heavy charge, heavy enough where we can make sure that you are remanded."

"For how long"

"As long as takes, three months tops."

"What about Rodney?"

"Oh, what a coincidence" Drummond pipes up. "Not one witness could identify 'The Ginge'"

"All they got was a license plate, your license plate. If you are not up for doing a little time, I would not worry about the charges, we will make sure one of the letters on your license plate changes in the witness statement and you can get yourself an alibi. That will cover you for any suspicion that arises in the future. Seriously though, I think this is a great opportunity for you."

I lean forward in the seat and put my hand over my mouth in a thinking motion. Both Drummond and Whyte look at me intently as they wait for a reply.

"What about Ginge? He offered me a job the other day."

"Doing what?"

"Working for him, driving and stuff, he's obviously taking over from Ryan while he's away. Would that not be a better lead to follow than going to prison?"

Drummond shakes his head. "We've told you, Ginge is not our concern, he's just a Saturday afternoon part-time thug. We want Buster, The Wise Man, and all their contacts."

"I really don't know if I can do this."

"Brody we read your file, you signed up in the possibility of becoming a detective. You have stated that this is all you ever wanted to be. From our first meeting, we told you that to do the job you will need to make sacrifices. I know that we have thrown you in at the deep end with it being your family, but this is undercover, sometimes undercover means going far beyond your comfort zone. You should know all about that, you were in the army for over five years."

"How am I going to explain this to my girlfriend? I haven't even told her about my job never mind going to prison." I say aloud regrettably.

"Sacrifices" Whyte repeats.

I nod at them.

"So you'll do it?"

I pause for a few seconds and nod again.

"Yeah, I'll do it." I hear myself say. I must be out of my fucking mind.

"Remember, we can pull you out anytime you like," Drummond says, obviously trying to sound reassuring.

"So what happens now?"

"Just go about your business and let things run their course over the next couple of days. We'll be watching closely to make sure everything goes to plan."

"The next couple of days, I thought this would take at least a couple of weeks. I have a fight next week."

Both Drummond and Whyte shake their heads at me.

"Have you any questions or queries before we put this into operation?"

"Yeah, what happens if this proceeds to trial, like months down the line?"

"It won't reach that, I've already told you we can get the statements changed when the time comes."

"Yeah, and if we run into a problem I'm sure your family will knock on a few doors and get the witnesses sorted," Drummond adds with a smirk.

This must be his attempt at humour...Arsehole.

Chapter 4

During the drive home, I tried to sort out in my head all that had just happened and the one major thought I kept coming back to was Leanna, my girlfriend. I had not even told her about my job, she knew that I had applied to join the force and attended the training program, but with everything happening so fast, I had never been in the correct frame of mind to tell her. She knew of my 'Dundee' side of my family but I had not told her much about them. So, along with explaining that my new job was to investigate them because they are all drug dealing thugs, I also had to explain that I was about to do time behind bars for assault.

I arranged to meet her a few hours later and this had given me time to think about my situation. I went over it in my head so many times that I had decided that the best thing was to keep the set-up going for the time being. The less she knew about me being undercover the safer it would be for both of us. We went out for a meal and my plan was to tell her about the assault while in the restaurant whereas there would not be a scene and she would have calmed down by the time we left. Well, that was my plan, but although the whole time it was on my mind to tell her, I just could not find the moment.

Arriving back at her parent's place, I wait until we are relaxed and comfortable, then I casually let it slip. Attempting to mention that the police are looking to speak to me, due to a fight that I was involved in sound random, is not as easy as I thought it would be.

"What was it about?" She says, sitting up and looking very grim.

"They were attacking my brother Ginge, I mean Rodney. I went to help him and they turned on me."

"But that's self-defence."

"There's a bit more to it than that honey."

"What do you mean?"

"Well, the guy that Rodney was fighting with was a witness against my father."

"What's that got to do with you?"

"It kind of makes things a lot more serious."

I can tell by her expression that she working herself up so I try to play things down.

"Look it might not come to anything but I just thought I'd let you know in case the police come crashing through the door looking for me." I attempt a smile but she is far from smiling.

"Wait a minute, so your brother assaulted some guy that is a witness against your father? And what is he a witness too, exactly?" She snaps.

"Assault"

"And who did your father assault?"

"Well, the guy that Rodney was fighting with, it was his father."

She stands up and when I look at her she has her hands on her hips with a fierce expression. In the hope of justifying the assault, I keep with the original story and not the updated version of the person running up debts.

"He was a beast. He had been interfering with some young girl."

Leanna puts her hand to her mouth. "This makes me feel sick. Has the guy that your father beat up been charged?"

"I don't know."

"I can't believe you've got yourself involved in this? ...I will tell you what though, that application that you have put into the police, and all the training you have done, it is all fucked. There is no way they're going to let you join now."

"Leanna, it's not like that."

"Look I think you'd best just go."

"What?"

"I want you to go."

"You're throwing me out?"

"Yes. I cannot believe how stupid you are. Is this what the meal was all about tonight? To soften me up before you told me that you have just fucked your whole life up."

"I've hardly fucked my whole life up?"

"Are you really that stupid? If you have an assault charge you have not only fucked it up with the police, you will be lucky to get any job. Nobody's going to employ you with a criminal record."

I want to reply but I find myself standing up and walking to the door. I am desperate to tell her the truth, but the whole time the word

'Sacrifices' keep going through my head. I bite my tongue and close the door behind me.

It is another few days before I receive the knock on the door. They are officers from Tayside and I assume that the heavy police presence is due to me being a sibling of the McNaughton's. Their excessive show of force is not needed though as I go willingly. During the journey back to Dundee, the detectives accompanying me comment on my lack of abuse directed at them. I can only imagine what it must be like when they arrest someone like my father. I prepare myself for their questions but with the advice from my solicitor, I make a 'no comment' remark throughout the interview. They formally charge me with intimidating and seriously assaulting a witness, and then transferred to the cells to appear in court the next morning. Throughout most of the night, as I lie back in the cell my thoughts are filled with the events of the last week. Due to me already knowing the outcome of the morning's court appearance I begin to think over different scenarios that I could possibly encounter in prison and how I am going to react to them. My whole objective is Ryan; I have to do whatever is possible to get him talking. Just by being there behind bars with him is probably enough to gain his trust, as me being a cop is the last thing he would expect, but to get him to open up and tell me what I need to know is a totally different matter.

The following day goes by very slowly for me. Having not slept much the previous night, The Turnkey wakens me with my breakfast, a dry bacon roll and a weak, sugarless mug of tea. I hear shouting between the cells all morning and the conversations are mind numbing. If it is not would-be hard cases, taking about which scheme they are from and how long their record is, it is junkies thinking they are talking in code about who is selling the best gear. From the time they call up my name to appear in the dock, to hear the judge refuse bail, is all a blur to me. Ginge was at the back of the court along with Ritchie and they both looked shocked. It happened so fast that I was back in my cell before I knew what was going on. I felt sorry for my solicitor who turned up at my cell looking down heartened and beaten, he could not understand why the judge would not even listen to his argument for his request for my bail. I, on the other hand, knew exactly why.

"You're not being processed to Perth until late this afternoon. Your brother is outside asking to see you but the Police are having none of it."

I shrug and make a face as though I really did not expect anything less.

"Brody, that judge wouldn't even listen to me, I think someone has seriously got it in for you."

"It's alright, I can handle it."

"Brody don't worry I'll appeal this, you're a first offender and let's face it, it's not as if you're up for murder. They have had it in for your family for a long time."

Late in the afternoon, as we approach the prison I glance up through the tiny window of the Reliance van and I catch sight of the razor wire topped walls and it makes me feel a little anxious. This is not a fearful anxiety; it is more like the anticipation of what lays ahead for me. Once the van passes the large gates, I and two other prisoners are marched out and given the rigmarole of being strip searched, allocated our prison numbers and read the riot act. The screws leave me standing while the other two prisoners are marched away to their allocated hall. The governor then appears in front of me with an open file in his hand.

"Buchanan" He says looking down at the file. "Do you think I don't know you're a McNaughton?"

I know not to answer.

"If you think you're going into 'B' Hall beside that fucking lunatic brother of yours then you can forget it. Put him in 'A' Hall" He nods to one of the screws.

"Are you sure that's a good idea Governor?" The screw asks.

The Governor gives him a serious stare. "He'll be transferred to 'B' Hall once that brother of his stops his shit and toes the fucking line. Wise Man, he won't be so fucking wise when I send him to Carstairs." He looks at me threateningly, before tucking his file under his arm and marching off.

Ryan's nickname 'The Wise Man' had come about many years ago. It was a sarcastic term that my father used for him due to the spontaneous acts that would result in him ending up in prison. Although technically it is a nickname, I have never actually heard many people call him by this term in person, it was used more to describe him in his absence.

The screw orders me to follow him and with another tight behind me I am walked through to 'A' Hall. This is seriously not going to plan. They introduce me to my cellmate, a tall, slim-build lad with very bad skin. He stands up from his bed and comes up close to me; it is hard to tell if he is squaring up to me or if personal space in prison is non-existent. He introduces himself as Stanley and I stand firm while he stares at me up and down with his sunken eyes before turning and sitting back on his bed and staring at the wall. My anxiety has disappeared fast and reality is beginning to set in. Being here is pointless; this whole fucking set up is pointless. It was set up for me to get close to Ryan and it does not look as though this is going to happen anytime soon. I need to get to a phone, Whyte or Drummond had better get this sorted out as soon as possible.

Chapter 5

My first night is more of a wakeup call to my situation than I could ever imagine. Stanley makes no effort to be sociable and stares into space as though he is stoned, which suits me fine. As I lie back on my bed and stare at the close walls and ceiling I start to have negative thought of being stuck in here permanently, and makes me feel like I am about to have a panic attack. I have never had one before but I am struggling to breath and my chest feels very tight. Luckily, it passes quickly and I accept there is nothing I can do about the situation tonight. The thoughts gradually fade out of my mind and I eventually drift off to sleep.

In Perth Prison, some prisoners have a pass, which means they have permission to keep their cell door open during the day while others, are on lock up 24/7. The prisoners with a pass do not have anywhere to go outside of their cell, but it does give them that small piece of liberty. At meal times, there is a rotation for a number of cells to go to the hot plate at the opposite side of the hall to pick up their meals. It is my first morning as a prisoner, and as I return to my cell after picking up my breakfast from the hot plate, Stanley is already there. He has his back to me and when I enter, a strange overpowering smell immediately gets my attention. I move in closer to see him inhaling fumes from a small piece of foil. I feel the rage come over me and knock it out of his hand. He makes some sort of effort to hit me but I grab him by the throat and watch as his eyes go wide scanning the floor to see where his drugs went. I pin him back against the wall and feel tempted to hit him but hold back as I know he is just some wasted junkie.

"Look I don't care what you do outside this cell but you're not doing that shit in here. You got that?"

I watch as his eyes fill up with anger so I squeeze my fingers tighter around his throat. He put his hands up in a pleading motion and I release my grip slightly.

"I said have you got that?"

He makes an attempt at a nod. I release my hand and watch him dive to the floor and salvage the leftovers on the foil. He stands up and grunts before walking out the door. I sit down on my bed and begin eating my breakfast, moments later he returns with a small, heavyset man in his late forties. I can tell by his expression that he is not about to shake my hand and welcome me. It is not until I stand up to face him that I notice another two inmates at either side of the door. I know what is coming so I keep a space between us, ready for the attack.

"I hear you have a problem with my cousin?"

I shrug. It is not in me to back down no matter what the odds are but I am certainly not about to act the tough guy either because I know I could be out of my depth here.

"Oh, so you think you're a wide-boy yeah? Well, let us get this straight, he is going to do whatever he likes in this cell, whenever he likes. Is that clear?"

Still not saying a word, I keep his stare.

"Listen, you look like an intelligent sort of fella, well obviously you're not that intelligent as you've ended up in this shit hole, but I hope you're intelligent enough to understand so that I don't have to spell things out for you."

He sneers at me before stepping back from the doorway. He then turns to his mates outside and nods for them to walk on. I know this is not the end of it, not by a mile. Stanley sits on his bed and I walk to the cell doorway to see the three of them strut slowly to another cell.

Over the next couple of days, I keep myself to myself and try to avoid any contact with my Stanley, although, this is proving to be extremely difficult in such an enclosed space. I am also trying to keep my anger under control as he continues to goad me by burning his heroin in front of me in the cell. I have also been informed, in the passing, by another inmate that my cellmates name is not actually Stanley, it is a nickname given to him due to his weapon of choice on the outside. His relation with who had words with me is also an acquaintance of the Donaldson crew. I remember the name when I was growing up but I never thought that they were much of a threat. Their reputation never really took off until they latched onto the Glasgow firm. When I heard this information, I realized why the screw questioned the Governor about putting me in the same hall as them when I arrived. I am not sure if the other inmates know I am a McNaughton but judging by the way gossip spreads through the place, I am sure it will not be long until they find out. I have used every opportunity to contact Whyte or Drummond but each time I call, they explain that they are working on it.

    It is my Forth day inside and I feel the anxiety building up inside of me. I receive another pass for the phone and try calling again but no answer. I return to my cell to see an agitated Stanley throwing things about while punching walls and kicking the beds.

"What the fuck is going on?"

"You stole it, did you?" He says in my face squaring up to me.

"What are you talking about? I haven't stolen anything."

"It was there this morning and you were the last person in the cell."

I feel a little spit landing on my face as he speaks.

"I haven't stolen anything and you had better get to fuck out of my face."

"And what the fuck are you going to do about it?" He spits at me again.

I bring my head back slightly and bring it forward fast onto the bridge of his nose. He crumbles to the floor and puts his hands over his face.

"You wanker, you wait till my cousin gets a hold of you."

Hearing this riles me and I step forward and smash my fist into his face several times. When I see the blood spray from his nose, I stop and drag him out of the cell.

"Go and get your fucking cousin" I demand.

I stand just inside the doorway of the cell, my adrenaline pumping. I watch as he crawls away out of sight. I know what is coming but at this precise moment, I could not give a shit. I only have time to catch my breath when the party of three arrives. I square up to them in the doorway. To them, it looks as though I am ready to stand my ground with all three of them, but in my mind, this is only so that they cannot all get into the cell at once. The cousin pulls out a makeshift blade.

"I fucking warned you" He says through gritted teeth.

My eyes go from the blade to his eyes continuously. He keeps it held tight by his waist but for me to get it from him I need to entice him to come at me. There are a few seconds of a standoff as each of us tries to lure each other to take the decisive step forward. His two minions are on either side of him are also inching forward. I know they will eventually work their way into the cell and if one of them gets to the side of me, or worse, in behind me, I am finished. I suddenly leap slightly and reach over with a punch and it comes downwards catching Donaldson on the side of the face. He swings the blade and I feel it graze my arm. They inch forward once more and I fake another leap which makes him swing the blade upward, I quickly slam my rear leg forward catching him in the stomach, this pushes them all backwards further from the cell door and I can see in his eyes that he is about to go for it. He lunges forward with the blade and I throw out both my hands grabbing his wrist, by using his momentum I pull him further forward into the cell and down to the floor. I stamp on his hand releasing his grip on the blade and I quickly kick it under a bed. His two sidekicks use the chance and push their way into the cell and I know that in such a confined space I would struggle to land a decent kick or punch so I think fast and give the one closest to me a hard poke in the eye. He makes a squeal and goes down with both hands covering his face. Donaldson is in the process of getting up off the floor and is near my waist level when I grab his head and smash it against the wall. As I turn my head his other sidekick catches me with a punch, we trade a few blows before ending up in a wrestle and fall onto the bed. I manage to get on top of him and with all the force I have I smash my forehead into the side of his face. His head goes back slightly, I grab his t-shirt with both hands, and sink my forehead into his face repeatedly until the screws come in team handed, dragging me off. With my arms pinned behind my back, the screws force me to walk through a long empty corridor and they place me in an isolation cell they call the Digger. With my adrenaline still pumping, I continually bang on the cell door and plead my innocence that I was the one who was attacked. Once I have calmed down the prison doctor arrives accompanied by several screws, as he examines me I start up again, about why I am in here as none of it was my fault. The screws stand stone-faced and do not even look me in the eye when I speak to them. When the doctor realises that none of the blood on my clothes is actually mine he steps out of the cell and the door and slam it shut. A few hours later I am informed by a screw through the hatch on the door that I won't be going back in 'A' hall and I will be transferred as soon as an appropriate cell becomes available.

  The Digger is a lonely place, the first couple of days for me do not feel that bad as I am just glad to be away from the tension and intimidation, but having no communication with anyone takes its toll. I constantly harass the screws for a phone call or to see my solicitor and each time they ignore me. It must be hard for any prisoner in the Digger, but for me, knowing I do not even have to be in prison, is a real struggle. By the end of the week I am very close to revealing my identity, then out of the blue my cell door slams open and I am told to get cleaned up as the Governor wants to see me.

"Well, it certainly didn't take long for you to make your mark" He says looking me up and down.

The whole time that the governor is talking all can think about is that as soon as they allow me my phone call I will be informing Whyte and Drummond that I want out of here.

"I had your brother in here earlier. I don't know what kind of statement he's trying to make by refusing to wear clothes but it certainly isn't working."

This comment has caught me off guard and I look up at the Governor confused.

"Oh don't you know that your brother walks around my prison naked?"

I am starting to think where this conversation is going as the Governor is pacing about in front of me as though he is thinking of what to say next.

"It looks as though due to the 'friends' that you made in 'A' hall you have now put me a position as you are obviously a risk and I can't put you back in there."

Friends, I am guessing that it is sarcasm day for the Governor.

"You are about to be put in 'B' hall but I want you to understand, if there is the slightest bit of trouble you will be transferred to Saughton, or better still, it will give me a good enough reason to transfer that brother of yours."

The governor dismisses me and informs the screws to take me to 'B' hall. There is a screw at either side of me and as they open the main door of the hall, they enter first leaving me standing. My view out in front is blocked and I am sure I can see a slight smirk on one of the screws faces as he lets me pass him so that the door behind me can be locked. When the other screw moves to the side, I can now see the reason for the smirk.

I had grown up hearing stories of Ryan's aggressive and violent attitude but I had never once seen that side of him. I had thought that of all the places I would witness his tough bravado; it would be in prison, but no. Standing before me was my eldest brother; over six foot, sixteen stone, a reputation that nobody in their right mind would want to fuck with and here he was, naked and leaning against a wall with his legs crossed and his dick and balls tucked underneath him. He is pouting his lips and winking as he says "Welcome to 'B' hall" before blowing me a kiss.

I stand in shock as the other inmates around him all laugh. Ryan walks towards me and the two screws take a back step as he puts his hand out for me to shake. He tries to grab me in a bear hug but I manage to push him away. Eventually, after a small wrestle and putting me in a headlock, he leads me to my cell.

"Right numb nuts you're fucking out of here" He says to his cellmate.

"I take it your Brody" He stands up to shake my hand.

"Thank fuck the Governor allowed you in here. It'll give me a break from looking at his fucking balls all day."

"Hey all you had to do was ask and I would have put them away for you" Ryan says tucking them between his legs again and pouting.

"Is that what you do for the Governor?"

"No this is what I do for the Governor."

We both cringe as Ryan turns and bends over to reveal them dangling from behind.

Chapter 6

I have been in prison less than two weeks and my experiences have gone from the constant stress and tension in 'A' hall to the loneliness of the Digger, to the now relaxed and joking environment of 'B' hall. I have been somewhat preoccupied with dealing with the prison regime that there have been moments when I have forgotten the reason I am in here. These moments do not last long though as there is always something or someone that brings me back to reality, most of the time it is down to hearing some of the desperate acts of junkies and the lengths that they go to for their next fix. From one who would perform sexual favours for drugs or cash to buy them, to other vulnerable inmates who bank their stash (conceal it up their anus) and other ruthless junkies who overpower them by pinning them to the floor face down, and forcibly removing the drugs by penetrating them with a spoon or some other similar instrument. The Prison is rife with junkies and quite a number of them did not enter prison with a heroin habit but they will most certainly leave with one and there are different reasons for this. A prisoner doing a short spell that maybe likes to smoke a little Cannabis will experience the longevity and intensity difference of the high. Heroin is more available as it is easier to conceal and there is more profit for the dealer. If an inmate was randomly drug tested and it showed up positive for Cannabis, they would lose their parole in the same instance as they would for Heroin. Cannabis stays in a person's system for up to ten days whereas, with Heroin, it is only a matter of twenty-four hours so there is more of a risk using Cannabis. There are ways around this but they are not always successful. One is that that if an inmate receives information that he is about to be drug tested he would drink several pints of water in the hours leading up to the test to flush out his system. The problem with this method is that a person's system shuts down after consuming a high quantity of water in such a short time and when the person urinates it is diluted so much the authorities can tell and the inmate is still classed as failed. To get around this, the inmate, before the test, would pull back his foreskin and place coffee granules on the end of his penis; therefore, the test for urine would show positive for caffeine. For an inmate to go to these lengths and gamble on his parole for the sake of a joint of Cannabis, it does not take long before they concede to Heroin.

Ryan is quite vocal about what goes on, and chastises the junkies, sometimes taking advantage of their vulnerability. I found this hypocritical, as he had explained to me that some of the profits from the drugs in the hall go to him.

"I don't consume them, I don't handle them, and I don't even fucking lay eyes on them. All I see is the cash; even then, I do not see that until I get out. Whether it is someone's boyfriend, husband, son, nephew or even a mate, if they have a habit on the inside, they will pay for it on the outside. It is not too often that I have to go looking for the money, but if you witness an inmate sucking another inmate's cock for a hit, you know their cash has dried up on the outside and I have given the nod to cut their supply in here. I do not offer them drugs; I do not tell them to become junkies. If they want to destroy their lives that is their choice, I cannot stop them from bringing it in but I am not about to sit back without a pot to piss in and watch someone else rake in the cash. I'll be taking my cut thank you very much."

After witnessing the damage the drugs do to people in here, I feel justified in the thought that I am betraying my whole family. I am not that naïve though; I know that demand far outweighs the supply and someone will replace them within a day. However, if I can get their connections at the top, it will eventually have the domino effect on the rest of the whole set up.

Most of the days I sit amused as I listen to Ryan's stories, he has always been one to talk up his past activities but it is always done in a way that you are led to believe it is all a bit of fun for him. He never once mentions the details of the planning or the financial gain. Sometimes he only mentions the criminal activity as the setting for most of his funny or out of the ordinary events that have happened. There is the odd occasion when another inmate tells me the same story but their version has the added effect of how ferocious and violent Ryan turns when things go bad. I have never witnessed this side to Ryan and when I hear this, it reminds me of the same things I heard about my father while growing up.

"So what's with the no clothes thing then?" I ask.

Ryan looks himself up and down and pauses before answering.

"Do you know what? I actually do not know, I think it just felt like a good idea at the time. You can probably ask me on a different day and I'll probably give you a different answer."

We both laugh.

Due to Ryan being almost ten years older than me, and with me brought up partly in Edinburgh, we have never really bonded properly as brothers. I find the situation quite ironic that it is now happening while we are stuck in a jail cell together.

There is a new inmate transferred into B hall, his name is Ferguson and straight away, the gossips start that he is on remand for the murder of a young girl. I remember seeing her photo in the papers for weeks after she went missing under strange circumstances. They found her body in some undergrowth and the CCTV captured him as the last person seen in the area.

"That's the evil murdering cunt over there Brody." Another inmate points him out to me in the passing as I collect my dinner from the hotplate.

"Is that Ferguson? The one everyone's going on about?"

"Yeah, you wouldn't think he was a cold-blooded killer would you?"

"Why? Do you know what a cold-blooded killer looks like?"

"You know what I mean; he just looks timid and a bit soft."

"Maybe that's what you see, but I don't," Ryan says butting in behind us. "Look at his eyes. You see how he keeps his head straight but his eyes are moving from side to side, he does not lock them with anyone but he is watching everything going on around him. He's a first class schizoid."

"Yeah I never really looked at it that way, I just see a guy scared, or even petrified of his surroundings" The other inmate continues.

I look away but when I turn my head back, I catch the murderer giving me a cold stare. I feel a little uneasy and I glance at either side of me thinking that it must be staring at someone else. I realize it is definitely me and I keep my stare back at him. Ryan obviously catches on, and not being one to hold back, launches a plate of food in his direction then attempts to make a lunge for him but the screws are quick off the mark and have Ferguson boxed in. His evil stare is firmly on Ryan now who smirks as they lead both of them him back to their cells.

Two more days pass and each time I see the murderer he is giving someone the evil stare. I look around for Ryan as I am expecting things to kick off but he is always somewhat distracted and it is hard to tell if he has not noticed him or if he is making out that, he has not noticed him. I know something is going on as I can feel the tension all around, as though the whole place is ready to erupt at any minute. I am beginning to think I am being paranoid until I catch the inmates giving each other strange looks. I know something is up when I return to my cell and there is a small container placed near Ryan's pillow. I open it and look inside.

"It's cooking oil" Ryan says entering the cell behind me.

"Oh, I thought it was a weapon or something."

"It is, well sort of."

"What do you mean?"

Another inmate appears at the cell door behind Ryan.

"Do you want it done now?" He asks.

"What? What's going on?"

Ryan smiles and sits on the end of his bed. The other inmate covers his head in shaving foam and begins slowly shaving it close to his scalp.

When he finishes, Ryan stands up and begins rubbing his fingers over his baldhead.

"How do I look?"

"Like a peanut" The inmate smirks.

"What's this for?" I ask.

"It's time for 'The Wise-man' to be let loose" He winks at me.

Several hours later, I am lying back on my bed in my cell and one of the screws passes the doorway giving Ryan a sneaky nod. Ryan takes out the tub of cooking oil and starts rubbing it all over his head, chest and arms. He does not say a word. The look in his eyes says it all. He tilts his head for me to follow him. When we step out into the hall, there are no screws to around. There is one other inmate in his cell doorway and he quickly follows in behind us. We walk straight to the shower block and when we enter, Ferguson, the murderer, is cornered, it is as though he has been expecting this. Ryan takes a few steps in front of us. There is nothing said between them but under the circumstances, there is no need. The murderer knows his only chance is to go for it. He puts his head down and dives forward to grab Ryan's waist, I'm sure his intention is to grapple him to the ground but with Ryan covered in oil he cannot keep his grip. Ryan brings up his knee and catches him on the chin. This stuns him enough to land a couple of punches. The murderer takes them well and straightens up to land a few of his own. They stand toe-to-toe trading blows for a few seconds and the murderer tries once again to grab him. This time he goes for the headlock, it is a typical thing to do when being overcome with a barrage of punches. He manages to pull Ryan's head down and they wrestle to the floor, the cooking oil shows its worth as Ryan easily slips out of his grip even under the flow of the shower. He reaches up grabbing the murderer by the face and continuously smashes his head back against the tiled floor. He lets his head go and it flops back as though severed from his body. Breathing heavily, Ryan stands up and casually picks up a bar of soap and begins washing the oil off his body. The inmate, who has been at my side the whole time, walks over and starts swinging kicks at his head continuously. I am about to pull him away when Ryan looks at me and shakes his head, a signal that I take to imply, leave him be. Ryan steps out from under the shower and as he dries himself off the other inmate is still launching kicks and stamping on the murderer, as he lies motionless on the floor. We walk back to the cell, Ryan leading the way, with not a mark on him. He lies back on his bed composed and does not say a word. Moments later, the alarm sounds and there is chaos as the screws rush around ordering everyone back to their cells. For someone who, most of the time is usually quite talkative and boisterous, for the next few hours Ryan still hardly says a word. It is during this time I realize, that after being in a cell with him for 24 hours a day, and for him, to not even once hint about his intentions towards the murderer, I have probably gathered all the information from Ryan that I am ever going to get. It is now time for me to make that all-important phone call.

Chapter 7

Upon leaving prison, I receive an urgent message from my bosses for a meet. They are obviously desperate for me to brief them on any information I have obtained but I swerve them and head straight back to Edinburgh. I know they will be pissed off and I have more determination and enthusiasm for my job than I have ever had, but there is something else on my mind or should I say someone, and she deserves an explanation. For as much as I want to keep my double life a secret, she deserves the truth. I pull up outside her parents' house, it is a small dead-end street with a lot of nosey neighbour's and as soon as I step out of the car, I notice a couple of curtains twitching. I walk up the path and press the buzzer and judging by her expression when she opens the door, I can tell that I am not welcome.

"I came to explain."

She lifts up her trademark one eyebrow and folds her arms.

"Please, can I come in and talk?"

"You must be joking; you've just been in prison for assault. I read about the case. You're nothing but a thug; your whole family are thugs."

"Look I can explain, it was all a big set up."

"So you didn't beat up someone?"

"No, well yeah, but..."

She goes to close the door.

"Leanna, I'm working undercover."

She stops and looks at me. "What? Piss off, you're full of shit."

"I'm serious. Can I come in? I really don't want to talk about this out in the street."

She looks me up and down and then opens the door wide to let me pass.

I walk into the empty living room. "Is nobody home?"

"They're all at work. Brody, what do you want? I wrote to you several times for an explanation and you never replied. I put in a request to visit you and it was denied."

"I never got your letters."

She lifts her eyebrow again.

"I swear it, I never got them. And I couldn't write to you or let you visit, I couldn't risk it."

"Risk what? What are you talking about?"

"I had to go to prison so that I could get close to the people that I am investigating."

"What people? The last thing you told me was that you were waiting on the results from the police training and the next thing I know you are on remand for serious assault against a witness. What's going on?"

"If you let me explain..." I plead. "I went to my final interview and they offered me a position there and then to go undercover and investigate some people."

"What people? They can't do that before you've even joined up yet?"

"Well, I couldn't exactly go from walking the streets in a uniform to trying to fit in with these people. If they get the slightest hint that I am a police officer it wouldn't just be a case of them not talking to me, there's a chance I could get seriously hurt."

"Who are they?"

I hang back and stare at her.

"Well, you obviously can't tell me. Do I know them?"

I look her straight in the eye. "It's my family."

"What? I don't understand."

"They've been under investigation for years."

"In all the years I've known you, you've hardly even mentioned them."

"Do you blame me? It was hardly going to be a great conversation. 'Oh by the way my father and half-brothers are all drug dealers and thugs who have been in and out of prison since they were teenagers.'"

"Are you going to have to arrest them?"

"I don't know, at the moment I only have to get close to them to get their contacts."

"I can't believe this. When you said you were applying to the police, I imagined you in a uniform helping old laddies across the road or something, I never expected this."

I shake my head. "Just remember the kind of things I had to in the army."

"That's different and you know it."

"Look, since I was a kid all I ever wanted to do was join the police, but my father and brothers have so much hatred towards them I couldn't even mention it. I thought by joining the army it would have helped put it out of my head, but all it has done is given me with the confidence to pursue it."

"So it wasn't just for the steady job and pension then?" She forces a smile.

"Oh yeah, I was like five years old and thought, you know what? I want to be a policeman because of the great pension that I'll retire with."

We both smile at each other and she puts her arms out towards me. I hesitate slightly but she pulls me close and it makes me feel comfortable after spending weeks in a cell with my naked crazy brother.

"So what happens now? You won't have to go back to prison will you?"

"I don't think so. I have to meet up with my bosses and if they agree with my proposal then I'll be back to Dundee."

"When time is your meeting?"

"An hour ago"

"Do you think they could wait a bit longer?" She smiles and puts her hand out. I take it and she leads me to her bedroom.

"What time do you call this?" Drummond demands.

"I had to take care of something."

"Look I know this isn't a 9 to 5 job but if we get in contact for a meet we expect you to be there."

"What, like when I was trying to contact you from prison? As I said, I had to take care of something. It was important."

Drummond is about to speak again but Whyte gives him a look and he lets out a sigh before speaking again.

"Ok, so what have you got for us?"

As I explain in detail my new plan of action to them, I start to feel a new enthusiasm for my job and it gives me that extra bit of confidence.

"So you've spent weeks alone in a cell with 'The Wise Man' and all you got was 'The Ginge' does his dirty work while he's inside?" Drummond looks at Whyte and shakes his head.

Whyte sighs. "Brody, we could have told you that."

"Look, forget about Ryan for the moment, he's never going to give up his contacts. You need to look at the bigger picture. Before I went inside Ginge offered me a job, he said that with Ryan away he could use me. Therefore, if I am working alongside him it is only a matter of time before something slips. I'm telling you now; Ginge is your only hope."

"You don't get it. Our intelligence believes there is a contact of Ryan's inside. That was the whole point of you going in" Drummond says.

"But Ginge is out here running things, surely it would be better trying to build a case up rather than waiting on Ryan letting slip who his contact is, which actually might never happen."

They look at each other and Drummond shrugs and makes a face.

"Well, to be honest with you Brody, after what has happened, we can't exactly risk putting you back in again anyway?" Whyte says.

"What do you mean, after what has happened?"

"The contract"

"Contract; you've lost me."

"Ferguson."

"The murderer; what has he got to do with it?"

"He's still in hospital on a life support machine. It's possible if he survives he could be a vegetable for the rest of his life."

"Well, you know what prisons like" I say looking away.

"Just like that, beat up and brain dead, no trial and no possibility of defending himself." Drummond retorts.

"Brody, even we know that Ryan did it" Whyte says.

"Only 'you' obviously don't know the reason why" Drummond snipes.

"No Drummond, I guess I don't, but no doubt you are about to tell me though right?"

"Will you two give it a fucking rest? Brody, Ferguson was about to pay you a visit. We do not know what he had planned if he was going to stab you or what but the Donaldson's were behind it. We don't know what deal they made with him, probably some sort of protection."

"So Ryan done over Ferguson, to protect me"

"Well, we were thinking that it was more along the lines of him sending out a message to the Donaldson's."

Hearing this gives my newfound enthusiasm a little knock.

"So where do we go from here?" I ask, knowing the decision is all in their hands.

Drummond looks at Whyte and speaks as though I am not even here.

"If he works for the Ginge, learns the ins and outs it will be easier for him to keep in there for when Ryan gets released. You never know, Ginge could let something slip."

"But Ginge was never involved in that side of things, occasionally his names been linked alongside Buster or Ryan but all he's doing is collecting cash."

"Someone has to be connecting things up for him while he's inside and it's certainly not Ritchie."

"What about Buster?"

"It's possible; Ginge could just be fronting to keep the heat off."

"Either way, he's involved."

"Yeah, I suppose you're right."

They talk quietly among themselves for a few minutes and eventually they turn to face me.

"Okay, we'll run with it and see where it leads" Whyte says.

"But we want regular contact, with week by week reports, and remember, this is not going to happen overnight. We've said from the start this could be a long-term investigation, learn the ropes, everybody likes to talk but the information you need will be given on a trust basis so don't go asking too many questions, let them tell you."

I nod at them and then Whyte puts his hand out for me to shake.

"Welcome back" He says.

To my surprise, Drummond also puts his hand out. Reluctantly I shake it, but there is no smile or expression from me, I keep it all contained until I am out of their office then I have a little smile to myself.

With my recent spell in prison, my bosses advised me to take a week off, relax and get my head together before rushing in feet first. I had a lazy couple of days with Leanna but she was due back at work so after sitting around on my own, bored, it was not long until I was travelling back to Dundee and my first port of call, my father's house.

"What the fuck do you want?" Ritchie grumbles as he answers the door.

"I'm looking for Ginge," I say following in behind him.

"Well, he's not in."

"What about Buster?"

"He's not here."

"What are you doing here?"

"I live here and what the fucks it got to do with you?"

"Fuck you, you arrogant prick, I was only making conversation." I nudge his shoulder as I march back out of the house and slam the door.

Out of my three brothers, Ritchie is the closest to me in age and from as far back as I could remember he is the first person in my life that I can ever say that I truly hated. He has bullied me since I was a kid and it was not until my late teens when I grew bigger than he was that he backed off. He still likes to tempt fate though by niggling at me and I know I could probably put him in his place with a good hard slap, but it would be like a liberty now and I do not think that would go down too well with the rest of the family. I am still fuming when I make the short journey to the Claverhouse pub. I take a deep breath before entering and see the same worn faces that had stared me down previously, doing the same again. The barman is serving but gives me a nod as though he will see to me in a minute.

"Hey I know you, you're Buster's young lad," a grubby looking man says as he slouches on a stool near me.

"That's right, have you seen him?"

"Nah, he's not been in here today son."

"What about Rod...I mean Ginge?"

"Ginge; he'll be in the Stoby gathering his troops for the game the night."

"Thanks." I nod at the barman in acknowledgement as I leave.

Chapter 8

Arriving near the Stobswell bar I have to drive several streets away until I find a space to park. I walk up by the side entrance and there are a couple of people outside having a smoke and one of them gives me a nod and smiles at me as though I know them. When I enter, the place looks near empty with only two older men at the far end of the bar.

"Way hey" I hear the voice of Ginge.

I look to my side and in a secluded corner of the pub; Ginge is sitting with several of his football crew. He stands up with his arms out wide and then pulls me into a bear hug. He introduces me to his football acquaintances and tells one of them to order me up a pint. One of the bigger lads, Hunter, reaches out his hand for me to shake and I feel like I recognize him from somewhere. It takes a few seconds but it comes back to me, it is from the surveillance photos from Ginge's file. The two that had been outside having a smoke have also joined us and the one that had nodded and smiled introduces himself as Joe.

"Joe the Bull" I say smiling.

"Yeah that's right, you remember me? I was only a young nipper the last time I saw you."

"Yeah, he's now just a big nipper" Ginge says playfully grabbing him and putting him in a headlock.

Joe was also on a number of Ginge's surveillance photos.

"So how are things? When did you get out?"

"A few days ago"

"A few days ago" He says surprised.

"Yeah, I had to smooth things over with Leanna first."

"So how's Ryan? I take it he's still walking about naked?"

"Yeah, what the hell is that all about?"

"I think it was some sort of protest years ago. Now anytime he gets put away he has to keep it up."

"I asked him why and he says he can't remember the reason but it seemed like a good idea at the time."

Ginge shakes his head. "That's why I never go and visit him. He's not allowed an open visit, so even when his missus goes up she's got to speak to him through the glass, fuck that!"

"He thinks it's funny, he actually laughs to himself anytime anyone mentions it."

"I can't believe I'm fucking related to him."

"He's like a celebrity in there" I say, shaking my head.

"So what's the crack? Are you up for the game the night, Motherwell in the cup."

"Yeah right, I've never been to a football game in my life."

"Neither has some of these guys...Most of them get arrested before they even reach the stadium" He jokes.

I am about to speak when one of the three phones that he has lined up in front of him starts to ring.

"This is The Ginge speaking, how may I help you?" He says putting on a polite voice.

"...How are you doing mate? Are you up for the game? I'll be back in a minute" He winks before taking off out the pub.

I sit quietly sipping my pint and listening to the loud banter of Ginge's crew before he bursts back in the door and shouts up another round of drinks.

"So what were you saying...Oh yeah, Ryan..."

I nod to him leaning forward and tilt my head so that he does the same.

"Ginge I was wondering if that job was still open" I say quietly.

"Sure. Is something up? Do you need cash?"

I shrug "Well, sort of?"

"Missus on your case is she?"

"No, she's more concerned about me having a criminal record now."

"Hey, don't worry about it, we'll get something sorted" He lifts his glass and nods at mine. He gives me a wink as the glasses clink together.

Over the next couple of hours, the pub starts to fill up with more of Ginge's crew. I can distinguish them from the normal punters due to their subtle designer labels. I have never understood why football hooligans spend so much money on clothes and then wear them to fight with the possibility of them ripped or torn in some way. When it comes to game-time, the whole crew leaves the pub together and walks towards the stadium. With the young team swaggering out in front, the crew is close to forty strong, which is apparently above average for a mid-week game. I am in the middle of them by Ginge's side and I am feeling slightly intoxicated. I look around at the faces near me and I can feel for a split-second the adrenaline that all of them have when walking together. I now understand the purpose of the dress code. The labels are like their symbol and it gives them that extra confidence as though they are dressed for war. We get closer to the stadium and I can see the opposition in the distance, their crew is roughly about the same in numbers, which would look good for a battle, but there is a major problem, there is a line of police between us, escorting them to the game.

"Don't worry lads. We'll get on the blower and get a meet up later" Ginge says aloud.

Once they all realise that there is no way of getting anywhere near the opposition, we all stop in our tracks and about turn to walk towards the home end. As we do this, a couple of unmarked cars that had been following us attempt manoeuvres in the street to keep on our tail. Hunter points them out and the whole crew laughs as the cars cause long queues of traffic in both directions. I notice that Ginge does not even bother to turn his head in their direction, he only smiles at the commotion and appears to walk faster and uses the opportunity to break off from the crew.

"You don't seem worried about them" I say picking up the pace to keep up with him.

"I've been watching them from the minute we walked out of the pub. I'll show you something when we get into the game."

Ginge then pulls out a baseball cap, pulls his hair back from his face and puts it on. He pulls it down to slightly to cover his eyes and then puts his collar up to hide his hair at the back. We pass a few police officers on the way to the turnstiles and not one of them gives him a second look. We meet up with the crew inside but Ginge keeps a low profile by standing to the side of them and blends in with the Scarfers. During the game, he starts pointing out random people in the crowd.

"Yeah I see them, what about them?"

"They are all C.I.D."

I look at each one of them again.

"How do you know?"

"Well apart from a couple of them that I've already had dealings with, the others I can tell by looking at them."

"Yeah okay the" I smirk.

"You obviously don't believe me. Have a proper look at them and I'll guarantee you that at least one of them will turn up at whatever pub we end up in after the game."

I watch them closely and notice that each one of them that Ginge had pointed to is not paying any attention to the game; they turn their heads shortly and try to discreetly eye up the crew.

"Can you not see the uncharacteristic look about them?"

"Uncharacteristic?" I smirk again. "What the fuck does that mean?"

"All cops are uncharacteristic, especially C.I.D. from the way they talk, to the way they dress, right down to the fucking car they drive. They look and talk like fucking bank managers. If any of them had the slightest hint of character, they would not have joined the fucking police in the first place.

I find myself discreetly looking myself up and down at my clothing and then scanning some of the crew. 'Hmm, maybe he's right' My thoughts then drift to my car.

"Listen, this what I'm saying. I've met and dealt with so many coppers over the years and I've yet to meet one who has his own point of view that hasn't been handed down to him from some other prick that's also had it handed to him. Everything they think or say has been drilled into them."

I smile as I immediately think of Whyte and Drummond and wish that they had been listening to this.

"When I was growing up Brody, I always used to hear people shout 'Fascist bastards' to them and I never really understood what it meant. I remember asking someone, and they told me it was because they do what they are told without thinking about it or even questioning it. Well as I got older, I eventually looked up the meaning and came across many definitions. The one that stood out to me was 'Faceless Puppets' imagine that, being described as a Faceless Puppet."

Unbeknown to me, several of the young team had left the match early and headed around to the travelling support turnstiles to arrange a meet. Ginge's phone rang.

"Joe, what's happening? ...Coppers everywhere" He says turning to me, then shouts over one of his crew and tells them to pass the message on.

"Star and Garter" He winks.

"What's that?" I ask.

"The pub near the train station, we'll meet there, try and cut them off before they reach it."

The game ends in a draw and as the supporters file out of the stadium with their grim faces, Ginge appears to be upbeat and still has his usual spring in his step. This I find out is that due to the match being a draw, it means an away trip for the rematch. Outside, I try to stick close to Ginge as he marches out in front of his crew. Having ditched the baseball cap on exit from the stadium, his long ginger hair is flowing in coordination with his bouncing swagger. We pass a few isolated officers in uniform and the anti-police chants go up to intimidate them, they put on a brave face to ignore it but once they recognise Ginge they are straight onto their radios informing their fellow officers to request back up. We are only streets away from the stadium when a meat wagon and two patrol cars gather at the street ahead of us. Ginge manages to stop a taxi and I get in along with two more of the crew. I look back to see the rest of the crew dispersing before they reach the police. Ginge is in the front of the cab giving directions to the driver to avoid certain roads where the traffic has built up. We pull up outside the Star and Garter and I can easily see why the football crew frequent this pub. From the front door, there is a full view of anyone entering or exiting the train station. Some of the young team have already been over and checked it out for any early arrivals from the game.

"The stations empty Ginge" One of them says as we enter the pub.

"Good lads, keep an eye on it and give me a shout if you see anything happening."

It is not long after the rest of the crew start to arrive that the drinks begin to flow fast and there is a constant stream of people in and out of the toilet powdering their noses. The more drink and drugs that they consume the more agitated they become. 'What's happening?' 'Any sign of them yet?' 'Is there any movement at the station?'

"Right I'm away to find out what the fuck is going on. They should have been here by now." Ginge pulls out one of his phones and heads for the door.

He is only gone a few minutes before bursting back in the door smiling with a surprised look on his face.

"You're not going to believe this" He says aloud to get most of the pub's attention.

"Guess where the Motherwell crew are? They have been packed onto two minibuses supplied by Tayside Police and are being escorted to Perth train station to by-pass us."

There are a few shocked expressions and headshakes but most of the crew appear to accept this, and I notice their attitude turns quickly from tension to hilarity once it sinks in that there will be no battle for them tonight. I do not know if it is due to me being intoxicated but for some strange reason, given the position I am in, I am feeling a little disappointed that nothing is going to happen. I would never in any way condone what the crew are all about but due to the excitement of being at my first football game, listening to all the hyped up talk, I feel caught up in the moment and had been anticipating some sort of action.

"Hey cheer up; we'll still have a good night," Ginge says as he places another pint in front of me.

"Does this happen a lot?"

"Only occasionally, I have most of the numbers of the top men of every crew, so I usually get it all arranged with them beforehand and they don't let the rest of their crew know the plan until they arrive. It just takes one text to the wrong person and it is all over. It's never once happened with our crew, so it makes me wonder if some of the other crews do it on purpose because they've lost the bottle."

I cannot figure out if he is trying to explain that other crews are afraid of him or he is showing how tight his crew is. He tilts his head towards the toilet and taps his nose.

"Do you fancy a line?" I shake my head and smile.

I always knew this situation was going to come up at some point and I never really gave it much thought as I always said I would deal with it when the time came. This is now that time, and although it is only a matter of a few seconds my mind is going crazy trying to think of a good reason to refuse. I mumble and stutter something about a fight coming up and even to myself I cannot make out exactly what words I blurt out, but I now have my long-term answer. I have a fight and I am in training.

"You won't have a line but you'll knock back those pints quick enough. When is your fight?"

"Well I've obviously had a couple of weeks off, so I'm just getting back to training. Possibly six weeks."

"Six weeks? Come and have a line, you big poof." He says putting his hands up in a boxing stance and pretending to taunt me.

"Piss off" I say pushing him away.

Ginge walks away but turns back after a few steps.

"Tony" He shouts across the pub.

One of the crew looks up and Ginge nods to the toilet.

"You sure you don't want one? This is some of the best shit around...apparently!" He says making a face as his mate Tony walks passed.

I smile and shake my head, then turn my attention to the TV screen above me. The scores are on from the rest of the night's games and although I am in amongst the 'Oohs' and 'Ahs' from the rest of the pub. My mind is in confusion, as I contemplate walking into the toilet and telling Ginge to put me out a line and getting it over with. My newly created excuse of 'I have a fight coming up' is not going to last forever. Everybody in the pub appears to be on it and they all seem fine, so why am I so afraid. I cannot decide if it is my morals or my job, or it is maybe a concern that I will like it too much. Gladly, these thoughts do not linger too long as I am distracted by two new faces at the end of the bar. I think I know one of them from somewhere but through my semi-drunken haze, I cannot quite place him. They appear as though they are trying to blend in with the crew but their nervous mannerisms and their constant checking of their surroundings make it clear they are not part of the scene. My first thought is that they might be from the Motherwell crew and things are about to kick off. In the few seconds that I am deliberating where I know one of them, someone throws a pint glass from behind me in their direction. It misses one of them by inches and smashes on the wall beside them. I look around to see Ginge leaning over to the bar and grabbing an empty bottle.

"Fucking scum" He shouts charging forward.

He pushes some of his crew out of his way in a desperate attempt to get to the other side of the bar. My thoughts on the customer's identities could not have been more wrong as the realisation of where I know their faces hits me. They are the coppers from the game and they now have an expression of complete fear as they disappear out of the pub door. Moments later, Ginge emerges next to me by the bar, breathing a little heavier.

"I told you they would turn up, the fucking cunts."

"Where are they now?"

"Fuck nose, I chased them to the top of the street but as I turned the corner they were off."

"You just chased two coppers up the street?"

"Yeah, why" He says with a serious face while I shake my head at him.

"Ginge, you fucking madman" A voice shouts across the bar.

"Fuck them" He shouts back.

"What? What are you shaking you're head at?" He says.

"I just have a vision of you chasing them up the street. Is it not meant to be the other way around?"

"No, that's exactly the way it's meant to be" He smiles.

Chapter 9

Sometime later, the pub begins to empty. The young team do not have the funds to keep drinking so leave early to catch the last bus home. Most of the older lads also make their excuses to leave with some of them pretending to go outside for a smoke and then sneaking off with saying a word. Those are the type where that one more drink will lead them to making a night of it, so they know to head off before the moment catches up with them. The rest of the crew decide to move on to another pub.

"Where are we going now?" I ask.

"Hey Tony, what pub are we heading to?" Ginge shouts at Tony who is leading the way.

"The Old Bank Bar" He says looking around for approval.

"Bit of a coincidence this is on the way to the strippers eh Tony?"

Tony does not answer but gives a cheeky grin and continues on his way.

The Old Bank Bar is near empty and although the barman welcomes us in and looks happy that he actually has people to serve, upon seeing Joe the Bull, he asks if he has I.D., Ginge overhears this and steps forward.

"He's eighteen, what's the problem?"

"It's over twenty-one's."

"Look he's with me. He's not causing any trouble."

"I can't serve him. He's going to have to leave" The barman says quite abruptly before standing firm with his arms folded.

It is fair enough what he is saying due to his position with licenses and stuff like that but his smug attitude is enough to rile anybody up, never mind someone with Ginge's temper. His crew obviously knows the scenario all too well as their smiles drop and they assume the wide-eyed stare.

"Just leave it Ginge, I'll head to another pub with Tony and meet up with the rest of you later" Joe says, trying to calm the situation.

"Stay there Joe, you're going nowhere" Ginge demands, while still eye balling the barman.

"I'll have a bottle of..." Ginge attempts to order but the barman cuts him off mid-sentence.

"...I'm not serving any of you" The barman says, keeping up his smug expression.

"Is that right?" Ginge smiles "Do you really want to go down that road; because that suits me fine."

The barman shrugs "Do what you like, but you're still not getting served."

Ginge takes a step back from the bar and looks as though he is ready to jump over it. There is an uncanny silence from his crew as they all look on as if they know what is coming. I watch as Ginge casually puts one of his hands in his pocket but as he does this, the manager appears from behind the bar.

"Ginge, what brings you down here?"

Ginge gives him a nod and stays still in his aggressive stance. Feet wide apart, back rigid, eyes fixed. "Your barman here has a bit of an attitude. He's refusing to serve us."

"His friend is underage" The barman states

"He's not underage, he's fucking eighteen. And he's with us."

The manager nods at Ginge to come around the side of the bar. As he walks over his hand slowly comes back out of his pocket. I have no idea what is in there but to my relief, whatever it is, stays there. The barman speaks to him quietly and Ginge turns and tilts his head at Joe to follow him.

"Brody" He says, also tilting his head at me.

As we walk around to the side of the bar, the manager tells the barman to serve them. The barman looks as though he is about to give the manager some attitude but he snaps at him.

"Serve them."

He lifts up the hatch and guides the three of us through to the office in the back. Ginge introduces us and explains that he and the manager go back a long way. After a quick nod of the head in acknowledgement, there is no fucking about, he pulls a bag of coke out of the desk drawer and passes it to Ginge.

"Here, put them out, I'll be back in a minute."

Ginge smiles at Joe and then nods at the bag, Joe uses the tips of his fingers, to empty an amount onto the desk, being very careful not to get any lasting prints on the bag. In this way of life, I am guessing you cannot be too careful. He then proceeds to put it into lines. I cannot tell if they are large or small but Ginge makes a comment about them and Joe laughs before emptying out more from the bag. The manager returns with a bottle of beer for each of us and he and Ginge chat about old times as they take a line. Joe hands the rolled note to me, I hesitate at first but then find myself stretching over the desk and snorting one. None of them bat-an-eyelid and why should they? It is no big deal to them. They do not know that I am actually an undercover copper who has just stepped up, voluntarily, with no peer pressure, no persuasion and without a second thought, to snort a class A drug. I take a drink of my beer and sit back down. I can taste some of the powder going down the back of my throat so I take bigger mouthfuls from the bottle. My mouth has started to go a little numb. Ginge and the manager are talking but all I hear is gibberish with Joe butting in every now and then with a smart-ass comment. As we finish our beers, the manager hands us another one before leading us out to join the rest of the crew. As we stand at the bar I feel myself a bit more talkative than usual, then I clock Ginge eye balling the barman again. This has put me on edge, as I know it is only a matter of time before Ginge leaps over the bar. He locks eyes on him several times but the barman keeps his head down and makes himself look busy. I am relieved when Tony tells everyone to drink up as we are moving to another bar. Once outside, and I hit the fresh air, my body feels tingly, it is not as powerful as it was in the bar but I am still in a talkative mood. I overhear the words 'Strippers' again and before I know it we are queued in a small side street waiting at the door of a club 'Private Eyes.'

"Ginge, how are things?" One of the Doormen asks.

"Not bad mate, Is it busy?"

"There are a few footballers in splashing their cash but that's about it."

"They've got a hard neck being out celebrating after their show earlier."

"Were you at the game yeah? I thought you were banned?"

"Ah well, you know how it is" Ginge winks.

As we stand in a disorderly queue, the Doorman nods at the cashier and allows Ginge to walk past, while the rest of us pay to go through. I walk inside and the place is very dark compared to most clubs. I find a seat with the rest of the crew at a large table in the corner out of the way. The bar looks busy, as the girls, all dressed in sexy lingerie, mingle with the punters. I watch as they chat, flirt, and try to persuade the punters to open their wallets for a private dance. The crew appears to know most of the girls as they engage in friendly banter with each other. One of the girls who had been talking to the crew walks off and one of the punters by the bar slaps her across the arse. She gives him a look and keeps walking. Ginge is sitting sideways across from me, but has a view over the whole club. He stands up and casually walks over to the bar and has a word with the punter. He then comes back and sits down. Moments later, he shouts the girl over.

"Do you know the guy that slapped your arse there?"

She shakes her head "No, he's with the group at the bar, bunch of arrogant pricks."

"Oh, it's just that I asked him if he knew you and he said yeah."

She shakes her head again and walks off.

Ginge stands up. Heads straight over to the punter at the bar and punches him twice, the second punch putting him down. One of his mate's steps forward and Ginge quickly turns and throws a punch at him. He stumbles back against the bar and the rest of his mates put their hands up in an 'I don't want any trouble' gesture. The Doormen are on the scene and once the girl has a word with them, they escort both of the punters out of the club. It is all over in a matter of minutes. Ginge comes back to the table, sits down, picks his beer up off the table and carries on as though nothing happened. Moments later the bouncer that he knows comes over. I watch as Hunter is standing near the bar chatting with someone but clocks the bouncer moving in and hovers closer to the table. His head is facing to the side but he does not take his eyes off the bouncer. It is like no matter how much drink and drugs they all have, their instinct to protect each other's back is still very much present.

"Ginge, can I have a word?" He says with a serious look about him.

Ginge does not move straight away, he takes another sip of his beer and slowly places the bottle back on the table. I notice this is only a distraction as his other hand craftily slides into his pocket. When he stands up, I also notice his trademark defensive stance that I witnessed earlier.

"Look, just to let you know, we appreciate what you did there but next time can you let us do our job?"

"No problem."

They both smile at each other and Ginge walks slightly around the table and sits in a vacated seat next to me. Hunter moves back over to the bar and carries on chatting as normal. I am leaning back subdued with my beer and apart from trying to take in the completely bizarre scene; all I am thinking is that I would like some more of that coke. One of the girls comes over and Ginge slips her some money.

"Come on, I've got a treat for you." He stands and nods for me to follow him.

Two girls in front of us lead the way and take us across to one of the larger private booths. Ginge takes off his jacket and throws it on one of the stools beside him. It slides off and as it hit's the floor I find out the reason why his hand slips into his pocket when he thinks things are about to kick off. Lying next to his jacket is a mean looking knuckle-duster. I catch his eye and nod at the floor. He makes a face and waves it off. The girls hardly have time to close the booth curtain when Ginge pulls out a small wrap. He opens it and pours some coke onto the back of his hand and one of the girls leans over and sniffs it up. He does the same for the other girl and then sits down next to me. We both have our backs against the wall as the girls begin their raunchy routine. There are two lovely, near naked girls in front of me, touching, kissing and licking each other's breasts and the whole time my mind is on the small wrap clenched tight in Ginge's hand. I look on as one of the girls comes closer to Ginge, arches her back thus pushing her chest up. Ginge tilts the wrap and lets a small amount of coke drop on her nipple. It is as though they have done this many times. Ginge looks at me and nods at the girl. I stand up and lean over to sniff the powder. I get most of it up my nose but the girl pulls my head tight to her cleavage and rubs my face in it. I sit back down and Ginge laughs as he points at my nose. I assume the remainder of the powder is on my face so I give it a wipe as the girls finish their routine. Ginge picks up his coat and puts his knuckle-duster safely back in his pocket and we make our way back over to the bar. I feel the sensation of the coke kicking in and I am amazed that something can make you feel so good. After a few more drinks the lights come on, I look down at my watch, two thirty, closing time. I feel like I have only been in here for half an hour. Ginge walks swiftly towards the door with Joe the Bull following on behind him. By the time I get outside, I have to jog to catch up with them. There are several nightclubs that are situated close together, not too far from the strippers, so at closing time when they start to empty, a crowd of revellers congregate in the adjacent streets in drunken chit chat. Even though it is only mid-week, there are still plenty of people around. Ginge, accompanied by his bouncing swagger, is a couple of meters out in front of Joe and me as we walk through the crowd of people. He has a serious stare and appears to be scanning faces as though he is looking for someone in particular. We reach the taxi rank at the far end of the street and there are around ten people near the pavement. As Ginge walks passed, one of them nudges his shoulder, I assume they know each other as Ginge smiles before making a comment but the person then squares up to him. Their faces are only inches apart, and with Ginge grinning I'm still thinking it is friendly banter but then the person pushes Ginge back and within seconds they are trading blows in the middle of the road. Another one of the crowd steps towards me and I clock him about to swing a punch. I lean forward and land one first which puts him down. I turn slightly to see the person trading blows with Ginge going down. The rest of the group spreads out in front of us like a standoff and as Ginge and Joe move in on them, two police officers appear and the whole group scatter including both of the people that had been on the ground. The police have the three of us lined up against the fence that runs parallel with the taxi rank.

"Why are we being pulled? They started on us" I hear myself say.

One of the police officers is a woman and she is nodding at me and telling me to calm down. I suddenly realize that I am in her face with my teeth clenched. I feel slightly embarrassed and sink back against the fence behind me. Ginge is standing firm, shoulders back, and legs apart with his eyes never moving from the male officer in front of him.

"Am I about to be lifted?" He asks.

The officer does not answer him. He puts a hand up in a calming motion as he talks into his radio.

"Are you calling in to get me lifted?" His eyes bulging like he is ready to explode.

"No, we just have to check the CCTV" The female officer says. "In the meantime, I'll just take some of your details. Can I have your name?"

"You know who I am" He says not moving his eyes from the male officer.

"Can I have your address?" She asks as she writes in her notebook.

"You know where I live" He answers and still does not take his eyes from the male officer.

"I just need you to confirm it."

"It's confirmed."

I stand in silence next to Joe watching the scene in front of us. We both know that Ginge is listening to the conversation that the male officer is having over his radio and if the information comes back that they are to detain him, we know this will kick off big time. The message comes back clear as the CCTV obviously shows that the group on the pavement had started it and they inform us to go on our way.

"I like how you arseholes were quick enough to try and arrest us, but I don't see you running to catch up with those other pricks" Ginge mouths as he goes to walk off.

"Can you refrain from swearing please?" The male officer says smugly as he turns to face Ginge.

"Do you believe this shit?" Ginge looks at Joe and me and shakes his head. He then turns back to face the officer "What are you going to do? Arrest me for swearing you prick."

"Look I've already warned you, now can you go on your way please or I will arrest you for breach of the peace."

Ginge leans in towards the officer as though what he is about to say is for his ears only. "No, I'll fucking warn you, you cunt. If you even think about arresting me for a breach I'll make sure it's for a serious police assault, so you just keep that in mind the next time you slip into your nonce bravery costume."

Ginge stares him out for a few seconds before moving away and I cannot help but feel sorry for the officer. If I was in his position and was being belittled like that I seriously doubt if I would have the same self-control. As I turn to walk away I see his panicked expression and realise it has nothing to do with self-control.

Chapter 10

Ginge flags down the first taxi that passes and gets in the front.

"How are you doing Rodney?" The driver says a little too enthusiastically.

"Not bad mate. How are things?"

"Ah, could be better, you know how it is. Where you been the night then?"

"Just a few pubs and that, how's your night been?"

"Steady. I haven't had to wait too long between jobs."

"Good stuff."

I lean forward in the seat and am about to make a comment about what happened but Ginge snaps his head around and gives me a quick wide-eyed stare, shakes his head and then faces the front again. I look at Joe who is staring out the side window minding his own business. I have an anxious urge to talk but I sit back and listen as Ginge continues his small talk with the driver. The driver is doing most of the talking, with Ginge keeping it going by adding the odd question here and there, if I did not know him better he could actually be quite convincing at sounding interested. The taxi pulls up a few streets away from my father's house and as Joe and I get out of the car, Ginge is doing the handshakes and hi-5 with the driver.

"Who was that?" I ask as the driver pulls away.

"Fuck nose. I have never spoken to him before in my life. He gave us a free taxi though."

Joe laughs "Did he? What a tube."

"Oh, by the way, Brody, just a bit of advice, never talk about anything in a taxi. Never tell them where you have been and if possible, where you are going. Same goes if you're standing near any sort of bar staff."

"Except if you're in the Claver" Joe adds.

Ginge smirks. "That's right, I'm sure you'll be safe in the Claver because, the

Bar man is probably in on it anyway."

We cut through someone's back garden whose back gate leads to my father's street. I remember the shortcut from my childhood. Before we reach the gate, Ginge disappears into the darkness and I can just make out his shadow climbing over a large fence. His head reappears moments later sticking out over the top.

"Joe, here give is a hand."

Ginge passes over a large box and I can hear the bottles inside clinking together.

"Is he still up?" Joe asks.

"Doesn't look like it. His lights are all out, he left us a bottle of vodka as well."

"What about the gear?"

Ginge holds up a small bag, similar to the one he had earlier and even though it is dark, I can see that it contains an amount of white powder. He climbs back over the fence and we make our way to my father's house. Without switching a light on, Ginge makes his way through the dark living room and turns on the stereo. The volume must be near full as the bass makes the room feel as though it is vibrating. Joe turns on a lamp in the corner and sits down near the small table; he wastes no time in putting out lines from the bag of white powder.

"I take it Buster won't be back." I ask as Ginge passes me a beer.

"Are you joking, he's hardly set foot in this house in over six months…"

He is about to say something else but Joe shouts him over. I watch as he leans down to take a line, stands up and makes a howling noise, then whips off his t-shirt revealing his tattoo-covered body and starts dancing around like a mad man. Any thought I had of a conversation has just gone straight out the window. I am already eyeing up the other lines laid out before Joe turns and nods at me to take one. I try to act cool, but as I stand up, I feel I am rushing as though I cannot get there quick enough. He hands me a note and without even a hint of contemplation, I sniff the powder up my nose. I sit back down but I feel the powder going down the back of my throat and the taste is awful. I take large gulps from my beer and it eventually settles. My mouth starts to feel numb, like a tingly sensation. This is different from earlier and I cannot figure out if this is due to the lines being bigger or the purity is more. Ginge is still jumping about the living room swinging his t-shirt above his head but occasionally he works his way over and peers out a gap in the blinds. On the third time of doing this, he howls again and goes to the front door. He walks back in with Tony and a few others; quickly followed by some of the strippers from the club. Ginge turns the volume down slightly but is still jumping up and down in time with the music.

"Hi, its Brody isn't it?" One of the strippers says as she squeezes in next to me on the chair.

She is one of the two that put on a show for Ginge and me earlier.

"I'm Tanya." She says putting out her hand for me to shake.

"Are you Ginge's brother?"

I nod and smile.

"You don't really look alike."

"He's my step brother. We have different mothers."

"So Buster is your real father?"

"Yeah, do you know Buster?" I ask surprised.

"No, I met him once though. There was a bit of trouble in my work a while back and he came in to have a word and sort it out."

"Oh right."

For some reason, I have an urge to keep talking and even though I am now in a conversation with Tanya, I keep scanning the room and feel quite alert. My beer is finished and I badly need to go to the toilet but I cannot stop talking. Thankfully, Tanya breaks my momentum when she sees my empty bottle.

"Is that empty? I'll go and get you another one?"

As soon as she gets up, I make a move upstairs for the toilet. I hardly have time to zip up but she appears at the door.

"Hi, I've got you another beer."

"Thanks, I would've got…" She pushes me back into the toilet.

"You can guard the door." She smiles. "Joe just gave me this, you can put them out" She hands me a small wrap.

"I don't think you need to guard the door for that."

She laughs, "It's not for that. There's no lock on the door" She then indiscreetly pulls her knickers down and sits on the toilet.

I put my beer on the side of the bath and look at the wrap. What the fuck do I do with this? I look around the bathroom for some sort of flat surface and am about to open the wrap then I just think fuck it. I sit on the end of the bath and look her straight in the eye.

"Look, Tanya, I'm not really sure what to do with this, I've never taken it until tonight."

She laughs "Yeah right."

"I'm serious."

"But...oh look, I'm finished here now. I'll do it."

She flushes and I hand her the wrap.

"Get your beer, come on."

She takes my hand and leads me to the bedroom next door, one that I used to share with Ritchie when I was a boy. I sit next to her at the end of the bed and I can feel the bass from Ginge's music thumping from downstairs through the soles of my feet. I watch her put out two lines on the back of a CD box. They are roughly the same size as what Joe put out earlier. She hands me a note and holds up the CD box while I sniff up the line. She then re-rolls the note and takes a line herself. We start chatting again and each time Tanya talks to me, she touches my arm or her leg brushes against me. I feel a little uneasy, as I know where this is going. I should make my excuses and leave. Just get up and go. However, I feel drawn to her and I keep watching her lips when she talks. I know taking the drugs can be justified as part of my job, a reason to fit in, but how do I explain this to Leanna. She starts rubbing her hand lightly on my thigh and my stomach is feeling tingly. Her face is getting closer to mine as she talks and when I turn to look at her, she is staring into my eyes. She leans closer and kisses me. I can feel her trying to pull me back onto the bed but I am hesitating.

"I have a girlfriend."

"Oh, that's okay...I won't tell her" She whispers in my ear.

I know that I should stand up and get the fuck out of there but I feel myself sliding further back onto the bed with her. She removes the bottle from my hand, takes a drink and leans backwards to place it on the floor. She leans back and her top slides up slightly revealing her tight body. I do not know if she meant this to happen but it certainly has my attention. She pulls herself towards me and my hands are all over her.

Sometime later, the bedroom door slams open, waking me up.

"What the fuck are you doing in my bed you prick?"

Before I even open my eyes, I know that it is Ritchie. I lift my head to see him standing near the bed with an aggressive look on his face.

"Ritchie fuck off. Go and crash someplace else."

"I'll crash you."

"Yeah okay Ritchie." I put my head back and shut my eyes in the hope that he will go away but then I feel a jerk as he kicks the bed.

What the fuck, I dive up, inches from his face, taking in the smell of the stale alcohol on his breath.

"You and your slapper can get to fuck out of my room."

I push him back towards the doorway and he stumbles slightly but does not fall. He takes a swing and lunges forward at the same time, I pull back slightly and the punch swings passed me. I grab him by the throat and walk him backwards out of the bedroom. I pin him against the wall with my forearm under his chin.

"Listen you arrogant prick. Brother or no fucking brother, you swing at me again and I will seriously smash you. You got that?"

"What the fuck is going on?" Ginge shouts as he steps out of his room.

"This cunt just took a swing at me."

"Brody let him go."

I release my arm and Ritchie leans forward into my face with a growl.

"Ritchie, get to fuck and sleep it off someplace else."

Ritchie ignores him and keeps his stare on me.

"Ritchie" Ginge shouts louder "Get to fuck or I'll smash you myself."

Ritchie does not even look around at Ginge. He takes a few steps down the stairs, looks back at me then carries on.

Ginge looks at me and smirks. It is only then that I realise that I am naked. I quickly walk back into the bedroom and close the door. Tanya is peering up from the covers at me and I sit down on the bed beside her. It is not until I hear the front door slam shut on Ritchie's exit that I relax. I lift up the covers and lie back and Tanya curls into me, resting her head against my chest.

"What time is it?"

"Half six"

"I take it everyone has left?"

"Well there's no music on downstairs and Ginge was in his room, I don't know if anybody's with him."

We lie in silence for a while and I hear her breathing heavy as she falls asleep again. I start to get flashbacks from last night; they are like a continuous film reel going around in my head. Then the questions; What if they test me for drugs; What if my bosses see the CCTV of me fighting at the taxi rank? It has been less than a week since they released me. What if they pull me off the case, Reality is kicking in fast and my head feels like it is pounding and spinning at the same time. Leanna, shit. What the fuck am I going to tell her? I cannot tell her. What if she finds out; how could she find out? I never used anything and she is a stripper. What if I have caught something; well she is not exactly a hooker, I am probably best to get myself tested. Shit, why did I not just go home after the football? I cannot believe I took that coke. Fuck! I really need to get out of here. I gently pick up Tanya's hand and slide it away from me so that I can get up. I am nearly dressed when I catch her looking at me.

"You weren't away to sneak off and leave me sleeping were you?"

"Truthfully yeah I was. My head is pounding, I need to get out of here and get some fresh air."

Tanya sits up in bed and I turn to look at her. She gives me a little smile and just like last night, her piercing blue eyes are drawing me in.

"Felling a little guilty are we?" She smiles.

"Sort of"

I sit on the end of the bed to put my trainers on and she stands up to put on her underwear. I glance up at her tight body as she stands in front of me. She smiles as she catches me looking at her and the wave of guilt somehow disappears for a few seconds.

"I'll need to phone a taxi. Will I order one for you too?"

I think for a few seconds.

"Shit, my car. It's parked at the Stoby bar."

"Do you want me to drop you off? I pass that way anyway."

"No, it's okay. I'll just walk; I need to clear my head a bit."

Her taxi arrives by the time we get downstairs, which saves one of those uncomfortable moments of small talk.

"Are you sure you don't want me to drop you off?"

"No, I'll be fine. Thanks though."

Before she walks out of the door, she leans towards me and kisses me softly on the lips.

"Well, you know where I work. I'll leave it up to you to get in touch" She smiles at me again and I close the door behind me as I follow her out.

The taxi drives away and I glance up a couple of times so that I do not look ignorant in case she waves. She does not even look back but I guess I never gave her much reason to. I think I made the correct decision to walk as the fresh air really is making me feel better. My thoughts are still all over the place though and the guilt is slowly creeping in again. I reach my car, and the sweat is running down my forehead and the back of my t-shirt is damp with sweat. I drive away thoughts immediately hit me that I am being followed. I keep checking my mirror for something or someone out of place and everyone I see, I think they are staring at me. I guess this is the paranoia side effects of taking drugs. I do not like it. I do not like it one little bit. I arrive back at my flat and after a few hours' sleep; I wake up to a couple of missed calls, with both of them being from Leanna, I am thankful that neither is from my bosses. I laze about for the rest of the day and with the paranoia now subsided, it is only the guilty feelings from what I did last night that I have to deal with. By evening time, I am in Leanna's company and I place any thoughts of last night firmly to the back of my mind.

"So how is the job going?"

"Yeah okay, I was at the game yesterday with Ginge, met a few of his crew."

"The football game" She smiles.

"Yeah" I smirk.

"You're not into football."

"I know. My first game and I was chaperoned by the soccer casuals."

We both laugh.

"So when are you back in Dundee?"

"Not until tomorrow night, I'm planning on going to the gym during the day."

"So I can have a long lie with you then?"

"Are you not working?"

"I can go in late" She smiles and curls up to me tighter.

The innocent situation seems so far from where I was at this time yesterday or from where I will be this time tomorrow. After falling asleep late, Leanna wakes me up early by straddling me. This appears to be a good start to my day until I close my eyes and Tanya flashes through my mind. I try to stay with the moment as I keep thinking that I will do something stupid like blurt out her name. Thankfully, I keep my composure until she rolls off to my side. She smiles and kisses me before announcing she is away to have a shower. I pull the covers back over me as

I lie watching her walk around the bedroom. I think to myself that I really do love her and I trust her more than anybody I have ever met, yet here I am, comparing everything about her, her looks, her figure, how good she is in bed with some stripper I met just over 24 hours ago. I really need to get this shit out of my head. Maybe I should just tell her and get it over with; it was a one-off so maybe if I tell her she might forgive me. I had taken lots of coke; it is not as though it will happen again. Well, I might be in the situation where I have to indulge in the coke but I am hardly going to be in Tanya's company again. Fuck, I cannot get her out of my head. I keep picturing her face, her eyes, her body...Fuck!"

  With Leanna off to work, I make my way to the gym. I have not been here in weeks but I am welcomed as though I was here only yesterday. The place is a rundown hall that the boxing club took over many years ago. I have trained with this club since I was a young teenager and I still fought for them when I was on leave from the army. After a short warm-up, the sweat is pouring out of me. I put on a brave face throughout the circuit but truthfully, I am just going through the motions. There is a mention of a fight locally in six weeks' time. This should be enough incentive for me to cut out the drinking, especially after indulging last night with Ginge and his crew. I think I have proved myself enough to fit in, so it should be a good enough reason for me to refuse any future offer of drugs when the moment arises.

PART 2 - THE GINGE

Chapter 11

"Is that fucking right?" I smile to myself. "Well, you tell them that if my gear isn't back by tonight I'll be paying them a visit" I calmly say down the phone.

I am saying these words and am meaning them in the same way that in most situations people would be shouting angrily at someone. Do not get me wrong, I am seriously pissed off but I know through experience not to let people know this. It gives them a false sense that they are still in control of a situation. There is no point in me ranting and raving or spitting down the phone like a maniac. You see, my anger could generate opposing reckless anger on the other end, and as I said, being calm, gives them a false sense of control. I hang up and put the mobile next to the other two on the table in front of me. The three of them are cheap, run of the mill, pay as you go identical phones. There is one simple reason for this; if I have to ditch them, it is no big loss. Why do I have three? Well, one is for the everyday use, the 'how's your family?' type numbers. One is for the 'local business and threats procedure' and the last but not least is my 'out of town contacts'. This phone only contains two numbers, no names. The two numbers that they belong to will also have identical phones, one of which will have the number from this phone, with no name. You see the coppers nowadays have the powers to confiscate your phone, pass it to some snotty nosed tech person who has the latest technology and can retrieve all your past data. I mean absolutely everything, your contacts, random numbers, calls and text messages. Now if the data from one of these mobile phones just so happens to contain some sort of threat towards someone or details of an illegal activity stored in them, and my fingerprints were all over it, there would not really be much point in me denying that I had handled it. So my defence is simple, 'Oh look, I must have picked that one up by mistake. Excuse me judge but that phone in question is very similar to my phone.'

"So what's happening?" Joe enquires as he walks back from the bar with the round.

"They're not answering to that number I was given so I've phoned that little prick that gave me it and told him to pass on the message. He says they're in a flat up Fintryside."

"Partying on your gear?" Joe smirks.

"Yeah, apparently they knew it was ours, but they robbed it anyway. They're acting all the big shots saying I'm nothing without Ryan, and with him in the jail, I could basically go and fuck myself."

Joe laughs when he hears this and I smile back.

"Who is going up with you?"

"You and Hunter obviously, Larnio is looking for a bit of work. I phoned Brody earlier, he was on his way through."

"Brody, but I thought he didn't want to be involved in anything heavy.

"He thinks he's coming through for a bit of driving" Joe smiles and shakes his head.

I receive a one-ringer on my 'number two' mobile. Larnio, he does this all the time, instead of topping up his phone he just keeps enough credit to give people one-ringers knowing that they will call him back. I step outside, as I always have to be cautious with overeager listeners near the bar. As I talk details with him, I spot Brody walking towards the pub and I immediately clock his attire.

"You're definitely taking this casual thing seriously."

He smiles and proudly looks himself up and down. I cut Larnio off and head back inside the pub with Brody behind me.

"Guys, we have a new member of the Utility."

Brody squirms a little as everyone look him up and down.

"Get a seat, Joe just got the roundup. Joe!" I lift my pint and nod at Brody.

Joe stands up and gives him the nod of approval before he passes him to go to the bar.

"I take it you've spent all that money I slipped you" I nod at his new jacket.

"Most of it" He smirks. "So what's on tonight?"

"Just a bit of door chapping"

"Door chapping, I thought you said on the phone you needed me for a bit of driving."

"Well, you'll be driving to the door that we'll be chapping it, obviously."

"So there is the possibility of violence then?"

"Violence, this is possibly going to be more on par with twisted evil."

"You should have said."

"Don't worry. You can stay in the car."

"I'm not worried. I just don't want to get my new clothes all dirty" He smiles.

"Oh, so you do have a sense of humour. I did have a nights work for you but there has been a change of plan. It's only going to be one job but it won't be until later tonight."

"What's happened?"

"Well." I lean forward and talk quieter in his ear. "I had a stash that was about to be cut and divided up for you and Hunter to deliver. But an acquaintance of the Donaldson's have taken it upon themselves to walk into a flat, give the occupant a bit of a slap and walk out with all the gear, it was uncut by the way."

"Are they okay?"

"Who"

"The occupants"

"Fuck nose. Who gives a shit, they obviously could not keep their trap shut that they had my gear and that is why the Donaldson's have found out about it. I'm glad it's happened though because it would have only been a matter of time before it got back to some copper and they got busted."

"Brody" Joe shouts from across the table. Joe touches his nose and nods towards the toilet.

"No thanks. I really have to cool it with that shit. I've been offered a fight in six weeks."

"You need to cool it?" I nod, questioning the pint in front of him.

"Well I am allowed a couple; I just can't kick the arse out of it." He lifts his pint and smirks before taking a sip.

"Well, I'm glad you cleared that up because we're probably going in town later, and if we happen to venture into the strippers and Tanya's working I'll remember and tell her to stay clear...as you are in training." I make a face.

He shrugs. "It's cool I explained to her that I have a girlfriend."

"A girlfriend, I think Tanya might say differently."

"The other night was a one-off" He says with a serious look on his face.

"Ooh, guilt still eating away at you then?"

He nods and takes another sip of his pint.

"You should just be like me, single, nobody to answer to and no crazy wenches to give me any shit."

"Yeah but I don't think you're single by choice. I just think there's nobody prepared to put up with your lifestyle."

"That's ironic coming from you who has left his 'pretty little girlfriend' tucked back in Edinburgh so you can be part of 'MY' lifestyle."

He takes him a few seconds to think about this before answering and nods in acknowledgement as he says "Point taken"

After numerous more drinks, several of the regular faces turn up and the pub banter is in high spirits. Joe looks over and taps his watch then gives me the universal action for phoning someone. Even before I reach over to pick up one of my mobiles, I clock Brody trying discreetly to watch the exchanges. I pick up mobile number two and head off outside. A quick call to the little prick and I am informed that my threat fell on deaf ears as the acquaintances of the Donaldson's have no intention of returning my gear. I return to my vacated seat in the pub and give Hunter a wink.

"It's on?" He asks.

"Hunter, it was always on, even if they returned all the gear."

Usually, when I am out, the decision of where I will venture is a spur of the moment decision but I make a point of mentioning the strippers several times over the next couple of hours. The sole intention of this is so that the information reaches certain faces in the far corners of the pub, as I know it will reach the occupants of the on-going house party. After they hear that I am off in the town to the strippers they will still sit for hours telling each other that if I turn up at the door they'll do this to me and that to me...blah de fucking blah. I can actually picture them all coked up while sitting around thinking they are Tony Fucking Montana. Eventually it will justify to them that my message was an idle threat. Come the early hours of tomorrow morning when I go through their door, they will be flapping about that living room like a budgie in a cage.

I noticed earlier that Brody had switched from beer to juice. This has worked in my favour as he will be sober to drive and more alert for the job but it has not stopped me from belittling him about it. When I tell him the 'I'm training for a fight' excuse is wearing a bit thin, he does not look too amused. I have let him think I need him as a driver but I can very easily get a taxi, slip the driver an extra big tip to wait on us and to keep his mouth shut. It gets nearer to closing time so I down my last pint and a few of us pack ourselves into Brody's car and let the others follow us down in a taxi. As soon as we walk into the strippers, I clock Brody checking out Tanya. She gives him a wink as she walks past with a punter to a booth for a private dance. Although the rounds of drinks are flowing just as fast as they were in the pub, Joe and I have started to slow it down, but not so much that anybody would notice. Hours later the place closes and we are on our way back to mine with the strippers in tow, and Joe and I we have discreetly sobered up. A few friends of friends have tailed along with the crew back to mine for a beer, but this has suited me fine as it means more witnesses to say I was here all night. I check the time and it is close to half four, the music is still blasting out and the lines being put out like a barcode, it's time for Brody to earn his pay. I make a call to Larnio and then give Joe the nod. He goes to find Brody and returns minutes later.

"Where is he?"

"He's just coming."

"What's he doing?"

"What do you think?"

"Is he with Tanya?"

Joe nods.

Minutes later Brody comes down the stairs with a guilty look on his face.

"Got a girlfriend huh" I tut.

"Fuck off."

Chapter 12

We head off in Brody's car but I tell him to stop a couple of streets from mine.

"Wait here." I jump out of the car and into someone's garden, through the back and over a few fences. I then double back through heavy bushes until I reach a shed belonging to a mate. There is a quicker way to get here but then it would be too obvious of where I was going. I always have to keep one-step ahead; you never know when prying eyes are watching. I pick up the key that only he and I know is under a certain brick around the back. There is a small torch near the inside of the door and I know exactly what I am looking for so am in and out in under a minute. I put on one of the ski masks and when I approach Brody's car I sneak around to the driver's door and hold up the chainsaw to the window.

"Give me all your fucking money" I shout.

Brody jumps back from his seat. "You fucking dick" He shouts.

I take off the ski mask and get into the back with Joe and Hunter still laughing.

"What the fuck is that for?"

"To cut those fuckers up"

"Listen I'm not about to get involved in some murder" He says all serious.

"Get a grip Brody; it's for their front door. Here, you'll need these" I throw him a ski mask and a pair of gloves.

"I thought these people knew you?"

"Yeah, but that doesn't mean I'm going to blatantly pop my head around their living room door and ask for my drugs back."

I hear Brody mumble something to himself but I do not take him on. My head is buzzing so I could not care less if he bottles it and sits in the fucking car. I just want to be in and out; get the job done and back in the house before most of the party have even noticed that we were gone. On the way, we stop off to pick up Larnio, who knows the score and comes prepared for the job with his own ski mask and machete. Larnio is old school, a mate of the old man's from years back. He is a six foot four black man and I can see Brody taken aback when he jumps in the front beside him. I only brought them along as a cautionary measure, safety in numbers and all that shite.

I get Brody to park up a few blocks from where we are going.

"Leave it running but turn the lights off."

I hand Joe, Hunter and Brody a baseball bat and Joe opens his jacket to place it inside it.

"Joe, what are you doing?"

"Hiding it until we get to the flat"

"Joe, you do know that I will be walking in front of you with a fucking chainsaw" I shake my head and then notice something else under his jacket.

"Is that my Kevlar vest?"

"Obviously"

"You're starting to get a bit safety cautious nowadays Joe."

"Well if any of them try and get a sneaky blade in me I'm not going to be the one lying on the deck with my guts hanging out."

"Joe, you don't half know how to put a dampener on our fun nights out do you?" Hunter tuts and shakes his head at him.

With the ski masks on but not pulled down, we walk in silence towards the block of flats. I reach the door and notice that it is a security entry. It is not the new steel doors so a quick shoulder charge by Joe and we are in. If it did have a steel door, it would not be too much of a problem, just an inconvenience, as we would then have to come back later when the timer on the service button activates. The timer is for the post or the milkman or for someone sneaking in to shag someone's missus once the person has left for work. The coppers usually use it for their early morning raids, as there would not be much point in them buzzing up to a tenant beforehand and explaining that they have a warrant. With our ski masks down, we quietly creep up to their door. I lift the letterbox and can hear faint voices over the low music. I quickly start up the chainsaw and it slides straight through the door. Joe goes in first with his baseball bat held above his head. He barges into the living room where the occupants are already on their feet holding swords and various other weapons. Joe does not hesitate, he smashes the nearest one to him over the head with the bat, he falls to the floor and some skanky girl in the corner of the room starts screaming that it is her boyfriend. I clock each one of their faces and although none of them is an actual Donaldson, they are all close acquaintances. Brody enters the room behind me and has his bat down by his side. The person with the sword obviously sees this as an opportunity and charges towards him. Brody manages to get the bat up in time and with both hands, he blocks the sword. It looks like it is away to be a struggle and I am about to step in when Brody takes one hand off the bat and in a quick flash he jabs forward with his finger and pokes the guy hard in the eye. He drops the sword, falls to the floor cupping his eye with both hands, and screams in agony.

"Where's my fucking gear?" I shout.

There are two people in front of me with blades, I take a step towards them with the saw and one of them drops his blade and tries to climb out of the window. Hunter swings his bat and hits the lower part of his legs. He crumbles to the floor clutching his ankles shouting that it was not him that took my gear.

"Where the fuck is it?" I take another step towards them.

The last person standing with the blade leans over to the couch and starts lifting cushions. He holds up my bag of coke and straight away I can tell just by looking at it, that there is a fair amount missing. I already clocked the small baggies and scales on the coffee table when I came into the room, and judging by the length of time they have had my gear in their possession, and also allowing for the fact that four or maybe five of them have been hitting it non- stop, I know they couldn't consume all that.

"Where's the money?" I shout.

The person does not answer but stands firm still holding his blade.

I switch the power off on the chainsaw, place it on the floor and pick up the sword that is near me.

"You have one chance. You either hand over the money or I'm going to cut your fucking hands off."

I can tell by looking at the sword that it is not sharp, so cutting the persons hands off would be near impossible, but the threat sounded good to me. It obviously did not sound like a real threat to him as the look in his eyes does not change and he still has a firm grip on his blade. I should have kept the saw in my hand, bit late to backtrack. I take another step closer to him.

"Where's the fucking money?"

I bring the sword up slightly to the side as though I am about to pull it down towards him. I can see the fear in his eyes. Actually, when I think about it, this person is high as fuck, it is more likely anger or maybe it is a bit of both, either way, he's not fucking backing down. Fuck it! I change the angle of the sword and pull it down to hit the side of his leg. For how blunt this fucking thing is, it still makes a fair slice. A moment ago, I could not tell if this fucker's face was full of anger or fear, well now I know. He lunges forward in a rage and manages to stab me in the side with the blade. Thankfully, it is only a flesh wound.

"You little bastard" I lose it.

I pull the sword from one side to the other hacking the person to pieces and stabbing him. Someone is in my ear shouting 'Stop it; you're going to fucking kill him' while pulling me back. I do not even have to look around but I know it is Brody, as nobody else who is with me would bother to stop me, even if I was attempting to cut his head off. I look at him cowering in the corner of the room covered in blood. Most of the cuts are on his arms and legs after he tried to protect himself. I step forward and push the tip of the sword at his chest.

"Where's the money?"

He nods to the couch.

"Get it!"

I step back and he lifts up one of the seat cushions, he puts his bloody hand down the side and pulls out a thick wad of notes all conveniently rolled together with an elastic band. 'Thank you very much' I stab the sword deep into the back of the couch and turn to Larnio who is standing guard in the doorway and give him a nod. I pick up the chainsaw and follow them out. We head out the back door of the block, over a few fences and back out onto the street.

"I can't believe that fucker managed to stab me."

"You should have worn your vest" Joe says smugly.

"Oh smartass, you won't be wanting paid then?"

"Fuck you, keep it. After witnessing you getting chibbed, it was worth it."

The fuckers carry on laughing at my expense as we walk back to Brody's car. I squeeze into the back with Hunter and Joe and pull out the roll of notes. I can tell without counting it that there is at least a couple of grand. We drop Larnio off first and I peel off a few hundred and pass it forward to him. I also hand Brody his share, he gives the notes a quick glance and stuffs them into a pocket before driving off. Hunter and Joe know that I will sort them out later.

"It's okay; you're allowed to smile Brody, that's happy money" I catch his eye in the mirror and he forces a smile.

I place the weapons and ski masks, along with the coke and rest of the money back in my mates shed to sort out later, then we go back and join the party before most of them even notice that we are even gone. As I attend to my wound in the kitchen, Brody appears looking a bit wired and takes a beer from the fridge.

"How is it?" He nods to the wound and steps closer.

I look down at it and am about to make a smart-ass comment until I look up to see the remnants of powder under his nose.

"Thought you had a fight coming up?"

He wipes his nose and gives me the wide-eyed stare as though I am disappointed in him or something.

"Look, Brody, I'm not your coach or your fucking mother; I don't give a shit if you have a line or a beer, or even twenty fucking beers."

"It's not that, you getting stabbed put me on edge, kind of freaked me out a bit. I just felt like I needed something to take my mind off it."

"Brody, you were on the front line. You must have seen guys get their fucking heads blown off."

"It's not what you see it's how you react when you see it."

"And how did you react?"

"I dealt with it!" He says sternly, almost killing the conversation.

"Well, well. Brody here has a few things he does not like to talk about; I have been stabbed before you know? Because of you"

He looks at me confused.

"Yeah, I suppose you were a bit too young to remember."

"When was this?"

"It was a long time ago"

He looks even more confused now.

"You must have been about ten maybe eleven."

I watch as Brody's expression changes to a look of shock.

"Shit, I do remember. Ritchie was slapping me around and you started on him, the next thing you were on the floor covered in blood.

"Slapping you around? He was kicking the shit out of you. I gave him a couple of slaps, the next thing he stuck a fucking blade in my stomach."

"Yeah, I remember I ran and got Buster, he never even asked what happened. Instead of grabbing something to stop the blood, he scooped you up and put you in the back of the car. The whole way to the hospital, he was shouting 'You fell on something, remember, you fell on something.' Buster got my mum to pick me up from the hospital; she did not allow me to visit for months. What happened after that?"

"I was kept in overnight. The next day, Buster turned with Ritchie, he had a black eye. I found out later that Ryan had flown on him and Buster had to pull him off. We left the hospital and went straight to the Claverhouse, Buster bought us all a pint and it was never mentioned again."

"Well Ritchie's never changed anyway. He's still a horrible cunt towards me."

"Ritchie's a horrible cunt to everybody" Joe adds after walking in the kitchen and catching Brody's last comment.

"He has his uses"

"Yeah maybe he does, but to me, he'll always be a horrible cunt."

"Well, I'm glad we cleared that up" I smile

Chapter 13

"Did you get everything, Joe?" I ask as he dumps the black bag on the living room floor.

"Nah I only managed to get two florescent waistcoats, we are short of a pair of steel toe caps as well."

"Who for"

"Well, you or Brody, depending on who these will fit."

"I'm sure Buster has a pair lying around, I'll just use those."

"I hope he doesn't need them. Remember, he'll not be getting them back."

"Joe, he probably only had them for the same reasons as us."

"Yeah probably, where is Brody?"

"He's on his way."

"Why does he not just move here?"

"He's got a girlfriend through in Edinburgh."

"Is he still with her? It seems like whenever he's through here any chance he gets, he's away with Tanya."

"Yeah, but have you noticed it's only once he's had a few lines that he goes near her?"

"And he only seems to have a few lines after there's been a bit of work."

"He bitches all night about not taking a line because he has a fight coming up, then the next thing you know he's following someone into the toilet."

"Maybe he should take a line before he does a bit of work."

"Joe you know me, I'm not one for doing any kind of business while in party mode and I sort of make it a golden rule for anybody else that's coming on a job with me. I like to keep a clear head and all that shit. I mean, don't get me wrong, sometimes it can't be helped as in our line of work business can creep up when you're already in party mode. I do try not to let them clash if possible but in Brody's case, I think a slight party mode might actually sort him out before he gets involved in any work."

"Speak of the devil" Joe says looking out of the window."

I rise up to see Brody walking towards the house.

"Don't mention Tanya to him, I think it's a touchy subject. I need him alert and concentrating on the job at hand, the last thing I need is him pitying himself because he has a guilty conscience."

"Brody, why do you knock before coming in?" Joe asks.

"Manners"

"But it's your old man's house."

"But it's only Ginge that lives here, and I wouldn't want to enter if he's in a compromising position. So if I knock he can either shout 'I'm busy' or 'don't come in' or, well, something along those lines.

"By compromising position, you mean like catching him wanking over gay midget porn or something?"

"Well not entirely, but if that's what he's into then I suppose yeah."

"Hmm, I guess that's where we differ because if there was the slightest chance I was going to catch that ginger cunt in a 'compromising position' I'd be bursting through that door with a video camera and half his fucking neighbours as witnesses."

"I guess that's where we all differ because every time I do go to have a wank over gay midget porn I always leave the door wide open, just on the off chance that one of you will come and catch me. Here was me thinking everybody was into this danger wanking...I guess it's just me."

"So you've really got gay midget porn?"

"Yeah, I stole it from your mum Joe."

"Bitch, she must have been in my room again." Joe shakes his head disapprovingly.

"So what's the job then?" Brody asks putting an abrupt end to our banter.

"Joe's mum! ...Here try these." I throw him a pair of overalls.

"What are these for?"

"Just try them, I'll tell you later. What size of feet are you?"

"Eleven."

"Eleven? Fuck sake flipper!"

I dig out Buster's steel toecaps and hand them to Brody. "Here, try these. They are a size twelve, you definitely have your old man's feet, and actually, I am sure Buster is only an eleven as well but he needs the extra room for his long filthy toenails. I can only remember him wearing them a couple of times to the pub, and that was only to kick someone in the balls.

I don't even think the guy had done anything wrong, Buster only wanted to try them out to find out how effective they were!"

Once we are all satisfied that our made to measure suits fit us, I throw them into a holdall along with the steel toecaps.

"Why are we not keeping them on?" Joe asks.

"Joe, if we walk out of here with overalls on that's probably on par with writing the coppers a note telling them we are up to no good."

We head off in Brody's car and I give him directions to a lockup. I tell him we are borrowing a mates van for the job. What I have not told him is that the mate stole the van two days ago and he changed the plates early this morning. So technically, I have not really lied to him, although he did look at me funny when I handed him a pair of gloves to put on before he got in. He hasn't mentioned anything but maybe his minds preoccupied wondering what kind of job I've brought him in on or it's quite possible he hasn't asked because he knows what the answer will be. Either way, he is keeping his fucking trap shut, which suits me fine. The job is in a small country village about sixty miles north of Dundee but we need some supplies so we have headed west, to a builder's merchants on the outskirts of Perth. If Joe or I were to enter a certain merchant in Dundee there would be a very high chance that somebody would know us and clock every item we were buying. I know there is still a chance of this happening in the Perth store but it is less likely. We also could have chosen a small off the main road merchants but that kind of place would have fewer customers so then the staff would be more likely to remember our face's and what we bought. This Perth store has served me well over the years. I instruct Brody to park at the far end of the car park and reverse into a parking space so that we can see who is entering or leaving the store. We climb into the back and put on the overalls and boots.

"Brody, you're staying in the van. Remember the type of people and cars I told you about." I say tapping my temple and pointing out the window at nothing in particular."

"The uncharacteristic dress sense" He nods.

"He gave you that lecture as well?" Joe laughs until I give him a little slap on the back of the head.

"Now now Joe, there is a time and a place for taking the piss. Brody, keep your head low and if you notice anybody checking out the van, phone me."

I know there was no one following us but it will keep him on his toes and make him think he is useful. Joe grabs a trolley and we head into the store. There is only a small selection of items needed, but if it is in the trolley, nobody will bat an eyelid. If I happen to be walking about the aisles with an axe in my hand, people will fucking notice. I go through the list in my head as we approach the last aisle just in case I have forgotten anything. We arrive at the checkout and it is self-service which means that we will not even have to face some spotty teenager sitting at a till who would no doubt clock every detail of our description. I scan the items and as I put some money in the machine, Joe places everything back into the trolley. We casually walk out of there with pliers, a drill, Stanley blade, six-inch nails, a hammer, cable ties, duct tape, a hatchet and of course the axe and not one person has given us a second look. If that had been some supermarket and we scanned cutlery, a beeper would go off, we would be asked for I.D. and the security cameras would no doubt follow us out of the shop into the car park and record our registration. We load up and I give the car park a thorough scan before Brody drives off but nothing appears to take my eye. We head out of Perth and back onto the motorway and I am still regularly looking back and checking the side mirrors. It is not the driver who speeds up and overtakes to keep up that would concern me; but the ones who appear as though they are a boring ordinary couple, out for a Sunday drive, they keep a steady distance, just close enough to see the top of your vehicle. We pass the border of the Perthshire area and I direct Brody onto the road towards Inverness, we are now in the Northern Police district so I reach into the back of the van for the holdall and feel about until I find the scanner. This was top of my list of requirements that I requested when I agreed to take the job. It has full surveillance of Police and C.I.D. radios.

"What's that?"

"A Police scanner, we'll know from here on in if we're being followed."

"Why didn't you use it earlier?"

"You're not clued up with this shit are you Brody? Scanners are all tuned and coded to their own radio frequency for each district."

I do not say anymore as I play around with the scanner but I can tell Brody is anticipating on me explaining what the job is. A few minutes later, I look up and I can tell he is ready to burst.

"We're away to do over a beast."

"By beast, you mean a sex offender?"

"Oh no, the words sex offender are thrown about far too easily nowadays, the range of that word could mean some loner who has looked up Kiddie porn on the net, to some guy who has put his hand in his pocket to scratch his balls while walking past his local shops during the school dinner break. The evil rodent we are about to encounter is a top of the scale Paedophile, a sick twisted beast. I'm not about to fill your head with the gory details, but there are a number of young innocent minds that are going to be tormented for the rest of their lives due to what he has put them through."

"I don't mean to sound like some do-gooder but should you not wait at least until after the trial, I mean, if he's guilty would it not be easier to get him cut up inside."

"Come on Brody, you've been inside, you know how protected they are. Anyway, it's been to court."

"What happened?"

"The dirty fucker got off with it" Joe snaps.

"I can see the wheels turning in your head Brody. So before you attempt to argue the guys case of 'what ifs' let me tell you, these kids were so traumatized by what this beast done to them that no matter how much counselling they receive, the social workers report says that they will be lucky if they will ever get over it."

"The fucking judge threw the case out due to them not being able to testify." Joe snaps again.

"Did you know them, or the family?"

He looks over at me and I shake my head.

"So why are you involved?"

"Brody, this is a professional job. Do you know what that means?"

"Sort of"

"Clearly not, listen, money was put up by someone to get this fucker cut up. If any of the faces from their end are even seen in the same street as him, they will be onto them and he will be moved, another new identity, the works, hence the reason I was offered the job. At first, when I read the file I told them I would do it for nothing, then I was informed that it was actually a copper who put most of the money up."

"A copper" He looks at me unconvinced.

"How do you think we got the address?"

Joe nods at the scanner.

"Oh yeah, where do you think this came from?"

"Was the copper investigating the case or something?"

"Apparently he's a distant relative."

Brody does not say anything for a couple of minutes. I do not know if he is taking this in or having second thoughts about the job but I have come prepared either way.

"Pull over at the next lay-by."

"What? Why?"

"I think I need to explain, just so that we are all on the same track here."

He indicates to slow down and the cars and Lorries speed passed us. I reach into the holdall and take out a file.

"I was going to spare you the gory details but I guess it's one of those 'need to know' times of exactly what this job is about."

This was very unprofessional of me to have brought this on the job in case the coppers gave us a pull, but I now feel it is justified. I hand him the file. Out of the corner of my eye, I can see Joe leaning forward in his seat to see Brody's reaction.

"This file didn't come from just any old run of the mill uniformed copper; this is case sensitive and could only have been copied from someone high up."

"Fuck, you're not joking" He says as he turns each page slowly.

Joe and I sit in silence as Brody carefully scans each page. There are photos of all the kids involved, both girls and boys aged between eight and ten.

"The guy was a teacher" He looks up and I nod back at the folder for him to read on.

He eventually reaches the pages that made my decision to take the job. It contains photos, close up photos of the bruises that the beast inflicted. There are bruises at the top of the inner thighs on the girls and on one of the pages is a photo of one of the young boys from behind where there are marks on the top of his legs that resemble thumbprints. Brody closes the file and hands it back to me.

"I've seen enough" He lets out a sigh "And he got released?" He says angrily.

"Brody, these politicians, prosecutors, judges and high ranking coppers look down their noses at people like us, they insist that we should be locked up for public safety, but who do they turn to when they need a bit of dirty work done?"

He does not say anything and indicates out to get us back on the main road.

Chapter 14

I have directions written down and in between telling Brody the next left or right I am constantly looking at Joe, he has the scanner close to his ear listening for any sort of message or code that would indicate that we had a tail. Once we find the street, I do not have to worry if the beast is under surveillance or bother about nosey neighbours. I do not even have to search for house numbers, as along with the case file I also requested one with specifics for the job. It had photos of the beast's house, the neighbours, their cars, the ones who go to work, and the ones who do not, what time they leave and return. I memorized everything and then burned it.

Brody pulls the van up outside the beast's next-door neighbour and I walk to the front door and ring the bell. I know there is no one in but this is just a distraction as Joe has nipped around the back. He drills the lock on the door, walks through, and opens the front door for me. I signal to Brody and he brings in the tool bag.

"Brody, gloves on" I demand as soon as he walks in the door.

"Shit! Sorry."

"And you were in the army for how long?"

He gives me a look.

"So what's the plan?"

"Well, first thing is, you can put the kettle on."

"What?"

"Put the kettle on."

"You're joking right?"

"No, put the kettle on, Joe's going to nip next door with a bucket and tell the cunt 'we're doing a bit of plumbing and the waters been turned off, could you possibly fill this for me?'"

"And then what?"

"By that time, you'll have made us all a cup of tea" I smile.

"Is this so that he thinks we're genuine?"

"Military huh" I shake my head. "Oh Joe, remember, a bit of a west coast accent."

"I basically served my last two years training in a gym" Brody says trying to justify himself.

I look at Joe and make a face toward Brody. Joe smirks and walks off with the bucket in hand. I go through to the living room, switch on the TV and sit back in one of the large comfortable recliners. Jeremy Kyle is on and he is giving some poor lad a talk after finding out that some slut he obviously thought he had up the duff had been telling a few porky pies. I pick up the remote to change the channel but the only way to press the button is if I take the gloves off. Therefore, Jizzy Kyle, it is. Joe returns through the back door into the kitchen and Brody is still making the tea.

"I'm in here Joe."

"Jeremy Kyle?" He gives me a raise of the eyebrows.

"I can't change the fucking channel can I?"

"I'm not here to judge you" He smirks.

"Fuck off! So what is the crack then? We good to go"

"We're good to go."

"Brody, what's happening with that tea?"

"It's coming."

Minutes later, he comes through with the mugs of tea.

"Brody, for fuck sake"

"What?"

"Gloves"

"Give is a break; I only took them off to carry the fucking tea through."

"Brody it just takes you to touch a door handle and if they get one print your fucked. Ex-army, do you believe that shit, Joe?"

Joe tuts and shakes his head.

"Well if I do get caught, I'll be taking you two down with me for your fucking cheek."

As we sit back in our overalls and steel toecaps discussing how much of a cunt Jeremy Kyle is, I am thinking, we could probably pass as a few workies on a tea break if it was not for the job at hand. With the last gulps of tea finished, I stand up and have a stretch as Joe collects the mugs and places them in the sink. I help him give the kitchen a wipe down before we stand by the back door putting on our ski masks. Joe has his rolled up from his face as he is going to the front door again with the bucket.

"Joe, are you ready?"

He gives me a nod.

Brody, this is a way to get nasty but just remember what this beast has done. All I need you to do is be alert for anything or anyone coming near the house. Just let Joe and I get on with it.

He also gives me a nod.

"Right, let's get this fucking job done."

Joe goes out first and heads to the front door with the bucket. I have the axe in my hand and head to the back door with Brody following me with the tool bag. I hear Joe knocking on the front door. I give it a few seconds for the beast to walk through the house then I nod at Brody to drill the lock on the back door.

"It won't budge," Brody says, trying to put the drill in at different angles. We only have a matter of seconds until Joe is in a position that he does not want to be.

"Fuck it, out of the way."

I lift up the axe and tell Brody to move out of the way, I bring it down hard on the lock. It sticks in the door splitting the panel of wood that holds the lock. I pull it to the side and give it a kick. Brody realizes what I am trying to do and takes a few steps back before giving the door a hard kick. It bursts open and I step in and pull the axe up above my head just as the beast is walking back into the kitchen. He looks like a rabbit caught in the headlights, as he freezes just long enough to get a vision that will probably haunt him for the rest of his life.

"What the..."

The beast attempts to make a run for it but Joe is in behind him and smacks him hard in the mouth knocking him back towards me. I turn the axe sideways and smack him in the head with the flat end. He lets out a yelp like a wounded dog but unexpectedly he does not go down. Joe grabs him by the throat and drags him through to the living room. I follow on with Brody close behind me. I give him another blow to the head with the flat side of the axe and this time he does go down. I look at Brody and point to the window. He drops the tool bag at my feet, walks over and closes the blinds but leaves a small enough gap so that he can see out, but not so much that any passing snoopers would be able to see any movement inside. Joe goes to work with the cable ties and duct tape, gagging the beast before bounding his feet together, and his hands clasped firm up his back. Joe pulls out the Stanley blade and starts cutting at his clothes, I give him a hand to tear them off until he is completely naked. This is not some twisted perversion of ours but we need to do this to make him feel vulnerable, just like he did to those little kids. Joe grabs him by the hair and pulls him up at an angle until he is in a sitting position. I watch as he pulls his knees up towards his chest in a typical way as though to cover his groin area. After several hard hits to the shins with the handle of the axe, he still holds them tight to his chest. It is amazing how much pain a man will take to protect his balls. Brody taps me on the shoulder and holds up a finger before walking out the living room. I look up at Joe who shrugs back and we both take a defensive stance as we assume that we have company. Brody returns carrying a chair from the kitchen, he turns it upside down and kicks out the seated part. He turns it back up and nods at Joe to give him a hand to lift the beast up onto it. Brody stands behind the chair and points underneath. Both Joe and I move to the back of the chair to see the beast's balls in full view dangling underneath. I am impressed. These military boys know all the tricks. I give Brody the thumbs up and he takes his position back at the window. I swing the axe handle under the chair and we all hear the effect even through the duct tape. The beast closes his knees tighter together to try to give him some sort of protection but this pushes his balls further back and even easier to hit. After a couple more blows, I have to add more duct tape as the muffled yelps become not so muffled. I have the impression that this torture method came about while trying to obtain information from a prisoner of some sort and it could possibly go on for days if need be, without the recipient passing out or dying. Well I do not have days, and I certainly do not need any information from this beast, but the method has certainly been educational. I pass the pliers to Joe and he immediately goes to work crushing the beast's thumbs and attempting to pull his fingernails out. In the meantime, I am digging out the six-inch nails from the tool bag. I bought a box full and I know they do not cost much but I grudge the extra cost, as I only need three of them. Earlier I had considered getting Joe to use the pliers on the beast's teeth but after weighing up the noise level and the possible mess involved I decided to stick with my original plan. By the time I fuck about trying to open the box of nails with the gloves on, Joe has been busy. He has mangled the beast's thumbs and several of his fingertips are now dripping blood. I tap him on the shoulder and when he looks up, I nod for him to move back. I pull the Stanley knife across both the fuckers' cheeks and it easily tears through part of the duct tape. This is a jail thing, if someone has scars diagonally down either cheek towards their mouth, nine times out of ten it be due to them being a nonce and they will have did time where another prisoner has managed to gain access to them. I kick the beast out of the chair and as he lands on his side on the floor, I notice that the most vulnerable to him is still his balls as he curls up into the foetal position to try to protect them. Joe cuts the cable tie around his ankles and sits him upright. As I stand in front of him with the hammer in one hand and a couple of nails in the other, the beast is staring at me with his eyes bulging through fear and pain. For a split second, I feel like I want to ask him if the expression he has is the same as what those little kids had before he forced himself on them. Joe grabs one of his legs, pulls it out wide and sits on it with his back to him. I prize the other as far as possible but he is fighting against me. I look over at Brody to give me a hand but he is busy looking out the window. There is no fucking about with soldier boy when he is on duty. I cannot shout for his attention, as the beast will hear my voice so I decide on the easier option. I turn with the hammer and hit his balls. With his mind concentrating on the pain I pull his leg easily out to the side, I hold the tip of the nail to the centre of his foot and smash it through with the hammer. I hit it a few more times until it goes hard into the floorboard. 'Huh,' I really thought there would have been more blood. I move over to the other leg that Joe is holding steady and drive another nail into that one. Again, surprisingly, there is very little blood. Both of us stand up and take a step back. The job is nearly over but there is one last thing to do and I feel quite hesitant. Having nailed this beast's feet to the floor, some would think I was capable of anything, but as I stand in front of this pathetic excuse for a human being, hammer in hand, and knowing every detail of what this beast has done. I still cannot bring myself to do the one last little bit of torture to finish the job. If it was simply to put a bullet in his head, I could possibly be fine with that. I look at Joe and he nods down at the beast and then looks back up at me as though telling me to hurry up and finish it. I look straight at him and hold out the hammer. He puts his hands up and refuses to take it. I look back at the beast. It is a simple task, one nail, hard through his ball sack, job done and on our way home. I kneel down and lean forward with the nail. I lift the hammer. One hit and we can pack up the tools and we are out of here. I rest back on my heels and look at the beast. I try to think of the photos from the file, the bruises on the little girl's legs, the thumbprints on the young boys. I lean forward again and hold the nail in place. I then stand up and force the hammer and nail into Joe's hand and nod at the beast. He tries to hand them back to me. We nod at each other with wide eyes as our only way of communicating. Joe tries to force them back to me, I then feel myself nudged out of the way. Brody grabs the hammer and nail out of Joe's hand, kneels down and puts the nail towards the beast's ball sack and hits it. I can hear it going on the floorboard with the first hit but Brody does not stop until the nail is flat on the floor. He stands up, throws the hammer into the tool bag, and walks towards the door. Joe and I are still standing in the same spot admiring his work when he stamps his foot on the floor to gain our attention and tilts his head for us to move. I have a quick look about to make sure that we have not left anything before picking up the tool back and following Joe out the back door. We go into the neighbour's garden, and one by one, we roll up our ski masks and casually walk out to the van. Brody drives off and even though we can now talk to each other, there is silence between us for at least ten minutes.

"Can we stop at a shop?" Joe asks.

Brody looks at me as though waiting for me to give him the okay to stop.

"Are you off your fucking head Joe?"

"I'm hungry."

"Well apart from the fact that your overalls are covered in sprays of blood, think about it, if the shop has CCTV outside, it will get the van. If it has cameras inside, it will record you."

He appears satisfied with my answer and puts the scanner closer to his ear. My focus switches from one mirror to the other for the next fifteen minutes. I know if we are going to get pulled it would have happened by now, but I'd rather be that extra bit cautious than be sitting in a cell telling myself I wish I had been that extra bit cautious. We arrive back at the lockup, and once we are in and the shutter is down, we strip off the overalls and boots. I throw them back into the van beside the tools. I lift up the shutter door just enough for Brody to slip under and he goes out and starts his car. Joe jumps in the back of the van and covers everything in petrol then climbs back out and stands next to me by the door. He lights a rag and throws it into the van. We watch for a few seconds as it goes up then I remember I still have the scanner in my hand. I launch it into the flames and then with my foot I slam the shutter down tight. We both walk sharply to Brody's car. It will be a good ten minutes before anyone notices the smoke and by that time there will be no trace of us.

Chapter 15

Who the fuck is that at my door at this time? Surely not the coppers if they are knocking.

"Hunter! What time is it?"

"It's early" He says sternly.

I nod for him to come in "This doesn't sound good."

"It's not" He says walking in behind me.

"What's up?"

"I tried to phone you last night but all your phones were off."

"Yeah, I was busy."

"While Brody and I were collecting last night, we went to Little Liam's door. Somebody got there before us; they took the lot and also gave him a few slaps in the process."

"Little Liam got bumped?" I smile as though he is taking the piss but I can tell by Hunter's expression that this is no wind-up.

A dealer with the nickname 'Little Liam' actually sounds as though he should get bumped. His real name is Liam Ross and he is a big fucker, so naturally, they call him Little Liam. Although he is part of my crew, I do try to keep him out of any harm's way. Tommy, his father, is doing life in prison for killing a copper, and many years ago, I did some time with him down south. I was a young lad in a man's prison and he made sure I wanted for nothing. Upon my release, he asked me to return the favour by looking out for Liam while he was still inside. If Liam comes to any serious harm under my watch, Tommy is the type that would hold it against me. I have taken Liam on a few low risk jobs and he has shown that he can handle himself. He is very sharp and knows when to keep his trap shut, actually, it is sometimes hard to get the fucker to talk at all, but he does take everything in.

"I take it I'm not going to like what I am about to hear."

Hunter shakes his head.

"Who was it?"

"Ritchie"

"Ritchie" I say surprised.

Hunter nods.

"But he knows Liam. He knows he's one of our crew"

I sit down feeling a little confused.

"Is Liam alright?"

Hunter shrugs "There are a few marks on his face, it probably looks worse than it is."

"What the fuck is Ritchie playing at?"

"Liam said he looked as though he had been on it for days, he only let him in because he thought he was collecting for you; there were a couple of other guys with him. When he saw the state they were in, he knew something was not right. He refused to hand it over and went to call you, the Ritchie pulled out a blade. Once he handed it over they laid into him."

"What did Brody say about it?"

"Well Liam wouldn't tell me at first, you know what he's like. I knew something was up though. Brody was a bit worse for wear anyway so I told him to drop me off and call it a night and I would sort it out with you later. When Brody took off I went back up to Liam's and that's when he told me."

"Wait, what do you mean Brody was a bit worse for wear, was he ill or something?"

"He looked like shit and he was talking like he'd been on downers. Listen Ginge, I know he thinks he's only driving me to collect money but I think you need to sit him down and explain to him what that really involves because, well you know what it's like, some people don't like to pay their debts so if something kicks off I need to know he's got my back."

"I'll have a word."

"What are you going to do about Ritchie?"

"Fuck nose..." I put my hand over my mouth and stare at the floor as I think.

"...I'll need to go looking for him. Have you any ideas where the fat bastard could be or who the fuck was with him when he turned up at Liam's?"

"Don't have a clue mate, but with the Wad that he's taken off Liam he'll certainly not be short on mates."

"There's got to be a few likely suspects that know where he is."

"What will I say to Liam?"

"Give him a phone later, tell him not to worry about the money, I'll get it sorted. Have you got anything on just now?"

"Nothing important"

"Good. I might need your help. Do you want to stick the kettle on while I go and get my phones and try to get hold of that fucking waste of space?"

Hunter raises his eyebrows and walks off to the kitchen.

"Never a dull fucking moment" I mumble to myself.

From 'no answer' to 'not seen him' to a few leads of other numbers. I eventually receive a text with an address of some junkie scumbag's house. I say scumbag as in someone that is just like Ritchie who would rob and steal anything if it not nailed down.

"Did you get the address?" Hunter asks.

I nod at him but I do not read the address aloud, I know Hunter knows it and I think he can tell somethings up by my expression. I try to hide it by flicking through my phones pretending to be checking something.

"So what's the plan? I know he's your brother and all, but do you want me to go to the door and see what's what?"

"I don't know mate, I haven't really thought that far ahead. I'm raging right now so I know if I turn up there and he starts acting wide, I'll really fucking do him, and as you say, he's my brother."

I take a deep breath and put my head in my hands as I think about the best way to go about this.

"I know what I'll do" I flick through the names on my phone.

"Hello Buster, I need a favour. Do you have transport? ...Can you come pick me up? ...I will tell you when you pick me up...half an hour. No probs."

"Do you want me to hang about?"

"No it's cool; I'll get this sorted out. I will give Brody a phone later as well and have a word with him. If he's still fucked I'll come with you tonight and we'll go around the rest of those doors."

Hunter finishes his cup of tea and heads off then moments later Buster pulls up and blasts the horn.

"So what's going on?"

I look at him angrily "Ritchie."

"Fuck, what's he done now?"

"He bumped Little Liam last night."

"How much for"

"The lot, Brody and Hunter were on their way to collect. Ritchie turned up before them, Liam obviously thought he was collecting for me and let him in. He was with a few guys; Ritchie pulled a blade and took the lot."

"How much"

"Three grand"

"What is the fuck is he playing at?"

I shrug. "Apparently he was wasted and looked like he had been on it for days. By the way, Hunter said Brody wasn't looking too great either."

"Is he not meant to be fighting in a couple of weeks?"

"Supposedly, I'm going to phone him later and have a word with him, tell him not to bother coming through until after his fight."

"So where are we heading?"

I show Buster the text with the address.

"I know that address, that's the fucking Duggan's."

"That's why I phoned you and sent Hunter on his way. I never even showed Hunter the address, I felt fucking embarrassed."

"Bunch of junkie bastards. He'll be lying up there smacked out of his nut."

"That's why I phoned you. If I go up there and he gets wide I'll really fucking smash him, this is the third time he's done this."

"The third time" Buster growls.

"It wasn't a lot of money and Ryan covered up for him both times, he told me about it months later. Ritchie doesn't know that I know about it."

"And this was last night; I hope you're not expecting any of this three grand to be left are you?"

"Right now, I couldn't give a fuck about the money."

"He obviously thinks with Ryan in the jail he can do what he likes and by the time he gets out it will all be forgotten."

"He couldn't have gone and bumped one of the Donaldson's. No, he goes for the easy target, Little Liam."

"And at that, he couldn't just take the money and walk off; he laid into him after it. I swear if he wasn't my brother he would have been done in a long time ago"

Buster does not say anything but I can see the rage building up in him as he drives. We arrive at the address and Buster tells me to wait in the car.

"That's not fucking happening" I mumble as I get out and slam the door.

"Ginge" Buster shouts.

"Look if you go to that door with that head on it's going to kick off straight away, at least let me try and find out what he's done with the money first."

"I told you, I couldn't give a fuck about the money."

"Exactly, now wait here."

I take a deep breath and lean against the car. I have learned over the years that if Buster gives you an order for you not to get involved, he has a good reason. I look up at the house and all the blinds are closed. There is no spy hole in the door so they will not know who it is. I watch Buster walk up the path and ring the bell and I can see his chest lifting up and down as though he is heavy breathing. Then I notice his hands. He stretches his fingers out wide and closes them into a tight fist continuously. He does this when he is gearing himself up. I have also learned over the years, never to trust Buster when he pretends to be diplomatic I take off from the car and run towards the house but before I get there the door opens and Buster has stepped forward and nutted the guy in front him without saying a word. He crumbles to the floor and Buster steps over him and walks into the house. I storm in behind him and when I walk into the living room there are about six or seven people lounged around. Empty vodka bottles, cans and used needles strewn all over the floor. The coffee table looks as though it has the remnants of every different drug imaginable. I clock the wraps of foil and among them are small blue pills, and with the way Ritchie is laying crashed out in a chair and it looks as though he has consumed a vast amount. Buster grabs him and starts slapping him hard in the face but Ritchie is out of it. One of the rough looking females in the room makes a comment towards Buster in his handling of Ritchie and he swiftly turns to face her.

"Wench, shut your fucking trap."

"Are you going to let him speak to me like that?" She says turning to her man.

He looks up at Buster and turns to have a quick glance at me. He knows he is out of his depth but he also knows if he does not stick up for his women he is going to lose face. He stupidly decides to stick up for his women and attempts to get up from his seat.

"Hey man, don't speak to my missus like…" Smash!

Buster punches him back into his chair. He certainly will not need any of those little blue pills for a while. Buster starts searching Ritchie's pockets; he finds a role of money and throws it towards me. I can tell without counting it that there is about a grand.

"Empty your pockets, all of you" He demands.

Not one of them move

"I said empty your fucking pockets."

A couple of them do as he says and turn out at the most, fifty quid. Buster takes it and hands it to me.

"You, empty your pockets" Buster singles one of them out.

"Fuck you, who the fuck do you think you are, coming in here. You're just a fucking bully."

"Bully" Buster leans down; he grabs him out of his seat by the throat and pulls him to his feet.

"Bully" He repeats. "You turn up at a young kid's door, pull a blade, take his money, beat him up and you sit there like some smug bastard calling ME a fucking bully.

"It wasn't me; I never turned up at anybody's door."

Buster releases his grip and goes to turn away but then in a quick flash he swings his arm around and catches him with a backhander, as he falls back to his seat the blood splatters against the wall from his nose.

"You've sat there all night with this lot banging that shit up your veins knowing exactly where the money came from to pay for it. So do not get on your fucking high horse that it was not you. Now I better not have to say it again, EMPTY YOUR FUCKING POCKETS." Another couple of tens and twenty-pound notes appear and Buster snatches them and hands them straight to me. He picks up an empty carrier bag off the floor and in one large swoop; he clears the whole contents of the coffee table of all the drugs, cigarettes and even their mobile phones.

"And you can tell that fat bastard when he wakes up to come and see me."

Buster nods at me and follows me out. I get in the car and he dumps the bag on my knee.

"What the fuck do I want with all this shit?"

He shrugs. "I don't know, it just seemed like a good idea at the time."

I place the bag on the floor and pull out the role of money to count it.

"How much is there?"

"Altogether, just short of fifteen hundred"

I split it up and put half in his pocket while he is driving?

"What's that for?"

"A couple of hundred for you, the rest you can put through Ryan's door for me when you're passing."

"I'm not taking that."

"It's up to you. Just put it all through Ryan's door then. I'm sure his kids will appreciate it."

He pulls up outside the house and he goes to hand me the carrier bag.

"I'm not taking that shit" I laugh.

"Put it in the bin when you're passing."

"Why don't you pass it around the punters in the Claver; I'm sure they moaning old bastards will appreciate it."

I go to shut the car door then turn back.

"Oh, if Ritchie happens to surface tell him to keep out of my fucking way."

Buster appears to be content with this and nods before driving off.

I try to put all that has happened out of my mind but even after I have sat down with some breakfast, I still keep thinking about Ritchie. After everything I have done for him, he still goes behind my back and does this shit. When he is with me, he never once has to put his hand in his pocket. I have always looked out for him, stuck up for him, as a brother should do. I have lost count of the number of times I have had to sort out shit with other people due to him being an arrogant prick. He has crossed the line now though and with Ryan out soon, I think it is time we had a talk.

Chapter 16

"Hold on a minute, there's Joe on the phone. Joe, I am in the Claverhouse having a pint with Buster...no worries."
"What's he up too?"
"He's on his way here."
"Have you heard from Brody?"
"Not since I told him not to bother coming through this week."
"Did you have a word with him?"
I shake my head "Not yet. I told him that there was no work for him this week. I will have a talk with him though; the last thing I want is for him to end up like Ritchie.
"Ritchie phoned me the other day."
"What, asking for the money back that he stole?" I smirk.
"He started ranting and raving about me being a fucking bully and that I was out of order hitting his mates like that."
"Mates" I laugh. "What did you say?"
"Nothing I hung up. He phoned back a few times and I kept hanging up. Eventually, I answered and told him if you have anything to say I'm in the Claverhouse, get your arse down here."
"I take it he never turned up."
"Did he fuck?"
"He'll surface at the end of the week, feeling sorry for himself and looking for money.
"There's Joe now. JOE" Buster shouts past me and cuts me off.
"How are you doing Buster? Not seen you about for a while, what have you been up too?"
"Nothing much, I had to keep a low profile for a bit, you know how it is."
Joe gives me a lift of the head "What's on for tonight then Ginge?"
"Just going over a few debts, there's a couple of big ones been outstanding for a while."
I flick through the names on my mobile number two and lean forward to show Joe the screen. He reads the name and shrugs.

"Maxi, I think I remember you mention him before; did he used to play for Dundee or something?"

"Yeah, Steven Maxwell, he signed for Rangers and sat on the bench for a season then got punted down south for a bit, he came back up here thinking he was some superstar. He talks as though he is middle class because he has a big house away from the schemes, drives a flash car and has money to throw round. He seems to forget we knew him when he was running about with fucking holes in the soles of his trainers, I remember he had to borrow boots from other players just so that he could get a game."

"I can't remember us ever having to go to his door before."

"He's always dealt with Ryan and with the amount of money he's now due I wouldn't exactly expect him to hand it over in a carrier bag on his doorstep."

"How much are we talking here, a few grand?"

"Try twenty."

"Twenty grand" Buster buts in

I nod.

"How the fuck did that happen?"

"Ryan just kept laying him on; he was hanging out his arse, they were old school buddies so he obviously thought nothing of it."

"What's he saying about it?"

"The cunts not been answering, he's obviously changed his mobile number, which is fair enough, I always give people the benefit of the doubt if they've lost their phone or whatever, but I got his house number and left messages through acquaintances for him to get in touch weeks ago and I've not heard a fucking thing."

"Why don't you get Ryan to phone him from the jail?" Joe asks.

"Fuck Ryan. It's me he's dealing with now, so if he wants to blank me that's fine, I've never liked the cunt anyway so he'll play right into my fucking hands. I hope you have your best togs on Joe because we are going 'uptown.'"

"Perth road" Buster smirks.

I nod.

"Do you want me to come with you?"

I smile. "Nah it's cool, I'm only going to show face, let him know we're onto him. I might give you a shout later though, depending on the outcome."

The last thing I need is Buster jumping about the Perth road and the attention that cunt could create. These fucking pricks would not hesitate to name names if the shit kicked off. They are the type of people who swagger about thinking they are all that when they have put enough powder up their nose but they are the first to run to a copper when they realize they are in over their heads.

The Perth road is unfamiliar territory to me, but when I say unfamiliar it does not mean I do not know every pub on every corner or what street their fire exit leads to, or which ones have CCTV and which ones do not. All it means is that I do not know the Doormen, and they do not know me. If the Doormen know you and something kicks off, they deal with it there and then. If it is something that has gotten out of hand and the coppers become involved, the Doormen are good for their wall of silence. If they don't know me, then there is the whole irritation of coppers on my case, getting hold of the Doormen's names and addresses, the slight persuasion to their loss of memory to a full on intimidation to what will happen if they turn up at court. I have gone through this scenario with Buster and Ryan many times over the years and believe me, in this line of work; sometimes all that hassle is worth it, just to get your point across. As always when I have business to take care of, I keep a cool head in the drinking department but Buster is none too happy as I refuse his constant top-ups. When Joe and I finally decide it is time to make a move I can see the disappointed look in Busters eyes that he is not coming with us. If it was some scheme pub I would gladly take him along, point the fucker out that's due money and within minutes Buster would have him dragged to the toilet, pinned up against the wall by the throat and threatened that if the debt's not paid in three days he'll hunt him down and torture him. However, with these jumped up would-be middle-class pricks you cannot get away with that shit. I have to do this in stages, first its diplomacy, a persuasive word in their ear to pay up. Two is tactics, a course of action and third is all out fucking war. If the course of action is done right and proper, it should never reach the third stage, unless of course you are dealing with someone on a power trip who has more than likely taken too much of their supply and actually wants to take you on. An example of this would be the Donaldson's and their ever-growing entourage. A never-ending battle that I am happy to keep going, and it will never escalate to anything more than what it is. They swagger around acting and talking themselves up like gangsters, which is good for business as it takes up many of the coppers resources and keeps them away from us.

  The taxi pulls up outside Braes bar and we walk in without even a second look by the Doormen. The place is busy and as I wait for the bar staff to serve me; I discreetly scan the faces near me. I recognise one of the girls working there from way back when I was a young boy at school. Rachel O'Neil, I never forget a face. She was an overachiever, one of those with top grades in everything, to me she was a snotty nosed bitch who would look you up and down before considering whether you were good enough for her to talk to. Funny how things turn out, I am here chasing someone for twenty grand and here she is collecting tumblers. If I was not so wired due to the matters at hand I would gladly shout on her to get her attention just to piss her off, but the last thing I need is people remembering my face. With a beer each, Joe and I walk through the bar until we find a space where we can overlook the whole pub and have a view of the front door. I start to feel that it is obvious that we are looking for someone as people are catching my eye as I scan their faces. The toilets are at the far end of the pub and down the stairs so I decide that my best option would be to head near there, that way I have a purpose to walk through the crowd and see if that cunt is in here. I squeeze through the groups of people and a few faces give me a nod but I do not know who the fuck they are. They could be fucking coppers for all I know; actually, given their dress sense, it is highly unlikely. I pass the Doormen at the top of the stairs and head down to the toilet. What a surprise! One of them follows me. I stand at the urinal and can hear him behind me opening cubicle doors as though it is his routine check. I feel like turning around and nutting him just for being a smug bastard and following me. By the time I zip up and turn around, I see the back of him walking out the door. I feel the growl coming on so I think it is time for Joe and I to leave. Walking back through the pub I pass by the snotty nosed bitch and she looks up and smiles at me, then turns to clear a vacated table. After all that studying and acting as if her shit doesn't stink and here she is probably earning minimum wage and waiting around to pick up my empty bottle.

"Drink up Joe."

"Where are we going?"

"Next pub"

"Hi, Rodney" The snotty nosed bitch appears at my side.

I look at her as if she must have the wrong person.

"I'm Rachel. I was at school with you."

"Hi, how are you?"

"I'm fine. I didn't think you would remember me?"

"Of course I remember you. I just didn't expect you to be working in a pub. I thought you would be a doctor or a politician or something by now"

"Oh definitely not, I can't stand politics. I was an accountant for ten years but got bored of it so I'm back studying again."

"What are you studying?"

"...Law"

"Law, that's good, I can maybe hire you to sort out a few cases I have pending" I smile.

She smiles back "Yeah, you were always a bit of a tearaway weren't you?"

She turns to Joe who is half walking off."

"Is that you leaving?"

"Yeah, we just popped in for the one. Are you on all night?"

She looks around the busy pub and then nods. "Afraid so"

"Well I'll no doubt still be out and about later, if you're up for it, you're more than welcome to tag along with us to some dodgy party when you finish."

"Yeah okay, sounds like fun, give me a second I'll give you my number."

She places the empty bottles on the bar and pulls out her mobile. I search in my pocket and pull out my number one phone. As I flick down the screen, I turn to Joe and smirk as he makes a face. I give her the number and she rings me once so that I have hers.

"Well I'd better get back to work; I'll give you a text later okay."

"Yeah okay...Oh eh, Rachel!" I nod for her to come closer and she smiles and tilts her head towards me.

"Do you take drugs?"

Her smile widens as she walks off.

Chapter 17

"Do you take drugs?" Joe laughs as we step outside the bar.
"What?"
"That's some fucking chat up line that."
"Well there's no point in fucking about is there?"
Joe shakes his head and keeps walking. The cunts got me paranoid now.
"What? Do you think that was out of order?"
"Fuck sake Ginge. Next, you will be asking me 'do you think she'll call?'" He says in a high voice.
"Fuck you" I walk on.
We come to a choice of three pubs at the next junction and I know that our friend Maxi boy frequents all of them.
The closest one is the Arts Centre, which has high stairs leading down to a large open plan area where you can overview everyone in the bar, which is not the ideal place for us to go unnoticed. We cross the road and head towards a smaller bar called Medina. There is one young person on the door and he lets me pass but stops Joe.
"You'll have to take the badge off."
"What?" Joe smiles at him as though he is joking.
"You can't wear that badge in the pub" He nods towards the label on Joe's Stone Island jacket
"Are you taking the piss, you're not letting him in because of his jacket?"
"He is allowed in, but he'll have to take the badge off."
"What's the problem with the badge? It's not offending anybody."
"It's associated with the casuals and it's the bar's policy."
"Associated with the casuals? You're about ten year too late mate" Joe says.
"Look I can't let you in with the badge on."
"Well, I'm not taking it off" Joe stands firm.
"Well, you'll not be coming in then" He abruptly says.
"I'm a casual" I say leaning in towards him.

He takes a step back and looks up at me "Well, you're not getting in either them."

I look at Joe but tilt my head towards the Doorman and smile. We both laugh but it is more in shock at the balls he has.

"Mate are you fucking winding me up?"

I step closer towards him as though I am about to hit him but in the split second I do this I stamp my foot and pull back. The Doorman jumps back and puts his hands over his head as though protecting himself, his face has the image of fear. Joe and I walk off laughing and glance around to see him back in his bravado stance, chest out, looking as though he is ready to take on the world. We walk around the corner and cross the road to The Cul-De-Sac Bar. There are two parts to this bar, a large dance floor area with a DJ and the other is a quieter area containing small enclosures with seating booths. Unlike the last bar, Joe and I walk pass the Doormen without them giving us a second look. Both sides of the bar are crowded so I make a quick decision to head to the quiet area. We find a space near the bar and while waiting on the bar staff to serve us I glance around and spot Maxi. He is standing at the far end of the bar, in a group of about eight; clean cut, tanned, shirts open and labels everywhere. They are the stereotypical football players who would not look out of place in a poofters boy band. We move further into the crowd and I find a space near the doorway that leads down to the toilet. I now have a full view of Maxi and his whole group. He looks straight at me and then carries on his conversation with his mates, there is no lift of the head or any sort of acknowledgement whatsoever, so now I am starting to get a bit annoyed. A few faces I recognise stop and chat in the passing but the whole time I am clocking Maxi.

"What's happening?" Joe asks.

"I've been watching him knocking back those bottles like 'fuck nose what' so I've been thinking, he's either got to pass me to go for a piss or if he's half the pop star that he thinks he is he'll be off for a line very shortly. All I want from him is a quick word to arrange the repayment of his debt and we will be out of here and on our way. I am not here to kick off; I will give him the benefit of the doubt, as he has been good for it over the years. I really do not like the prick and there is too much money involved to let this drag-on. Every time I look over at him, I feel as though he is specifically blanking me and it is starting to wind me up. I'm actually on the verge of sending you over and telling him to get his arse outside."

Joe gives me a shrug as if to say; well what the fuck are you waiting on.

"Wait a minute Joe, I've spoken too soon, I've just clocked one of his mates tap his nose and nod in the direction of the toilet."

I watch him down the dregs of his bottle and walk casually towards me. I stare straight at him and he turns to his mate as he passes me. I tap him on the shoulder.

"Yeah, what is it?"

"What do mean? What is it? A word" I tilt my head for him to come closer. The prick actually stands in front of me as though he is about to square up to me.

"I've been trying to get in touch with you?"

"So I heard."

"Oh, so you got my messages?"

"Well obviously, you have left enough of them" He says quite snide.

"So why have I not heard back?"

"Wait a minute, my debts not to you. It actually has fuck-all to do with you."

"Is that right?" I smile. "I will tell you what. For the sake of you being, just that bit ignorant, I'll explain something right now." I move in closer. "You're debts mine and you've got three days."

"Three days till what?" He says pushing me back.

Out of the corner of my eye, I see Joe go to make a move but I shake my head at him. Within seconds, Maxi's mates are around us.

"Do you really want to go down this road?" I smile again.

"What; who the fuck do you think you are?" He steps forward as though he is about to go for me but I don't even flinch, one of his mates pulls him back and this sets him off on a little rant. I turn to Joe and I can tell that he is waiting on the nod from me to let loose on the cunt. The two Doormen have appeared and typically, they side with the boy band, even though they are jumping up and down as though someone has stolen their bottle of fake tan. Joe and I stand firm not saying a word, as we know what is coming.

"Guys I'm going to have to ask you to leave" The taller of the two Doormen says.

The shorter of the two, puts his hand towards Joe as if to guide him back but Joe does not move and the Doorman's hand touches Joe's shoulder.

"Take your fucking hands off me."

The Doorman appears to take offence to this and squares up to Joe. I am all for playing it cool and not kicking off with Maxi and his gay boy band because that's just one of my ploys. I like to give people a false sense of control of a situation when in reality the wheels are already in motion as to what I am going to do to them. However, when it comes to a jumped up Doorman that has taken too many steroids, I draw the fucking line. The difference in attitude between Maxi and this Doorman being wide is that this Doorman does not owe me twenty fucking grand.

"What the fuck are you doing? You little steroid monkey" I step in closer to him.

He does not answer but I can see him clenching his teeth, he is bursting to have a go. The taller Doorman steps in between us and I watch the smaller one take a step to the side, he places his hands on his hips, in a catalogue-posing stance.

"Look, guys, we've asked you to leave."

"I'll go when I've finished my fucking drink," Joe says taking a sip from his bottle, still not taking his eyes off the Doormen.

I know the expression well, he is about to kick off, then suddenly, he downs the rest of his drink before slowly to walking away. What the fuck, I follow Joe towards the small-enclosed doorway that leads out of the pub and as I glance back, the smaller steroid monkey is behind me, his arms now folded, like some smug prick. I know there is CCTV outside the pub so I slow down and just before I exit, I turn back and throw a punch that lands clean to the side of his jaw. He stumbles back and I continue towards him throwing a couple punches putting him to the floor. I turn and walk swiftly out of the pub before the other bouncer gets a chance to jump about and make a scene.

"I thought you said before we came out not to kick off" Joe says, somewhat annoyed.

"That was only meant towards that fucking Maxi."

We head for the taxi rank at the end of the street and I know once the call is put through the CCTV will probably be tracking us, so with a generous tip to the driver he is informed that we were never in his cab as he drops us back at the Claverhouse.

We walk in and Buster is over at the pool table. "Fuck that was quick. I never thought you would be back up here."

I nod towards the enclosed area at the back and he puts up his hand to signal he will be five minutes. No sooner has the barman passed over drinks for Joe and I but the coppers have walked in the front door. Obviously, the generous tip for the taxi driver was not generous enough. Joe and I slide under the hatch at the bar and head out the back door. A few minutes later, the barman comes out and gives us the all clear. When we head back inside Buster is waiting with our drinks.

"What the fuck have you two been up to?"

"Oh Joe at his best, hit a doorman" I shake my head.

"I fucking wish I had hit him, now that I know he stuck us in. I can't believe he was acting all the big man then as soon as he gets a slap he goes running to the coppers."

"Joe I've seen that shit my whole life mate. Coppers, screws, bouncers, they are all the fucking same, hard as fuck until you get them on their own, then they shit themselves." Buster says.

"Did the coppers say anything?"

"Not a word son. They had a quick look around, checked the bogs then fucked off."

"The doorman had no witnesses and it wasn't on CCTV, but I bet if they got a hold of me they would have still pushed for a remand on Monday morning in court."

"Too fucking right they would've. So what happened? Did you find him?"

"Oh yeah, we found him" I raise my eyebrows.

"That bad" He says surprised.

"That bad" I nod.

"What was said?"

I smile before I tell him. "Listen to this, He said his debt is not to me and it has fuck-all to do with me. Those were his exact words."

Buster growls, "So when Ryan's in the jail he thinks he can swan about and not pay his debt?"

"Obviously"

"I can see this getting out of hand, are you sure you don't want to give Ryan a phone and let him sort it out?"

"Fuck Ryan, he's the one that let it go this far. No, the cunts had his chance, more than I would give most people."

"This has got nothing to do with the money anymore is it?" Buster says.

"Not really." I smile. "I was hoping this would be the outcome, but I honestly never thought he would have the balls to take me on."

"So I guess that's the reason you didn't want me to come with you earlier"

"Pretty much"

"So what's the plan? Are you making a few calls?" Joe asks.

"Not this time Joe. I can probably manage this one on my own, but you're welcome to tag along."

"I'm not doing much else" He shrugs.

"Have you got his address?"

"I could make a call to get it but I already know he stays out by Clearwater Park and it will not be too hard to figure out which house is his because I would make a million pound bet that he has a car sitting in his driveway with a personal reg."

"Clearwater Park" Buster says.

I nod.

"What are they worth about two hundred grand?"

"About that"

"So he has a house that's possibly worth give-or-take a quarter of a million but he can't pay off his 20 grand coke debt?"

"What pisses me off more is that Ryan was giving him a good deal and he was obviously charging his mate's full price, which is fair enough, but then why the fuck was he running to Ryan and asking to get laid on?"

"He's maybe got a massive habit" Joe says.

"Oh I know he has a massive habit Joe, but even taking that into account he should have been making enough to feed several habits."

"There is a possibility that he is waiting on debts to himself being paid" Buster adds.

"Come on Buster, you know I always give people a chance, all he had to do was pick up the phone and explain. He is the one that decided to take this route. So right now, I could not give a fuck what his reasons are. He has run up a twenty grand debt and now thinks that he is too good to pay it back. Drink up Joe. We've got work to do."

Chapter 18

Joe and I walk the short distance to my house and after a quick scan of the adjoining streets for preying coppers; we enter through the back door. I am not planning to do a major job on this prick but I am going to give him a clear message not to fuck with me. After a quick change into some old clothes, I pick up my knuckle-dusters and a couple of spare pairs of socks before heading off out the back door again. We make the short journey over some fences to my mates shed. I open the door and hand Joe the ski masks.

"What do we need them for anyway? It's not as if he won't know it's us."

"Joe, how many times do I have to explain this? When was the last time I was locked up for anything other than football?"

He does not answer.

"Exactly, trust me, we'll need them."

I search around for the keys for one of our lockups and Joe picks up the metal detector. "Have you got a new battery for this yet?"

"Yeah but it's still not working. I'm just going to have to buy a new one."

"Yeah well, take your time; I'm in no hurry to spend another night digging fucking holes."

"It keeps you fit you fat cunt."

"I'm obviously fitter than you, you lazy bastard."

"I'm only lazy because your mum wears me out."

"Fuck you."

"Actually she's quite fit. I'll maybe ask her to help dig the holes."

"Anymore talk of my old dear and the only hole that'll be getting dug will be your fucking grave."

"Now now Joe, there is no need for that. Who is going to pay your pocket money when I'm gone?"

"Pocket money, is that what you call it?"

"Yeah, what did you think it was? Maintenance"

"I always thought it was protection money."

"I'll tell the jokes about here."

I find the lock up keys and jingle them in front of Joe.

"Come on Joe; let's go earn your pocket money" I laugh. "Grab those cable ties? Oh and that crowbar as well, we might need it."

We leave the shed and climb over another few fences until we reach the lockups. These lock-ups have been here from as long as I can remember and in all that time, I do not think anyone has used them for anything other than illegal activity. In one of them, I have a scooter hidden away, collateral for an unpaid debt. We put on our helmets and gloves and I kick-start it, while Joe jumps on the back. We take off at the breakneck speed of thirty miles per hour! I am sure I could get it up to forty if fat boy here was not weighing me down. I have had a few bikes over the years; they are handy for certain jobs. One of the good points is that nobody recognises you with a helmet on and nobody takes much notice of someone on a scooter. You see, a witness will hardly even remember what colour it was, whereas a car is much more identifiable and they can narrow it down by make, model, colour or even just part of the reg. If the coppers give chase when you are on a bike, they are highly unlikely to catch you, unless you are stupid. The downside is that you are limited to who and what you can take with you on the job, for instance, if it is a job needing more than two people. There is the possibility of using more than one bike, but then two bikes travelling together attract attention, also, if certain tools are required, for example, a chainsaw or a sledgehammer, forget it. I take the back roads through the different schemes and come out at the end of Douglas to join the dual carriageway; I turn off at Clearwater Park and follow the winding road. I pass each of the large houses and I notice that the occupiers all have one thing in common; they all park their cars on their driveway, which means that I do not have much difficulty finding what I am looking for. Parked on his driveway, out in front of his large expensive house, only feet from the doors to his double garage, is a top of the range BMW with the registration M14 XII. I make an about-turn on the scooter and drive back out of the street. Before joining the dual carriageway, I exit right, drive up a small dirt track, and park up beside some thick trees near a field.

"So what's the plan?"

"Are we coming back early doors?"

"No, we're going back on foot, leave the helmets here."

"Ginge we can't walk up that street wearing balaclavas."

"I know. We're going the long way, through the field."

"Ginge are you joking? It's just started fucking raining."

"I know we'll have to be quick, come on."

We begin walking towards the back of the houses and by the time we reach the wooden fences that run parallel to their gardens, the rain has started to get heavy.

"Ginge it's fucking pissing down. How far is it?"

"It's four from here, I think."

"You think? What do you mean you think?"

"I had the number in my head and I was counting them down from the start of the street, but I've lost count now and I can't see how many we've passed from around the corner. Fuck it! All the rest had lights on so it's got to be that one." I point further up to a house that is in darkness.

"Right Joe, pull the balaclava down. You never know if these posh cunts have their own CCTV."

"Yeah and it's probably not even for crime prevention, just for spying on their own neighbours"

I use the crowbar to wedge one of the spars in the fence; Joe gives it a pull and slides it to the side.

"Are you going to fit through there Joe?"

"Fuck you."

I laugh as he nudges me out of the way and squeezes through the gap. The house has two back doors and one of them is a patio. Joe pulls the handle on the single door; locked. I check the patio, also locked. Joe takes a step back as though he is about to give the single door a shoulder charge.

"Joe, hold on. Give me a hand here" I say in a quiet voice. "I am going to pull the handle and then nudge the patio door upwards. This should make a gap at the bottom corner. Try and force the tip of the crowbar in."

I lean against the glass and take a deep breath as I heave upwards. I hear the crowbar clatter off the metal strip along the edge.

"No not like that Joe. Look, you pull the door."

I take the crowbar and place the tip against the corner of the door. Joe pulls it and I manage to slide it in just enough to make a lever. I pull it back towards myself and there is a low snapping sound as the lock on the patio releases and the door slides open. I stand up and walk around the side of the house to have a quick look.

"What's going on, Is somebody there?"

"No, I was just making sure it was the right house."

"Fuck sake Ginge."

"Well, you never thought about checking either did you? Come on, pull the door over, and let's go."

"Why, is it the wrong one?"

"No, but he's not fucking in is he?"

We make our way back out through the gap in the fence and place the spar back in place. By the time we get back to the bike, we are soaked through and up to our knees in mud. I start the scooter and after revving it a few times, it cuts out. I turn the key a few times, nothing! We manage to get it going with a kick-start but it cuts out again.

"Fuck!"

"Do you think the rain has got into it?"

I shake my head "I think we've actually run out of petrol."

"You're fucking joking?"

"No, come on, there's no point in fucking about with it. There is a garage along the road. Grab one of those helmets."

We keep away from the main road and trudge through the thick mud around the side of the field. Joe is moaning the whole time. I can see his point, if there was not 20 grand at stake here, I would be fucking moaning as well. We reach the garage and after checking where the cameras are situated, Joe puts the helmet on with the visor pulled down just enough to block their view of his face. I wait out of sight as he walks across the forecourt towards the cashier before he reaches the counter; I look on as he puts his hands in his pockets and then marches back over to me.

"Ginge, I've no money. I left it all in my other jeans at yours."

"Shit. Did you bring your mobile?"

He shakes his head.

"Fuck!"

"We can flag down a taxi and pay it at the other end."

"Oh, that's real discreet Joe, and who do you think the coppers will ask for info first? Nah I never saw anybody on a scooter officer, but I did pick up two dickheads, one had a helmet and the other had long Ginger hair."

"Well, it's either that or we can walk but how many witnesses are going to see us then? Or we could go back to Maxi's house and see if he has any spare cash lying around?"

I think for a few seconds as I consider Joe's options and then a car drives into the forecourt and stops at the pump closest to us. We cannot see the faces of the occupants due to the tinted windows but we can hear the bass thumping from where we are standing. We stand in silence in the shadows waiting to see who will emerge then the music gets louder as the driver's door opens. A young person gets out with slick hair and spray-on jeans and before he even reaches for the fuel pump, Joe slams the visor wide open and makes his way towards him.

"Here mate, I've run out of petrol along the road, you couldn't spare me a couple of pound could you?"

"I've only got a fiver mate and I'm already driving on the red. I could give you a lift if you want."

A fiver, he will be lucky to get to the end of the road with that. What is it with these boy racers, they spend their last on doing up heaps of shit with tinted windows and alloys that would fit a fucking tractor but never have money to drive the fucking thing. I see Joe weighing up his options and goes to walk away.

"You're okay mate, cheers though."

"I have a spare petrol can if you want it, I don't have the funnel part but I'm sure you could tilt it."

"I appreciate that mate. Thanks a lot."

He goes to his boot and hands Joe the can. He thanks him again and walks back towards me. He drops the can and lets out a sigh as he slides the helmet off. We do not have to wait long when a taxi pulls in. An older man gets out and starts filling up, he looks well into his sixties, he's either finishing before the crazy drunks start crawling out of the clubs or he's filling up mid-shift for a busy time ahead, either way, I just hope that he's a good-natured old cunt who is willing to help us out.

"Joe!" I nod towards the driver. He looks at me and lets out another sigh. I know he is about to moan again so before he gets the chance I grab the helmet from him, put it on and pick up the can before making my way across the forecourt.

"Excuse me mate, you couldn't do me a big favour could you, I've run out of petrol along the road and don't have any money on me, I was wondering if you could spare a couple of pound."

He quickly gives me the once up and down.

"Just a minute" He sighs and gives me a scowl.

He takes his time filling up and climbs into his car. I cannot believe how ironic it is that I am standing here in the pissing rain waiting on some old fart to hand me money like some beggar, while I am due in twenty grand from one person alone. He grudgingly hands me a pile of small change, I feel like giving him a slap for being a miserable bastard but under the circumstances, I'll just say 'thanks, buddy' and be on my way as I have bigger fish to fry. I count it out and start filling up the petrol can. I fill up to exactly two pounds and when I lift up the can, it is less than half-full. I walk over to pay the cashier with the visor covering most of my face. He does not even bat an eyelid; he counts the change double quick and gives me a nod. The rain appears heavier as we walk back to the scooter and Joe is moaning the whole time. It makes me feel a bit negative about the job and I start to think that maybe I should have taken Buster with me, did Maxi over there and then in the pub, and that would have been it, done and dusted. But then again, there is a high possibility of us all lifted and remanded for months, then it would be the whole process of threats to witnesses and courts appearances, and in all that time, Maxi, the prick, would be swaggering about and still not stumped up a penny. The pissing rain, the mud and Joe's constant moaning does not really seem that bad now.

With no funnel for the petrol can, I get Joe to hold up the bike while I try to aim the fuel towards the hole at the top of the tank.

"Fuck sake Ginge, you've got it all down my jeans."

Well, it's fucking hard to see in the dark Joe."

"Pity we don't have a lighter or something."

"A lighter Joe"

"What? Oh right yeah."

"Ah fuck, you know what I mean, a torch or light of some sort."

"A lighter"

"Ah fuck off."

I shake the last few drips out of the can and we get the bike started.

"So where are we going? Back to yours"

"The town"

"The town, why the fuck are we going back there?"

"Well, there's no point in hanging about here all night if the fucker doesn't come home."

"Do you know where he'll be?"

"Yeah, but we'll have to be quick. Come on, jump on."

Chapter 19

There is the possibility that this could be a wasted journey but instead of hanging about for a few hours in the hope that Maxi does actually go home tonight, we head back into the town. Most of the pubs are closing by the time we get there and with this weather; people are either rushing to get to a nightclub or trying to flag a taxi. Joe taps me on the shoulder and points across the street. It is the bouncer from earlier who refused him entry due to his Stone Island badge. I stop further up and pull over to the side of the road and we watch him walk up the opposite side on his own. Joe gets off the bike and goes to walk over.

"Joe, not now"

"What do you mean, not now? I'm away to give that jumped up prick a slap."

"Joe there's CCTV at both ends of the street."

"So fuck, I'll just walk passed and nut him with the helmet."

"And then what; jump back on the scooter? Really clever"

"It'll take me two minutes."

"Save it, Joe. I did not go to all this trouble for an arsehole like that. He'll keep."

Joe reluctantly gets back on the bike and we drive off. I know he is raging but if I let him confront that bouncer they will pick us up on CCTV in no time, and we would not last five minutes on this scooter. It would be different if we were up in the scheme but the chances of outrunning the coppers in the city centre are slim. I drive to an empty car park situated not far from the entrance to two of the nightclubs.

"Why are you stopping here, you can get a better view from over there?"

Joe nods to another car park across the road belonging to a supermarket.

"Joe it is filled with boy racers standing about talking shit and admiring each other's cars. They rip in and out of there, passed the nightclub queues and through the town and back again just to let everyone know how loud their exhaust is, attention that we do not need. That reminds me, I received a phone call from Ryan's missus the other day, one of her neighbours is one of those boy racers and has been giving her shit, she wants me to nip past and have a word with him."

"I take it he's not met, Ryan?"

"No, he moved in not long after Ryan was remanded."

"What's he been doing?"

"Revving his engine at all hours and generally being a little prick. She mentioned something about bothering the dog."

"I never knew Ryan had a dog."

"Yeah they've got a Staffie, it's called Biscuit. It used to belong to one of Buster's drinking friends, Big Danny. He died last year and his wife couldn't look after it so Ryan took it in."

"I remember a dog called Biscuit when I was growing up. It was a guy named Gaz that had it"

"It's the same dog Joe. Gaz was Big Danny's grandson; they used to live not far from you."

"He was murdered was he not?"

"Yeah, someone stabbed him about ten years ago."

"Did you know him?"

"Yeah, I knew him well. I just didn't like the company he kept."

"What do you mean?"

"He was always with that Junkie Jamie and he used to deal a lot with the Donaldson's. I liked him though, he was never flashy and he knew how to keep a low profile."

"Who killed him?"

"I'm not sure. There were a few names thrown about at the time. There was a guy Murdo, don't know if you remember him, crazy fucker back in the day."

Joe shakes his head.

"Well he took a bad beating for it but it turned out to be nothing to do with him. It was apparently a mix up with that Junkie Jamie's brother or something."

"Junkie Jamie" Joe snorts.

"Remember he wasn't always a Junkie. After Gaz died, he tried to step into his set up. He was swaggering about like some sort of gangster; name dropping whatever Glasgow firm he was working for at every opportunity.

It was inevitable that the coppers were going to bust him. He did a few years inside and came out a Junkie."

"Now all he does is goes around robbing other junkies for a fix."

"Exactly, he's a horrible, nasty piece of work."

Joe and I sit for a good half an hour watching the doorway to both nightclubs. Every now and again one of the boy racers cruises into the car park opposite and sits for a few minutes before wheel spinning out passed us.

"Joe, look who's just stumbled out of the club looking a bit worse for wear? And it looks like he has a hot pair of tits to keep him company."

"Hopefully he's going to his place and not hers."

"Good point Joe."

Maxi walks around the block towards one of the takeaway shops, we follow on, but keep our distance. From across the street, we can see him through the window of the shop. While he is talking sweet nothings into the girl's ear, she is giggling and pushing her tits out towards him. They receive their takeaway and climb into the first taxi outside. The bike struggles to keep up but we manage to catch them as they stop at several sets of traffic lights. When it hits the Arbroath road, the taxi takes off but I am not that bothered about keeping up, as I know now that they are heading to his place. We reach the dirt track and stop under the tree as before. With our helmets off and balaclavas down, we make our way towards Maxi's house. The rain has stopped but Joe is still moaning about having to walk through the thick mud. As we approach his fence, I can see his living room light on; I pull the loose spar to the side and enter his garden. We can hear music, as we move closer to the house. I hand Joe one of the pairs of socks and we both put them over our trainers. The patio door blinds are closed but there is a small gap just big enough for one of us to see in. I watch as Maxi is lying on his back on his fluffy rug on the floor and the girl is straddling him. She still has her dress on, draped around her waist and is nearly hitting herself in the face as her large tits bounce in time with their movements. It is like a carry on film, he stretches up now and again to put one or her tits in his mouth but she is grinding so fast he keeps missing it. He gives up and lies back but moments later he goes for it again.

"Joe, come over here" I whisper.

"What is it?"

I move out of the way to let Joe see through the gap. He has a look in and then turns to me, and all I can see are his white teeth, smiling through the hole in his balaclava.

"He doesn't waste any time does he? I mean, they never even touched their food."

Joe has obviously eyed up the bag from the takeaway shop.

"Hungry Joe"

"Fucking starving"

"So what would you rather have? Whatever is in the cartons or what he's eating?"

"Well if I was having as much trouble as he's having I would probably rather have what's in the cartons."

We both have a silent giggle to ourselves and as I move back to the gap in the blinds I watch as they start moving a little faster and grunting a little louder, minutes later, it's all over. She lies back on the rug and slides her arm around his waist. With her tits pushed tight against him, she reaches up to kiss him. He gives her a look that he seems more concerned about her smearing his cream rug with her orange tan than puckering up to her sweaty lip. The forced returned kiss is enough for her to get the message that she has served her purpose. He reaches down to pull up his jeans and she sits up to put her tits back into her dress. She mouths something to him and he snaps back at her before picking up his phone. This is all going in my favour, well probably Joe's favour, as he would have had to keep her quiet while I dealt with Don Juan here. There are a few nippy exchanges between them and then total silence until the phone rings to let them know the taxi is here. There are no goodbyes between them and as expected, she slams the door shut behind her. He does not hang around, as soon as the taxi drives off he puts the light out and trails upstairs to his bed. Joe slides the patio door open.

"Joe, not yet, a couple of minutes" I whisper.

He ignores me and creeps in anyway. I follow him and although I cannot see him in the dark, I know exactly where he is heading. Seconds later, I hear the rustling of the takeaway bag and then the sound of Joe munching.

"Fuck sake, Joe" I say in a loud whisper.

"You've got to get it while it's hot" He mouths back.

"It's not that, the cunt will know we are here with the sound of you eating you noisy bastard."

He does not answer back which tells me the fat cunt has stuffed that much food into his mouth that he cannot talk.

"Give me the cable ties."

I can hear him chew faster as if he wants to say something and he eventually blurts out. "What for, I'm ready."

My eyes have now become accustomed to the dark as I see him place the takeaway carton on the floor. I head out of the living room door and start to creep slowly up the stairs. Joe's munching has stopped but I know he is right behind me due to him now smelling like a cooked rat. There are several doors at the top of the stairs and I open each one and pop my head around until I find sleeping beauty in his bed. I step back and tap Joe on the shoulder. He pulls out the cable ties and steps in front of me. I take off my gloves and slide on the knuckle-dusters. Maxi is lying on his side, which means it is possible his legs are far apart so Joe joins two cable ties together. He goes on his hands and knees and reaches under the covers to slide an end under one of his feet. I walk over and stand by the bed and in one quick movement Joe lifts up the covers, pulls his legs together and bounds them tightly with the doubled up cable ties. I dive on top and straddle him, which wakens him up. He jolts upright and makes a high-pitched scream. I swing from the side and catch his cheekbone with the knuckle-duster. He is still in the fear mode as he screams again. He tries to wriggle his arms free from under my legs. I swing again from the other side and as his head is turned, I catch him square on. This stuns him long enough to relax his arms. I give him another quick left and right and his hands are soon flapping about again as though he is learning to swim. I grab him by the throat and put my mouth towards his ear.

"You've got until next week to get your debt paid you arrogant prick."

I release my grip and then swing a couple more times. At one point, I hear his teeth crunch as the metal connects with them. Joe taps me on the shoulder and I swing one last time. As I climb off him I look down, and even in the darkness, I can make out his face covered in blood. I move off the bed and Joe pulls out a blade and slices through the cable ties. I take off the knuckle-dusters and put my gloves back on just in case I touch something on the way out. We head back downstairs and Joe picks up the takeaway as he is leaving.

"There's no way he's going to be eating it now" He mumbles.

I pull the patio door back over and replace the spar on the fence before making our way back to the scooter. Joe moans that the rain is coming on again but it is a relief for me as all our footprints and tyre tracks will be long gone. To most people, it would appear that this job is done and dusted, time to piss off home and sort out the finer details later, and believe me, the way I feel right now, I could think of nothing better than to park up the scooter and jump in my bed. This could be due to the eventful night or the fact that I have been wearing soaking wet heavy clothes for hours. However, in this line of work, the difference between finishing the finer details of a job and doing things half-arsed would depend on whether you were prepared to rot in a cell for a few years. We dump the scooter and the helmets back at the lock up and make our way back to mine. After changing clothes, Joe heads home with a full stomach while I head out the back door start climbing over a few neighbours' fences. I have the bag of wet clothing in tow; it is too wet to burn so I dispose of it into several different bins along my street. I make my way home before switching off all my phones and going to bed.

"I thought you would still be sleeping" Buster says barging into the room.

"What time is it?"

"Just after eleven, you must have been busy when you left the Claver."

"Why, what's happened?"

"I received a call from the pub early this morning, there was somebody waiting for you when they opened up. They couldn't get a hold of you, so they phoned me."

"Who was it?"

"Fuck nose. Some guy in a suit."

"What did he want?"

"He gave me something to give to you."

I look up to see Buster smiling and can tell he is dragging this out on purpose.

"Come on then. What is it?"

"An envelope, it's pretty thick."

"How thick"

"Oh, I'd say about twenty grand thick!" He pulls it out of his jacket and pretends to examine it.

"That does look pretty fucking thick" I smile.

He throws it towards me and then smiles again before walking out the door.

I do not know what goes through some people's minds. They go for these huge mortgages, expensive flashy cars, exotic holidays and designer clothes all on credit and the person they try to rip off is the local drug dealer, a person who has no rules or laws when it comes to recovering his debt and will stop at nothing until it is paid.

Chapter 20

"Ginge, how many tickets have you got?" Buster shouts from the other side of the bar.

"Brody gave me five."

"How many are going?"

"Including you? Five."

Buster shrugs at someone sitting next to him, he must be bending his ear about going to watch Brody fight tonight. I've spotted a few plain clothes coppers randomly tailing me today so having Buster with us has kind of worked in my favour, as with him around it will take some of the attention away from me. The fight is in Edinburgh, and part of the condition that Buster is coming with us is that he has to drive us through. Hunter could have driven us, but I had already asked Buster to come along and if he was not driving, then that means he would get pissed and I have arranged to meet up with a few Hibs boys before the fight, so having him pissed around them would be like babysitting. Fuck that. He has a pint in front of him and I am standing opposite, watching closely. I know he would not hesitate to rope some other tube into driving, so that he could get pissed up. My original plan was to take a busload through which meant that if any would be coppers were on my tail I would've slipped off quietly and back again without them noticing.

"Ah is that fight tonight? I was really wanting to go," Says some random that is sat next to me at the bar.

I've had this shit all day, I told everybody the dates of the fight and when the ticket money had to be in, we had a flyer up on the door of the pub but only three people got back to me, Larnio, Joe and Hunter. It is now the day of the fight and every cunt and their fucking dog wants to go, including the knob-head who has piped up next to me by the bar. He is one of those weirdos who will pop in for a pint about once a month and talk shit to anyone who will listen.

"What time are we leaving at?" Hunter asks.

"We're leaving before Buster tries to sneak in another pint and tells us that he can't drive."

"I told you earlier I would drive."

I shake my head "Believe me; you don't want to be driving when Busters pissed later on. If he's coming with us, he's fucking staying sober."

"Ah, I hear you" Hunter winks.

"So who is your brother fighting?" The weirdo asks.

I shrug "Someone from Dundee, I think his names Navarro or something."

He raises his eyebrows and gives me a look.

"What's up, do you know him?"

"I think your brother might be in for a hard fight" He nods as though confirming to himself.

"Why, is this Navarro any good?"

"Good, oh he's a mad brawler, very tough."

"Yeah well, I've seen Brody handle himself. I don't know what he's like in the ring but he boxed in the army for years."

"I'll be surprised if your brother lasts the distance. Navarro goes for it right up to the final bell."

"So what are you trying to say, that Brody doesn't have a fucking hope in hell?"

"Well..."

He starts to give me the statistics on this Navarro, about how many people he has knocked out and how he beat this fighter and that fighter...blah de fucking blah. I really cannot tell what is getting me more agitated, this weirdo talking absolute bollocks in my ear, or that Buster now has a fresh pint sitting in front of him or maybe it is that I have just clocked an undercover copper pop his head around the door and scanned every face in the pub. Whatever it is, it is time for me to get to fuck out of here.

"Look my brother's no mug, he's been training hard and I'm sure his club wouldn't put him into the fight if they never thought he had a chance."

"Yeah, I suppose you're right."

"Exactly, now shut the fuck up, you're really starting to piss me off. You've never even seen Brody box, yet you're sitting here putting him down before he's even had the chance to throw a fucking punch."

"Oh, Ginge I didn't mean it like that."

"What's this 'Oh Ginge' you don't even fucking know me."

He gives me one of those wide-eyed stares and stands up from his stool. I take a step towards him, leaning in with my head and smacking it off the bridge of his nose. He falls over the back of the stool and crumbles to the floor.

"There you go, Mr Statistician. Add that to your list of fucking knockouts...you prick."

Nobody really bats an eyelid except the barmaid; who leans over the bar to see him flat out on the floor.

"Rodney! Is there any need for that?"

I do not answer. I pick up my jacket and turn to walk away but then turn back towards Buster.

"Buster" He looks up and I nod towards the door.

He looks at me and gives me the thumbs up. I watch as he picks up the fresh pint in front of him and downs it in one go, the sneaky bastard. I go to the door and glance back to see the other punters, drinks in hand, stepping over the weirdo on the floor as though he is just a small puddle in the rain.

Before getting in the car, I glance up the street and as predicted, the coppers have parked up in an unmarked car.

"Buster, do you still have a warrant out?"

"No why?"

"We've got company" I tilt my head back.

"Is that right?" He says checking his mirrors and looking alert.

He starts the car and pulls out from the space slowly while continuously checking his mirrors. Once he is comfortably out from the parking space, he puts the foot down and takes off around the corner like a rally driver. You see Buster's usual scenario when the coppers are onto him is to pull up to their car and demand to know why they are following him. Well, I say demand, on some occasions that could be putting it mildly. I have witnessed him walk straight over to them, tap on their window, lean into their car, grab one by the throat and threaten them. It never works out that great for him but that is just his way.

"Do you know them? What are they C.I.D. or Drug Squad or what?"

"Who cares, just fucking lose them."

He does a sharp U-turn in the street and gives them an evil stare as he doubles back and passes them. I look behind to see them pull out and hold up the traffic as they also attempt a U-turn. They speed up and eventually pull in behind us and Buster slows down so that the gap is only meters between us. He stares at them in the rear view mirror, taunting them and talking to himself as though they can hear him. I look back to see Joe, Larnio and Hunter all with a face of concern. You see, although they have dealt with coppers all of their lives, and possibly had as many run-ins with them over the years as me. They have never actually dealt with them quite like Buster and it is a worry that they could get pulled in on a police assault charge and face two, maybe three years inside, whilst never even setting foot out of the car. Whereas this does not faze Buster, he would look on it as just another day in the life. From my point, it does not really faze me either as I look on this with two different opportunities, one is simple enough, that Buster will hound them, and lose the fucking tail. Two, would be for me to find out exactly whom they are really on to, and what they know. You see if Buster flips and we are all pulled, they would question each of us separately, they'll mention a few incidents that have occurred, usually the ones where they have fuck all leads, if any of us have cases coming up they'll give us the old line 'If we help them they'll help us.' It is all lies. Sometimes they will even throw in a random name just to see if our expression changes and then pounce on it with all sorts of accusations. You see coppers would think nothing of making up charges to get the five of us put away, this is due to them being a bunch of lying, corrupt bullying bastards. There is the odd one who is decent and tries to be diplomatic but then it is like the old saying good cop, bad cop, but for every good cop there are about twenty fucking bad ones, all fascist cunts with major chips on their shoulders.

    With the C.I.D. tight on our tail and Buster driving at a high speed he decides to break suddenly and swerves into a tight lay-by, the coppers are now so close that they have two options, one is to go straight into the back of us, or two, make a sharp turn outward and overtake us. For their own safety, they go with the second option and Buster gives them a wave as they pass us before quickly pulling out behind them. At the first available turn off the coppers keep going straight ahead but Buster takes a left and rips through various streets, he then doubles back to make sure that he has lost them. Once we get back onto the main road heading south out of Dundee, Buster floors it again, as although they are not in sight, it does not mean we don't have another tail, and if it needs to be flushed out, Buster will get it done. There is no fucking about when he is behind the wheel but I do not think this is due to any expert driving on his part. I think it is down to him having no fear whatsoever of extreme velocity, sharp bends or any on-coming traffic. His foot is practically on the floor nearly all the way to Perth as he switches lanes to overtake anybody and everybody. He slows down slightly as we approach the Friarton Bridge on the Perth bypass as there is a build-up of traffic, but as soon as we are over the bridge, we are once again at maximum speed. I have seen this scenario many times. There is a blind bend a few miles up the road before the Edinburgh turn off and if there is a tail on you, which is too far behind, there is no chance for them to know which road you have taken. For any coppers on our tail to keep up before the bend, we would spot them easily, if they kept their distance, took a guess and got lucky at which road we had chosen, they would still have no chance, as Buster will continue flooring it all the way to Edinburgh. If it was down to me, I would have taken one of the random turn-offs and parked up on the flyover just to see if there was a tail, but Buster is in control and whether there was or there was not a tail, I do not think he would have driven much differently.

Chapter 21

The boxing show we are attending is in a community centre in Leith not too far from Easter road, the home of Hibs football ground, but I have some other business first. I have arranged a meeting of sorts with a close acquaintance who, like myself, happens to be part of his local football crew. With the armed robbery of the building society still under investigation, it is probably not in my best interests to be seen having a drink and banter in one of the Hibs boozers with one of their top boys. This probably does not seem much for the coppers to go on, but if they were putting a case together and they allege that we staged the Hibs clash to set up a diversion for the robbery, it would not look good. My Hibs acquaintance would have ditched the mobile that he had in his possession that day, the minute he stepped off the train in Dundee. Likewise, the one that was in my possession should also have been disposed, but stupidly, I had handed it to Ritchie to send the final 'all clear' message to Ryan. That same mobile is now in Police evidence, and is the only thing that can tie it together. In this game, ditching phones is standard procedure, whether tied to an armed robbery or not, as football violence now comes under the mobbing and rioting act, and this comes with a sentence of up to twenty years. If I were in possession of a phone, which contained documentation of an organised meet, especially with my record, I would receive more prison time than if they prosecuted me with the armed robbery charge. They do not have enough evidence to place Ryan on trial and even the smartest lawyer in the country could persuade them otherwise so he will be out soon. His remand is nearly up but I know they will hold him for the full term and not a minute less.

We stop outside the Artisan on London road, and Buster abandons the car as we swarm into the pub. We instantly receive a few dodgy stares from a large group in the corner of the pub but once they recognise me, it is all smiles and banter. Joe knows some of them through dealings with me so receives the handshakes while Hunter and Larnio stand by the bar and give the few nods of acknowledgement. They stand with their drinks next to Buster, whom I know is completely out of his comfort zone of the Claverhouse, and is meaninglessly saying to himself that he hates everyone. I keep the banter flowing until I manage to manoeuvre myself unsuspectingly next to my main contact in their crew. The jukebox is on and the banter around us is providing enough background noise for us to swap the much-needed information between us away from the bar, the toilets, suspect punters and any sneaky acquaintances. While his crew are shouting and informing each other of their sexual conquests, we both add to the banter while exchanging our information. To someone who did happen to be listening, this is similar to prison talk, a broken conversation of words that to an outsider would not make sense. Having learned this trait from my own unfortunate prison time up and down the country, it does have its uses on the outside world. While serving time in prison, I managed to perceive some of the main reasons why people ended up there. I was never interested in the social aspect of crime, as in the, why they committed the crime, more the reasons why they were caught. Depending on the crime, there were those blatantly caught on camera and others that stupidly left a fingerprint behind, and then there were the institutionalised. By this, I mean the ones who needed their sanity checked. For instance, when someone walks out after a ten stretch for armed robbery, they go and commit another armed robbery; they go on the run and live-it-up for a few weeks, until the money is spent. Unsurprisingly, the coppers catch up with them, and they smile at the judge as he hands them another twelve to fifteen. Those are the exceptions, but other than the aforementioned, the main reason these people have ended up in prison is not due to the coppers great detective skills, but due to loose lips. Whether it is a wife, girlfriend, mistress or hooker, if they boast about their crimes, they would be as well walking into the court and telling the judge 'it was me.' Pillow talk is not always the case though; sometimes it could be someone in your circle of trust. You see, someone that you consider to be in your circle of trust might think that it is okay to blab about certain jobs in their own circle of trust; this could very easily go on until it leads straight back to those it concerns. My circle of trust involves only those that are directly involved with the job at hand. For instance, my acquaintance here from the Hibs mob did not know anything about the armed robbery. The clash between our two crews was in the planning for nearly a year in advance when the football fixtures date came up. He's not stupid, he probably knew I had an ulterior motive that day, and it's not that I don't trust him to know about it, but if he did, and one day, maybe a year from now, he could get chatting to someone that he considers that he is tight with and mention the job. Before I know it, the coppers are back on the case. If I bring someone on a job for a particular skill, I never talk about any other job that I am, or have been involved with, reason being, is that if that particular job I am on is brought down, that person could then use the information that I was bragging about to cut a deal. All these high profile busts that the coppers make, they don't just stumble upon them, and they certainly don't offer rewards for information or employ people to work a hotline twenty four seven, if it isn't beneficial. The seemingly, random suspicious person, who the coppers pounce on when he steps off a train, due to him carrying a package containing a few ounces of cocaine, does not seem that random if he has been tailed since he left his house that morning. The information has come from their drugs hotline, in an anonymous tip-off. Possibly from the person who has passed him the drugs in the first place. It is a set up to divert the attention away from the unsuspecting grandmother who is pushing a pram only feet behind him carrying half a kilo.

 Before I get a chance to down the rest of my pint I happen to glance over and catch Buster giving me a smug look and he nods towards the door. I return him a mean stare, which in my mind means 'cool it, you impatient bastard' but to him, it means I have five minutes then he is fucking out of here. The stubborn prick would actually think nothing of jumping in the car and leaving us here or start downing drinks to make sure that he is in no fit state to drive back. Either way, if I drag this out I will be paying for a taxi back to Dundee. With only dregs in the bottom of my glass, I exchange my new number and make our excuses to leave. I walk outside to see Buster already sitting in the car.

"What was the smug look for?" I ask.

"You coming to this fight night was all business for you wasn't it?"

"Among other things"

"You're a right sneaky bastard" We both smirk.

 Due to his erratic driving and spontaneous road rage, we struggle to find the community centre where they are holding the boxing show. At one point when he realises he has missed a turn off, I look at him and think that a vein in his neck is about to explode. We eventually find it and

I give Brody a call. He comes out to the front door to meet us and then leads us through to our seats. The place is packed and already there are two fighters going at it in the middle of the ring. One of them must be local as there is a large part of the crowd on their feet cheering him on. I clock a few familiar faces from the across the hall and I notice Hunter giving them a wave. Buster picks up the program on the table in front of us and scans down the list of names; he looks at me and makes a face.

"What's up?"

"Brody's opponent"

"What about him?"

"Navarro" He shakes his head "I've heard of him."

"Oh, you're not another one that thinks Brody doesn't have a hope in hell."

"I wouldn't go that far, but I think Brody might be in for a hard fight."

"I'm sick hearing about this fucking Navarro. I'm telling you now, If Brody gets knocked out, he had better not fucking come over and talk to me."

"That's your brother you heartless bastard...But you're right, if he gets knocked out, he better not come over and talk to us."

We both laugh

We sit through an exhibition bout and a few more matches until Brody's fight. They call Navarro's name first and he appears in the corner of the hall with a small entourage. He marches forward towards the ring like a man possessed. The spotlight shines on him and the whole crowd can see the look in his eyes, like venom. They announce Brody's name and it seems as though half the hall are whistling and cheering him on.

"He had better not fucking lose with this crowd behind him," Buster comments while looking around the hall.

Brody appears in the doorway at the opposite end of the hall, he looks relaxed, a bit too relaxed for someone about to fight. He walks slowly towards the ring and climbs through the ropes. The two fighters stand about two feet apart in the centre of the ring as the ref recites the rules. Although they are the same weight, Brody is a couple of inches taller but Navarro has the wider frame. The bell rings and every person in the hall is on their feet, Navarro steams across the ring like a tank; head down with big wide swings making Brody cover up straight away. He makes a sharp slip to the side and Navarro's momentum makes him stumble into the ropes. Brody uses the advantage to throw a couple of punches; Navarro does not even bother to cover up. No matter what Brody throws at him, he just keeps coming. He gets Brody in the corner a couple of times and this forces Brody to go toe to toe for a few seconds but this appears to be only to get Navarro on the back foot, just enough to give himself space to slip to the side and get around him. Navarro wants to brawl and spends most of the fight chasing Brody around the ring.

"This guy is like a pit bull" Buster comments

"I know if Brody wasn't so fast on his feet I think he would get smashed."

"What's going on? Why won't Brody stand and fight him?" Buster growls

"Well, I think the objective is to hit and but not get hit."

"Fuck that, I was looking forward to a good tear up. Brody looks as though he needs someone to break his temper; he's been brought up too soft from his mother."

Hunter overhears this and looks at me. We both raise our eyebrows.

"Break his temper? He's not a fucking dog Buster."

"Ah, you know what I mean."

The weird thing is, I do know what he means, but I would not have put it in the same context as to 'break his temper.'

The fight is a split decision and Brody nicks it. He climbs out of the ring with a few marks on his face and what looks like a black eye about to form. After a few pats on the back and some encouraging words that mostly consist of telling him that it was a 'good fight' from Hunter and Larnio and myself, Buster doesn't hold back and gives it to him straight.

"What the fuck was that? Did you leave your handbag in the car or something? I came all this way to see you dance around that ring like you were playing a game of fucking tag."

Brody looks at him and smiles; he knows he is only taking the piss. Well, I think he is taking the piss.

"You need some aggression in you" Buster clenches his teeth and makes a fist.

"I'll see about getting you on the next show then Buster."

"I've been there, done that."

"What? You used to box?"

"Of course I used to box."

"Fuck off!" I laugh "What weight did you fight at, extra super heavyweight!"

"I wasn't always this size you cheeky Ginger prick. I was a bit of a liability when it came to fights though; they disqualified me a few times. I was a dirty fighter."

One of Brody's corner men appears with a fresh ice pack for his eye and this gives us an excuse to leave him to lick his wounds. I tell him to give me a call during the week and with his good eye, he gives me a wink as we walk away. The journey home is much the same, with Buster's foot to the floor as though he is attempting to travel back in time. He comments again about Brody being too soft and I feel myself backing Brody up, but I do know where Buster is coming from; his temper is far too controlled. The wheels are now turning in my head as to how I can 'break his temper' as Buster would put it.

Chapter 22

"So what happened last night?" Larnio asks.

"What do you mean?"

"One minute I was standing talking to you and you mentioned about heading into the town, the next thing you disappeared. I tried to phone you but it was switched off."

"I had something to take care of, a bit of business" I wink.

Larnio would have accepted that answer and thought nothing of it, until Joe pipes up.

"Sneaking off to meet his new posh missus" He smirks.

"Posh missus, what's this then Ginge; do you think you're too good for the skanks around here?"

"Missus, I've met her twice. And she's hardly fucking posh if she went to school with me." I say in-defence.

"Twice, that's a fucking record for you."

"Not only that Larnio, she's a fucking lawyer."

"Whoa! Good shout Ginge." Larnio gives me a high five.

"You're meeting a lawyer?" Brody asks.

"Well, she's training to be a lawyer."

"Where did you meet her?"

"I sort of bumped into her the other week while Joe and I were out on the Perth road for a few."

"The Perth road, what the fuck were you two doing up the Perth road. Sipping Pims"

"You know me Larnio; I like to soak up the culture and that. So are you up for the game tomorrow then Brody?" I quickly change the subject.

"Yeah of course, who's playing?" He smiles.

"Hearts, some of your old local boys"

"Not a football man Brody?" Larnio asks.

"Not really, but I'm enjoying going to the games now though."

"I bet you are. That was a good fight last week, I really enjoyed it, it looked a hard fight though and that guy was solid."

"Tell me about it." Brody turns his head slightly to show the remains of his black eye.

"Have you got any more fights coming up?"

"I've been asked to fight on a show in Dundee. This fighter is a bit lighter but a lot more technical."

"Where is it, in Dundee? We'll have to get a few more of the boys through this time to support you."

"It's at the Bonar hall."

"The Bonar Hall" I say surprised. " Just let me know when the tickets are on sale, and I'll get the full squad out to support you...Oh and another thing, you better not be getting any more black eyes, I can't have you collecting money when you're standing there looking like someone has given you a slap."

"Right then" Brody makes a face.

"Listen Brody, if some arsehole approaches us and says, look, I have a debt of five grand that is due-in and the prick that owes me it is refusing to pay up. We would take on the collection of said debt, minus our fee of twenty percent. If you are sent to knock on this persons door, they will take one look at you with that black eye and say 'Jog on pal, I am not paying any debt' and probably tell you to go fuck yourself. Then you could have a fight on your hands that would escalate to a lot of noise, damage and nosey neighbours. Then the coppers turn up. 'What were you doing at this person's door? Oh, you are a McNaughton, and you are out on bail?"

"You got all that from a black eye" Brody smirks.

"Brody, this is our way of life. Yeah, we can all joke about these things but in those types of situations, that is how quickly we can size things up. Larnio, if somebody turned up at your door with a big fuck off black eye demanding money, what would you do?"

"Well you see, he wouldn't have to be demanding money and he probably wouldn't even have to be at my door. You see if I happen to bump into some arsehole in the pub, you know, the typical pissed up punter with a chip on his shoulder, I spill his drink, then I apologise, but he still gets mouthy. I'd be thinking, he must be able to handle himself if he's mouthing off to a six foot five black man, so I say 'Oh wait a minute pal, I've apologised, I don't want any trouble' then I notice the black eye, and I would be like, right then, you're fucking mine."

Brody looks at him for a few seconds as Larnio keeps a straight face.

"Fuck off!" Brody laughs.

"We nearly had him" Larnio and I laugh.

"What's this job tonight anyway Ginge?" Larnio asks.

"We're away to sort out some sneaky prick that was working for us."

"Who's that? Do I know him?"

"Mikey McCash"

Larnio shrugs. "Name rings a bell, but I can't put a face to it."

"He just some jumped up clown from the Ferry end. Well, I am not actually sure if he is from there, but he lives there now. Always at the gym, full of the steroids" I smile and pose with my arm as though showing my muscle. "He used to jump about with that junkie Jamie."

"Jamie the mad stabber, runs about for the Donaldson's?"

I nod.

"How the fuck did he end up involved with us?"

"Well, he and that Jamie had a falling out. Then he somehow latched onto Ryan. He started punting an ounce here and there; all between him and his mates, low key. Then out of the blue, he starts buying five ounces, then a week later ten ounces."

Larnio raises his eyebrows.

"Yeah, exactly, it was all cash up front so Ryan wasn't really giving a fuck. It was not even a huge amount and if he had built it up gradual, I probably would not have taken any noticed. However, to go from buying an ounce to ten ounces in a matter of weeks was enough to get the wheels turning in my head. Obviously, I ask about, and I find out that the Donaldson's are onto him. Larnio if they had gotten a hold of him they were ready to cut this fucker up. In the meantime, they remand Ryan, so now this fucker he has to deal with me. He is on the blower saying that he needs another three ounces and he has the cash waiting. Instead of sending someone around with the gear, I arrange to meet him. Joe, what was he like?"

Joe shakes his head.

"Larnio, he turned up in a top of the range sparkling white BMW jeep, he jumps out and comes bouncing over to me, chest puffed up, tanned and a gold chain hanging around his neck that was thick enough to anchor off the fucking Titanic."

"Just a pity it wasn't still attached to it" Joe says.

Larnio laughs.

"You get the picture though mate."

Larnio nods.

"Anyway, I'm looking at this fucking idiot and thinking this cunt is on the gear. So sarcastically, I ask 'you been going to the gym?' As soon as I say this, his chest grows about another six inches, looks himself up and down and says 'Yeah, I'm not working now so I'm there every day.' I already know what is coming but I ask anyway. 'Why are you not working?' He goes 'I ditched my job. There wasn't much point in working if I'm making more from selling coke.' I had to walk away. I swear it, I could have fucking choked him there and then.

"What about the jeep?" Joe says.

"Oh yeah, as we walked off, I turned back and said 'Get rid of the jeep, if you don't get rid of it I'm going to fucking burn it.' How stupid could someone actually be, he's driving about in a twenty grand motor, he does not work and is at the gym every day pumping steroids in his arse. I cut the cunt off and ditched the phone. I told anybody that had contact with him to do the same. A few weeks later I started receiving messages informing me that Donaldson's were away to come through my door because I bumped so and so. I started laughing, 'why would I bump any of the fucking Donaldson's? One thing, their gear is shit and they cut it to fuck. Two, we have our own supply and three, well three was that I did not need another fucking reason. Tell the cunts they know where I live, my door is always open.' Then I start to think, hmm, Ritchie. I hunted Ritchie down but he swore blind that he had not bumped anybody, well not at that point anyway, then I make a few enquiries and find out it is this cunt McCash. He had been bumping people left, right and centre and swaggering about telling anybody who will listen that nobody will fuck with him because he now works for the Wise-Man. I mean, does anybody actually still call him that?" I look at Larnio who smiles and nods then I turn to Joe who does the same.

"Really" I shake my head.

Brody, tactful as ever says "So why don't you just let the Donaldson's catch up with him."

"Well I would Brody but there's more to it than that. You see, due to me cutting him off and the Donaldson's onto him he has been doing deals up and down the country with anybody that would take him on. The other week, the inevitable happens, the coppers bust him. Apparently, he was caught with at least a key, kept in until Monday, no court appearance, no charges and let out the front door, off you pop son."

"Probably gave him his drugs back as well" Larnio says.

"Well depending on what he's told them, I wouldn't be surprised."

"That's Hunter outside" Joe says looking at his phone.

"Right Joe, you go with Brody in his car, Larnio you come with me in Hunters."

We down the rest of our drinks and make our way out of the pub.

"Where are we going?"

"Just follow us, Brody, Joe will keep you right."

There is no need for directions, as Hunter already knows the finer details. We have gone over this several times in the last couple of days. He heads for the Ferry road, over a small bridge to a narrow lane where we have two other cars waiting for us, both stolen. We quickly switch over and Brody follows in tight behind us. I have a scanner with me so we will know if we have a tail, or are about to be pulled. We enter a retail park on the outskirts of the city centre, it has a large gym above one of the retail units and we know McCash is in there right now as Hunter followed him here earlier while we were in the pub. Hunter drives around the car park and points out McCash's jeep. We find a space several rows back but not too far from the view of the entrance. Brody parks up further down the same row. I look up and clock the CCTV on the buildings that overlook the car park and then phone Joe.

"We can't do it here Joe. There are cameras attached to the buildings."

"Well, we know where he's heading to after the gym so we'll pull him on the main road."

"Piggy in the middle" Joe says

"It will have to be. We can't exactly ram him off the road with that fucking jeep."

"Remember this is just after rush hour, there'll still be a lot of witnesses."

"Witnesses I can handle, cameras, not so much."

I overhear Brody asking what piggy in the middle is.

"Joe you'll have to enlighten him, but make sure that when he moves, he keeps it as tight as he can."

I hang up and the three of us sit in silence watching the front door of the gym. Our eyes widen when we see a few of the steroid monkeys come out of the gym and head towards us. McCash is not with them, but like him, they all have the same pumped up build and walk as though someone has shoved a baseball bat up their arse. They walk past the car one of them glances over and looks away then does a double take and stares. Our eyes follow him. He mentions something to his cronies and they all discreetly turn and look. We all turn our heads and stare at them and they quickly look away.

"Do you think they felt intimidated?" Larnio sniggers as we watch them walking faster towards their cars.

"Bunch of Poofters" Hunter mumbles.

Moments later, McCash appears at the gym door.

"Get ready Hunter."

He starts the car and we watch and wait as he jogs slowly towards his jeep. As soon as his lights go on, Hunter pulls out and drives slowly towards the car park exit. The second we pass him, he pulls out of his space and drives right up our arse. As we turn the corner at the traffic lights, Hunter checks his mirrors to make sure Brody is behind him.

"Brody is on his tail but I can't see Joe with him, did he get out of the car?"

"No I told him to keep down, McCash knows who Joe is, so if he looks in his mirror and sees him he'll know something is up."

The lights turn green and Hunter moves off slowly to make sure that McCash stays tight behind him.

"Just say 'when' Ginge."

I pull out my handgun, point it towards the floor and cock it.

"When"

"Whoa! Someone's eventually dug up their stash" Larnio says.

"It only took him six months" Hunter laughs.

"Six months? It felt more like a year."

Hunter slams on the breaks and McCash has driven too close to drive around us. I jump out and even before McCash spots the gun, I can see the fear in his eyes. He tries to manoeuvre back but he is going nowhere, as Brody is hard up against him. There are other cars behind sounding their horn at the sudden disruption to their journey and some swing out into the fast lane to overtake us. I open McCash's door and point the gun at him in full view of passers-by. He puts his hands up to cover his face and looks as though he is trying to say something but no words come out.

"Get out."

He does not move.

"Get out of the fucking jeep" I grab hold of him with one hand and pull him out while still pointing the gun at him.

Larnio is out of our car and standing with the boot open.

I push McCash towards him.

"Get in."

"What have I...?"

I smack him in the back of the head with the handle of the gun. "Get in the fucking boot."

He climbs in and Larnio slams it shut. I get back in the car with Hunter and Larnio gets into McCash's jeep. We all drive back to the same place where we had stashed the stolen cars and no sooner has Brody stopped, but he is out of the car and marching towards me.

"What the fuck is this Ginge?"

"What are you talking about?"

"What am I talking about? Guns; kidnapping; what the fuck do you think I'm talking about?"

"Kidnapping?" I laugh "You watch too much TV. This is all just friendly banter."

"Friendly banter, are you off your fucking head? There must have been about a dozen witnesses that drove passed you. We are all looking at ten to fifteen years for this shit."

"Ten to fifteen, Brody you really need to take a pill, or maybe that's your problem you take too fucking many"

"What's that supposed to mean?"

I ignore him and turn to give Hunter the nod. He goes to the boot of his own car and takes out bottles, half filled with petrol. Larnio starts tearing up a rag.

"What the fuck is this?" Brody says continuing his rage.

"Well we can't have our DNA all over the cars can we?"

"Are you fucking kidding me? I'm not away to be part of this."

He storms over to the car that McCash is in, and goes to open the boot, but I grab him and pull him back. He turns as though he is about to square up to me but stalls when my hand slips into my pocket.

"Brody you better back the fuck up" I stand my ground and smile at him.

Larnio and Hunter stop what they are doing and look on. Brody glances at each of them.

"Fuck you, I'm not away to be part of some murder."

"Murder" I laugh and then shake my head at him.

"So what is this then?"

I put my finger to my lips and nod for him to move back. I open the boot and point the gun at McCash.

"Get out."

He climbs out and I push him towards the back of Hunter's car. Hunter grabs him by the throat and gives him a few punches before practically throwing him into his boot.

"Hunter, hold on, I want him to see this."

Hunter opens up the lid of the boot, just enough for McCash to see his jeep parked close by.

"Remember I told you that if you didn't get rid of the jeep I was going to burn it?"

Larnio hands one of the bottles to Joe, he lights the rag that he has stuffed into the top. Joe holds it out in front of him for a few seconds to let the flame take hold. He turns to face McCash who is peering out from the gap in the boot, Joe cheekily grins at him before throwing the bottle inside the window of his jeep. Hunter slams the boot shut. Larnio lights the rags of the other two bottles and throws them into the stolen cars.

"Right let's move. Brody, Joe is going with you, he will give you directions, do not speed, you will only attract attention. We'll all be miles away by the time the smoke is noticed anyway."

"What's happening? Where are you going?"

"Funny you should ask. I thought I would introduce Hunter and Larnio to one of your methods, as Mr McCash has some vital information" I wink

"So where am I going?"

"I told you, Joe will give you directions. I will meet you back at mine later. Joe, phone me when you're done, any problems, walk away and ditch your phone."

Joe nods before getting into Brody's car.

Chapter 23

"So what is this place, Hunter?" Larnio asks.

"It's a mate's garage."

"Looks more like an oversized lockup."

"It's the type of place where they'll fix your car really cheap as long as it's not too technical."

"You mean they're not proper mechanics?"

I glance up at some dodgy looking certificates framed on the wall.

"They must be qualified, they have certificates up there. Framed as well"

"Must be genuine if they're framed then?" Larnio says with a straight face.

"Eh, none of you cunts even have a car so why the fuck would you give a shit if they are qualified mechanics?"

"Just saying" Larnio shrugs

"The chair you required" Hunter points to an old wooden chair similar to the one Brody used in the beast's house.

"Cable ties?" I look at Larnio. He pulls them out of his pocket.

"Right let's see what this cunt has to say."

Hunter opens the boot and we both drag him out and pin him to the floor face down. He attempts to fight back but Hunter gives him a slap on the back of the head, making his face smack off the floor.

"If you move again I'll do it harder."

He lies still. Larnio slips cable ties around his wrists and ankles and pulls them tight. We lift him up and sit him on the chair.

"What do you want? What have I done?"

"Well to start with, I want to know who you were punting the gear to."

"Just people I know, my mates."

"Your mates" I pick up a hammer off one of the workbenches and hit it off his kneecap. He makes a cringing noise as though he is trying not to show that it hurt.

"Who were you selling the gear to?"

"I undercut the Donaldson's and used their dealers to sell it."

I turn to Hunter and Larnio who look as confused as I do.

"How is that possible if they are after you for bumping them?"

"I only bumped them after you cut me off."

I think about this for a few seconds.

"So, you went to the dealers that were working for the Donaldson's and undercut them with the gear that Ryan was selling you. I cut you off so you then go to the same dealers, who are now back selling for the Donaldson's, you get laid on and then bump them."

He nods.

I turn to Larnio and Hunter and shake my head. "Do you believe this shit?"

They both smirk and still have the same puzzled look on their face.

"Well truthfully, I couldn't give a fuck about any of that shit; I'll let the Donaldson's catch up with you for that. What I want to know is how much you got busted with?"

He looks at me shocked as though he thought nobody knew about it.

"I never got busted."

I lean over with the hammer and tap it harder on his kneecap, this time he lets out a yelp.

"We both know what I'm talking about so I'm going to ask you again. How much did you get caught with?" I lift the hammer higher above his knee again to remind of what is coming if he lies.

"Ten ounces" He blurts out.

"Ten ounces" I do a quick calculation in my head. "That's 280 grams...The coppers would take the street value which would work out at close to... fourteen grand?" I look at Larnio and he gives me a nod. "That's enough, give or take your previous, to be locked up for a couple of years. So what I want to know is why the fuck you were in and out of there in less than twenty-four hours without even being charged?"

"There wasn't enough evidence" He mumbles.

I lift up the hammer and bring it down hard on his other knee. He makes another loud yelp and I can see him gritting his teeth.

"Okay, I'll make this simpler for you. Who did you grass on?"

I keep eye contact with him and watch as he looks to my side as I raise the hammer.

"I never grass..."

I bring the hammer down hard on the same knee.

"The Donaldson's" He cries.

"Now I know they didn't just get lucky catching you, they had to have been onto you for a while. So who else was mentioned?"

I look down at the hammer and as my hand twitches, he answers.

"Ryan...but they already knew I was working for him."

"Well apparently so does the whole of fucking Dundee due to you dropping his name left right and centre. Ryan's been locked up for three months so I want to know what you told them."

"Nothing, I never told them anything."

"Was my name mentioned?"

"No. Not once."

I lift up the hammer.

"It wasn't, I swear it."

I let the hammer drop to the floor and lean forward tipping him out of the chair. Hunter and Larnio go to work on stripping him naked from the waist down while I turn the chair upside down and kick out the seat. They lift him up and place him back on the chair.

"Right Mikey, I'm going to ask you again. Was my name mentioned?"

He shakes his head and winces, obviously feeling vulnerable as though he knows something is about to happen. As I had hoped, he also closes his legs tight together in an attempt to protect his balls, thus pushing them back further and making them more prominent to hit. Having explained this set up to Hunter and Larnio earlier, they both come to stand behind the chair, arms folded, looking at me and then nodding to each other in agreement that this works. I have no intention of going to the extreme of what we did to the beast; I am only applying this method on Mikey to find out what the coppers know. I skim the hammer along the floor towards Hunter, he picks it up and without any instruction, he leans down and taps the side of the hammer off McCash's balls making them swing slightly.

"Mikey, tell me what I want to know."

"I swear I never mentioned your name."

I stand up straight and shake my head, then look up at Hunter. He leans down and smacks the hammer hard off his balls. McCash makes a strange wincing sound and looks like he is about to throw up.

"You had better tell me now. Was my name mentioned?"

He shakes his head.

"Hunter" I nod.

Hunter brings the hammer down harder and again, he makes a strange noise.

"WAS MY FUCKING NAME MENTIONED?" I shout leaning in towards his face.

With his eyes wide with shock and pain, he shakes his head again.

I kick him out of the chair and he lies in a heap on the floor.

"That's enough. Untie him."

Larnio reaches down with a blade and cuts the cable ties. He wriggles on the floor as he attempts to put his trousers back on.

"Put him back in the boot."

Hunter grabs the trousers from his hands and throws them across the garage. He makes a struggle while they march him across towards the car and Hunter smacks him across the head. He stops struggling and crawls back into the boot without any assistance and Hunter slams it shut. We drive out towards the Ferry. I know McCash's place will be buzzing with coppers due to his Jeep going up in flames so we stop short of actually entering the area. We pull into a quiet side street and I step out of the car and open the boot. I point the gun at McCash. He puts his hands up to his face and makes a muffled squeal.

"Get out"

He struggles to climb out and is unsteady on his feet. I push the barrel of the gun under his chin.

"Now you fucking listen to me, if you ever mention my name. I am going to fucking bury you. Now fuck off."

I get back in the car and we all glance back as Hunter drives off to see him naked and limping away.

Due to my little stunt earlier we are now limited to where we can go as there is no doubt that the description from witnesses will be, someone with long Ginger hair and a tall black man, which will lead the coppers straight to me. They will also know that Hunter will be involved so there will be a raid on his place at some point tonight along with Larnio's and of course mine. Hunter heads straight for an address that he already had lined up, it is a female acquaintance of his that knows the score and will let us hole up there until tomorrow.

"We need to stop by Little Liam's first."

"Ginge we really need to get off the street. Remember, they only need to get lucky once."

"I need to ditch this shooter. Nothing's come up on the scanner yet, so go straight to Liam's."

"Little Liam" Larnio says, concerned.

"He's okay, he's solid."

"You're putting a lot of trust in him."

"His old man is Tommy Ross."

"Tommy Ross, that rings a bell. I know that name. Did he not kill a copper?"

"Allegedly, he did twenty-two years, I ran into him when I was banged up after a Scotland clash with England at Wembley many years ago."

"When was that, ninety-six?"

"No, ninety-six was the finals. We had them again in ninety-nine for the qualifiers. We played them twice in four days, Hampden and then Wembley."

"Twenty-two years" Larnio whistles. "What was he like?"

"He taught me a lot" I nod,

Hunter makes the detour and we pull up outside Liam's block. I leave Hunter and Larnio in the car and enter Liam's block. I run up the stairs to his door.

"Ginge, what's up?"

"I need a favour"

"Sure, come in."

I step into the doorway but stay by the door.

"Liam, are you on your own?" I say quietly.

"Yeah mate, nobody's in."

"Good."

I follow him into his living room and pull out the shooter.

"I need you to hide this, for me."

He looks at it and smiles "Not a problem.

"It has to be a place where nobody but you has access to it, but also, if I call at short notice, you can get to it."

"I can do that."

He reaches over to take it from me but I pull it back.

"Do you have a cloth or a rag or something?"

He walks to the kitchen and returns with a small towel. I give the gun a hard wipe and wrap it up in the towel.

I hold it in front of him but as he reaches to take it, I pull it back once again.

"Liam, before you take this you have to understand, wherever you hide this it can't lead back to you or me if it is found."

"Do you want me to hide the fucking thing or not."

I hand it to him and smile.

I walk towards his front door but turn before I leave. "O and eh...whatever cash you pull in this week, just keep it."

He nods in acknowledgment as I close the door behind me.

I jump down the steps several at a time as I hurry back down to Hunter's car.

"All good" Larnio asks, still concerned.

I smile reassuringly "All good."

I instruct Hunter to take the long route using the quiet back streets to avoid any patrol cars. This is only a precaution in case they are using a different frequency. If his registration is out for detection, we would have picked it up on the scanner but nothing about the McCash incident has come through or even a mention of the burning cars. It may just be me being paranoid but either way, Hunter feels the same, so it suits us both. We arrive at the block of flats and Hunter drives around the back and into a small-secluded parking bay allocated to each numbered flat.

"We can't just turn up here empty handed Hunter. Should we not have stopped at the off-licence for a few bottles?" Larnio asks.

"It's all taken care of mate" He winks.

We walk around to the front door and I can hear the music from outside. Hunter leads the way and walks in without knocking. He introduces us to the host and several of her friends. One of them acknowledges me and mentions that she has met me before, I nod in agreement but I am none the wiser as to whom she is. Several beers later and I have already forgotten all their names. I receive a text from Joe that the delivery is done and I reply with the address of where we are. Larnio passes me another beer and as one of the girls across from me holds out a tray with several small lines on it, one of my phones starts ringing.

"Give me a minute." I wave the girl off that is trying to hand me the tray, but I give her a wink as I stand up to walk out of the room.

"Buster, what's up?"

"Coppers were just here, they were team handed."

"Where are you?"

"The Claver"

"That means they've already been to the house, Hunter's house and possibly Larnios'"

"They'll no doubt have left here and went straight to the Stoby."

"Give it a couple of hours they'll be knocking on anybody and everybody's door."

"That bad"

"Pretty much"

"You safe"

"For now"

"Good, fuck them, keep them on their toes for the rest of the night."

I hang up and turn to see the girl that was handing me a line has followed me out into the hallway. Before I get a chance to put my phone away, she is reaching up and kissing my neck and her hand works over to the crotch of my jeans. I pull her into the bathroom and she locks the door behind us. She goes straight to her knees and pulls down my jeans and boxers to my ankles. I try to shuffle back so that I can sit on the edge of the bath or the toilet but she puts both her hands on the back of my legs to stop me from moving. I stand still and let her get on with it. Over the loud music, I can hear the door going and a few raised voices. The door goes again then I hear my name someone calling my name. It sounds like Joe. He bangs on the bathroom door.

"Ginge, are you in there?"

"Fuck off, I'm busy."

I hear more talking but it gets faint as they walk away from the door.

The girl stops and I look down and pull the back of her head towards me for her to keep going. A few seconds later, she stops again. She looks up and shakes her head. She stands up and moves over to the mirror and starts fixing her hair while I pull up my boxers and jeans. I barely get the button fastened on my jeans but she turns and gropes my crotch again.

"We'll finish this later."

She unlocks the door and I follow her out. She walks into the kitchen and I head for the living room. As soon as I walk in, I clock Brody about to take a line. He sees me and hesitates.

"Don't let me stop you."

He quickly takes a line and then gives me that guilty look. Joe stands up and nods me over; I can tell by his expression that it is business. Joe knows what is what. If the music were low enough for anybody else to hear, he would have waited for a better moment or followed me outside.

"What's up Joe, did everything go okay?"

"Yeah, the job went smooth. No worries, but just thought I'd let you know I've had a call from my old dear, the coppers are parked up outside my house."

"It's okay Joe they're only looking for me."

"Yeah I know, she said they knocked and asked if they could come in and have a look."

"What did your old dear say?"

"What do you think she said? She told them to piss off and get a warrant."

I smile.

"Are you all set for tomorrow?"

"Of course"

"Good. Remember what I said, do not get involved and keep your distance. Oh and don't worry about the coppers, they'll be off your case by tomorrow."

"What are you going to do about the witnesses from earlier?"

"Well, the coppers will no doubt put me and Larnio in a line-up. If they pick us out, they pick us out. They have no gun, no victim and McCash is not exactly going to open his mouth. Even if they did find something to charge us with, what is it going to be, setting fire to a car? Damaging property?"

As we are talking, I see Brody hovering near me and as soon as he gets his opportunity, he is all in my face apologising for going off on one earlier.

"Brody forget about it."

"Yeah but I feel bad that I thought…"

"…You thought that I was away to kill somebody for grassing? I'd do it for a lot less than that!" I smile hoping that my sarcasm will be the end of it, but I can sense that Brody is high and needing reassurance.

I notice my drink empty so I use the excuse to end the conversation but mostly it is to go on the hunt for that girl. I go to the kitchen and there she is standing chatting with another couple of girls. I go straight to the fridge and take out a beer, by the time I close the door, Brody is in my face again.

"Ginge I just need to say, about that..."

I give him a look "Brody, not now." I tilt my head towards the company. He goes quiet but I can tell that he is not hearing me. I nod for him to follow me outside the kitchen.

"What have I told you about mentioning things in front of people?"

"Yeah I know but I thought these people knew you?"

I shake my head "Are you taking the piss?"

He looks at me confused and I feel like slapping him for being that stupid, but then I remember what I have lined up for tomorrow, if all goes to plan he will soon have his eyes opened.

"Look Brody, forget about all that shit from earlier, we'll talk about it some other time okay."

He nods.

"Now let's go and have a good night."

The next couple of hours go in fast as the banter is flowing and I indulge on the coke a little more than I had planned. I over-hear someone mention the game tomorrow and this gives me a slight wakeup call, this makes me start passing on the lines when they come my way. The last thing I need is to be too full of it and turning up to the game with my head up my arse. The girl from early on discreetly works her way over to me until we end up sat next to each other. We make small talk for a while but the whole time, all I am thinking is that I do not even remember her name. All I know is that we have some unfinished business. I notice her empty glass and it crosses my mind to ask her if she wants a refill, this would be my subtle way of getting her to follow me to the kitchen but making a detour to one of the bedrooms. Then I think about her performance earlier and I change my approach as I think she deserves a bit of charm.

"Do you fancy coming next door to finish what you started?"

She nods.

With the party in full swing, the volume up full and Hunter standing on the coffee table giving the house a dancing lesson, it is a big enough distraction as she follows me through to the hallway. I make a swift turn into one of the bedrooms before reaching the kitchen and she enters behind me and locks the door.

Chapter 24

It is late morning when I emerge from the bedroom and most of the people have gone. Larnio and Brody are in the living room, awake, wired and a beer in their hand. Joe is asleep in the corner.

"Where's Hunter?"

"He's with Sophie" Larnio mumbles.

"Who the fuck is Sophie"

"That's whose house you're in."

"Oh."

Through his bloodshot drunken eyes, Brody lifts up a small tray with a line on it and passes it towards me. I make a grunt and wave him off.

Larnio laughs.

"Are there still beers in the fridge?"

"Yeah, there's plenty. Oh and Tony has been on the phone. They are in Stoby bar now, he says there is a riot van parked up around the corner and a few plainclothes have been in."

"I don't think it would be a good idea to turn up there then. Tell him to let us know when they're leaving to go to the game."

"What's the big deal about this game or is this all because of what happened yesterday?" Brody asks.

"It's probably a bit of both"

A few beers later and Hunter eventually appears from the other bedroom looking a bit unfocused.

"What time is it?"

"Nearly game time, you look rough" Larnio comments

"I feel rough."

"Have a beer, that'll sort you out."

His face cringes "I don't think I'll make it the day lads."

He about turns and makes his way back towards the bedroom and receives the ultimate of abusive comments to which he gives the two-finger salute. He turns with a sly grin then closes the bedroom door behind him. Due to the raised voices, this awakens Joe from his slumber.

"What's going on?"

"Nothing much, just Hunter being a lightweight"

"Nothing new there then."

"I heard that you little fat prick," Hunter shouts from the bedroom.

We all laugh.

Larnio receives the call from Tony.

"They're about to leave the pub to go to the game."

"Right let's get our shit together."

A taxi pulls up outside and I let Larnio and Brody walk ahead as I pull Joe aside and hand him my phones and knuckle dusters.

"Remember Joe, not too close where you'll get pulled in, but not too far that you can't get the footage."

"Which one will I use?"

"Joe, they're three identical phones. Does it really matter?"

During the taxi journey, I start to go over in my head how I can get things to kick off, but just my presence will no doubt be enough. As we near the stadium, Larnio calls Tony who informs him that they are about to head onto Court Street. He directs the taxi driver and we manage to catch sight of Tony and the rest of the mob. We pull up alongside them and make our way to the front of the crowd, all excluding Joe, who singles out Little Liam and they walk separate from us. Halfway up Court Street, we turn onto Sandeman Street and not too far ahead, there is a copper directing traffic. He becomes aware of us approaching, and is straight onto his radio. We march towards him and the mob watch him squirm as they give him some light hearted verbal. We approach the queue at the turnstiles and I clock a number of coppers scattered around, with one signal, they close-in and group together. I also notice a riot van creep around the corner and mount the kerb. The side door opens and they all pile out in full gear. They have been well informed. One of the bigger coppers comes storming over; he must be the one they all bow to, the one with the stripes on his lapel.

"Trotter, where do you think you're fucking going?" He stands in front of me with his chest out as his minions quickly file into rows beside him.

"Trotter... the names Rodney"

"Look I don't want any of your shite you Ginger bastard." He says aggressively.

I need to hold my smile when I hear his comment as this is a great sign that his temper is already near the surface and it will not take much intimidation for him to pop. I keep the stare on him. One of those long-range stares, the one that says 'you are mine, you cunt.'

"Ginger bastard? What sort of way is that to talk to a member of the public?"

"Just piss off, and take your group of fucking girl guides with you."

"Girl Guides, you're saying that while standing here in your poofy outfit. Bit ironic is it not?"

"Fuck off now" He puts his arm out and points his finger over my shoulder.

"What was that? That was close to being a Nazi salute. Is that you practising you fascist cunt?"

"I'm fucking warning you Trotter."

"You keep calling me Trotter but the only pigs I see around here are you lot."

He grits his teeth and goes to take a step closer to me then one of the officers next to him taps him on the shoulder, this backs him up and he talks into his radio out of earshot. I am lining up my next taunt to try to provoke him, but when he looks up from his radio and makes a smirk, I know our small talk is over.

"Well well Trotter, looks like you're coming with us. Some of my colleagues would like a word."

My face lights up with a big smile and I put my arms wide out to my sides.

"So come and arrest me then."

I watch his eyes look at the faces on either side of me. I do not need to look, I know that each one of them is looking at him the same way that I am. He turns and proudly inspects his own mob of uniforms. He knows this is about to turn ugly, but I can tell that he wants it to. I have been here many times, up and down the country and I know the look in his eyes, that sadistic look from every copper. He wants to show his authority. He wants to put his stamp on the situation. It feels like a standoff. It is all a matter of pride now. He turns his head and whispers something to his colleague again, then I watch as the line behind them link in like a wall. I put my hands out in front of me, palms up, provoking him to step forward and cuff me.

"Come on then"

I look at his colleague and mouth the word 'nonce' but do not actually say it. The word is like the old saying, a red rag to a bull. His hand goes to his belt and he pulls out his can of CS gas. In one motion, he takes a step forward and sprays it into my eyes. This does not take effect straight away and I stand firm without even a flinch.

"What is that, aftershave?" I smile at him.

With my arms still out in front, he knows, and every copper in front of me knows, that I am not resisting arrest, but he plays right into my hands as he steps forward and sprays me again. Unexpectedly, out of all our mob, the first person to react is Brody, but not in the manner that I had hoped. He grabs the coppers wrist and twists his arm with some fancy manoeuvre. In a split second, the copper is on his knees and the can of CS spray is rolling along the ground. I am still standing in front of the big copper and my eyes are now starting to sting a bit, but I do not even think about touching them, I purposely keep my arms out in front to entice him to step forward with his cuffs, but I know he has a different agenda. He pulls out his baton and without warning or any attempt to control the situation; he sidesteps me and leans forward to smash Brody in the side of the head. Brody puts his hand up and crouches slightly. He looks up at the big copper and then lunges forward with a punch to his jaw. It does not appear to have much of an impact as the big copper comes at him again with the baton. Then it all kicks off. Our mob charge forward and the big copper goes to work by repeatedly lashing out with his baton, trying to hit anyone that is in his range. I move in quick to get under his arm and am now too close for him to hit me. We end up in a wrestle but with my mob pushing behind me, he is over-powered and I pull him to the ground. I lean over him and land a few punches before the other officers pull me forward and out of the reach of my mob. I feel the batons smack off my head but I try to stay upright. I know if I go down, I am finished, so I start punching my way upright; it is moments like this where my knuckle-dusters would come in handy. I manage to catch a couple of them and this makes them back off enough for me to stand straight, but the blows don't stop. As I stand toe to toe with one of them, there are on-going battles either side of me, and one of them is Brody. He has one officer in a headlock and is holding his own by fighting several of them off with one of their own batons. A number of officers soon surround me and I feel myself going down once more. I put my arms up to cover my head to try to protect me from the blows from their batons but they rain down on me from all angles. I soon find myself pinned to the ground with a knee in my back. While they struggle with me to put the cuffs on, Brody slumps to the ground next to me with several officers on top of him. They manage to put the cuffs on Brody first and as they lift him to his feet, he launches forward cracking his forehead on the nose of the copper in front of him. They force him to the ground once again. With my cuffs now on, they drag me to me to my feet and walk me towards the meat wagon. The officers are about to push me in, when an order is shouted to hold me back. Four coppers rush passed us carrying Brody, he is face down, with his wrists cuffed and his legs are cable tied. They launch him into the meat wagon headfirst. They march passed the meat wagon to a waiting car. Joe appears with Little Liam, both holding my phones, videoing the whole event. I cannot tell if it is due to the knocks over my head but for some reason, I remember that I was supposed to meet Rachel tonight.

"Joe, go through my phone and find Rachel, tell her I've been lifted" I wink.

He gives me a weird look and shrugs before one of the sadistic pricks turns and tells him to piss off. With a copper squeezed in either side of me, the car makes a U-turn in the street and I catch a glimpse of my mob scattering while the coppers make the chase. As the patrol car drives off it passes Joe and Little Liam, I laugh when I see them, leaning against another car, videoing each other, smiling and waving.

During the journey to Bell Street station, the C.S. Gas is in full affect, and even though my eyes feel as though they are on fire, there is no fucking way I am going to give them the satisfaction of letting them know this. They drag me out of the car and one of them trips me up. With my cuffs still on, I have nothing to break my fall, but I manage to twist quickly so that I land on my side when I hit the ground. As expected, the four of them swing the boot into me while I lay unable to get up and helpless to defend myself. I am still mouthing off at them when they pick me up and march me into the charge room. I inform the desk sergeant of the assault and he instructs them to back off, as this is now formal complaint. I smirk at them as the desk sergeant takes over. Any thoughts they had of escorting me the cells to continue their assault are now over. The desk sergeant passes me to an assistant who searches and processes me before placing me in a cell. My adrenaline keeps me going for a while as I pace back and forward and although the pain from the batons has not kicked in yet, it is coming. I eventually sit down and close my eyes to try to stop the burning but it does not help. I know there is the option of pressing the buzzer and ask to have them rinsed, but they are hardly going to drop everything and run to help me. The burning will have stopped by the time they get around to me and I will have given them the satisfaction of knowing they have hurt me for nothing, fuck them. I keep my eyes closed and put my head back against the wall. I can overhear shouting and banging in the distance and it is not until it gets closer I realise that it is Brody's voice. He is kicking off big time and it sounds as though he has hurt a few coppers in the process. They manage to get him into a cell and I hear the door slammed. Heavy footsteps run back and forward in the corridor outside the cells and a few raised voices of someone giving orders. This can only mean one thing. Those pricks are away to do-him team handed.

"So this is the new McNaughton on the scene. Let's see if he lives up to the name" I overhear a copper say before they open his cell door.

There is a lot of shouting and I smile to myself I think of Brody's trademark move after one copper screams 'my eye, my eye.' when moments later I hear another shouting 'get him off me' Brody is clearly giving as good as he gets, but then I hear more footsteps.

"Quick grab his legs. Pull him back."

"Hold him down, hold him steady."

Brody is still shouting abuse at them as they beat him on the ground. Then it goes quiet and all I can hear is the low continuous thud of the batons echoing through each cell as they lay into him. I stand up and join the others in their cells by banging on the door and shouting for the bullying bastards to leave him alone. The beating goes on for several minutes and it sounds as though they are taking it in turns hitting him.

"You bunch of fucking animals. Leave him alone. He's had enough" I shout.

The hitting eventually stops and the corridor is quiet except for a few of the officers muttering between themselves. They are probably congratulating each other on a job well done, a job of beating a man with a stick, while several other men pin him to the floor. I sit down with a worried thought that Brody is okay, hoping that he is still breathing. Moments later, I hear more banging on a cell door and a voice shouting.

"You bunch of fucking cowards. I'll to take any of you on, one on one."

I lay back and smile, thinking, they have broken his temper.

Interlude – Part 1

Chapter 25

Brody lies still on his cell floor battered and bruised. Every now and then, the cell door opens and he can see a blurred vision of someone in front of him. They check his pulse and ask him a few questions. It is always the same questions, repeatedly. It has come to the point that he now replies with a distinct mumble of 'Fuck off.' He has lain in the same position for a few hours now, as the last time he turned to lie on his opposite side was so painful to move he did not think it was worth the effort. He can hear faint voices from the other cells having conversations through the walls with each other. Most of them are junkies, in for the weekend having been caught doing petty crimes to feed their heroin habit. Much of what they say is repetitive and along with their slurred whining speech, it starts to annoy Brody. At one point it gets to him so much that, even though it causes him severe pain he manages to lift his chest and shout 'shut the fuck up.' A bombardment of insults and stabbing threats towards him soon follow. He then overhears Ginge's voice shouting at them and they immediately apologise. Things go quiet after this and Brody enjoys the silence, it gives him time to think about things, which in turn, takes his mind off the pain. A pain caused by his fellow officers, his fellow boys in blue.

It is early Monday morning and Brody stirs in his sleep while slumped on the cell floor. He overhears a familiar voice shouting, accompanied by a continuous banging on a cell door. It is Ginge's voice, shouting for a doctor.

"Why, what's wrong with you?" The Turnkey says as he opens the hatch on his door.

"None of your business, I just need a fucking Doctor"

It goes quiet again and Brody is about to drift back to sleep when he is startled by the Turnkey serving him breakfast. He manages to sit upright but he still cannot lean back due to the kicks to his spine. He can hear the Turnkey making his way around each cell with his trolley containing the food trays and then he overhears Ginge's voice once again.

"I don't want your fucking breakfast. I told you, I want to see a fucking doctor."

"And I told you, if you tell me what is wrong, I'll get you one" He says smugly.

The whole hall echoes with the noise of Ginge's breakfast launched against his cell door.

"I've requested a doctor, so you had better fucking get me one."

The junkies from the other cells join in by shouting abuse at the Turnkey and begin banging their metal food trays against their cell doors in protest. The Turnkey marches out of the hall with his trolley in tow. Soon after, Brody is startled as his cell door opens. The Turnkey stares down at him and grunts before stepping back from the doorway, a small older man wearing a suit appears from the side and enters his cell.

"Hi. I'm Dr Taylor, I've been sent over here by your brother to check on you."

"What do you mean? I thought he needed a doctor."

"No, there's nothing wrong with him. He demanded that I come over and check on you. He said he had been shouting at you for hours and you hadn't responded."

The doctor has to help Brody lift up his t-shirt. He then places his stethoscope on his back and asks him to breathe in. Brody attempts to lift his chest but stops suddenly due to a sharp pain. The doctor moves the stethoscope to different areas while continually asking him to breathe hard, each time the pain shoots through his body. He struggles to hold himself steady and begins to shake. The doctor steps back and looks at the Turnkey.

"He has cracked or quite possibly broken several of his ribs, the damage is definitely what is constricting his breathing. I am concerned that he cannot fully lift his chest as this can make him susceptible to infection. I would like him transferred to the hospital immediately."

The Turnkey gives him a look and the doctor follows him outside of the cell. He makes an unconvincing excuse for not transferring Brody due to his expected court appearance in a few hours. The doctor listens to his concerns and then makes him aware of the proper incident procedure and the consequences of what could happen to Brody if the correct treatment is not given. The Turnkey steps in very close to the Doctor and lowers his voice to a whisper; he knows that behind every cell door someone is listening intently to every word spoken.

"Now you listen here Doc, I don't give a flying fuck about your 'proper incident procedure' I am not about to fill in a mountain of paperwork because some fucking thug turns up in my cells with a few broken ribs, especially after assaulting several of my colleagues. He is about to be transferred upstairs to the court in a few hours and once he is signed over, his broken ribs are not my fucking problem. Technically, your call was to that Ginger cunts cell behind me and there is fuck all wrong with him. So, as far as I'm concerned, you can either write up your little report that this was a wasted journey, or you can go back in there and slip him some painkillers to see him through the next few hours, because but there is no fucking way he is being transferred to any hospital."

The Turnkey shuffles forward into the doctor's comfort zone with an intimidating stare, forcing the doctor to take a step backwards. He hesitates for a few seconds as his eyes move from Brody to Ginge's cell door and back to the Turnkey. He puts his head down and walks passed the Turnkey into Brody's cell. He places his stethoscope back into his briefcase and locks it.

"What's happening?" Brody asks.

The doctor turns to him with a guilty look. "When you breathe, try and open your lungs by slowly lifting your chest a little more each time."

The cell door slams shut and as the key turns in the lock a shout of 'Shitebag' comes from inside the cell, it is loud enough for every other cell to hear it including Ginge, who smiles when he realises it is Brody. The doctor squirms with embarrassment. Before the Turnkey and the doctor exit the hall, there are a few cheers from the other cells and Ginge shouts a few words of encouragement to Brody. There is silence once again and Brody's mixed emotions about his situation are making him feel confused as to where he goes from here. After witnessing an officer influence an independent doctor's decision about treatment for someone he has examined, he knows there is no middle ground when it comes to the Police. There is no question that it is 'Us' and 'Them' The only problem he has is that as much as he wants to be part of the 'Us' he now feels that he is part of 'Them.'

Over the next few hours, the cells begin to empty as each prisoner makes their plea in front of the judge. Brody's cell door opens and he is surprised to see a different Turnkey. He struggles to his feet and shuffles out of his cell. Two G4S officers are waiting to escort him up in front of the judge. He nods to the cell opposite.

"Has he been up yet?"

"He's been remanded. He's in a holding cell waiting to be transferred to Perth" The Turnkey confirms.

One of the officers cuffs Brody's wrists before they slowly escort him up to the courtroom. His solicitor approaches him and attempts to smile, but this soon turns to a look of concern when he senses the tension in Brody's face.

"Brody I can only apologise for not talking to you sooner but as you can probably tell, it's been a hectic morning. I assume you are pleading not guilty?"

Brody nods.

"Well the judge is being, how can I put this, a bit problematic, and I think I am going to struggle to persuade him not to have you remanded."

Brody shrugs. He glances around the court and notices someone waving near the back. It is Joe the Bull and Hunter. They had turned up to see Ginge and decided to hang around. Joe gives him the thumbs up and Brody forces a smile back and nods. As he turns to sit down he looks over at the prosecutor's table and the two dull suits of Whyte and Drummond catch his attention. Whyte looks up and makes eye contact but is professional enough to look away without acknowledging him. The judge appears with a face like thunder and once he settles into his chair he listens to the charges and shakes his head. The prosecution passes over some paperwork to the judge and he puts his glasses on before leaning forward in his chair to read it. With Ryan still inside and Ginge awaiting transfer, Brody knows that Whyte and Drummond are here to make sure that he is banged-up alongside them. The whole room is in silence as the judge takes his time to go over the documents in front of him. Now and again, he lifts his head and glances up at Brody with a disdain expression before looking back down to continue reading. He eventually leans back in his chair and slowly removes his glasses. Without any objections or even a comment from the judge, he grants Brody bail and the court is quickly dismissed. Brody is shocked. He felt sure that he was about to be remanded along with Ginge. He looks at his solicitor and gives him a nod. He turns to face Hunter and Joe who gesture to him that they will see him outside. Brody gives them a nod. He turns to look for Whyte and Drummond but they are already exiting the courtroom. When Brody steps out of the court building, it is overly busy, as various groups of people have gathered to support their friends or relatives who are up for trial. Dressed in their best clothes, each accused looking more prominent from the rest of their group as they await their appearance in front of the judge. Brody shuffles slowly through them and catches sight of Hunter and Joe standing on the pavement at the bottom of the steps leading to the court. He reaches for the handrail of the ramp to the side and slowly walks down to meet them.

"Fuck sake Brody, are you okay?" Hunter asks.

"I think those fuckers have broken my ribs."

"Yeah, Ginge told us. We got a chance to talk to him before they took him down."

"That was a turn up for the books, you getting bail" Joe says.

"I know. I was sure I was going to be remanded."

"We're away to meet a few other boys for a pint, you coming with us?"

"That sounds good lads but I think I'm going to have to go up to the hospital to get checked out."

"Do you want us to come with you?"

"No, it's okay Joe. I could be a while. I'll give you a phone once I'm done and catch up with you though."

Hunter waves down a passing taxi and holds the door open as Brody struggles to get in.

"Give us a text or something later and let us know how you get on" Hunter says before closing the taxi door and waving him off.

On arrival at the hospital, Brody gives his details to the receptionist before taking a seat in the waiting area. He turns and quickly scans the busy room of would-be casualties, all with various ailments. He notices a vacant seat at the far wall and makes his way past the rows of fixed seats. He feels the whole room's eyes on him, no doubt wondering why he is cringing in pain with each step. He sits down and looks up at the information screen above him 'approx. 3-hour wait.' he looks around the room and studies each person while trying to work out their reasons for being here. Each one of them has a story but some are a bit more obvious, as in, the person closest to him in dirty work overalls holding a bandage to his bleeding head or the child opposite, in school clothes with his arm in a sling. All of them are typical Monday morning casualties. He wondered if they were looking at him in the same way, thinking if he had some sort of accident that was making his face cringe every so often and grip the chair due to the pain. They would never guess that it was a beating he had taken two days earlier, a beating from the Police, people who are placed in a position of trust to protect them, to protect the taxpaying public. He put his head back against the wall and closed his eyes, moments later he hears the nurse calling someone's name and his eyes ping open. He looks up to see her standing in the passageway with her clipboard, waiting for her new patient before disappearing down the corridor with them. He closes his eyes again and his thoughts drift off to Leanna. It had been five days since he had talked to her. He received a text on Friday but due to the number of drugs he had consumed, he was in no fit state to reply. He had been contemplating finishing with her for a while now. She understood that getting involved with his 'family' was part of his job but she did not know to what extent that involvement meant. She knew nothing of his new lifestyle, his new friends, the violence, the drugs, and not forgetting Tanya...actually, most of all, Tanya. She was not part of the job but she was like an addiction and she went hand in hand with everything else. It did not matter what drugs he had taken, she understood. If he turned up at her door looking rough from days of no sleep and feeling wired from too much coke, she understood. She would welcome him in, slip him some Valium and cuddle into him until he fell asleep. If he had turned up at Leanna's house in that state she would probably phone an ambulance and have him booked into AA meetings for the next six months. He felt a sharp pain in his side, which made him jerk his head forward, he tried to lift his chest to catch his breath but this in-turn caused him more pain. He gripped the chair next to him and took several shallow breaths until his breathing returned to normal. With Leanna on his mind, he searched in his jacket pocket to find his phone.

"Another eventful weekend for you I see"

He looked up to see Whyte standing in front of him. He clocked the cheap suit, the fresh white shirt and the squint tie. Brody did not say a word. He stretched his neck out to the side and made it obvious he was trying to see around him. He was waiting on Drummonds' head to appear like a hand puppet and fire out his usual derogatory insults.

"It's just me." He says before sitting down next to him.

"I thought it would look less conspicuous if you were talking to one suit instead of two."

"I'm still wondering why I'm not halfway to Perth right now."

"Well, we decided it would be best to keep you out. There have been a few developments. I cannot go into much detail right now, but with the way you're looking, I think it would be best if you take a couple of weeks away from the case."

"The way I'm looking? Do you know what those arseholes did to me?" Brody raises his voice, sounding angry.

Whyte notices a few heads turn in their direction.

"I understand."

"You understand? No, I don't think you do, those bastards kicked the shit out of me."

"Brody you were involved in a standoff with Police officers, one of them is a sergeant who is in the hospital with a concussion, there is a possibility another could lose an eye."

Brody lifts his shirt up just enough for Whyte to see the severe bruising that has now surfaced on his rib cage.

"Those fucking cowards pinned me to the floor and each of them took it in turns to beat the shit out of me. If they are injured they fucking brought that on themselves."

Whyte raises his eyebrows at Brody's comment. He is about to speak when he sees Brody's face become distorted and looks on as he grips the chair again due to the pain.

"Look, Brody, you know there's nothing I can do about that just now. I can't even file a report against them without jeopardising your position." He says softly as though trying to sound sympathetic.

"Both of Ryan and Rodney are now inside and Buster doesn't leave the Claverhouse. So where do I go from here?"

"As I said, there have been a few developments, take a couple of weeks off, go home, relax, and spend some time with your girlfriend."

Brody looks at him with contempt.

"I'll be in touch." He stands up to leave and Brody's eyes follow him until he disappears out the main door.

Brody felt more confused than ever, as too many things did not seem right. Whyte had approached him in a public place to discuss the case and at the same time commented about not jeopardising his position.

Sending in Whyte alone to talk to him, was definitely a tactical decision, but it had nothing to do with 'looking less conspicuous' as he had put it. They both knew that if Drummond had shown his face near him the way he was feeling, there would have been a lot more than raised voices. He put his head back against the wall and began to plan his report.

Interlude - Part 2

Chapter 26

Brody's sleeping pattern had been erratic for over a week now. With Leanna sound asleep next to him, he tried not to disturb her as he lay staring into the darkness. His entire thoughts focused on his meeting with his bosses later that morning. It had been two weeks since he had spoken to Whyte in the hospital waiting room and he still felt the same about quitting his job. He had told Leanna that he would request a transfer to another department, but this was only for her benefit to keep her happy. In truth, he had lost his respect for the force. His whole childhood dream had been shattered that day in his cell. He attempted to turn over and face Leanna but felt a dull stabbing pain in his side. The hospital had confirmed that he had two cracked ribs, severe bruising to several others and slight internal bleeding, as there was no treatment for this type of injury, he was injected with a strong painkiller and sent on his way. His own doctor had prescribed him Tramadol and even though he had upped the dosage, they were having little effect. He had started with the recommended two tablets every four hours, but after only a couple of days, he was taking them every two hours. By the end of the first week, his body had built up a tolerance to them that it had now come to the point where he was popping them whenever he felt the need. Leanna complained that he was slurring his speech and talking nonsense but he did not care, he was enjoying the spaced out feeling that he got from them. He managed to slip out of bed quietly so as not to wake her and made his way to the kitchen. He switched the kettle on and turned to the cupboard containing his pills. They were gone. He searched in the other cupboards thinking that he had mistakenly moved them. He was sure he had some left. He took a step back from the cupboards and thought that maybe he had gotten up during the night and finished them. Maybe Leanna had moved them. He was about to wake her up and ask her but decided to double check the cupboards first. He began slamming each cupboard door shut in frustration then a shadow appeared in the kitchen doorway and a slight panic came over him. He turned and froze, Leanna was standing with her arms folded and her expression said it all. He quickly put on his face of pain and held his hand up to his ribs for added effect.

"Have you seen my tablets?"

"I flushed them."

"What. Why would you do that?"

"Why would I do that? Because I'm sick of seeing you wandering about like a zombie."

"Hardly"

"Are you fucking kidding me? I can't get a conversation out of you and when I do it is fucking gibberish."

"Gibberish, I'm in fucking pain here" He raised his voice.

"Don't shout at me."

"I can't believe you flushed them. You bitch."

"Don't you dare talk to me like that?"

She pulled his tablets out of her housecoat pocket and threw them at him.

"Fucking take them all and when you meet your bosses later today you won't have to bother asking for a transfer because when they see the state of you, you'll be bloody sacked. She slammed the kitchen door.

"Arsehole" She shouted

He looked down at the small strip of tablets on the floor but stood frozen to the spot. In all the years he had known her, he had never seen her act like that. The steam coming from the kettle distracted him and he turned and placed some coffee into a mug along with some sugar. The row with Leanna had caught him off guard and as he stood stirring the spoon around the bottom of the mug, he started to think about his situation. The officer's faces flashed through his mind, the smug look they had each time they kicked and punched him. The beating he would get over, but the look on their faces while they did it, he would never forget. He started to feel angry, angry that the last three months work had all been for nothing. He looked over at the kitchen door half expecting Leanna to burst through and start shouting at him again. He looked down at the strip of tablets on the floor. Before leaving the kitchen, he popped two from the strip and swallowed them. He walked into the living room with his coffee and noticed the bedroom door closed. He was still angry. He was angry with Leanna for being angry with him. He finished his coffee and the mellow effect of the tablets had started to kick in, he then found himself creeping through to the bedroom to apologise.

Whyte and Drummond received a call from the reception at the Edinburgh Police Headquarters to let them know that Brody had arrived. They sat back in their chairs and waited patiently. His final report was on the desk in front of them, attached to the last page of the report were photos of Brody's injuries, the bruising on his spine and rib cage. A civilian employee knocked and held the door open for Brody to enter. After a quick nod in the direction of Whyte and Drummond, she left and closed the door behind her. They both stayed seated and looked Brody up and down as he walked towards them.

"Have a seat Brody." Whyte gestured to a chair placed directly in front of them.

"How are you feeling?"

"I'm fine, well for now anyway, the painkillers kicked in about an hour ago." He said half-jokingly.

Although Leanna had filled him with strong coffee to try to counteract the drowsiness, she had warned him to get his point across to them straight away in case they noticed that he was acting peculiar. Drummond picked up the file in front of him and Brody recognised it straight away.

"Would you care to elaborate on this?" He said as he flicked the pages and gave Brody a look of contempt.

"Elaborate?"

"Yes, elaborate. We expected your monthly report to contain your investigations into the McNaughton family business and supply us with names of contacts or evidence that would lead us to prosecute them. All we have read in this are accusations towards individuals whom that the McNaughton family clearly have a grudge. I mean, whose side are you on?"

"Whose side am I on?" Brody shook his head.

"I've given you enough evidence to put Rodney away for at least ten to fifteen years. I've basically lived in his shadow for three months and you're questioning whose side I am on?"

"Exactly, three months and you haven't given us one name."

"A name, I am a witness to kidnapping, drug dealing, serious assault, firearms, extortion, what more do you need?"

"We can only charge him with these crimes if we have solid hard evidence. The kidnapping charge would only happen if the victim actually made a complaint, never mind give evidence in court." Drummond said sternly.

"He pulled him out of a jeep with a gun pointing at his head. There must have been at least twenty cars went by."

"As I said, the victim would have to give evidence in court. Do you honestly see that happening? And the firearms charge would only stick if we caught him in possession of the actual firearm."

"Ginge knows all this. He wanted to be seen with that gun" Whyte added.

"What do you mean?"

"He was going inside one way or the other. If we didn't pick him up on suspicion of the firearm charge, football was the next obvious thing."

"Did you not think it was suspicious that he turned up at Tannadice knowing full well that he has a lifetime ban? I guess your judgment was a bit clouded that day." Drummond said.

Brody knew this was an obvious dig at him being intoxicated that day. He ignored it.

"Why would he go out of his way to get himself locked up?"

"To get to someone inside, you know how it works. They won't put him inside with Ryan, and so to keep them both separated they are placed in different halls, now they have more chance of getting to someone."

"What about the drugs? I have given you dates and times when they've been picked up and dropped off at different addresses in nearly every scheme in Dundee."

"No, you have picked up and dropped off packages that you assumed was drugs. You are not present when any of these packages are open, as far as a jury is concerned, they could contain absolutely anything. And also, none of this leads back to Ryan."

"What about all the money I collect?"

"There is no evidence that it has come from drugs, they would plead that it was a loan. Do you really want to go to all this trouble so you can face them in court over a possible loan sharking charge?"

Brody thinks about this. He felt defeated and let out a sigh.

"Brody, maybe now you can understand our position. We could have pushed to get them put away on any one of these charges. These crimes brought your family to our attention in the first place, but if we don't get the person at the top, we will be chasing them for the rest of their lives."

"It's like the old saying, get the person at the top and the rest will fall."

"What makes you so sure Ryan is the one at the top?"

They both looked at each other and shrugged.

"Well if he's not, you tell us who is?"

"I don't think it makes a difference whoever is at the top, you've seen how they work, as soon as one gets locked up, someone else takes over."

"Brody I don't know how many times I have to repeat this to you. We are only after 'their' contacts, we don't actually need to put them away, we only need to get something big enough on them that will make them talk, but if it's anything less than ten years, forget it, they would do that time standing on their heads."

"Well, except one" Drummond added.

They both gave each other a look. A look that does not go passed Brody.

"Am I missing something here?"

"Whyte gives Drummond a nod as though giving him permission to talk.

"The reason we know it is Ryan running the show is that Ritchie is an informant."

"Yeah right, he's an arrogant fat prick but he's no grass" He looked at Whyte for reassurance.

Whyte nodded at him "He's an informant."

Brody smirked and shook his head. Both Drummond and Whyte kept their eyes on him but did not say anything. It took a few seconds for it to sink in but Brody realised they were telling the truth.

"No fucking way."

Drummond nodded at him "You would be amazed at the things you find out when an addict needs a fix."

"Sneaky bastard" Brody muttered to himself.

"Do you not think that's something I should have been told at the start?"

Drummond nodded. "We discussed it and decided to hold that information back until you were more involved in the case, so, now you know."

Whyte leaned forward in his seat and placed his elbows on the desk in front of him. "Brody, this investigation is about to step up a level. Ryan's remand is up and is about to be released from prison any day now, we need you back in there."

Brody leaned back in his seat. He now realised why they did not let the judge remand him;. They need him out. This was not where he saw this meeting going. It was like a fresh carrot dangling in front of him.

He nodded at them.

Whyte turned to Drummond and shrugged.

"Okay, but you must understand, that any court appearances you face from here on in, we won't be able to step in without arousing suspicion, so if you are caught up in any serious charges where you face being remanded, we will have to pull you off the case."

"Or you can do the jail time" Drummond said, accompanied by his fake smile.

"So are we done here?"

"I suppose we are" Whyte said turning to Drummond to see if he had anything to add.

Drummond screwed up his face and nodded at Brody's folder still on the desk. He then swiped his hand towards it as though brushing it away.

"Well actually, this...this report. You need to forget about this."

"Forget about it?" Brody's eyes widened.

"For now" Drummond added.

Brody nodded unconvincingly and then stood up to leave. Drummond walked him to the door and made a snide comment on his designer clothes as he passed him. Brody stepped out of the doorway and turned back to face him and looked him up and down.

"I notice you're still keeping up the good cop, bad cop act. You know that only works with criminals, to everyone else it just makes you an arseholes."

Brody walked away and thought of Ginge's talk about coppers having 'no character.' He smirked and carried on along the corridor.

"Well, that's that then" Said Whyte

"Did you see him look me up and down?"

"Yeah, like you were the shit that he just wiped from the sole from his designer trainers."

They both laughed.

"Do you think we're making a mistake putting him back out there?"

"Definitely, he should be taken off this case immediately, but if he comes up with any leads from The Wise Man, it will be worth it. He's the best chance we've got."

"I know but what if the risk leads to nothing, it could also let The Wise Man find out we are onto him."

"Oh, he knows we are onto him. Brody was sharing a cell with him twenty-four hours a day and he said nothing. Come on, you know from experience they like to talk. They 'all' like to talk."

"Do you think he suspects Brody?"

"No I wouldn't go that far, some people get a bit paranoid in prison and think that others could hear. Maybe once he is out, he will start to let a few things slip. Our problem is Brody, knowing he is going off track is our biggest risk"

"He's a risk alright. He was out of his fucking head."

"He's on painkillers!"

They both smirked.

PART 3 - THE WISE MAN

Chapter 27

"About fucking time, I phoned you over an hour ago."

"You're only out five minutes and you're already fucking moaning. Do you think we just drop everything to come and meet you?" Hunter says with a wide grin.

"I'll remember that the next time you're being released you selfish cunt."

Hunter squares up to me and I clock Brody getting ready to step in between us until we both laugh and Hunter puts his arm around my neck and pulls me towards him for a welcome man-hug, at least I hope it's a man-hug, otherwise I'll need to start looking for some new acquaintances.

"So where's the car?"

"It's the blue one up ahead" Brody nods to a small rusty old fiesta at the end of the car park.

"Are you taking the piss? I'm just out after three months and you pick me up in that pile of shit."

"What were you expecting a fucking limo?" Hunter says.

"Yeah a big pink one"

"I thought after three months you'd have had enough of big pink ones."

"I don't know why you're laughing Brody, I never heard you complain about my big pink one."

"Yeah, because waking up to that every morning was the highlight of my day. I take it Ginge has just had that pleasure."

"I never saw him; thankfully he was put in C hall. Not to worry though, they'll get the message."

"Who"

"Whoever thinks about stepping into my shoes when I'm gone?"

"What do you mean?"

"Come on Brody you know the governor is never going to put me and Ginge in the same hall. He was banged up to send a message."

I get in the front of the car with Brody and once we are out of Perth and hit the main road, Hunter pulls out a large sheath from inside his jacket and passes it over to me. I open it up to reveal a large machete.

"What the fuck?" Brody takes his eyes off the road for a second to admire the recently sharpened blade and swerves slightly into the next lane.

"What the fuck is that for?"

His eyes move from the blade and back to the road several times.

"What? Or who?" I ask.

"What do you mean what or who? What is it for?"

"Or who?" I smile.

"Or who?" He says sounding annoyed.

"It's for fate."

"Who the fuck is fate"

"Fate is a what not a who"

"Actually, it could be a 'who'" Hunter adds.

"You're right Hunter, it could be a 'who', but until I encounter who the 'who' is, it will just have to be a what."

"Ryan, who or what is that fucking thing for?" Brody demands.

"Well, I don't know yet. It might not actually be for a 'who' or a 'what' You see I've heard a few people mention over the years that I had better watch out as fate will one day catch up with me. Well, I don't know who or what that fate is going to be, but if, or when that day comes, I'm going to be fucking prepared for it."

I see Brody shaking his head.

"Ryan, that's not what fate, is about; you can't be prepared for it. It's not a particular person or a thing, it's like if we were to be involved in a car crash right now, that would be our fate, you can't prepare for it."

"Well, I notice that you're wearing a seatbelt? Because at the back of your mind you are preparing for fate, just in case you are involved in a car crash. What do you think Hunter?"

Hunter nods in agreement. "I quite like your speech for carrying the machete Ryan, but somehow I don't think the coppers will buy it, and Brody, if a mob turns up at the pub looking for you, I don't think that wearing a seat belt is going to do you much good."

"I never mentioned…" Brody stops mid-sentence and shakes his head when he catches Hunter smirking in the mirror.

"Does the machete bother you?" I ask.

"Yeah, it bothers me." He nods with a scowl not taking his eyes off the road.

"Good, because that's what it's supposed to do"

"What do you mean?"

"Do you really think that I'm stupid enough to walk about with a machete tucked into my jacket?"

"Yeah" He nods as though it was a rhetorical question.

"Exactly"

"What, so you want people to think that?"

"Now you're getting it."

We reach Dundee and Brody signals in the direction of my house.

"No, we're going to the Gang Hut."

"The Gang Hut, you mean the Claver?"

I turn to face Hunter "Do you see what we're dealing with?"

Hunter shakes his head and scowls as though disappointed.

We pull up outside The Claver and as soon as I step inside, all the heads at the bar look up with wide eyes. In the split second that it takes for the punters to recognise me, I know most are thinking, who the fuck is this entering that I can tap for a sub. The barman smiles and points to the corner where Buster is sitting with a few of his cronies.

"Hoi, what sort of welcome home is this you fat old cunt?"

He looks up and gives me a grin.

"Well maybe if you gave me some notice I would have dished out the ice cream and party poppers."

"Just get the fucking drinks up."

During the usual small chit chat as we stand near the bar waiting for the drinks being served. I randomly pull out the machete in full view of the customers. I slide it over to the barman as though I am trying to be discreet knowing every pair of eyes in the pub is watching.

"Here, put this somewhere safe for me will you."

I wink to the barman and he picks it up and walks out the back with it. He knows it is all a show but the regular customers, who love to talk, will no doubt inform everyone in the next pub, the bookies and the taxi drivers. You see, people love to gossip, and by the time it reaches those intended, they will have added a few arms and legs to the story so the machete will end up being three times the size and I will probably have been swinging it around the pub threatening to slice everyone up with it. The upside of this, which is obvious enough, is that it makes other people think twice before attempting to fuck with you. The downside is that if there is someone with an intention of taking you on, it is a guarantee, that if they are going to come for you, they will be well tooled up, especially if there are rumours that you walk about with a machete tucked in your jacket. I sink the first pint in minutes and as Buster leans in front of me to shout up another round, he sneakily slips me a tightly rolled wad of notes. I turn to put them in my jacket pocket and I notice the barman passing Brody a glass of orange juice.

"Brody, what the fuck is that?"

He screws up his face "I'm on painkillers and I have to drive later."

Buster turns and looks at him "Supposed to be family eh? You couldn't even have one pint with your brother?"

"Speaking about family, where's Ritchie?" I ask.

Buster makes a face and quickly changes the subject. I know my old man is not one to hold back so whatever it is, it must be bad or someone in our company does not need to know. He is now giving Brody advice about his last fight and by the looks of it, it is not the first time he has heard all this.

"So when is your next fight?" I step in as Buster begins to repeat himself.

"Well it was supposed to be this week but due to my cracked ribs, I had to pull out. There's a show in six weeks that I've been asked to fight on but I'll see how the training goes the next couple of weeks."

"Where is it?"

"The Bonar Hall"

"In Dundee, great, I'll finally get to come and watch you fight."

"As I said, it's not definite; I'll have to see how quick my ribs heal."

Buster starts up again and now has his fists up trying to give Brody tips. The way he was talking you would think he had fought for a world title. I catch Brody's expression, which to me looks like a plea to get Buster away to fuck from him so I decide to save him. I nudge Buster out of the way and grab a hold of Brody; I playfully put him in a headlock and rub my knuckles on the top of his head.

"I don't give a shit about your boxing I'm just glad you're back here and not still away chasing bullets in Iraq or Afghanistan or wherever the fuck you were."

He kicks the back of my leg and puts me off balance and as he tries to pull away, we both stumble around knocking over tables and drinks. I pull my grip tighter on his neck and he kicks my leg again. With a little push from Buster, we both end up on the floor.

"Oh yeah, that's right. Never mind your wife and kids who have not seen you in three months. Might have guessed your first stop would be the fucking Claverhouse"

I look up to see Nikki, my missus, standing with Davie and Mollie, my son and my young lass at either side of her. I pick myself up off the floor and crouch down towards Mollie.

"How's my little princess?"

I put my arms out wide towards her but she looks up at Nikki and copies her by standing firm with her hands on her hips. I stand up and keep my arms out wide as though pleading.

"You know how it is. I was just getting the banter, the business and bullshit out of the way so that I can spend the rest of the day with you." I wink.

She smiles and walks into my arms, then I pick up my young lass and she gives me a hug. Davie stands firm but gives me a nod as if to say, 'what's the big deal? You're back, so fuck, give me more pocket money.' I want to grab him and rub his head as I did to Brody but he is at that age where it is too cool to make a big deal out of shit. I understand. When I was his age and if I had come into the pub to see Buster and he put me in a headlock, he would have a got a good hard kick in the balls, I know he is not at that stage yet, but it will come. I put my fist out towards him and he smiles as he puts his up to meet mine. Buster sees this as an opening to talk to him and reaches over to ruffle his hair.

"So how is my mini Buster then?"

"Hey don't start with that shit. His name is Davie. We may have given him your name but there's no way he's become heir to 'Buster.'"

Buster laughs "We'll see."

I manage to prize my young lass's fingers apart as she is reluctant to let go of me. I pull out the wad that Buster slipped me and just like her mother, her eyes light up. I peel off a few hundred and hand them to her.

"Give that to your mother and tell her to get you a sweetie."

I watch her big smile as she hands over the money.

"Get something good for the dinner; I'll be home in about an hour."

"I'm sure you said the same to me three months ago." She smiles and winks before turning with the kids and heading out the door.

Chapter 28

As soon as I managed to capture Buster on his own, he updated me on the situation with Ritchie. He has been dabbling in that fucking smack on and off for a few years now and Ginge and I have tried everything but lock him up to try and help him. Each time I have words with him he brushes it off as if it is no big deal as though he has it under control. He always tells me that he only smokes the stuff occasionally but after hearing Buster tell me that he has been banging that shit in his veins, it has given me the fucking rage. Ritchie has been inside with me over the years and seen how low people can stoop with that shit. He has seen good friends of ours damaged and down a path, they are never coming back from. I have a more pressing matter at hand, so there is nothing I can do about it just now. The whole time Buster was talking to me, I could not get the picture of my young lass clinging to me out of my head. I downed the pint I had in front of me and before anyone could shout me up another, I got the fuck out of there. On hearing about Ritchie, it was easy for me to put on my 'stay out my fucking way' face on so that I could storm out of the pub without anyone coming near me. With my face like thunder, they probably thought that I was off to smash some fucker. It certainly would not be good for my reputation if they knew I had a lump in my throat the size of a golf ball at the thought of my seeing my young lass. Brody clearly does not read facial expressions very well, as he was the only one that attempted to step in my way; he was only offering me a lift as well. I just gave him a growl and a light shake of the head before barging out the pub door. If I had taken his offer I would have been here a lot sooner, but I needed the walk to clear my head. I do not like to take that shit home with me. I reach my street and as I turn the corner I have a view of the top of my house up ahead and all the tension and anger that I felt in the pub suddenly disappears. As I get closer, my fucking heart starts to melt as I see Mollie in the garden, she is sitting in her three-wheeler and pointing at Biscuit, our recently acquired dog and she is telling him off. Biscuit was part of another one of Busters sneaky ploys. After attending his mate's funeral, Old Danny, he turned up at my door a bit worse for wear. With Danny gone, his missus was a bit frail and felt that she could not look after the dog, so Buster thought it would be a good idea to bring it around to mine. I had no intention of getting a fucking dog, especially with my lifestyle, but Busters not stupid, he doesn't think of phoning and saying, here, would you mind looking after someone's dog for a bit, no, he just turns up at my door knowing full well my young lass would go mad for it.

    Mollie sees me approach the house and climbs off her bike and runs to the gate. Biscuit is not far behind her. I kneel down and both she and the dog are all over me. She puts her arms tight around my neck again and at the same time, the dog is climbing up on me and trying to lick my ear. Nikki appears at the door.

"Just so you know, he was licking his balls earlier."

"That's okay; it will save me from doing it later."

"You're disgusting" She smiles.

As I take in my happy moment, Biscuit suddenly climbs down off me and bolts away into the house with his tail between his legs.

"What's up with him, I wasn't really going to lick his balls."

Seconds later, I hear the noise from a car coming up the street. The sound is like a loud roar and obviously, the dog heard it well before us. It looks like some sort of rally car. I am still on my knees as it passes and I see the driver give a sideways look before slowly manoeuvring into his driveway. He lives a few doors down on the opposite side of the street. He revs his engine for about another 20 seconds, I do not know if this is to make sure that he has the whole streets attention, but he certainly has mine and that is definitely not good for him. The car makes a loud banging sound before he shuts it off, I can only compare the sound to that of a shotgun going off and if he keeps it up, it is highly likely that he is going to find this out for himself. I stand up with Mollie still holding onto my neck and I watch him as he gets out of his car. He is a big lad and looks in his early 30's, a bit old to be thinking he is a boy racer. He glances over and gives a little smirk before going into his house.

"Who the fuck is this prick"

"That's the guy I told you about. He moved in a few weeks after they remanded you. Come inside and you'll see the state of Biscuit."

I follow her in and she points to a gap between the couch and the chair. I look down to see the dog, wide-eyed and shaking violently with his tongue hanging out. I try to entice him out but he looks petrified. Mollie climbs down from me and leans in to pet him. He licks her and looks at her with sad eyes but he will not come out or stop shaking.

"He's like this every time he hears that car. I told you I went over and asked him if he could fix his exhaust because the noise was scaring our dog. He basically laughed in my face and shut the door."

"Did you not tell Ginge to have a word?"

"Yeah I mentioned it to Buster as well, but you know what they're like to get a hold of. I kind of thought he would eventually get it sorted but it's like he gets some sort of thrill out of it."

"I'll give him a thrill alright" I mutter to myself.

"What?"

"I'll try and catch him 'in the passing' tomorrow and I'll have a quiet word."

I watch as Mollie climbs through the gap and puts her arms around the dog's neck to comfort him.

"It's okay Biscuit. Don't be scared" She says.

I sit on the chair next to them and reach my hand down to pet him. His big sad eyes look up and go from me to my young lass continuously. I watch the bond she has with him as she talks to him like a human and how gentle he is with her. I stand up to look out the window then back at Mollie and then Nikki catches my expression.

"Ryan, don't. Not tonight."

"I promise. I'm just going to have a quiet word."

I take a slow walk across the street while telling myself to 'stay calm... do not hit him' I knock and wait while still saying to myself 'do not hit him' He opens the door and from across the street I thought he was maybe early 30's but seeing him close up he is at least 40.

"Yeah what's up?"

'What's up? What's up?' I will give you fucking 'what's up.'

"Hi, eh, I don't mean to bother you but it was about the noise from your car, the exhaust, I think my missus spoke to you about it."

"Yeah, I think I remember" He says opening his door a little wider.

Oh, you fucking remember all right

"Well you see, we have a little Staffie dog and he's really sensitive about loud noise, and well, every time you rev your engine near our house, he sort of has a panic attack."

"So what do you want me to do about it?"

If I did not know any better, I would say this cunt was getting wide with me. I turn and look back at my house to see Mollie in the doorway watching me. I take a deep breath and blow my cheeks out as I turn back to face him.

"Well, I was wondering, if it's not too much trouble, could you possibly see about getting the noise fixed?" I say in my most polite mannered voice.

"It's a Subaru Impreza. That's the noise they are supposed to make" He says smugly.

I know the noise your jaw is supposed to make when I break it you flash cunt. I look over at Mollie once again and force a smile. I keep it on as I turn to face him.

"Okay, no problem. I just thought I would ask."

I walk off, back across the street towards Mollie, still wearing my fake smile. I have asked him politely, being neighbourly and that. I have given him a chance, more than I would most people. I walk back into the house to a surprised look from Nikki. She can tell by my expression exactly what I am thinking.

"You should've slapped the smug bastard" We both laugh.

Moments later, I place it all to the back of my mind as I sit down with Mollie to watch some cartoons. Biscuit eventually stops panting and jumps up on the couch beside us, and I am once again, enjoying my family moment. It is times like this that I start to question my lifestyle. It is not as if I planned it though, and growing up with Buster as my role model, certainly did not help. These thoughts probably would not even cross my mind if it were not for Mollie here. I know I will never have to worry about young Davie though, as he is tough as they come. If something big ever comes up, somewhere down the line, where I am looking at a lengthy stretch, I know he will step up to protect her. Right now though, while sitting here watching cartoons with her and Biscuit, well, that is what it is all about, I wonder if Buster had a daughter, he would have reconsidered a lot of the shit he got up to over the years...hmm...maybe not.

Feeling stuffed with some proper food after three months inside, and a few hours of playing games with Mollie, I eventually get her to bed. I had to promise her about a dozen times that I would still be here when she woke up in the morning. Davie was staying over at his friend's house so

Nikki and I head off for an early night and a catch up of our own. Biscuit jumping on the bed wakes me early the next morning. I do not mind it too much until I feel the whole bed shaking. I sit up and tap my hand on the covers for him to come to me but he sits at the bottom with his tongue hanging out and looking at me with his wide fearing eyes. Then I hear it, the car engine. It starts and stops a few times then the loud bang like a shotgun. I jump out of bed and open the curtains. The arsehole from across the street has parked right outside my house. He catches sight of me at the window and gives me a smug grin. I grab a pair of jeans and quickly put them on before racing down the stairs. As I open the front door, I grab a small steel bar I have hidden, just for these kinds of moments. I am still in my bare feet but make a run for him along the path. His eyes widen when he sees me and revs his engine one last time before taking off along the street. I stand by the gate watching the back of his car disappear out of site. I turn to go back into the house and glance up to see Mollie looking at me from her bedroom window. The noise from me thumping down the stairs must have woken her. I smile immediately and wave at her as though assuring her that everything is okay. I cannot tell what has made me feel angrier, that arsehole for purposefully intending to piss me off, or that he nearly caused my young lass to witness me smashing the shit out of him. I walk back inside and as I slip the steel bar back behind the front door, I catch Mollie coming down the stairs with her sleepy-eyes and fuzzy hair. She looks at me with her innocent smile and I immediately melt into Mr Fucking Soft.

"Where's biscuit? I thought you were in the garden with him."

"No, he's upstairs with your Mum. What do you want for breakfast?" I quickly change the subject.

"Coco pops"

"Come on then, let's get some Coco pops"

I cannot help but think about how quickly my mood can change. Not five minutes ago I was ready to tear someone apart and not give a shit if it got me banged up for two years, and now I'm happily sitting with my young lass as we slurp our cereal.

Chapter 29

I am out of the big house less than 24 hours, when a call comes in from my court ordered psychiatrist. It would not be too bad if I was still at home with my feet up, but I am walking Mollie to the nursery when the call comes in. It is only for me to make an appointment, which is fair enough, but then he starts asking personal shit over the phone. I know he will not have taken too kindly to being hung-up on, but he can go fuck himself. For one thing, it is a bit of a handful holding Mollies hand and the dogs lead while trying to hold a phone to my ear, but more importantly, it is ignorant as fuck. I did not offer to walk her to the nursery, to ignore her while discussing some nonsense on the phone. My lawyer advised me to tread lightly with him, as his reports can determine what a judge dishes out to me in any up and coming cases. That is all fair and well, he has studied hard and received his certificates to be in the job, but to me, he is a fucking weirdo. He comes across as one of those little boys that someone tampered with when he was younger and he secretly enjoyed it, a stereotypical paedophile. When I talk to him, it is as though he gets excited if I mention any gory details about my life. The last session I had with him, I found myself making shit up just to see his expression. The appointment is not until next week so that will give me more time to make up some wild stories to tell him. My priority this morning though is a contact I have in Glasgow, an old cell-buddy of mine from way back. He has twenty grand's worth of dodgy notes. I told him that if they look and feel right that I would take the fucking lot. I could divide that shit up and move it on by the end of the day. My first stop though, is the nursery, I receive a big kiss on the cheek from Mollie, accompanied by one of her choking hugs, and then I watch her run off happily towards her teacher. I have an hour to kill so I decided to pop into the pet shop and pick up a new lead for Biscuit. The cheeky little fucker keeps chewing them and it only takes seconds for whoever is holding the lead to be distracted and that is it, his teeth have sliced through it and he is off. I do not think Big Danny, his previous owner, ever had him on a lead, he always seemed to walk by his side without any sort of control. I will maybe work on that later, in the meantime, I will need to upgrade from this knotted old washing line. Well, it is actually only knotted because he keeps turning his head to the side and chewing the fucking thing. After marching up and down the aisles in the pet shop and not having a clue what to look for, the Staff soon points me in the right direction. They also give me some advice about the correct type of collar and harness. I now stand in awe at the rack in front of me. What ninety-nine percent of people will see is a range of dog leads in all sizes, lengths and colours. What I, and the other one percent see before them, is an assortment of legalised weapons, from thin hard leather straps to solid chains. I lean forward and pick up the thickest chain off the rack. I cannot imagine what type of dog this would be for but it would not be out of place on a baby dinosaur. I place the leather handle in my hand and wrap the chain around my knuckles. The shop assistant looks at me as I make a fist and then slowly punch the air in front of me.

"That's it, I'll take it."

She looks at me then smiles before nodding at Biscuit.

"Don't you want to try it on the dog's collar?"

"Oh yeah, that would be a good idea."

I unwind the chain and then clip the end onto Biscuits collar.

"There we go. Try and get your teeth through that you little fucker."

I follow the assistant to the till where she scans the barcode.

"That's twenty pound please."

Twenty pounds for a fucking dog lead, I should have just tied a few more knots in the rope, or better still, come back here later and slipped the robbing bastards a faker. With his new lead sorted, he cannily walks by my side as I flag down a passing taxi. In typical taxi driver talk, he has a little moan about the dog in his car, but he is soon put in his place when I tell him that he shouldn't have stopped for me then as there are plenty other fucking drivers that would have appreciated my business. I pull up at the Claver and as I hand over the money to pay I can help but think that another faker would not have gone amiss here. Before I enter the pub I notice Biscuit's tail going, he knows this place well. I let him off his lead and before I even open the door he is nudging passed me to get in. This used to be a second home for him not too long ago as his previous owner Big Danny, was a regular. I notice my acquaintance by the bar, I give him a nod towards the back area of the pub and he picks up his drink and follows me through. I leave Biscuit to it as most of the punters in here know him, so he will be well looked after. I sit down next to my acquaintance in the booth. Even if he had sat in the opposite seat, I would have still chosen this one, as I like to oversee the doorway when I am doing business. It is not that I do not trust him, but he could have had a tail. He slips me a couple of notes from his holdall and through experience, I can tell by a quick glance and touch that they are good quality. I give him a nod and he passes over the holdall, I put my hand in and pull out a random roll of notes. I unfold them to check that they are the same and I give him a wink. He finishes his drink and stands up to leave. I move to let him pass and we both give each other a nod. As he goes out the front door I stand by the bar leaving the holdall where it is. I look over at Joe the Bull and tilt my head towards the booth. I had messaged him earlier to be here. He knows the score. He walks by me without saying a word, picks up the holdall and takes it out the back of the pub. He will transfer it to another bag before heading out the back door of the pub to a safe place and divide the cash. Joe will deliver it to other buyers and once I receive the money from them, my acquaintance will receive his end. That is how I work; it is a thing of trust. If someone does a deal with me and expect an exchange there and then, they can go fuck themselves. If anybody I know even asked me to tag along to a deal like that, alarm bells would ring. I order a drink and slip the barman a sneaky faker that I kept back from the deal. He goes over to the till with it and I notice him slide it several times between his fingertips, he gives it a quick look and then turns and smiles at me. I smile back.

"Just testing you" I say before I pull out a real note and swap it with him.

The bar staff in the Claver do not need any fancy equipment to detect a faker, much like the punters. I hang around until I receive a call from Joe that the rest of the cash checks out before deciding to head home, and then Buster bounces through the pub doors as though he is in the Wild West. His persuasion for me to stay is by way of calling me a big poofter and then ordering me another drink. I clock him looking around to see if anybody is in earshot and asks how things went on the deal with the fakers. I pull out my phone and show him a message from Joe saying, 'all good'. He nods and then ignores me to have a random conversation with

Biscuit, who has perched his arse on a stool next to us at the bar. He then grabs him and starts cuddling into it.

"If you like him that much why the fuck did you give him to me?"

"What's the problem? The dog just likes attention."

"Yeah, I know what kind of attention you want to give it. You sick bastard. Actually, I remember when I was growing up there was a rumour you stuck your dick in a Pitbull."

"Hardly, I probably made a comment about it, but you know how people like to talk. Seriously though, if it was a bitch then I'd probably consider it."

"You need help you sick bastard."

"What are you trying to say, that you've never thought about it?"

"Not in the fucking slightest. I can't believe that I am even having this conversation, and I think it's time for me and Biscuit to get the fuck out of here before you start laying a trail of peanuts to the toilet."

I pull out the dog lead and lift Biscuit from the stool to the floor.

"What the fuck is that?"

"What?"

Buster nods at the dog lead.

"The dogs lead?"

"Biscuit doesn't need a lead. He'll walk by your side."

"Who said anything about Biscuit?" I say wrapping the chain around my knuckle.

Buster nods approvingly.

"Will you be back out later?"

"I'm not sure. I'll see what's doing."

"You mean if you're allowed out?"

"Pretty much"

I take a longer way home to give Biscuit a good walk and once I am away from the busy roads I try him off the lead. He walks by my side most of the way until I reach a large grass area. He takes off and sniffs about as if someone has put out free lines of coke in the Claverhouse toilets. I watch as he lifts his leg and leaves his mark at nearly every bush and tree in his path. A white van passes me then circles around and doubles back. I put my hand into my pocket and carefully start to wrap the lead around my knuckle. I cannot believe I only bought this today and some arsehole is going to let me test it on him. I stand at an angle where it looks as though I am watching Biscuit but my eyes still have a view of the van. Biscuit moves back and forward over the same spot several times then squats to take a shit. I walk to the far end of the patch of grass and when he has finished he runs towards me. Seconds later the white van speeds across the road and stops next to me at the kerb. The driver quickly jumps out and he has one of those thick 'village people' style moustaches. He flashes some sort of I.D. but I do not even look at it, as I know he is not a copper, not with that tasher. He mumbles some shit about the environment and then enquires about Biscuit. When I tell him that he is mine, his tone seems to change and he becomes more authoritative as he explains the laws on cleaning up after your dog.

"Mate I've never had a dog before, it was sort of put on me. But don't worry I'll make sure I clean it up in future."

I go to walk away, happy in the relief that it was not a mob in that van about to get heavy with me. Then the little Hitler calls me back.

"Excuse me but can I have your name and address please?"

"What, what for?"

"Well, you see, under the fouling of dogs act you are hereby fined the sum of one hundred pounds. This will be reduced to fifty pounds if it is paid within fourteen days."

"A hundred quid, are you fucking kidding me?"

"Fifty pounds if it is paid within 14 days."

"I told you, I've only just got the dog."

"Do you know how many times that I have heard that?" He says smugly.

"Look if you give me a bag and I'll clean it up now."

"It doesn't work like that I'm afraid."

He stares at me with his pen and notebook at the ready. One of those creepy stares where his eyes do not even blink.

"Can I have your name and address please?"

I clench my fist and feel the chain tightening around my knuckle. I have a quick glance around for any witnesses and scan the windows across the road for any curtain twitches. Then just as I am about to move in closer to him, I remember the fakers that I have on me.

"Fifty quid you said?"

"If it is paid within fourteen days"

"And who do I pay this to, you?"

"No, it can be paid at Dundee House, the council building in the town."

I put my free hand in my other pocket and pull out a couple of twenty's.

"How about if I paid you now"

"Sorry I don't accept payments."

I take a step towards him a bit menacingly.

"I don't think you're hearing me, pal. How about you accept this and we both go on our way."

He looks at the twenty-pound notes and hesitates. I move in closer and give him a big smug smile as I put it in his pocket. I take a step back still smiling. His creepy stare eventually softens as he looks around to see if anyone is watching.

"Don't worry; this is between me and you" I wink at him and walk off with Biscuit at my side. Have fun spending that you jobs worth cunt.

Chapter 30

With my family time planned early on, one of the first things I did was turn both of my mobiles to silent to make sure there were no interruptions. This was possibly a guilty feeling due to me being away from them for 3 months, as I know it would only take one text or phone call about some shit going down and before I know it, I have my jacket on, tooled up and am out the door. It is late, and with both kids now tucked up in bed, I sit back with Nikki to watch T.V. The light has flashed several times on both of my mobiles but I have resisted the urge to pick them up. Nikki has also noticed the flashing, and whenever she has looked at me, I have smiled and turned back to the T.V. pretending not to notice the phones.

"Oh go and answer it" She demands.

"Nope, this is family time" I say stubbornly.

She shakes her head and smiles. Then both phones flash continuously several times. She looks at me and we both laugh.

"Ryan, go and see who it is. It could be important."

I eventually reach over, pick them up, and read the messages. I am relieved that I did not look at them earlier. Harassed acquaintances, people refusing to pay debts, debtors disputing what they owe and the usual updates of what the Donaldson's are up to, none of it is urgent and I will deal with it another day, but one message really strikes a chord. It is about Ritchie. He is my brother but sometimes I really want to give him a good hard slap. I know he has always been a bit of an arsehole but since he has started dabbling with that fucking heroin, he has taken the word arsehole to whole other level. He has a kid of his own and I am now reading a text from his baby's mother Emma, saying that he has just robbed her house. I put the phone down and let out a sigh. Nikki turns to me, raises her eyebrows and then turns back to the T.V. If I decide to get up and go looking for him, she would not even say a word. She would not even question me, she has known me my whole life and knows exactly what I am like, she trusts me and knows that if I stood up and left the house without any explanation it would be for a very good reason. I try to relax but the thought of Ritchie is making me angry so when I see Biscuit having a stretch and looking up at me it makes me feel glad that I have an excuse to go and get some fresh air before I storm off looking for him. As soon as I stand up and grab my jacket, Biscuit's tail is twirling around like a helicopter, it amazes me how innocent and happy a dog can be with the simple things in life, like going for a walk. I put his lead on but I do not even reach the end of my street when I think 'fuck it' and I unclip him. He does not move from my side, he does occasionally run ahead to leave his mark on a lamppost, or a tree and the random car tyre but he quickly returns. I end up back near the large grass area where I was earlier today, when I come across that fucking job's worth. I turn the corner and notice a group of people gathered in the middle of the grass with their dogs, some of them are on leads but most are running free and as soon as Biscuit notices them he takes off. I make a chase for him, but when I reach the group, I notice that none of them react or even appear surprised. I automatically had a vision of Biscuit fighting and me being the bad cunt because he is not on a lead. The whole group is polite towards me and this appears to be their regular meeting place as they all huddle around making small talk. I am took back at how relaxed they are at Biscuit as he runs from one dog to the other licking and then sniffing at each other's arseholes. I smile and return the small talk as I try to keep an eye on Biscuit. There is an older woman in the group who still has her dog on a lead and out of all the dogs; hers is the one that Biscuit tries to mount. I feel a little embarrassed and make an effort to get a hold of him but the sneaky little shit is too quick and takes off around the group, by the time I get near him he has done a full circle and is back trying to mount the same dog. She must sense my feeling as she tells me not to worry.

"That's just what dogs do" She smiles.

"Oh okay."

This makes me relax a bit and I stand back as Biscuit runs around tiring himself out, as fun as it is watching him, a few minutes listening to this group put the world to rights is enough for me, he will have to get his leg over another time. I manage to get a hold of him and clip his lead on; I give the group a nod of acknowledgement as I walk off with Biscuit straining to get back to them. Once I am out of sight of the group, I unclip his lead and he once again happily walks by my side. With a clearer head on me than what I had when I left the house, I start to make my way back. I can only imagine where I would have ended up tonight if not for the company of Biscuit. I start to weigh up if it is more therapeutic than kicking in doors and slapping around drug dealers. I approach the end of my street and I turn to see Biscuit with his head under a bush sniffing the leaves that another dog has obviously pissed on, then suddenly, he stands firm with his ears and his tail pinned. I turn in a half step as I think someone is there and when I turn back, biscuit takes off and runs past me. I am about to make chase, thinking that he is about to attack someone, then I hear it. That wanker of a neighbour of mine with the Subaru comes tearing around the corner. He slows down slightly when he sees me and revs his engine before speeding along my street. I get to my door and Biscuit is sitting on the top step panting and shaking. I look over to see that wanker's car parked in his driveway. I open my door and Biscuit runs into the house and sits at Nikki's feet still panting. I do not say a word. My expression is enough. I am about to walk back out my front door and head straight across and confront him, but I know where that will lead, so I think ...what would Ginge do? I go out my back door and search through some various 'items' I have lying around. I compare the thickness of several steel bars before choosing the appropriate one. This will save me an embarrassing double journey if one of the thicker ones does not fit. I walk around the side of my house and climb over a neighbour's wall, I walk through a couple more gardens and when I come around to the front, I am facing the wanker's car. I slide the steel bar into the exhaust and pull it from side to side. I can hear some of the brackets that hold it in place coming loose. I thought this would be a 2-minute job but as I pull and kick the steel bar, I start to break out in a sweat. Eventually, I get frustrated and jump on the end of the bar. The exhaust makes a loud clanging sound as it hits the ground. I pull the bar out and with a satisfied smirk and casually walk back home the same way that I left, happy that I have dealt with a problem without having to spend a night in the cells. I awake late the next morning by Biscuit jumping on the bed again, only this time there is no panting or shaking as he stands over me wagging his tail. I am still half-asleep and with Nikki already up, he makes use of her vacated space by curling up on the quilt next to me. This suits me fine as I try to drift back to sleep. Then Davie appears to disturb our peaceful moment.

"Dad, mum doesn't have any change, I need dinner money."

I look over at the chest of drawers where I usually dump all my change.

"Check on those drawers son."

"There's not enough Dad."

"Okay, give me a minute."

I sit up and it takes me a few seconds to get my bearings before pulling my jeans over and checking the pockets. I find a few crumpled notes and I check for a genuine one before handing one over."

"Thanks, Dad."

Like a typical kid, he is out the door in a flash before I even have a chance to say cheerio. I eventually get out of bed and reach up to have a stretch, I look out the window and notice the neighbours car still in his driveway and have a little smile to myself. I turn from the window to see Biscuit still curled up on the covers. I am now looking at the dog with a protective fondness that I would my own kids, I guess this now makes him officially part of the family. As I put my jeans on I catch sight of my phones by my bed and my little happy moment is conflicted with thoughts of the messages from last night. It all comes back to me of what I have to deal with today. Due to this being a family matter, I decide to call Brody. I do not explain the details; I only mention that I have a bit of work for him. He says that he is at Tanya's and not had much sleep, I do not know who the fuck Tanya is and the last time I talked to him, he was supposed to be in training for his fight. I tell him that it is only a bit of driving so he can get his arse around here in an hour and pick me up. I could have called a number of people but with this situation, the fewer tongues wagging the better.

I get myself ready and have some breakfast with Mollie before walking her to the nursery. I keep the same routine as yesterday and even though the rain is blowing through, she still seems happy enough to walk with Biscuit by her side. Only minutes after waving her off to run towards her teacher, Brody is phoning to tell me he is outside my house. I tell him to drive around and pick me up at Mollie's nursery. As soon as he stops his car, and even though he is metres away, I can tell that he is high. Whether it is uppers or downers, I can always tell when someone is, or has been on something. Due to him turning up like that, it immediately changes my mood. He also makes a face because I have Biscuit with me, which pisses me off. I had intended to place him on the floor at my feet in the front but that scowl from Brody was enough for me to change my mind. I open the back door and unclip his lead; he jumps in and leaps up onto the parcel shelf with his nose against the window. I get in the front and before I even say a word, he mumbles something about getting his seats all dirty. I look back to see it covered in muddy paw prints.

"What are you bumping your gums about? It is only a couple of paw prints. It's a fucking heap of shit anyway."

He lets out a sigh.

"So where are we going?"

"Well, back to mine obviously, unless you want Biscuit to make himself at home in this luxury motor of yours."

He lets out another sigh and drives around to mine. I can tell this is going to be a long day for him. I put Biscuit back in the house and pick up a small cosh, slipping it into my jacket as I leave.

"Right, the first stop I need you to take me to the best place where I could pick up most of this." I show him a small piece of paper with a list of electrical items.

He gives it a quick look.

"I hope I've not driven here just to help you with your fucking shopping" He snaps.

I give him a snort then pull out a roll of notes. I peel off five twenty pound notes.

"Here." I throw it onto his lap. "That will cover you for today and tonight, if today happens to go into tomorrow then I'll sort you out with more okay."

"What? I didn't mean it like that..." He mumbles as he attempts to hand back the money.

"Brody I phoned you specifically as this is a sensitive family matter so I'll explain this now before we go any further, I'm needing transport and possibly back up, what I don't need, are any wide, arsehole comments or judgements, as I'm really not in the mood."

He quickly puts the notes in his pocket and drives off without a word or even his usual sigh. He takes me to the nearest retail park and after a quick look at a couple of shops to compare prices; I manage to pick up everything on the list that Ritchie stole. TV, DVD player, microwave, a small stereo and a pile of kids DVD's. I get back in the car and tell him the address, he soon realises that it is Ritchie's address and I can tell the wheels are turning in his head to ask me questions, but he keeps his trap shut while he puts the car in gear and drives off. I know he deserves an explanation so during the journey I inform him of what Ritchie has done. He shakes his head and as soon as he opens his mouth to say something, I cut him off.

"Brody, remember what I said."

He nods at me and carries on driving.

We pull up outside the house and Emma is standing by the door.

"Brody you take the stuff into the house, while I go talk to her."

I follow her into the kitchen and straight away, she starts ranting about what a horrible person Ritchie is, that he does not give a fuck about his kid and that he is now starting to dispute that it is even his. I cannot really blame Ritchie for thinking this, as the way she used to carry on, I also had my doubts. She gives me the 'I can't take this anymore speech' which is far from Oscar material and when she sees that I am not buying it, she pulls out the obvious, 'the police are pushing for me to charge him' line.

"But I told them I would think about it."

I pull out a small roll of notes, real ones and her face lights up. I give her a wink and reassure her that it will not happen again. It is amazing how people's opinion on things change when you hand them money. As I go to walk away, she suddenly starts to get on her high horse, and mouths about Ginge and I always clearing up his mess. This annoys me more when I realise that Brody is standing outside the door listening. If she did not have that hold over Ritchie with those charges, I would have taken that money back and told Brody to reload all that shit back into the car, the ungrateful bitch.

"If you see him before I do, tell him I am looking for him" I say without turning to face her as I follow Brody out to the car.

Chapter 31

"So where are we off to now?"

"Give me a second. I need to think"

I know a few places where he would go to score but as soon as I show up at the first one, the word will go straight back to him and he will know that I am on his tail. I consider making a few phone calls to get a definite of his whereabouts before I go knocking on doors. I think about this for a few seconds and weigh it up, and then it hits me. Since when the fuck did I start thinking tactical, that must be Ginge wearing off on me. I am going to go through every fucking door until I find him.

"Do you know where Brownhill Street is?"

He shakes his head.

"Charleston, head for there, I'll keep you right."

We reach South road and after a few short lefts and rights, we reach Brownhill Street.

"Who lives here?"

"A dirty piece of shit smack dealer."

I take the cosh out of my jacket pocket and slide it up the inside of my sleeve.

"Do you have any sort of tools in here?"

"I have a wheel brace in the back."

"Go get it. I'm expecting trouble, so be prepared."

While Brody is raking in his car for a tool, I head straight to the door. I rattle the letterbox a few times and stand back from the step. I look up at each of the filthy windows but all the blinds are closed. I flick the letterbox once more and Brody appears at my side. I consider just kicking the door in, but at their level of dealing, it is a guarantee that there is a steel plate down the inside of the door. This is to give them an extra few seconds to flush their gear in the event of a bust. I give the window a little knock and the blind moves slightly with a pair of eyes now staring at me.

"I'm looking for Ritchie."

He opens the blinds and shrugs.

"It's important."

He closes the blinds and I overhear a few other voices but I cannot make out what they are saying, then I hear the locks being unturned. Dode opens the door with a half-smoked joint hanging from his mouth. He looks me up and down and then gives me a lift of the head for me to follow him inside. As I walk up the steps my decision not to charge the door is justified when I look down to see a reinforced steel plate running up the length of the door. I walk in the living room and stand a few feet inside the doorway, Brody is at my shoulder. There are three guys including Dode, looking a bit worse for wear, the T.V. is on but the screen is frozen like they have it paused on some sort of computer game. As stoned, as they are, the three of them appear to be edgy, as though they are ready to jump at Dode's signal.

"Have any of you seen Ritchie?"

"Ritchie doesn't come here, you know that."

"Do you know where I can find him?"

"Hey man, he's your brother."

"It's important."

"Yeah, you said. We can't help you."

"Look, Dode, I know he's been coming here."

"Yeah" He snorts.

"Yeah" I give him a stare but it has no effect, as due to his stoned state he does not keep eye contact.

He leans back in his chair and somehow appears overconfident for my liking. It is enough to make me hesitate before reaching over and strangling the fucking leech. His mate sitting closest to me looks up and makes a noise by pulling saliva through a gap in his teeth then gives me a sneer. I reach down and grab him by the throat and he slides up the back of the chair to pull away from me. I pin his head against the wall and his other mate makes a dive forward from the couch, I release my grip and slide my cosh down from my sleeve, I catch him hard across the side of his head. He falls back onto the couch and as I lean down towards him, I hear a clicking sound that makes me stop in my tracks. I turn my head slowly to see Dode still sitting back in his chair, with a gun pointing at me. He still has that smug, stoned look on his face.

"Get the fuck out"

I turn to Brody and nod for him to go.

As we walk out, I hear Dode mouthing "I'll sell to whomever the fuck I want"

We are halfway along the path when I hear the door bolted behind us.

"Well, at least we know Ritchie's not with them" I smile.

Brody gives me a look and starts the car.

"So are you going to explain to me what that was all about?"

"A while back when I heard that Richie was dabbling with the smack, I went through every dealer's door and threatened them that if I ever hear they are selling that shit to Ritchie I would burn their house down with them in it."

"I see that worked!"

"Yeah well, I sort of realised that if I had carried out my threat I would be burning houses down every day for months."

Our next stop is the Hilltown. We pass a few minor dealers on the way, but as Ritchie has bumped them in the past, I know they would not even open their door to him. One of the things I have always liked about Ritchie, if a person has something that he needs or wants, he will take it. He does not give a fuck. Well, I like it when it is someone that has latched onto the Donaldson's mob and are throwing their name about as if that is enough to protect them. Sending Ritchie onto them soon puts them in their place. Ginge always says that Ritchie has his uses but the only problem is that Ritchie does not have a cut-off switch to know when to stop. He would not think twice about bullying good, genuine people and that kind of shit will eventually reflects back on all of us.

"Right, park here, it's a block further down but I need you to wait in the car. I will press the intercom and he will come to the window. He will look out and see that I am on my own. This does not mean he will let me in, but it is less likely if there are two of us. Do not move until he closes the window."

Brody nods and looks up at the block.

"Who is he?" Brody asks as he stretches his neck to look at the windows above.

"Hardy, he ran about for Buster a while back. He sells smack now, that's all you need to know."

I slide the cosh back up my sleeve before getting out of the car and walk over to press the buzzer. Seconds later I hear someone shout from up above.

"What you wanting?"

I look up to see a young skanky looking girl.

"Tell Hardy I want a word."

"What? What do you mean tell Hardy you want a word, and who the fuck are you?"

"Is he there?"

She ignores me and closes the window. I press the buzzer again and step back from the door to look up at the window. Nobody appears. I press it twice more and eventually Hardy opens the window.

"What the fuck do you want?"

"I need a word. I'm looking for Ritchie."

"Well he's not here, so fuck off."

I had already clocked that the security door opens inwards and in the split second that it takes for him to close the window I have launched forward and burst the lock. It would not have been a big deal if it were a solid steel outward lock as I would have been back in twenty minutes with a crowbar. I run up the stairs with my cosh at the ready and by the time I reach the top, Hardy is standing waiting. As he stands with his screwed up face I catch sight of the long blade running up the length of his forearm. Hardy is the type who would not feel out of place cutting people's heads off in some Islamic country, so this confrontation with a blade is not for intimidation purposes. He would think nothing of plunging that blade into my stomach. The stairway is quite narrow which works in my favour as I am not one for thinking tactical or watching which direction the blade is about to travel. I do not even attempt to reach over with the cosh to get the first hit in. I put my head down and dive forward, grab him by the waist and pull him to the ground. I reach up to his face and manage to grip one of my fingers into his eye socket and slam his head back onto the ground. The skanky girl from the window appears and lets out a scream, before jumping on my back and digging her fingernails into my neck. I turn and place the palm of my hand on her face nearly covering it and launch her away from me. She stumbles back towards the stairs and Brody appears and breaks her fall. I turn back to Hardy and with the knife no longer in his hand, I punch him several times. When I get to my feet, I turn to see the skanky girl trying to scratch Brody's face, he has a hold of her wrists but she is kicking out and going crazy. He looks at me in a sort of pleading way then suddenly he lets go one of her wrists and gives her a good hard slap knocking her sideways. He looks back at me and shakes his head before walking off down the stairs without saying a word. There are not many situations where I would allow a man to hit a woman in my company without me stepping in to punish them for it, but I guess this is one of them. Brody is already outside but before I reach the security door I hear a shout from Hardy as he comes tearing down the stairs. He has blood running down the side of his face and the knife out in front of him. The skanky girl is nudging him forward and shouting at him to stab me

"Come on, I'm right here."

He edges forward as though he is about to make a run at me, then his eyes glance beyond me and he hesitates.

Brody's head peers around the door.

"Ryan, let's go."

I walk backwards out of the door still smiling. When I reach the car, Hardy is out on the pavement shouting to come back and waving the knife about above his head. I look at Brody and go to step away from the car.

"Ryan let it go, look around you."

I have a quick scan across the street to see several people who look as though they are on their way to work and have stopped to witness what is going on. I close the car door and Brody U-turns in the street to go back up the hill.

"You're bleeding."

"Where"

"Your arm"

I look down to see a slash in my jacket and a splash of blood around it.

"It's okay, it's nothing."

"And your neck is covered in scratches."

I pull down the sun visor and look at my neck in the mirror.

"Crazy junky bitch"

"I take it he's not seen Ritchie either then?"

"What? Oh yeah, I guess not." I smile.

"Where to now"

"Drumlanrig Drive."

He gives me a look.

"Mid Craigie" I confirm. "We shouldn't get much trouble at this house and there is a high possibility that Ritchie will actually be here."

"So why didn't you come here first?"

"Well the others were the less obvious ones and Ritchie knows I would be out looking for him, so depending on the company that's helped him shift the gear, he could be here."

When we pull into Drumlanrig Drive, I notice that something is not right. Parked up, half on the pavement of Fairhurst Walk is a random car that looks as though it is abandoned. As we pass, I turn to catch the faces in the front seats. Brody drives further down and facing us, parked up on the pavement, is another random car. I clock their faces straight away.

"Fuck!"

"What, what's wrong?"

"Look to your right. Quick."

Brody turns his head just as the occupants of the other car look at us.

"Who are they?"

"Drug Squad"

"How do you know?"

Brody quickly realises what he has said.

"Okay, stupid question" He turns up Mauchline Avenue and we are met with another unmarked car with four uniformed officers in it.

"What are they waiting for?"

"Looks like they've had a tip-off and are waiting on a warrant to arrive"

"What do you want me to do?"

"Just head for the Claver"

"Do you want to wait and see if they bring Ritchie out?"

"I'm not hanging about here. If he is in there we will find out soon enough. There's nothing I can do about it now."

Chapter 32

"Well, you've had a busy morning," Buster shouts across the pub with a big smile on his face.

I let out a growl.

"I've had a phone call about a little visit to Charleston. Apparently if you turn up there again you will be shot."

I raise my hands sarcastically surrendering.

"I've also had Hardy on the phone. What the fuck are you bothering him for?"

"I was looking for Ritchie."

He smiles "You knew fine well Ritchie wouldn't be there."

I shrug. "I know, but I've never liked him."

"So all that at the Hilltown, was for nothing?" Brody demands.

"Not nothing, I just said, I've never liked him."

"But you knew Ritchie wouldn't be there?"

Brody sighs.

"Brody he deals smack and Ritchie is a junky. Is that a good enough reason?"

He shakes his head and walks off to the toilet.

"By the way, there is about to be a bust on Drummy Drive, I wasn't hanging about to see if Ritchie was there."

"Ritchie isn't there."

"What, you know where he is?"

"I know where he is."

"Well...?"

"He's with the Duggan's."

"What the fuck is he doing with them?"

Buster shrugs.

"What's the address?"

"I can't remember the address but I know where the house is, the only problem is, I can't leave the pub, I'm waiting on someone, a bit of business."

"I'll get the fucking address" I take out my phone and start flicking through random contacts.

"If you don't want to hang about I'll get someone to show you…Stew!" He shouts over to someone sitting by the bar on his own. He turns his head and has distraught look about him.

"Stew is a window cleaner; he knows where the house is. Stew, I need you to go with Ryan here and show him that address. If you do him that favour he might be able to help you with your predicament."

I look at Buster "What fucking predicament."

"I'll let Stew explain. I'm sure you two can work something out" He smiles.

"Let him explain, he looks as though he's not left that bar stool for days."

"Yeah I know, he turned up here earlier like that. I wasn't going to let him in but…well…I'll let him explain it to you."

I give Buster a little growl and then walk over to the bar where Stew is sitting. "Do you know where this Duggan lives?"

He looks up at me and nods then reaches for his pint from the bar.

"Can you come with us and show us the house?"

He nods again and then makes a fair attempt at downing the rest of his pint in one go. Brody appears from the toilet and with his eyes wide and bulging, I can tell straight away that he has taken a line.

"This day is just getting better and better!"

Before leaving the pub, I turn back towards Buster and he smugly gives me the thumbs up and smiles. I return the gesture with the finger.

"So what's this favour you're looking for then Stew?"

"I need to get my hands on a gun."

I make a snort and turn my head to look at him as he sits in the back of Brody's car.

"A gun, no offence Stew, I know Buster obviously trusts you but you seem a bit troubled so if you don't mind, I think I would like to know why you want a gun."

"I've not seen my daughter for nearly two months since that sneaky bastard stole my wife and sacked me."

"Sacked you? But Buster said you were a window cleaner, are you not self-employed?"

"Yeah we are, but someone usually owns the round and this sneaky bastard I used to work for spread some shit about me so no-one will employ me."

"Who is he?"

"His names John Paul but he goes by Jay P. I was working for him for a few months and one day he came to pick me up for work and gave me the big sob story that his girlfriend had thrown him out and had nowhere to stay. I felt sorry for him and let him sleep on my couch until he got himself sorted out. Next thing I know he's banging my wife and they've moved in together, took my fucking daughter with them."

"They can't stop you from seeing your daughter. Have you been to a solicitor?"

"Yeah but because I'm not working I've had to apply for legal aid, they are accusing me of all sorts, so in the meantime, I'm not even allowed to contact her and if I go near them it will prolong the case."

"How old is your daughter?"

"Seven."

"So who is the gun for; him or her, or both?"

"Just him, I couldn't give a fuck about her."

"Stew I don't think you have thought this through. If I did manage to get my hands on a gun for you and you shoot him, you will serve maybe fifteen to twenty. How long do you think it will be before your wife has someone else moved in and is playing dad to your daughter?"

"I don't care about that, I just want him dead."

I am still trying to figure out why the fuck Buster would put this situation onto me, for one thing, he really can't be that stupid that I would go and put a gun in this guy's hand.

"Look I understand you're angry and if I was in your situation I would probably consider shooting some fucker as well, but I really think you should sober up and think about other ways to get at him."

"I just want my daughter back" He mumbles.

There is a short moment of silence, which makes me think about my own daughter, and how disappointed she would be if I ended up with a ten or fifteen stretch.

"So where am I going?" Brody asks.

Stew answers with a few drunken mumbled directions and eventually blurts out "That's it there?"

"That house there?" I point across the street and look back at Stew who gives me a nod.

Brody pulls over and stops the car.

"No Brody. We'll take Stew home first."

"It's okay I can wait."

"No, we'll drop you off first Stew. I don't want anyone in that house to know that you brought us here, they will use you for someone to blame."

Stew shrugs as though he could not care less, but I know Ritchie, if Stew thinks that his life is shit right now, it would be ten times worse if Ritchie was onto him.

"Tell you what Stew, before we take you home why don't you give Brody directions to where this Jay P lives, you can point it out for me and I'll get someone to nip up later and have a word with him."

Stew's eyes light up when I mention this and he edges forward in his seat slightly. With Stew's directions, we end up back at the Hilltown and the detour takes us to Milton Street, Brody slows to a crawl while we scan a row of fancy townhouses.

"I assume that one is his?" I point to a flashy BMW in a driveway with the registration J10 PEE

He nods at me and I notice the tears in his eyes. His face is full of anger.

"This Jay P can't be short of a few bob. This window cleaning business must be pretty lucrative."

He does not answer and when I turn to face him, I catch him leaning to reach for the door handle. I quickly grab him before he gets a chance to open it.

"What are you doing?"

"I want to see my daughter" He cries.

"I know mate but do you really want your daughter seeing you like that?"

"I don't care I just want to see her."

I tell Brody to keep driving and I keep a hold of Stew until he calms down a bit. The last thing I need is for him to cause a scene and have the place crawling with coppers. Brody drives him home and as he gets out of the car, his head is down as though he has the weight of the world on his shoulders.

"So are you going to get me a gun?" He mumbles.

I roll down my window and smile.

"I'll tell you what I'll do. If you go and get yourself cleaned up and come back and see me, then we will go and pay him a visit and get this sorted out. But I need you to be sober."

He looks up at me with tears still in his eyes "I just want to see my daughter."

"I know mate. Go and sleep it off."

He turns and trudges off towards his house. Brody drives off and we both look at each other and shake our heads.

"I can't believe he wanted you to get him a gun" Brody smirks

"It is a bit extreme, but I understand. I've been asked to get a gun for a lot less."

"Really, like what?"

"Just the usual drunken arguments that happen to get out of hand."

"Can you get hold of a gun that easily?"

"Why, what do you need a gun for?"

"I'm not."

"Well, then why are you asking?"

"Just curious"

"Have you ever heard of the saying curiosity killed the cat?"

"Yeah but, well what I mean is why would someone automatically come to you, thinking you can get one?"

"Brody whether I could or couldn't get one is beside the point. If I give off the impression that I could, how many people are going to think about fucking with me."

"You mean like Dode?" He says smugly.

"Listen, he's just some jumped up little smack dealer that thinks he's a gangster. He could not wait to pull that gun out, how long do you think it will be before the coppers catch him with that? I'll give it until the end of the day and he will have told that story to half a dozen people, that story will reach a certain person who will not hear it and think 'Oh he pulled a gun on McNaughton' they will hear it as 'Oh, so Dode has a shooter. Thank you very much. Hello Officer, remember that possession charge I have to go up for, any chance of a deal for some info on a shooter?'"

"So what about Ginge, he was waving a gun about in the fucking street."

I turn to face him "Brody, the only way Ginge will ever get caught with a gun is if he wants to get caught with one."

Brody now has a look of satisfaction on his face as though I have just confirmed what he already knew.

Chapter 33

We arrive back outside the Duggan's house and I tell Brody to follow me.

"Will I need this?" He picks up the wheel brace.

"I don't know, bring it anyway."

I approach the door and put my ear to the letterbox to listen for any noise. I give the door a loud knock, no answer. I bang on it several times with my fist but still no answer. When I go to bang again, I hear movement and then someone appears from around the door looking a bit dishevelled.

"I'm looking for Ritchie"

"Ritchie" He rubs his head.

"Yeah, Ritchie"

"What are you C.I.D.?" He says quite cocky.

"Do we look like fucking coppers? Go and get Ritchie. You little prick."

There are two reasons that I do not just walk in there and kick off, one is the rancid smell coming from the house and the other is that I really do not fancy walking in to witness Ritchie surrounded by dirty fucking needles. I stand back from the door to take a few deep breaths. Brody does the same. I overhear voices but cannot make them out, and then the same person appears once more, only he seems to be a lot less sure of himself this time.

"He's not here."

"He's not here" I say surprised.

"No sorry." He says shaking his head before attempting to close the door.

"You wouldn't happen to know where he is would you." I say as I shuffle closer to the doorway.

"No…" I quickly place my foot in the doorway before reaching in to grab him.

I pull him outside and force him against the wall with my forearm under his chin.

"Now you listen to me. You are going to go back in there and tell Ritchie that if doesn't get his arse out here, I'm going to come in and fucking drag him out"

I release my arm and he hurries off back inside.

Seconds later, Ritchie comes bounding out of the front door and into my face

"What the fuck is going on?" He growls.

I reach up, sink my hand into his jaw, and push him back against the wall. I press my thumb tight on his throat and he grabs my wrist with both hands. I realise what I am doing and let him pull my hand away.

"What the fuck are you doing? What the fuck is going on?"

"What do you mean, what the fuck is going on? I have been running about all morning replacing the shit you stole yesterday to stop you from getting the fucking jail."

"Is that what this is about? That fucking stuff was mine. I paid for it."

"Ritchie you took the kids fucking DVD's."

"So fuck, he's not even mine. I worked it out. I was in the fucking jail when she got pregnant."

I stand back slightly and notice Ritchie's eyes look passed me towards Brody.

"And what the fuck are you doing here?"

He attempts to go for him but I stand in his way.

"Never mind what he's doing here. What the fuck are you doing here? Do you want to end up like those filthy scumbags in the jail, sucking somebody's cock for a hit?"

"I'm hardly going to end up like that. It's only a little blowout."

"A little blowout, is that what you call it? You have just robbed your own fucking kid's house. If that had been anybody else you'd be the one coming to me asking me to hunt them down."

"Well if Buster hadn't cut me off, none of this would have happened."

"He never cut you off. He told you to come to the Claver after you bumped Liam."

"I never bumped Liam. I told him to hand me what he was due and I would pay it back to Ginge. He started getting all wide so I gave him a slap."

"Liam got wide with you?" I shake my head.

"I've been out for a few days now, why haven't you come to see me?"

"I was going to come later today. I know how you like your family time when you get out."

I stand back and shake my head again. I know that every word that comes out of his mouth is lies but what can I do, he is my brother, he is my blood. I turn and look at Brody and nod at him to go to the car. I turn back to see Ritchie giving him the stare.

"Ritchie"

"Fuck him. Who the fuck does he think he is?"

"Ritchie, why don't you come and stay at mine, and get yourself cleaned up?"

"I'm not away to put you out."

"You're not going to put me out. Come on, my kids think it is great when you are around. Come with me, we'll get you cleaned up then we'll go to Claver and talk to Buster."

"I'm not going to the Claver. If Buster wants to talk to me he can come and find me."

"You know he won't do that Ritchie."

"Well fuck him then."

"Ritchie, come on, you've got to get off this shit."

"I will, but I'll do it on my own, in my own time."

"Come on Ritchie" I plead.

"No Ryan. I'm staying here."

I take a step backwards and shake my head. He looks at me knowing that I am disappointed.

"Look, just give me a few days to get myself together. I promise I'll get cleaned up, I'll come and see you and we'll sort something out."

I know this is his way of passing me off so that I leave, and there is no way that he is going to come with me so I go along with it.

"Okay." I pull out a roll of notes from my pocket and hand it to him.

"I'm not taking that Ryan."

"Take it. Go get yourself cleaned up."

He puts his hand out to take it but I keep my grip on it.

"I'm telling you now Ritchie, if I hear about you robbing any more people, it will be the last you will ever get from me and it will be the last time I will ever talk to you. I mean it."

He nods as I let the money go and he heads back into the house. When the door closes, I stand for a few seconds before making my way back to the car.

"Go to the Claver."

"You know he's just going to go and spend that on..."

"HEY, what did I fucking say to you earlier? No judgments He's blood, that's all that matters" I snap

"I was just saying" He mumbles.

"Well don't just 'fucking say' I haven't said anything to you about whatever you've been on all fucking day."

He tries to put on the 'who me?' expression.

"And don't give me that fucking look. I can tell straight off when someone's high so don't fucking look at me like I'm some sort of mug."

I feel myself getting angry but I do not want to take it out on Brody.

"Do you know what? Take me to that fucking Jay D's house."

"Jay P"

"Whatever his fucking name is"

Brody seems to drive faster now, I don't know if it's because I've pissed him off or that he just wants this day over with but whatever the reason he should fucking drive like this more often. I get out and knock on the door and moments later a young woman appears, she has fake tits that are near bursting out of her top and a face that even a plastic surgeon would struggle to make half decent. If this is Stew's wife, I think that this Jay P has probably done him a favour.

"Hi, I'm looking for Jay P"

"Oh, I'll just go get him."

She walks off leaving the door open and seconds later, someone appears looking a bit too well groomed. He smiles as he approaches me with teeth that look as though they have recently had a fresh coat of white gloss paint.

"Yeah, can I help you?" He says in a slightly feminine tone.

I give him a fake smile back and nod my head towards his driveway. This is only to entice him further in to his doorway.

"I was just wondering if that was your car"

"The BM, yeah that's mine."

The second he steps into my range, I grab him by the throat and pin him against the wall. This manoeuvre works in many situations and does not leave any evidence of lasting marks, like black eyes or broken teeth, and if the person struggles or lashes out, I only have to squeeze tighter, they soon comply.

"I'm a friend of Stew and I'm here to discuss access to his daughter."

"It...It's nothing to do with me."

"Yeah, well you're going to make it something to do with you."

I apply a little pressure with my thumb and forefinger.

"You've got until the end of the week to get it sorted. I release my grip and go to walk away but I turn back before he closes his door.

"Oh and another thing, that window round that you have, it's no longer yours."

"I'm not going away to hand over my window round over to him."

I turn and smile.

"Oh no, you've got it all wrong. You're not handing the round over to Stew, you're handing it over to me."

"You can't do that. What am I supposed to do?" He pleads.

"You should have thought about that before sticking your dick into someone's wife."

"You can't just take my round, I've paid for that."

"Watch me. Oh and if you're stuck for work just come give me a visit, I'll be in the Claverhouse every Friday counting the takings."

"I'll go to the police."

I smirk before getting in the car.

"Back to the Claver"

"BUSTER" I shout as I burst through the doors of the Claver. "Get your buddy Stew on the phone."

"Why, what the fucks happened?"

"We're about to go into the window cleaning business."

"What the fuck do you know about cleaning windows?"

"No much, but I do know one thing. You can't go shagging your employee's wife and not expect it to have a repercussion."

"Did you get a hold of Ritchie?"

"What? Oh yeah, fuck him" I make a face.

Buster shrugs and makes the call to Stew. Twenty minutes later, Stew comes bursting through the pub door with a big smile on his face.

"I've just had a phone call to pick my daughter up from school tomorrow."

He stands by the bar and attempts to buy us all drinks.

"Put your money away, Stew. Use it to buy your daughter something."

"No, it's not only that, I'm getting my job back as well."

I turn and give Buster a look and then gesture towards the back of the pub.

"Stew can I have a word?" I tilt my head for him to follow me.

I take a seat at one of the booths by the side of the bar.

"Ryan I can't thank you enough."

"Yeah, I'm happy to help mate. Listen, Stew, what do you mean that you are getting your job back? What did he actually say to you?"

"It was my wife that called. She just asked if I could pick my daughter up from school tomorrow and also if I want my job back, Jay P said I could start back on Monday."

"Oh Stew you can start back tomorrow if you like."

"What do you mean?"

"Stew that round is now mine. You are now working for me."

He looks at me a little confused.

"No offence Ryan, but I never really pictured you being a window cleaner."

"I'm not, but what I need you to do is go around all of Jay P's customers and inform them that 'You' are now taking over the round, and if this Jay P makes any attempt to contact them, to let you know."

"But I can't manage it. I have no ladders or transport and the guys all work for him."

"Not anymore."

"I'll give you what you need to get started. Do you have a license?"

He nods.

"Come and see me or Buster tomorrow and we'll get you sorted out with a motor. Get in touch with the other guys that you worked with, tell them if they come work for me I'll pay them an extra fifty quid a week."

His smile does not move from his face.

"Now go and sleep it off, you've got a busy day tomorrow."

We shake hands and I watch him walk out of the pub still smiling.

I sit down and explain Stew's situation with Buster and that I am going to front him the money to get it up and running.

"Are you sure you know what you're doing?"

"Buster I know how these window cleaning rounds work. Heavy money is exchanged for these rounds that technically they don't actually own."

"Where are you going with this?"

"Keep on at Stew, get this up and running. We will muscle in on other rounds and take over one at a time. Most of these guys are on minimum wage, so if the word gets around that they are getting paid more than the going rate working for us, then we'll see how loyal their workers are."

Buster thinks about this for a few seconds "Cash business?"

"All cash"

"I see where you're going with this" He smiles.

"Get a few of our boys on the books" I wink.

Buster gets up to go to the bar but I wave him off before standing up to leave. After seeing Stew's face light up about seeing his daughter, it made me think of mine and I have been watching that clock above the bar as though it was a bomb about to go off.

"Where the fuck are you going?"

I point to the clock behind him "Nursery time"

"What are you going for, father of the year?"

"What the fuck would you know about that you fat cunt."

"Hey, there's no need for that, all those foster families did a fine job with my boys."

"Yeah, tell that to Ritchie" I smirk.

Buster gives me a growl.

I go to walk out the door and Brody stands up to follow me.

"It's okay Brody, that's us done for the day."

I walk over to thank him for today and put my hand out for him to shake. He places his hand in mine and I grip it tightly to pull him towards me.

"Now you listen to me. There are times and places for taking that shit, but not when you're working with me" I say quietly in his ear.

He pulls away and looks at me with his wide eyes, and then gives me a justified nod.

Chapter 34

After turning my phones off last night, I was expecting to wake up to the usual drama, and I am relieved when no texts come through. I have my voluntary work today, so with any luck, it will all run smooth. The courts have asked them for a report about me, so with this, added to my psychiatric report, they will both go towards any future cases that I have pending. The volunteering had come about from an old cellmate of mine, he informed me that even if it I turned up for only one day a month, the judge would look at it as though I was trying to see the error of my ways, like giving back to the community and all that shit. With my past record, it can only help. Before I found myself remanded, my volunteering was set up at a local centre that dealt with mental health. It was more for people that lacked confidence, for instance, being out in public. A simple task of going for their shopping stressed them out. The person in charge was impressed with me though, he liked me that much that he wanted to employ me full time, luckily for me I found myself remanded!

It is still a little early so I sit with my coffee in front of the TV while Biscuit and Mollie venture in the front garden. The front door is open and I overhear voices from outside which draws my attention away from some crazy talk show. I lift my head up to the window to see two smack heads leaning over my garden wall and attempting to reach over to touch Biscuit. By the time I reach the front door, Biscuit, being as trusting and friendly as always, has moved into the range of one of the junkie's hands. I stand by the door and my rage is ready to explode when I see for the first time in Mollie's life that she has a look of fear on her face.

"Hey pal, is that your little doggy? He's a cracker." One of them says through his slurred speech while the other has fallen over my garden wall while attempting to reach towards Biscuit with both hands. As soon as I see his hand touch Biscuit's head to pet him, my protective instinct takes over.

"Keep your grubby fucking hands off him."

"Hey pal, I wasn't going to hurt him" He drools.

"I'm not your fucking pal."

I step forward but Nikki nudges me out of the way, she races in front of me and picks up Mollie.

"Don't you dare talk to my daughter in the bloody state you are in?"

"The state I am in, look at the fucking state of you" He hisses.

"You should be ashamed of yourselves. Just get away from my house" She screams at them.

"Sake, there's no need for that."

"I suggest you both move on. Now" I demand.

As soon as Nikki passes me to go into the house, I dive forward and grab hold of the one lying on my wall. I throw him backwards and he falls towards his mate before stumbling to the ground. They start to mouth off again and I about to jump over the wall and give them both a slap when I notice my wanker of a neighbour from across the street standing by his car. He is the last person I need as a witness for these two wasters. He gives me a stare before getting into his car, which I assume he has had repaired. I reach down and pick Biscuit up before marching back in the house. I explain to Mollie that I have to leave to go to work and it does not go down too well when she realises that I cannot walk her to nursery today. I give her a hug and a kiss before heading off but not before I slip my cosh up the sleeve of my jacket as I head out the door. With the state those two were in, I know they will not be far. I spot them on the next street up and as much as I want to wait for them to stumble closer to a secluded area, I am a bit pushed for time. I walk straight up to them and luckily for me they both turn and square up to me. With a quick glance around me to check for witnesses, I don't even make a fist, two slaps from an open hand and they are both on the ground out cold. It seemed a bit of a liberty hitting them in the state that they were in, but if they were compos mentis enough to stand up to me then maybe they will think twice before approaching my daughter in that state. I keep walking until I am far enough away so that no one can place me at the scene before phoning a taxi. I manage to find a place to ditch the cosh before the taxi pulls up. I do not think it would look good if it accidentally fell out of my jacket while accompanying some schizophrenic to help with their shopping. It was only a precaution in case one of those slimy fuckers pulled a blade. The taxi pulls up outside the day centre and for some reason, I feel a bit hesitant, I think it is because I am unsure about how they will react towards me, as I have not seen any of them in three months. As soon as I walk in, they all greet me with big smiles and handshakes. There are a few new faces and I cannot tell if they are workers or clients as mental health is not exactly visible. Seeing all these new faces makes me think of the first time I came here, I casually walked, like today, and everyone was smiling and introducing their selves. Then I heard someone shout 'Arsehole' from across the room. When I looked over at whom I thought had said it, he turned away, and everyone around me continued as though it did not happen. Then I heard it again. 'Arsehole' There was still no reaction from anyone. I remember feeling somewhat paranoid and thinking did I really hear that. Is it possible that I am not a volunteer here and I am actually the fucking client? I heard it a third time and I knew for definite that it was coming from the person sitting on his own away from the group. He was about eighteen maybe nineteen and when he looked at me again and turned away, I thought, right this cunt is taking the piss. I was about to approach him when the person that run the place appeared in front of me, he walked me over and introduced us.

"Ryan, this is James. Well, Big James, we like to call him. James has Tourette's syndrome."

When he stood up to shake my hand, I realised why they called him Big James. He was huge. I thought I was big at six two but he towered over me by a few inches.

"Hi, I'm James. James Smith."

My first impression was that he was very polite and soft-spoken, well, when he was not having an outburst of abuse at no one in particular. My boss explained that I would be working with Big James. I smiled, but inside I was, well... still fucking smiling. The wheels immediately started turning in my head about how much of a laugh this would be. I already had a day out planned in my head to take him to the Claver and have everybody in the pub convinced that he was shouting at them. Maybe even treat him to the cinema and have Joe the Bull video him from a few rows back while he shouts abuse at the screen with updates every week of peoples reaction. Then, over the next hour as I sat chatting to James, he explained how the Tourette's has affected his life. The pointing, laughing and sometimes aggressive comments and abuse from strangers has destroyed all of his confidence, and has resulted in a long bout of depression. He has few friends and even his family are embarrassed to walk down the street with him. He also has had on-going intimidation and bullying from some of his neighbours, all from the unwanted attention he receives from his condition. I persuaded the boss to let me walk through the town centre with him to get an experience of what it was like for him. From the type of person who thinks nothing of walking about prison naked for months at a time, to walking through the town that day as he shouted random obscenities, it gave me a sense of paranoia as people stared at us, and I could not even imagine how it felt for James. The thoughts of having fun at his expense, soon disappeared. He never went anywhere; he could not get a job and sat in his room most of the time scared to leave the house. His situation was really affecting me until he mentioned that he liked football. I smiled and got straight on the phone to Ginge. United was playing at home the following weekend and I spoke to my boss about taking him to the game. He explained, 'he's not a kid, you don't need my permission to accompany him to the football.' The morning of the game, I picked him up in a taxi and took him in town. Ginge met us at one of his regular clothing haunts, we chipped in and rigged him out head to toe in designer gear then we made our way to the Stoby bar. Ginge's crew introduced themselves and made him feel welcome. We made our way to the game and anytime during the match that Big James had an outburst, the whole crew stood by his side and echoed everything he said. Witnessing this moment and seeing the smile on his face that day made me one proud as fuck volunteer. I accompanied Big James to every home game after that and even paid his bullying neighbours a visit, unbeknown to him or my boss obviously.

 With James being so tall, he would normally stand out in any room, but I find myself having to look for him in amongst the new faces at the centre. Then my boss calls me from across the room and waves his hand for me to come over.

 "I told him earlier that you were coming back today. When you didn't show on time he thought you weren't coming."

 He gestures at me to follow him and we walk towards the canteen. He stops a few feet from the canteen door.

 "He's been waiting patiently."

I look in to see Big James sitting on his own with his head slumped down staring at his cup of coffee.

"Oi Arsehole! What sort of welcome back is this?"

He looks up and like a loyal dog wagging its tail; he smiles and stands up with his hand out ready for me to shake. Sometime later I am in the bosses office as he informs me that he has been asked by my solicitor to give them a detailed report about me to be read out in front a judge.

"Look I know you have a reputation, but I try to take people as I find them and I can only go on what I have seen."

"Is that a good thing?"

"Of course, Ryan I would give you a fulltime job without a second thought, well, if it wasn't for your criminal record."

I nod with my fake sympathetic expression 'Ah well.'

"Ryan you are a natural people person. I see the way you talk to everyone in here; you connect with all of them. They all look up to you; you never judge them and treat them all as equals. And the confidence you have given young James." He lifts his hands up and gives me a surprised look.

"So I take it you'll be giving me a good report?"

"Don't you worry about that, it will be glowing."

I smile.

"Also, if you ever need me to turn up as a character witness in court, just let me know."

"Thanks, that's really appreciated."

I leave the centre on a bit of a high, feeling good about myself that I have done my good deed for the day. It also makes me consider my bosses offer of a fulltime job. This thoughtful moment lasts for approximately twenty seconds when my phone sounds and Hunter informs me that it has kicked off with the Donaldson's' I do not even ask for details.

"I'm tied up at the moment, I'll sort it later" I hang up.

I have a more pressing matter at hand, family time.

Chapter 35

I called Brody earlier with a time to pick me up and as I am about to have a last look in on Mollie and Davie, I hear his car outside. I mention to Nikki that I need to pop out for a bit and cheekily she tells me not to hurry back and blows me a kiss. I give her a wink and we both smile before I head out to Brody's car. I direct him to the spot where I ditched the cosh earlier this morning and thankfully, it is still there. This could have made an awkward situation if someone found it and used it with my fingerprints all over it. We drive to the Claverhouse where Hunter and Larnio are waiting outside.

"So what happened then?" I ask as they climb into the back of Brody's car.

"Joe dropped off an ounce at Tony's earlier on today. They were cutting it up and Junkie Jamie came through the door with hammers and blades.

"Junkie Jamie, when did he get out?"

"Yesterday"

"How are they?"

"They are both still up at the hospital, Tony was hit in the head with the hammer, he has a concussion and can't remember anything about it. Joe caught a blade in the hand and arm as he fought them off. His face is a bit of a mess as well."

"So how did they know about the gear, do you think they were following Joe" Brody asks.

"Not a chance" I shake my head. "Joe is far too careful for that, he has lived in Ginge's shadow since he was knee high. You have seen how tight our circle is Brody, occasionally there will be someone introduced to us in good faith, which may result in a word to the wrong person, i.e. the Donaldson's, I think maybe Tony has unknowingly let slip to someone."

"But why would Jamie attack Joe if he knows you'll come after him?"

"Because he's just out the jail and has been mixing with some of the Glasgow mob, they'll have filled his head with all kinds of shit about how they'll back him up to help him take over Dundee and he'll be the man. I have heard it all before. He believes it's a case of us receiving a phone call from them and nobody will touch him."

"Are you all tooled up?"

"Of course"

I pull out my cosh and look at it "Go back to the Claverhouse Brody."

"Seriously"

"Yeah" I nod.

He makes his way back and stops outside.

"Just wait here. I'll only be a minute."

I stand by the bar and wait as the barman finishes serving, he looks at me and I nod behind him. He goes out the back and seconds later, he appears with the sheath containing my machete. He slides it over the bar and I quickly place it inside my jacket before heading back out to the car. Hunter receives word that they are in a house somewhere in Ardler. As Brody puts the foot down and heads for the area, both Hunter and Larnio are on their phones trying to locate an exact address. I decide to phone Mick. Mick is the oldest of the Donaldson's, and appears to be the only one that was born with a brain.

"Hello"

"Is this Mick?"

"Who the fuck is this"

"Ryan"

There is a silence.

"McNaughton"

"I'm listening"

"Couple of my boys got hit earlier"

"So what the fuck do you want me to do about it?"

"It was Jamie that did them"

"As I said, what the fuck do you want me to do about it?"

"He's part of your fucking crew"

"They're fucking drug dealers" He laughs down the phone. "If they aren't hard enough to look after themselves then maybe they shouldn't be selling drugs" He starts to laugh again but I hang up the phone.

"I hope one of you two have that fucking address"

"Got it" Hunter says.

"Who was that on the phone?" Larnio asks.

"Mick"

"Mick Donaldson"

"Yeah"

"I never knew the two of you spoke"

"We don't. I had someone send me his number earlier. I had to make sure that he was not in on it with Jamie, otherwise, we would have had to go and find some bigger tools" I smile.

I really don't know what it is with these fucking Donaldson's, if they were dropped on their heads when they were kids or have just taken far too many drugs, probably a bit of both. It is like a vicious circle, whatever they do always appear to lead back to me and I have to deal with it. Their whole family seems to attract little loudmouth would-be gangsters, like Junkie Jamie for instance. Most of the time I leave them to it, but every now and then they get it into their heads that they can take on some of our boys so I have to go in hard so they will think twice about doing it again.

We turn off the main road into the Ardler village and under the instructions of Hunter; Brody pulls the car to the side of the road.

"Is this it?"

Hunter looks across the street to check the signpost and then back to the house.

"Twenty-five, yeah that's it over there." Hunter nods to the only house in the street with every light on. As I step out of the car, I can hear the music coming from the house.

"I'm guessing this is their subtle way of saying, here we are!"

I pull my machete out of its sheath and then I remember my cosh is on the floor. I pick it up and hand it to Brody. He looks at me and then at the machete. I take the cosh back out of his hand and swap it, handing him the machete.

"Remember and leave your fingerprints on it before you hand it back to me." I wink.

"No ski masks?"

"Do I look like I have Ginger hair?"

As we walk across the street towards the house, Larnio is holding a baseball bat inside his three quarter length jacket and Hunter has a sock wrapped around his fist that is weighed down with a couple of snooker balls.

"Ready?" I turn and ask as we reach the front door. They all give me a convincing nod.

I instruct them to step out of the way while I gear myself to launch a kick to the front door, when Hunter steps in front of me and tries the handle. The door opens. We burst into the living room and the first thing I notice is the large pile of coke on the coffee table. I grab the table lengthways and throw it across the room. A cloud of dust from the coke fills the air. This is my statement that I am not here for the drugs or their money. The girls in the room run screaming towards the kitchen. One of the guys pulls out a hammer and makes an attempt to come at me but Hunter steps forward and clocks him over the head with the sock, knocking him clean out.

"Where's Jamie?" I shout as I pull out my cosh.

"Fuck you." Another of them shouts as he takes a dive towards me and actually lands a punch on my jaw. He is in too close for me to hit him with the cosh so I let it go and grab him with both hands and bring my forehead down hard on the bridge of his nose. He falls back but I keep a hold of him to do it again, then I feel a weight on my shoulders and my head pulled backwards. Someone has me in a chokehold. I go to my knees and lean forward to pull him over me but it is no use as his arm tightens more around my neck. I look up to see Larnio near the doorway swinging the baseball bat and hitting anybody that comes in distance. Hunter is to the side of me but is having a standoff with someone who has appeared from the kitchen with a knife in each hand. Larnio starts to make his way across the room, he is swinging the bat and manoeuvring closer to me but before he reaches me, the person in the standoff with Hunter pulls one of the knives hard across the top of Larnio's shoulder. It slices through his jacket cutting into him. If he was not as tall as he is, I am sure the force of this would have decapitated him. The distraction is just enough for Hunter to step forward with a clean hit of his sock putting him down. Both Hunter and Larnio grab the person from around my neck and pull him forward. As I get to my feet, I look over to see Brody by the doorway. What the fuck is he doing? Someone is attempting to attack him with a hammer and he is bobbing and weaving in front of him. I am about to shout at him to use the machete but I know by the time that the words are out that hammer will be embedded in his skull. I grab the baseball bat from Larnio and dive forward smashing it over the persons head. More people start to pile down the stairs and the one at the front has his top off, he is shouting the odds like a crazed maniac with a large blade in his hand. I catch sight of the blood seeping through Larnio's jacket and I start to think that maybe this could turn bad. I signal towards the front door and stand with the baseball bat making sure I am the last to leave. We get out of the house to make our way towards the car.

"Come on then McNaughton. Let's do this."

I turn back to see the shirtless person with the large blade running towards us. I stand my ground with the bat out by my side. He has that crazy look in his eyes through too much coke. He runs straight at me and I swing the bat at his hand holding the knife but I reach out too far and it catches his forearm. He pulls back and attempts to come at me again. I pull the bat back ready to smash it into him when I hear a dull clunk from Hunters sock hitting him on the side of the head. He falls hard to the ground. I look up the small crowd appearing out of the doorway of the house.

"You give a message to Junkie Jamie. If he crosses any members of our firm again I'm going to fucking bury him."

We get in the car and drive off but not before a few missiles bounce off the roof of Brody's car. Larnio is still holding his shoulder tight to stem the blood flow.

"How bad is it?"

"It's a clean cut so I don't think it will be a hard job getting it repaired. The bloodstains probably won't come out though."

"I was asking about the cut but I'm glad that you have your priorities in order."

"It will definitely need a few stitches...I fucking loved this coat."

"Well, I'm glad that all went to plan."

We all laugh, except Brody.

"By the way, what happened to my machete?"

Brody reaches under his seat and hands it to me.

"A lot of good it fucking did under there."

"I wasn't going to attack someone with that."

"No, you just bob and weave people with hammers."

We all laugh, except Brody.

"Brody you're going to have to learn that these guys don't fuck about."

"I kind of know that now. And anyway that guy wasn't getting near me with that hammer."

"I hope you're right because if you go down in a situation like that, there's no referee to give you ten seconds to get up again."

Brody makes a turn onto the dual carriageway.

"Where are you going?" Larnio asks.

"The hospital"

"I'm not going to the hospital"

"I thought you said you needed stitches."

"I was thinking maybe you could do it"

"Me. I can't do that"

"You're ex-army; surely you've stitched someone up before"

Brody laughs. "I've never even stitched a hole in my trousers."

"Go to the Claver," I tell him. "We'll clean it up a bit there, then we'll drive to Perth or Sterling, or Edinburgh if need be."

"What do you mean, if need be?"

"Well we'll have to give the scanners a listen and if anything comes up about Larnio's description, we'll have to go a bit further afield."

"Sounds like you've had to do this before?"

"Once or twice"

Chapter 36

After reading the texts from Larnio when I woke up this morning, I am glad I decided not to accompany them to the hospital, as they never arrived back in Dundee until three this morning. If I had tagged along with them, I would never have surfaced in time to walk Mollie to nursery. The only problem I have now is this fucking machete tucked into my jacket. I had left it in Brody's car when we arrived back at the Claver and I only remembered about it when he was dropping me off before they headed onto the hospital. If I left it with them and they received a pull, one of them would have had to go down for it. It is the same reason that I do not leave it in the house, there are plenty of useful items that resemble weapons stashed all over, but nothing that the coppers can charge me with, this machete would easily put me away for two years. If I keep it in the pub, the barman can always say that one of the punters left it behind. At the nursery gates, I crouch down so that I can give Mollie a hug and I feel the machete come loose. I manage to grab it through my jacket and hold it secure until she runs off. As much as I do not mind tongues wagging about that kind of shit, it is usually contained to certain circles. The gathering of gossiping parents at the nursery gates is not one of them. I let Biscuit off his lead as I enter the Claver and he runs straight over to the cleaners, this distracts their attention and makes way for me to hide the machete in a safe place. Even though fingerprints do not mean too much nowadays as they can trace anything back to you through your DNA, but out of habit, I still find myself giving the handle a wipe down. I take a seat in one of the booths as I go over the business I have lined up for the day. Flicking through the names in my phone, I come across Stew and I remember that I need to sort him out with a permanent motor. Buster gave him the keys to one he had borrowed off a mate but it was only to get the round up-and-running. The barman appears and puts an orange juice on the bar for me and a bowl of water for Biscuit. I step over to put the bowl down for him and when I return to my seat, I notice a text from Nikki to phone her immediately. The first thing that flashes across my mind is Mollie but I know she is safe, as I have only just left her in the nursery. Then I think, must be coppers at the door. By the time I get through to her, panic is beginning to set in. She rattles on a bit but all I hear are certain words, Davie, school and missing.

"I'll be right there" I hang up.

I clip Biscuits lead back on and march out of the pub without saying a word. A few taxis pass me and eventually, one pulls over. I sit in the front with Biscuit on the floor at my feet. Two minutes into the journey and he puts his paw on my leg and attempts to climb up. The driver has a little moan about keeping him on the floor and I let out a grunt before gently pushing Biscuit down. He tries to make conversation but my mind is miles away worrying about Davie. For only being eleven years old and having to grow up around my lifestyle, he has turned out better than I could have ever imagined. Any time I spend with him I have been upfront about my lifestyle and never lied to him. He is a bright, tough kid and I have taught him to stick up for himself and those close to him. When I watch him with any of his friends, he is always the most streetwise out of them, a born leader. I know it is hypocritical of me but I have lost count how many times I have told him how disappointed I would be if he ended up down my path of being in and out of prison. With Davie on my mind, I suddenly start to feel anxious and the taxi cannot get me home quick enough. I then realise that the driver is still talking and I feel a bit rude when I cut him off by asking if he could speed up a bit. I pull up outside my house and Nikki is at the front door waiting on me.

"Where is he?"

"He's here."

"What's going on?"

She puts her finger to her lips and tilts her head for me to follow her into the kitchen.

"He's in the living room. I told him to wait there until I talked to you."

"Why, what's happened?"

"I received a call not long after you left with Mollie. The police found him and two of his friends hiding behind the shops near his school."

"He's a bit young to be starting this. I'll go and have a word with him."

"Wait, there's more to it. I think you had better sit down."

With the anxious feeling returning, I take a seat not knowing what I am about to hear.

"When I turned up at the school they showed me his attendance record and he's been missing every week at the same time for over a month. His class schedule is a trip to Lawside High School for swimming. I know he likes swimming so I could not work out why he was skipping it. I knew there was something he was not telling me so I asked to take him home. He told me that he doesn't like going because he doesn't like the way the teachers touch him."

"What?" I let out a half laugh. "He's having you on" I smile.

She raises her eyebrows to let me know that it is not a wind-up. My smile drops.

"When you say touching, what exactly do you mean?"

"Well, apparently when they come out of the pool they go into a drying area before they go into the changing room and the teacher touches them to make sure they are dried properly before they are allowed into the changing room."

"He's far too wide to let someone away with that. Why hasn't he said anything?"

"Well, he says he was worried that if he lashed out, you would find out what it was about and go after his teacher, and he didn't want you to end up back in prison."

I lean back in the chair feeling absolutely stunned. It takes a couple of seconds for it all to sink in.

"I need to talk to him"

I stand up and walk fast across the kitchen.

"Ryan"

I turn back.

"Calm" She says quietly, motioning with her hands.

I nod at her before entering the living room. Davie is sitting back on the couch flicking the through the channels on the TV, the volume is set way too low for him to have been watching anything, so I can tell that he has been trying to hear what has been said between me and his mother.

"Hey son"

"Dad" He looks up at me and then turns back to the TV.

I catch a look in his eyes that I have never seen before. I know it is not a look of fear, as I have never given him any reason to fear me. It is more a look of nervousness as he obviously thinks that he is in trouble.

"Davie your mum has told me what happened."

He does not take his eyes from the TV so I reach over for the remote and turn it off. He gives me that nervous look again.

"Look, son, I know how smart you are and I know I've taught you how to use situations to your advantage but this is serious. I need to know that what you told your mum, about the teacher touching you, I need to know what really happened."

"It wasn't a lie Dad, but I knew that if you found out you would go after him and end up back inside"

This stuns me even more hearing it from Davie, and I realise now that the nervous look in his eyes is more of concern.

"Son, you know I've done time for a lot of stupid things but I can assure you I will not be doing time for this, however, I am going to need some more details from you before this goes any further. I need to know, does he single you out or are there other boys that this happens to?"

"They do it to everybody."

"Wait. What do you mean they, how many are there?"

"There's my teacher Mr Andrews and the swimming teacher Mr Nolan. We all try and sneak past them from the drying area to the changing room, but they block the doorway and run their hand down your back when you pass them so that they can check that you are dried properly."

I try not to show my anger on hearing this but my son knows me too well. I see him look down at my clenching fists.

"I thought we had a bond son, why couldn't you tell me?"

"I wanted to Dad, but you were inside and when you got out I was happy having you around that I didn't want you to go back in."

"Son whatever happens, not just about this, but anything in the future, you must understand that you will never, ever, be the fault that I am in prison. Do hear me?"

He nods.

"I don't know what's made me angrier, those beasts abusing their position or the fact that they have come between me and you."

I put my fist out towards him and he does the same but when our knuckles touch, I grab him playfully and put him in a headlock.

"So you like having me around then do you?"

I rub my knuckles on the top of his head as he squeals and attempts to grab my leg and trip me up. Nikki comes through wondering what all the noise is and looks surprised to see us rolling about laughing.

"What's going on?"
"He's made his point. I'm not allowed to go to jail again."
"So what are you going to do, phone the police?"
"Phone the police?" I laugh.
"Well, they need to charged, they can't get away with this."
"It's okay. We'll do what his Uncle Ginge would do."
I wink.
"Glad to hear it" She smiles.

I will need to have both of these teachers done around the same time, as if I get to one of them and the information reaches the other, they will immediately have their guard up. I make a call to Hunter, as I know he attended Lawside back in the day, as soon as I mention the name Nolan, he laughs and comments about him touching up the young boys. I explain the situation and he says that he would gladly take the job.

"If you knew about it back then, why is he still teaching?"
"Remember Ryan, back then if a kid mentioned that a teacher touched him or her they would be accused of lying and made to feel guilty, it was very rare for a teacher to be arrested for that kind of thing twenty years ago."
"Well, what I mean is why has someone not fucking done him over if it's been going on for over twenty years?"
"It was sort of like an on-going joke between the boys. Like, 'Ha Nolan touched you'"
"You must have like it then" I smirk.
"What, he never came near me."
"Bit defensive there Hunter. Is there something you're not telling me?"
"Fuck off."
I laugh and hang up.

Chapter 37

Brody sounds his horn to let me know he is outside and when I look up at the clock on the wall, I notice that he is bang on time. All those years as a soldier have certainly made him punctual. I had not mentioned what the job was, so when I walk out of the house with Davie in tow, he has a puzzled expression.

"What's going on?" He asks as we get in his car.

"Brody I know you probably haven't seen him since he was a toddler but this is Davie, your nephew. Davie, this is your Uncle Brody."

Brody turns to Davie in the back seat and they both give each other a nod.

"Brody, Davie has a little bit of a problem with one of his teachers so we need you to drive us there so that he can point him out to us."

"You're joking right?" He shakes his head. "Ryan you can't just walk into the school and beat up a teacher, especially in front of kids."

"Of course I'm not going to do that, what do you think I am, some sort of a maniac?" I smile at him and look back at Davie. "Tell him Davie, what are we going to do?"

"We're going to do what Uncle Ginge would do."

"What's that then?"

"Davie" I nod for him to continue.

"If you are ever in a situation think, what would Ginge do?"

"So what would Ginge do?" He asks.

"Well, you know Ginge, the first thing he does is make a plan."

"So what is the plan?"

"Well right now, all we have is a name, Andrews, Cormack Andrews, and Davie here is going to help us put a face to that name."

"Where is the school?"

"It's St. Columbas"

"That's not far from here, why did you need me?"

"Because once Davie points him out, you are going to follow him."

I look at him with a straight face and he gives me a lift of the head as though he now understands.

Brody drives along to the school and joins the long line of parent's cars as they await the school bell to sound. I have already informed Davie to keep low and not to wave or try to get the attention of any of his friends.

"So what did this teacher do?" Brody asks.

"He gave Davie an F on his homework."

Brody gives me a look.

"Think about it Brody, what is the most obvious reason that I would be going to all this trouble for. There's another one involved but Hunter is taking care of him."

We hear the bell go and the three of us sit in silence, alert and watching all the faces pass us. The parent's cars disappear quite quickly and with only a few stragglers left coming out of the school gates, it gives us a better view of the staff car park. While I am busy focusing in on several teachers walking to their cars, Davie pipes up from the back seat.

"There he is Dad."

"Where, I can only see female teachers?"

"He's out the front door, walking towards the school gate."

I look to see a small man in a tweed jacket carrying a rucksack with what looks like a dark ginger afro.

"Why isn't he going to his car?"

"He doesn't drive."

"Davie don't you think that's a detail that we should have been informed about?"

I look back to see him shrug "I didn't think it was important."

"Your Uncle Ginge would be disappointed" I joke.

"Are we still going to follow him?"

"We're not, but Brody is."

I look around to see Andrews walking fast down the street.

"Come on Davie, let's go. Brody, you know what to do."

He mumbles something as I get out of the car and before I close the door I lean back in "Don't let me down."

I watch him turn in the street and speed off to catch up with Andrews.

"Well done son. You did a good job" I grab him playfully, and he pushes me away.

We arrive back at the house and with Biscuit and Mollie demanding my attention I soon forget about the job at hand. It is nearly two hours later that I hear from Brody, a text that goes into detail about how Andrews had met up with his wife and went shopping before getting another bus home. Not only does the fucking idiot mention Andrews by name but he also adds the fucking address at the end of the text. I do not even reply, I call Joe off my other phone and tell him I need two new mobiles. I also mention that I have a little job later. He is not long out of the hospital after his beating but I know this work would suit him. I give him a time to be at the Claver and instruct him to bring three hoods, my term for ski masks. I pick up the other mobile to message Brody, I give him a time to pick me up and make a point of telling him not to sound his horn when he gets here. I shake my head as I dismantle the phone and snap the sim card, before going out the back door and placing the pieces in my neighbour's bin. He has obviously learned nothing from shadowing Ginge.

As expected, I look out of my window bang on ten to see Brody pull up outside. I am sure he waits along the street or something because there is no way he can time a car journey to arrive here at the exact minute, every single time. I pop my head around the living room door and give my missus a nod before quietly heading out to meet Brody. As soon as I get into Brody's car, I ask for his phone. He hands it over without saying a word and I tell him to drive to the Claver to pick up Joe. He glances over at me as I dismantle his phone and he does not question me until I start to throw the pieces out of the window.

"Brody I can't figure out why you can time a journey to arrive at a destination at the exact minute but you are questioning me why I have had to destroy two mobile phones tonight because of your stupidity."

"The address in the text"

"Not just that Brody, you fucking named him"

"I'm sorry I wasn't thinking."

"I don't know what the fuck you did in the army but it certainly couldn't have been communications or any sort of fucking espionage."

Before we reach the Claver I see Joe waiting outside and even from a distance, I can see the black eyes and the swelling on his face.

"How's it going Rocky?" I say as he gets into the car.

He tries to smile but one side of his face does not move.

"Are you sure you are up for this?"

He nods "It looks worse than it is."

"I hope so because it looks pretty fucking bad!" I smirk.

"Did you bring the phones?"

"Of course" He hands them over to me. "I've put the numbers in each one."

I pass one to Brody but I do not embarrass him by bringing up the reason for them in front of Joe. I do give him a look though, which he acknowledges.

"Brody, you're up" I nod for him to drive.

He takes us to Menziehill and after doubling back several times along Glamis Road, he drives into Dunkeld Place and then into a connecting cul-de-sac called Birnam Place. He parks up and kills the lights.

"It's that one there" He points at a house to the right of us.

I start to look around at the adjoining houses and their side access. With only one exit and all the other houses overlooking each other, it seems far too visible for passing witnesses.

"I'm thinking we might have to exit that back-fence over there. Brody you will have to drive around and wait for us on the main road." They both agree and as Joe passes over a hood, I happen to glance up at Andrews's house and catch sight of a kid at the window.

"Wait, what the fuck?"

We all sit in silence looking up at the window. We watch as another kid appears and then Andrews's missus closes the curtain.

"Well, that's that then."

Brody starts the car and we head back out onto the main road.

"Wait slowdown"

"What is it?"

I tell him to pull over while I look up and down the road. I feel a little disorientated as I try to work out in my head the direction of the school from where I am.

"Quick, drive over to that bus stop."

I get out and scan the timetable of the buses. I give them a smile as I get back into the car.

"You two had better get a good sleep because we're coming back here early tomorrow."

Brody drives to mine first and before I get out I tell them both to leave their phones on, I will call them when I get up. They both nod and I quietly walk back in the house and sit down as though I had never left. If we had done the job there and then, I would not have given it a second thought but as the situation is about to drag into tomorrow I cannot get Andrews face out of my head. The thought of him touching up Davie is making me shake with anger. I know that if I do not calm down I will eventually end up back there later tonight to finish the job. I look down at Biscuit and it is as though he can read my mind. I smile as he stands up and then puts his front paws out to have a stretch. As soon as I reach for his lead, his tail starts wagging. Minutes after I leave the house I receive a text from Hunter. For anyone out-with our firm who reads it, it mentions the result of a football game playing earlier and who won. To me, it means they have taken care of Nolan. With no reply, he will know there is a problem at my end. I walk Biscuit around his usual route and feel relieved that I have missed the group of dog walkers at the park. With things on my mind, I am not exactly in the mood to listen to them talk the biggest load of shit just so that Biscuit can sniff at some other dog's arsehole. I get home and go straight to bed but I find that I cannot sleep. I roll about for what seems like hours, and just as I start to think about getting up again my eyes begin to close. The next thing I know, the alarm on my phone goes off. I reach over to put it off and slowly creep out of bed so as not to wake Nikki. I go downstairs and phone Brody, no answer. I try a few more times, still no answer. I phone Joe who answers straight away.

"Brody's not answering."

"Is the phone on?"

"Well, it's ringing. If he switched it off it would go straight to answerphone."

"What will we do if we can't get him?"

"Where did he say he was going when he dropped you off last night?"

"Tanya's"

"The Stripper"

"Yeah"

"Do you know where she lives?"

"Yeah"

"I'll give it a few more rings and if he doesn't answer, we'll have to arrange other transport."

"Not a problem."

I hang up and make myself a coffee, all the while I am still calling Brody's phone. I call Joe back.

"Joe, go get his fucking car."

"Ok, I'll give you a one-ringer when I am on my way."

I finish my coffee and moments later my phone makes a noise and then cuts off. I quietly leave the house and walk to the end of my street. Joe does not appear for another five minutes. I get in the car and notice a bunch of wires hanging down under the steering wheel and a screwdriver in the key slot as a replacement key to turn on the ignition.

"How long did it take you?"

"About twenty seconds."

We both smile.

Joe drives back up to Glamis road but when we approach the cul-de-sac, I tell him to drive past it. We end up parked in between several cars on the main road.

"There are no direct buses from here over to our end of town Joe, so I know Andrews would have to catch the circular which would be at least an hour's journey to the school. The only problem is that he might get a lift in the mornings or a taxi, in which case we're fucked."

"We'll just have to do what we planned last night."

"I can't do that Joe, not when he has kids."

"What about when he gets off the bus on his way home?"

"That would be home time rush hour Joe, too many witnesses. If he doesn't appear in the next half an hour we'll be in the same boat with everyone on their way to work."

We sit for over twenty minutes and with the constant sighs from both of us I am about to tell Joe to drop me back off when I notice the dark ginger afro walk fast out of the cul-de-sac.

"That's him, Joe. Let's go."

We both pull our hoods over our faces and with the car still running, Joe attempts to drive off and stalls it.

"Fuck."

"Come on Joe."

He tries it several times and although the engine turns over it cuts out. He lets it settle for a few seconds. I watch as he takes a deep breath and turns the screwdriver that is a makeshift key and this time, the car starts. Andrews is now at the bus stop looking in the opposite direction. Joe puts the foot down and as we approach the bus stop, he tries to break.

"The breaks are not working."

I quickly look down to see his leg slamming down on the brake pedal. I look up to see Andrews now facing us and in the split second as we approach the bus stop, I grab the bottom of the steering wheel and pull it towards me. The car swerves up onto the pavement and I see Andrews' eyes go wide with fear before the car smashes into him sending him into the air. We hit the bus stop and the pole bends to the side, thus, helping the car come to a halt. I look at Joe and all I can see is his wide eyes through his hood. Without hesitating, he slams the car into reverse and we take off leaving Andrews lying on his side in the gutter.

Chapter 38

While sitting in the waiting room at the Psycho Docs, I start to think about the events of this morning. After Joe dropped me off, I entered the house unnoticed, crept upstairs, changed my clothes and went back down to join the kids for breakfast. Davie seemed his usual self, more concerned that he had run out of hair gel than what cereal he wanted. I hope that was still his main concern when he turned up at school to find that he had a new teacher. As I was about to leave for my walk with Mollie to the nursery I was reminded of my Psycho Docs appointment, so after cutting Biscuits walk short, and rushing about to make sure I was here on time, I am now sitting pissed off as he's the one that's fucking late. He eventually turns up and his receptionist calls me through.

"Hi, apologies for being late Mr McNaughton but there was a detour on the way here, apparently there was a bad smash earlier this morning." He says putting out his creepy little hand for me to shake.

"Really, I hope no one was badly hurt"

"Well, it said on the radio that it was a hit and run and the victim was taken to casualty."

"That's terrible, probably a drunk driver"

He nods in agreement before leading the way into his office.

"So how are you today?"

"Yeah, not too bad, adjusting to life outside once again" I smile.

"Oh that's right, you had been remanded not long after our last visit weren't you? Please, take a seat" He points to one of the chairs in front of his desk.

"Yeah, three months"

He looks at me before lifting up a large notepad and starts writing. After some small talk about being inside, he wastes no time in getting straight to the personal questions.

"So how is that rage that you always refer to? Have you been keeping it under control?"

"Uh huh, pretty much." I nod. I know he is looking for some gory details but I cannot exactly mention that my rage was the cause of him being late for work. Then I think of my neighbour. If I get the psycho doc to put it on record that he is harassing and antagonising me, it will look good if I ever end up in court for smashing the cunt.

"Well, there is my new neighbour."

"What about him, do you not get along?"

I shake my head and put on a sad face as though I am disappointed.

"What's happened?"

"I feel that he is tormenting me."

"What do you mean by tormenting you?"

"Well he sits outside my house in his car revving his engine and he has one of those loud exhausts, it scares my dog."

"Your dog, you've never mentioned that you have a dog."

"Yeah my father came around with it one day, the sneaky bastard. The dog's owner was a friend of his from the pub and had not long died. Anyway, my daughter took one look at it and well, it's ours now." I smile fondly.

"And your neighbour, you think he does this on purpose?"

"Without a doubt"

"Have you spoken to him about it?"

"Yeah, I was polite and I asked him if he would mind fixing his exhaust as the noise was scaring my dog. Do you know what he did? The arrogant fucker laughed at me."

"How was your rage when he laughed at you?"

"I wanted to stab him."

He stops scribbling and looks up from his notepad. "You wanted to stab your neighbour for laughing at you?" He smirks.

I just made that up but if I did genuinely want to stab someone for laughing at me, I really do not think the Doc here is going the right way about it.

"He laughed at me as though I was stupid. Like you just did"

The Doc's face drops slightly and I keep my stare on him.

"So let's get back to the dog. How do you feel about it?"

"He's great, like part of the family. Some days I talk to it more than I talk to my wife."

"So you treat your dog as though it is a human?"

"Well yeah, sort of, doesn't everybody? I mean, I'm no Dr Doolittle but I am beginning to understand him."

"So the dog communicates with you?"

"Of course"

"And what does he say?"

"Well he's a dog, he doesn't actually fucking speak but I know what he wants to say."

The Doc gestures with his hand for me to continue while he scribbles away fast on his notepad. I am all for taking the piss here but if I go too far this Doc will have me fucking committed.

"Well, for one thing, I think if the dog could talk he would say, give me a different name. His name is Biscuit, who the fuck calls their dog Biscuit?"

"And what do think he would like to be called?"

"Something normal, like Harry or Barry, or maybe Garry, yeah Garry sounds good."

"So he would tell you his names Garry, what else do you think he would say?"

"Well, you see when you ask kids what they want to be when they grow up, and they say a Fireman or a Spaceman or something, I think if you asked Biscuit that he would say a Giraffe."

"A Giraffe, why would your dog want to be a giraffe?"

"Well so that when I take him to the beach and throw his ball into the water he can walk out and get it."

"Can he not swim out to get the ball?"

"I suppose, but if he was a giraffe, he wouldn't have to swim."

I see the Doc give his watch a little glance and I know the session is ending as his questioning quickly changes to advice about keeping my rage under control. I exit the psycho docs with a slight grin as I think about what he has possibly written in his notes about me. I am sure it will go down well in future court appearances. 'The accused has illusions that he is Dr Doolittle and he thinks that his dog 'Biscuit' is actually a giraffe named Garry.' I turn both of my phones on and big surprise, the new one that Joe gave me last night starts ringing almost immediately and as it can only be one of two people, it is a guarantee that it is Brody looking for his car. I do not even answer or divert the call I just turn it off again, he knows where to find me, if he ends up sending a text mentioning his car and I have to ditch another phone and he will end up with a hard kick in the fucking balls. Due to Brody's call, it reminds me to pop into the newsagents on the way to the Claver where I pick up a few car magazines and sales papers. I walk into the pub to find Joe and Hunter already there, unlike Brody, they have a filter in their brain of what information we can and cannot discuss on the phone. I do not even have to ask them about the job at hand, a confident nod from both is enough for me. I will no doubt hear the gory details in good time. I place my phones on the table in front of them along with the papers, I tell them a price range and they immediately go to work flicking through the pages and scanning the ads. Both of them have done this many times, and know exactly what to look for. I leave them to it and go to the bar to order a round. Hunter shouts me up that one of my phones is ringing.

"It's an unknown number."

"It'll be Brody just leave it."

He has obviously managed to retrieve my other number. Seconds later after the phone stops ringing, the pub landline goes. The barman answers and turns to me with a big smile.

"It's for you."

I am about to tell him to hang up when he adds that it is Ginge. They have given him a day for his release this week. I return to the table to enjoy our happy moment, when Brody bursts through the pub doors and comes storming towards us.

"Where's my car?" He says quite aggressively.

We all give him a blank stare.

"This isn't funny, I need my car, where is it?" His tone is settling now

We keep our stare on him, still saying nothing.

"Ryan I need my car" His eyes now pleading

"Now what would we want with a heap of shit like that." I smile.

"Ryan it's not funny, I'm stuck without my car. I'm supposed to be in Edinburgh today, training for my fight."

"Don't worry; we'll have another car for you by the end of the day, a much better car." I wink.

"So you did take it?" He stands back, picking up his aggressive tone once again.

"Look, we're on it" I glance down at the papers spread out in front of us.

"What have you done with it?" He demands.

I turn to Hunter who in-turn raises his eyebrows. I then have to remind myself that Brody is family.

"Brody, I said we're on it" I snap.

"But I need to be in Edinburgh today, they had the gym booked for me" His voice is now showing a strain of pleading once again.

"Well that doesn't look very likely, so may I suggest that if your car is missing, that you go and report it stolen and by the time you get back here later today we might have a shiny new one lined up for you," I say in my best posh voice. I watch his eyes look at both Hunter and Joe then back to me and not one of us take our eyes off him. He makes a huffing sound like a spoiled little school boy before turning and walking off. As soon as the pub door closes and we all laugh before I pick up my mobile and work on the calls to the selected adverts that Hunter and Joe have outlined. Most of them are genuine, and when they confirm that they are from listed garages I do not waste time, I hang up and start dialling the next one on the list. I eventually come down to a top of the range Mercedes, on paper, it appears as though it is an unexpected bargain, only a few years old, low mileage, one lady owner…blah blah blah. As soon as the person answers and I hear the strong Irish accent, I know it is the Gypos. We have dealt with them many times over the years. Buster did it the other week when I asked him to sort Stew out with a van for our new window cleaning business. If the Gypos are punting a motor, which is in a decent condition, it will definitely be part of a con. One of their favourites, which they are possibly about to pull today, once Hunter makes a call to confirm it, is that one of them have somehow managed to take a car on credit. They then sell the car on quickly at a vast discount to an unexpected buyer. Once the new owner has registered the car, the credit company will trace it to the new owner's address and give them the option, pay the total debt or hand the car over. The difference this time is that the Gypos will not be getting such a good deal. After asking the Gypo to repeat himself on the phone several times I eventually get an address somewhere in Stonehaven, he mumbles some nonsense about a supermarket, it is less than an hour away, somewhere between Dundee and Aberdeen. Hunter makes a call and confirms what we already thought, that the car has outstanding finance. Once the new owner's details are registered, the debtors will be on the trial for their money. The car will change owners so much that the debtors and they will never see the car or their money.

"Game on you Gypo bastards"

I phone ahead to a contact and tell him to have the cash ready; someone will pick it up in a couple of hours. I then call Brody, who is back at the Strippers place; he is apparently now at a loose end for the day. I inform him that we are about to pick him up to go and get him a new car but he does not sound too impressed, the ungrateful cunt. While Joe is out finding us transport to get to Stonehaven, Hunter and I manage to down a couple more pints while he fills me in on the antics of last night. As he is getting to the gory details of the torture of Nolan, I receive a text from Joe that he is out the back of the pub with our transport.

"This is a bit upmarket for you Joe, I thought you didn't know how to hotwire the new models."

"I've never said I didn't know, I just don't like them, they draw too much attention. If the coppers see someone like me driving around in a new car I'd have a tail about a mile long."

He throws Hunter the keys "Hunter's driving it so it's no big deal."

"Joe, I need to ask, if this is stolen, how come you have the fucking keys?"

"It's my neighbours; he's a miserable old bastard. I crept into his back door and picked up his keys, he probably won't even notice it's missing for days."

Hunter throws the keys back at him.

"I've had too much to drink."

Joe shrugs and gets in the driver's seat.

"We have to pick up Brody; he's back at that strippers pad. Actually no, go pick up the money first. I don't want him knowing what's going on until the deals done."

"Don't you trust him?"

"Of course I trust him, but he's very highly strung, you saw him earlier about his car, he needs to get that anxiety shit under control. If we turn up there and he appears even slightly hesitant, the Gypos will know straight away that something's up. They'll see it in him a mile off."

We pick up the cash, all neatly folded into bundles of five hundred. When we pull up outside the strippers pad, Brody is standing waiting. Joe gets out and hands him the keys.

"Is this car for me?" He says getting in and sliding his hands down the sides of the steering wheel.

"No this is to take us to go and get the car; we have something better lined up for you."

"So whose car is this?"

Hunter and I both look at each other, unsure if we are in shock at the actual question or that neither of us could come up with an answer. Then Joe pipes up.

"It's my uncles. He let me borrow it."

Brody gives a him smirk, he knows Joe is lying but lets it go and starts the car. Due to Brody driving like an old pensioner, the journey to Stonehaven takes longer than we expected. Hunter does the navigating and directs Brody to a supermarket car park where we are to meet the Gypo's.

"Drive up to the back, they should be waiting."

"Why are we in a car park, who are we looking for?"

I was about to answer the usual, 'a mate of a mate' but Brody's not that stupid, he saw the adds that Hunter and Joe were circling in the paper earlier. We all ignore the question. Joe points over to a shiny new Mercedes near the far wall and tells Brody to park near it. As we get out of the car, I spot the transit van nearby and seconds later a grubby looking man appears from it, he opens the car door and I nod for Brody to give it a look over. He walks around it as if inspecting it for scratches or dents and then he sits in the driver's seat and starts it up, a few revs of the engine and he gives me the thumbs up. He shows the paperwork and once everything checks out to be legit, Hunter does some negotiations on the price. I do not get involved as I get frustrated when they talk too fast and I become aggressive, nine times out of ten it ends up in an argument and turns physical. I do not mind that so much but it is not so good if the coppers appear and I am in possession of several thousand worth of counterfeit notes. A price is agreed and once Brody steps out of the car, I hand him the notes and he follows the smelly Gypo over their van to do the deal. I catch him glancing back and he has the look of a kid about to enter a sweet shop. His genuine expression goes down well as I watch the Gypos through the windscreen of their transit counting out the money. While Brody is out of earshot of the Gypo's van, Joe comments about following him to ditch the car that he stole.

"Just take it back Joe."

"Take it back?"

"Yeah, there's no harm done."

"Are you serious?"

He turns to Hunter looking for an expression that I am winding him up but Hunter knows my reason. He nods at Joe to look behind him. When he turns his head, he spots the CCTV on the side of a building opposite the supermarket.

"Judging by what you said earlier Joe, the miserable old cunt won't even notice it's missing. Hunter, you go with him, if the old cunt says anything, you only borrowed it."

I look over at Brody as he shakes the Gypos hand to complete the deal.

"Come on Brody, hurry up, you can drop me at the Claver then fuck off back to Edinburgh and get your training done."

Joe wheel-spins it passed us with Hunter giving the finger out of the window.

"Let's go Brody and you better put the foot down because if they beat us back to Dundee then I'm trading this in for a mobility scooter for you."

Chapter 39

With a mad rush to get through to Perth to be on time for Ginge's release, we ended up being here too fucking early, so we are now sitting here, suited up and waiting very impatiently on his exit. He has already made a call to my house and to the Claver to find out if someone was picking him up. He has no mobiles at hand so they must be the only landline numbers that he knows. I only received the call while I was walking Mollie to nursery earlier this morning, I was about to forward the message to Brody but as he has his fight next week, I decided not to bother him. As I stood with the rest of the parents at the nursery gates, I smiled at Mollie as she said her goodbye to Biscuit, pointing her finger and telling him to be a good boy while she was in the nursery. I watched her skip towards her teacher and found myself still smiling as my mind worked overtime on how to surprise Ginge. While walking to the Claver I phoned everyone for an emergency meeting, it was funny seeing each of them come bursting through the pub doors with their 'Let's do some cunt' face on. Once everyone was there, we put our heads together and come up with a few ideas, but it was short notice, so once we made a few calls, we had to settle for what was available.

"I'm sweating in this fucking thing. I hope the Ginger cunt appreciates all this" Hunter moans.

"Well, we're about to find out because there he is" I point towards the exit.

We are all crammed into a disused fire engine parked up by the kerb on the main road straight in front of the prison. He approaches us but stops short of the kerb and has no idea that we are all watching him. He looks up and down the main road at each passing car. Joe calls his mate who is waiting in his car nearby, and within seconds, he speeds around the corner and screeches to a halt. All the windows in his car are down and the music blaring. As soon as we hear it, the doors of the fire engine swing open and we bounce out onto the pavement in full firefighter gear dancing in front of Ginge. It takes a few seconds for him to realise it is us, and stands shaking his head in disbelief. Joe pulls out the fire extinguisher and sprays him head to toe in white powder. The traffic starts to build up on the main road, so we hurry back into the fire truck as people stop to video and take photos.

Back at the Claver, Buster had organised to have massive 'welcome home' banner put up above the pub doors. This was not really for Ginge's benefit. It was more of a big 'fuck you' message to any of Tayside's finest that happen to be passing. While Ginge stands by the bar surrounded by all of his well-wishers and enjoying his first pint in a while, Joe sneakily links up his phone to the big screen. He turns the volume up full and plays the footage from the day of the game. The pub goes quiet as everyone turns to see a close up of Ginge's face. His eyes are streaming from the C.S. Gas and there are tears rolling down his cheeks, you can overhear one of the officers escorting him demand that Joe put his camera away, a loud 'Fuck off' is heard from Joe and massive roar comes from everyone in the pub. As Ginge is about to be put into the back of the patrol car he looks over at Joe and mumbles into the camera. Joe has had the video altered and subtitles appear on the screen. 'Tell Rachel I love her.' We all turn to Ginge and give him the big 'Ahh' He tries to refute and announces that he was saying 'Tell Rachel I've been lifted.' Joe quickly rewinds it and plays it again..., again..., and again. Ginge finally concedes and nods. "Okay, okay, well played Joe...but I'll get you back you little cunt."

Joe puts his hand on his chest as though holding his heart and blows him a kiss. Ginge pulls his finger across his throat.

Everyone in the pub in high spirits and I notice Brody appear in the doorway, his head is a swivel as he looks around the pub for someone. My first thought is Ginge due to this being his welcome home party, but with the tension on his face, I have a feeling that he is here to see me, either that or he has diarrhoea and he can't find the toilet, I'm hoping the latter. I move slightly out of view so that he passes without seeing me, then I watch as he slips through the busy punters as though he is on a mission. He sees Ginge and his expression lightens slightly, they talk for a few seconds and then Ginge points him in my direction. I stand up straight with a wide grin and wave at him. The angst on his face appears to get worse as he approaches me.

"You're looking a bit nervous, have you just shit your pants?"
"We need to talk."

I tilt my head towards the back of the pub and he follows me over to one of the booths.

"The police came to see me about my car."

"Uh huh" I nod.

"Someone used it in a hit and run on a fucking teacher."

"Really, that's terrible!" I shake my head. "I wonder what disgusting thing that teacher done to deserve that."

Brody goes to say something but stutters a little and changes his words.

"Leanna has left me."

I put my hands out in front of me to accompany my confused expression.

"They are treating it as attempted murder and I needed an alibi."

I feel a little smile coming on but I manage to hold it in as I know what Brody is about to tell me.

"I was put on the spot and had to cite Tanya as my alibi."

I nod in agreement and this allows me to let my smile appear "That's good, she'll back you up."

"No, you don't understand. I had to confess to Leanna. I tried to say that she was just a friend but she kept at it and the guilt got to me so I told her everything, she flipped and packed her bags. She has left me."

"When you say you told her everything, do you mean…?"

"What? Of course not, I mean everything about Tanya."

"Ah okay" I say relieved and a bit happier that the cunt is finally starting to learn.

"I just don't know what I'm going to do."

I sit back and give him my confused look again.

"Brody I really don't know what you want me to say here. I mean, you have that miserable look about you like your whole world is falling apart but as far as I know, the last six months or whatever you've been snorting coke off some strippers arse and the same time you've been playing along at being the butter wouldn't melt boyfriend to some girl that lives sixty miles away. You've been found out, through your own confession I might add, and now you're sitting here in front of me, wanting me to feel sorry for you?"

Just as I say this, Ginge appears in my view "Well, speak of the devil."

"What's going on?"

"Brody here is having a bit of a domestic, but more importantly, I think he needs a drink."

"I can't, I'm fighting next week."

"Come on, one drink won't hurt you."

I give Ginge a wink before getting up to go to the bar. I give a shout to the barman and when I glance back around, I see Ginge, closely followed by Brody, heading towards the toilet, so much for willpower.

Getting suited up for a night out is a strange feeling, the only time I have worn a suit in the last few years is for court appearances. I walk into the Stoby bar and I do not feel too out of place as the whole of Ginge's crew are also suited up. I notice Buster by the bar, standing out like a sore thumb with his thick braces to hold up his trousers. I think his idea of getting dressed up is to give his Dr Martens an extra layer of polish. I am only halfway through my first drink when Ginge shouts out that he has called taxis for everyone. I overhear him telling his crew that he does not want anybody kicking off tonight.

"Pass the word around." He says before turning and catching my eye "That goes for you as well."

I give him a smirk.

"Both of you"

He gives Buster a stare and he, in-turn, lifts his hands pleading innocence.

We make our way into town and in the first pub we enter, there is another group of lads also suited up. With a couple of them acting out a few boxing manoeuvres on each other, it is obvious they are going to the same show. I overhear the name Kean mentioned a couple of times so I assume that they are friends of Brody's opponent. As more and more of them arrive, they become louder and more boisterous. Their obnoxious behaviour spills towards us and although Ginge's mob keep to themselves, the tension is there. Every now and then, I see him eye ball them to keep calm. As it is still too early to head to the show, Ginge makes the decision to move his crew to another pub.

"Why the fuck are we moving?" I ask.

"Ryan its Brody's night, I don't want any trouble."

"Fuck them. Bunch of little fannies"

"Ryan."

I respect Ginge's decision and trail on behind him but not long after we move to another pub I notice some of Kean's mob have followed us. With both parties knocking back the drinks quicker, and the thousand-mile hard-man stares becoming more frequent, I am expecting this to kick off at any minute. Buster, who is propping up the bar next to me, has also noticed this and I can see him trying to move discreetly closer to some of Kean's mob. He will be about to make his signature move by picking out the loudest and more irritating of the crowd, usually the one with the most arm movements. He will try to get as close as possible so that the person spills his drink, thus the ensuing argument and eventual mass brawl. Ginge has also clocked Buster, and as more of the Kean faces appear, he tells his crew to drink up to move us onto the show. We enter the venue and shown our seats. The ring is in the centre, circled by tables of ten all the way to the back of the hall. I don't know if this was intentional on Brody's part, or whoever bought the tickets had went for the cheaper option, but all of our tables are by the far wall, furthest away from the ring. The place fills up quickly and I clock the Kean mob as they enter, their tables are conveniently at the opposite end of the venue from ours. The meal is basic and exactly what you would expect at these functions but the way Buster is moaning you would think he had just been served someone's slop outs. It is waiter service only, and in hindsight, this should keep everyone's drinking under control but currently, this encourages more drug use and the continuous flow back and forward to the toilets confirms this. During the meal, one of the Kean tables becomes a little rowdy and an object flies through the air hitting one of Ginge's crew in the back of the head. It is one of the small French bread rolls, which they serve up to accompany the soup. He stands up from his seat and stares over at the rowdy table. He turns and looks at Ginge as though asking for permission to confront them. Ginge is also on his feet giving them the stare. One of the more sober from the Kean table looks over and mouths the words sorry, another stands up with his hands up in an apologise gesture. It feels as though the whole hall is looking in Ginge's direction and he knows that his whole crew is only waiting on his word and they will gladly storm the place, but with several apologies coming his way, Ginge has no option but to back down.

After the meal, the tables clear quickly and the bouts start to take place. The early fights seem to go like a conveyor belt, the minute one finishes; the next fighters are ready to enter and the atmosphere is still subdued. It is not until four or five fights in, that most people realise why they are actually here. The next fighters name is announced 'McKiddie' and the place livens up. He is fighting out of Kean's club but he seems to have a lot of support from both sides of the hall. I overhear someone mention that he is a Stoby boy so that would explain why most of Ginge's crew are cheering him on. He has a tough fight with what appears to be a more experienced fighter and they go toe to toe for the whole fight, both putting each other down. The last thirty seconds is a battle and the whole place is on their feet cheering. Kean's mobs are the rowdier of the two with a few standing on chairs and tables. The fight finishes and before they announce the decision, the security, along with some of the organisers are over at Kean's mob telling them to calm down and stay off the tables. Once they clear the ring, they announce Brody's name and a cheer goes up from our end, accompanied with a few boos from across the hall. As soon as Brody enters the ring, they announce Kean's name and his mob are soon on their feet once again, shouting their chant of 'Keano Keano.' Ginge, not one to see Brody outdone, gets his crew to chant Brody's name and it is soon echoing around the hall. I notice a few angry stares from Kean's mob in the direction of Ginge's table. The organisers also notice the tension and before the fight starts, the announcer makes a point of telling the crowd to stay off the seats and tables or the fight will not go ahead. The bell rings and both fighters seem very cautious as they circle each other around the ring.

"What's with this backing off shit? He did that his last fight as well" Buster shouts in my ear.

"He's countered everything that's been thrown at him."

"Fuck countering, he should go forward and be first to the punch every time."

"But if he does that, his opponent will counter him."

"Then he should just take it on the chin and throw another."

"Take it on the chin? I thought the whole idea was to hit and not get hit."

"If he keeps throwing while moving forward his opponent won't have a chance to hit him."

"Buster this isn't Rocky."

The last few seconds of the round, the fighters tangle up in a brawl.

"That's more like it. Knock his fucking head off" Buster shouts.

Brody comes out for the second round and starts moving in closer and trying to land the big punch. This gets Buster excited as he continually shouts instructions towards the ring. Kean slips to the side and counters most of Brody's punches and when Brody does land a good shot, he seems to pull back as though he is too tired to follow it up. This leaves Brody open for Kean to pick him off. The third round Brody is still moving forward and it seems like he is still looking to land that one big punch, the only problem is that he is tiring and his punches are now wider and more sluggish. He lands a few to keep him in the fight but Kean is in control and is moving around the ring with ease and picking him off. Brody looks exhausted and Kean's mob are on their feet chanting and encouraging their fighter to go for the knockout. At the end of the round, Brody trudges towards his corner with his head down. With two rounds still to go, he looks beaten. As I try to block out Busters continuous ranting in my ear, I clock one of Kean's mob move around the ring. My first thought is that he possibly knows someone at one of the ringside tables, but the whole time that he is walking, his attention is on Brody, who at the moment, is slouched on his stool in the corner taking deep breaths. His trainer stands over him and gives him, what I can only assume, are words of encouragement. It appears that I am not the only one to notice the intruder as the security are onto him, he slams the bottom of his pint glass on the ring to get Brody's attention before shouting abuse and trying to belittle him. One of Ginge's crew realise what is going on and attempt to get near him but the security warns him off. The bell goes for the fourth round and I look up at Brody, his gloves are held tight to his head, he knows Kean is about to step it up for the last two rounds and try for the knockout. The security tries to walk the person back to the other side of the hall but he is standing firm shouting abuse towards the ring. He then realises that some of Ginge's crew are shouting at him and his attention turns to them. The rest of Kean's mob is on their feet, some are shouting towards the security, standing up for their mate but not realising how much of a little wanker he is being. Buster is still shouting nonsense in my ear and I do not think I take much more of this. I glance over at Ginge, who is wide eyed and alert. I know he is struggling to keep his crew in check. He catches my eye. I shrug and he shrugs back. I take this as a green light. I pick up the chair that I had been sitting on. Buster knows straight away by my expression what is coming, he steps aside to allow me to pass. I lift the chair above my head and barge through the gaps in the tables until I reach the security. I step past them and pull the chair down hard onto the mouthy cunts head. He crashes to the ground and I turn to see the whole of Kean's mob coming towards me. I casually glide passed the ringside tables, the whole time gesturing to the coked up would-be hard men to come at me. A few brave ones put themselves forward and attempt to square up to me, one of them is a big lad who clearly fancies himself as some sort of tough-guy with a face full of ugly tattoos and biceps that are bulging out of his shirt that is easily three sizes too small for him. He is around my height and this works out perfect as he goes down like a tonne of bricks once my forehead crunches into nose. Ginge's crew are now by my side exchanging blows. Kean's mob start to launch bottles and glasses as they back themselves out of the fire exit located behind them. The ring announcer calls for calm and the fight is officially abandoned. There are a few skirmishes out in the street but as soon as the blue flashing lights appear, most people have disappeared. Ginge takes off with his crew but not before having a word with the security in case there are any fingers pointed in my direction. Brody calls me from his dressing room and I, along with Buster, decide to hang around for a bit and wait for him. More Police are arriving late on the scene so we casually walk over to the main road away from the venue, as once they have taken a few statements, it will only be a matter of time before a person with my description is given. A young male and a female officer with their notepads at the ready eventually work their way over towards us.

"Hi, you guys wouldn't have happened to attend the Boxing show tonight would you?"

We both give a slight nod, which encourages them to step closer towards us.

"You wouldn't mind if we asked you a few questions about what happened would you?"

Buster shrugs and casually leans back on the car closest to him.

"Did any of you observe the fracas that happened earlier?"

"Fracas" I let out a low laugh.

"Yes, the fracas. The mass brawl that has apparently taken place" The female officer says firmly.

I smile back at her.

"What, do you think this is funny?"

"I find it funny" Buster pipes us.

With the chip firmly on her shoulder and her face screwed up like a Pitbull that is ready to attack, she leans in towards Buster.

"Are you the owner of that car?"

"No, but I'm hot and I'm tired"

"That's someone's car, how would you feel if I sat on your car?"

"Well sweetheart, I don't actually own a car so that isn't very realistic now is it."

"You know what I mean. Something you own."

"I own a face, would you like to come over and sit on my face?"

She looks at her colleague who looks blankly back at her; she puts her hand on her radio about to call in when Brody appears with his bag over his shoulder.

"It's my car officer. They are waiting for a lift from me."

"Well, I suggest you go now and take your friends with you before you all end up spending the night in the cells."

"Ooh, saucy" Buster gives her a wink but his charm does not even make a dent in her expression.

Chapter 40

"Suited up twice in a week and no court appearance, this has got to be a first," Nikki says as she straightens my tie.

"Don't go jinxing it now."

I check the time. I am about to mention that Brody's actually late for once when I hear Davie shout from downstairs that he is outside.

"Okay son"

With my tie looking sharp and a promise not to get into any bother, I make my way downstairs and run into Mollie. She has her arms folded and a look that any finger-waving judge would be proud of, I again have to make a similar promise, only this time it is to make sure that I am not too late, as I have to be up early for our walk to nursery. After a hug and high five, I am out the door and on my way to the Claver.

"So what's this big event tonight; where are we going?" Brody asks.

"Do you not know?"

"No, Ginge just told me to get suited up and arrange a time for me to pick you up."

"Oh well, if he hasn't said anything, I'll let him tell you then."

The Claver is busy when we enter but I notice Larnio towering over everyone at the far end of the bar so I head for there. Before we reach them, Buster appears in our path.

"So I take it you're going to this big fight in Glasgow as well then. My invite must have got lost in the post did it?"

"Thanks for ruining the surprise, Buster."

"What are you talking about?"

"He didn't want Brody to know where he was going."

"Where are we going?"

"Ginge has tickets for the world title fight in Glasgow tonight."

"Oh well, that's what happens when you forget to invite family."

"It's a V.I.P. thing Buster. I can only imagine how you would be acting surrounded by all those suits in your turned up jeans and tartan braces."

"What? Like your behaviour last week you mean?"

"He had it coming."

"So it 'was' you that kicked off last week?" Brody's suspicions now confirmed.

I put my palms up and shrug.

He shakes his head as though I am some sort of disappointment and I am about to respond, when Buster jumps to my defence.

"Why are you shaking your head? If he didn't kick off we would have still been scraping you up off that canvas."

We both look to him for a comeback but in those few seconds I notice his shoulders deflating slightly, to me, this is as good as admitting defeat. I turn to walk towards Larnio when I hear Brody mumble. "I was saving myself for the last round."

I turn and give him a sympathetic smile and keep walking. I shout a roundup and Ginge has appears with a big smile on his face as he pulls the tickets from his jacket pocket.

"He knows"

Ginge's smile drops "What do you mean he knows? Who the fuck told him"

"Do you really need to ask?" I eye ball Buster.

"Ah, that's good of you Buster. It was meant to be a surprise."

"Well maybe if I got an invite I would've known not to fucking say anything" He turns to me "Snake."

I put my hands up and plead my innocence.

"Well, it was meant to be a gift for winning your fight, but you fucking blew that!" Ginge winks.

Brody responds by changing the subject "so who is all going tonight?"

"It's the five of us, oh and you're driving. Maybe if you never got beat we would have chosen a different driver."

"I didn't get beat" He pleads.

"But you didn't fucking win either did you. Come on drink up, we've got a real fight to watch."

We get outside and Brody presses his key to unlock the doors.

"Whose car is this?" Ginge asks.

"It's mine."

"No really, whose car is it?"

"It's mine" He confirms.

"Where did you get the cash for this?"

"Ryan" He nods towards me.

I put my hands up "Not me."

He looks back at Brody who in turn looks at me.

"Don't look at me, where the fuck would I get that kind of money?"

"Is that a new suit as well?" Ginge continues at Brody while we are in the car.

"Yeah, what do you think?"

"Did Ryan give you the money for that too?"

Brody realises what Ginge is getting at and tries to turn it round.

"What about yours, that definitely wasn't cheap. Where did you get the money to buy that?"

"Me, oh I have a job."

"Yeah"

"Yeah, I work part-time in the Claver. What about you Larnio?"

"Doorman at the Claver"

"Hunter?"

"Part-time barman...at the Claver"

"Ryan."

"I used to work at the Claver but I have recently started up my own window cleaning business."

"Okay, I hear you" Brody nods.

"Brody money and possessions can make a lot of people envious. If you show that your money's up that is when your enemies will come. Enemies that you never even knew were there."

The venue for the boxing event is the Plaza Hotel in Glasgow, and when we arrive, the car park is close to full. While driving around trying to locate a space, Hunter comments about some of the more expensive cars that we pass. After clocking a few of the registration plates, it is not hard for me to work out whose they are. I do not say a word though, as this will contradict everything Ginge had said earlier to Brody. We walk in the door and once we show our tickets, they direct us to a V.I.P. area where waiters are handing out glasses of expensive champagne.

I give Brody a nudge as we pass them "take two."

"I can't, I'm driving."

"Take fucking two"

He reluctantly takes two glasses and holds them as though they are the lit end of a cigarette. I gulp down both my glasses and smile as I take the two from Brody's hands.

"You had better take it easy with that stuff" Ginge says giving me a concerned look.

"Fuck off, it's like piss water."

Larnio and Hunter go straight to the toilets to powder their nose and I see Brody edging to go with them but I purposely send him to the bar to get me a proper drink. Upon his return, a who's who of Glasgow crime appears to have surrounded me. It is as though every would-be gangster who owns a suit is here tonight and is putting on a show that even royalty would be proud of, several of them introduce themselves and judging by Brody's expression, he seems to have now figured out the kind of company that he is in. Nothing much will be said from anybody on our side as we all know never to take things beyond the small talk at events like this. You never quite know who has put these events together. I can tell straight away that the security is a local firm as they blatantly ignore the drug taking that is going on around them. To me, it is like a set up to get people talking, not that some of these Glasgow boys need it, as they are not slow at talking themselves up. The people listening-in are not concerned with what these little Gobshites have to say though, as they would blab to anyone about their business, from the person in front of them at the queue in their local butchers, to the fourteen-year-old kid who delivers his fucking newspaper. It does not take long for one of these would-be gangsters to catch up with me and he is soon blabbing shit in my ear about his lifelong plan to run the whole of Glasgow, all from his two bedroomed flat he shares with his Gran in the middle of Govan. Brody is about to walk off and leave me listening to this clown, so I use him to break the conversation.

"Would you look at this?" I nod to Brody's tall glass of orange juice. "We tell him to get suited up, we bring him all the way here to mix with the big boys and he embarrasses us by standing with a fucking orange juice" I wink at Brody.

"Somebody's got to stay sober to scrape you up off the pavement," Brody says.

Larnio and Hunter appear from the toilet and as the Weedgie realises none of us are taking him seriously, he turns his attention to one of his own crowd to whisper sweet nothings in his ear about the size of the blade tucked into his sock.

"I see Ginge is enjoying himself" Hunter nods.

We glance over to see some skinny rough looking person with greasy hair stretching his neck up and covering the side of his mouth with his hand each time he talks. The movement is too perfect for it to be a random action so he definitely has a touch of paranoia about people lip reading him, we all have the little traits that we bring from the jail, and I am guessing this is his. I had an idea of who he was when we first came in, but with a nickname like Screw-face, it is not hard to realise why, as his face distorts each time he leans in to talk to Ginge. He has been in and out of Barlinnie prison more times than Ginge, Buster and I have been in Perth put together. Ginge is totally unfazed by him as I'm sure he shared a cell with him back in the day and saw him for what he really is, a jumped up bully with a blade. One of the staff announces that the buffet is open but there is hardly a mad rush from the clientele in here to eat it, there seems to be a bigger queue for the toilets than there is for the buffet.

"Are we heading through to watch the fights?" Larnio asks.

Ginge, who is still in deep conversation, glances up and catches my eye, I point over towards the doorway of the main hall, and he gives me the thumbs up and gestures for us to go ahead. When we enter the hall, one of the fights has already started and after saying our name to one of the staff, they lead us around the ring to our table.

"Oh, very posh" Hunter says as he points to the gold nameplate in the middle of the table with McNaughton printed on it.

"Gentlemen, if you would like to take your seats, one of the waitresses will be with you shortly to take your order"

"So we can't go back to the bar?"

"Yes, but you can't bring your drinks through with you, it is waiter service only in the main hall during fight times."

"Oh okay."

"We take our seats and I am immediately on the lookout for one of the waiters, but by the looks of it, there are about three of them covering the whole VIP area. I eventually get the attention of one of them to order us a round of drinks but by the time they return, the bout that was taking place when we entered, has finished and another one started. There is still no sign of Ginge. Due to waiting so long for a drink, I end up downing it and I quickly make a start on Ginge's drink. I look around for one of the waiters, but they all appear to be at the opposite end of the hall.

"Fuck this."

I down the last of Ginge pint and stand up.

"If any of these waiters happen to venture near our table, get another round of drinks up and give me a shout, actually get two rounds up. I'll be at the bar."

I go to walk away then turn back.

"Oh and keep this cunt out of the fucking toilets he's driving us home" I nod at Brody and put my finger to the side of my nose.

I walk back through to the reception area and it looks as though several other people have the same idea as there are a few more suits holding up the bar.

Ginge appears "I was about to come through."

"Well if you need a drink I wouldn't bother, it's fucking waiter service."

I head straight to bar and order a pint, and no sooner has the barman placed my drink in front of me but another would-be gangster appears giving me the whole, I run this and I run that bullshit. This saying, a rock and a hard place comes to mind. I can either go back through and wait forever on a drink or stay here and listen to these jumped up little pricks. I down my pint and head back through, but not before downing a couple more glasses of champagne that is still flowing freely. When I get to our table, there is a fresh pint waiting for me.

"Just in time"

Ginge informs me that when he came through from the bar, he slipped one of the young girls serving a large tip and told her to make sure our table was priority. Upon hearing this, I relax into my seat to watch the fights. After the young girl serves our table for the third time, I overhear someone not far behind me shouting abuse at her as she apparently keep missing out his table. I turn to see a suited-up prick on his feet and throwing hand signals towards her and shouting for her to hurry the fuck up. He catches my eye as I turn and tries to justify his behaviour by showing me his empty glass.

"Place is a fucking joke" He shouts.

I am ready to tip over his whole table but due to the present company surrounding us, I try to be a bit diplomatic.

"Settle down pal, it's not her fault, she's trying her best to get around everyone, if you need a drink so badly, go through to the bar. Shouting abuse at her isn't going to get you served any quicker."

"Fuck her. She has purposely skipped our table twice, the SLUT" He shouts in her direction.

I stand up and am about to move when Ginge and Brody also stand up and block my path. The people at his table pull him back into his seat and make their apologies. I sit back down and take a sip from my pint. I can still hear him mouthing off but it is more subdued so I cannot make out what he is actually saying. I down the rest of my pint and stand up once again. Ginge tells me to leave it but I put my hand up in a calming motion and smile. I walk towards his table and when he sees me, his face drops, I give him the stare but keep walking towards the reception area. I enter to find the place empty as everyone is now through in the large hall, waiting for the main event. I head straight to the bar and shout up a pint.

"Make that two, Big Man"

I turn to see Screw-face walking towards me from the toilet."

"I thought I had the place to myself."

He makes an attempt at a smile and justifies his nickname once again.

"Are you not a boxing fan?"

"Not really. Unless it's someone I know that's fighting I don't really take much interest."

"I'll keep that in mind for next time you're through."

The barman put the pints in front of me and just as I am searching in my pocket for cash, Screw-face steps in front of me.

"It's okay I've got it."

For a split second, I feel like I have warmed to him then typically, he pulls out a thick wad of notes in my face and peels off a twenty.

"You keep that big man."

The barman looks at it and nods. "Thank you very much, sir."

"Not a problem."

He then lifts his hand up to his face and moves in closer to me. "Tips like that and he still can't put a smile on his fucking face the miserable cunt."

"He's maybe scared in case you make it permanent with that blade tucked into your sock."

He gives me his twisted smile once again. "Why do you lot have this conception that we constantly carry blades?"

"I don't know, experience, history, intuition?"

"I never carry a blade."

He comes up close to my ear still covering his mouth. "I would just get someone else to do that for me." He pulls back and winks.

"Yeah well, I guess that's where we differ, you see, if a job needs to be done from my side, it is all hands on from me."

"Yeah, I've heard. Like this thing with an acquaintance of ours, the Donaldson's"

"An acquaintance of yours you mean!"

"I suppose. An acquaintance of mine" He nods. "I wanted to discuss the on-going little tit for tat feud that you have with them."

"I'm listening."

"Well it's no secret that they get their supply from me, I know they've thrown my name about for some time now."

I nod. "Yeah to anybody that will fucking listen"

"The thing is, we are all connected from our source down south and I'm led to believe that if I ever gave my backing to the Donaldson's, my supply would be cut."

"Sounds as though you've already discussed this"

"With the way you boys carry on, I would be pretty fucking stupid not to. Listen, Ryan, nobody wants a war, both our firms have done each other favours in the past so I thought maybe you Dundee boys could at least call a truce so to speak."

I force out a laugh. "A truce, you're talking like you're the only firm in Glasgow, you boys shoot each other like it's the fucking Wild West"

He pulls back from me slightly and judging by his expression, I seem to have offended him. It does not faze me in the slightest and his talk of firms and feuds is making me think he is auditioning for a Scorsese movie.

"Ryan, I arranged this tonight so that we could discuss this on neutral ground."

"Neutral ground, this place is filled with tables of your boys all pissed and coked up."

"Ryan I gave my word to Ginge that I would be here with four of my top boys, same as you, to have a meet and greet. That's it."

"Your boys wouldn't happen to be the knob ends at the table to the right behind ours would it?"

"Ryan, my boys are sat ringside at the opposite end of the hall from you. I will admit I do know a few other faces here but they are not with me. If you need me to take care of someone, just say the word and ill have it sorted."

"No, as I said before, I'm hands on."

I pick up my drink even though there is only a couple of mouthfuls left in the glass, I sip it slowly as I try to think of the politest way of putting what I have to say to this cunt. The glass empties and I place it further back onto the bar.

"Listen, I appreciate you inviting us here tonight and I respect your reasons, but what you don't understand is that the only reason the Donaldson's are still around doing what they do. It is because Ginge needs them as it keeps the heat off of him, otherwise, I would've taken care of those horrible bullying bastards a long time ago, and I would've done it on my own without any help from Ginge's connections in Liverpool, Manchester or London, or wherever the fuck they're from. Now you know where I stand on this subject, so if you need to talk any other business, go and sit down with Ginge."

His body tilts away from me and I watch his eyes squint, which makes his face screw up more than usual. I know the look, it is a look that someone gives out just before they are about to kick off, a look I know all too well. I step back from the bar but keep my eyes firmly on him. I know what is coming but he does not scare me. Then surprisingly his expression changes, his screwed up face softens and he gives me an acknowledging nod.

"I understand."

He puts his hand out and even though I shake it, I am still expecting a blade to appear. I give him a nod and in the split second that I turn to head back through to the main hall, I freeze.

"Brody"

"Ryan" He says smugly, leaning on the bar immediately behind where I was standing.

"Sneaky bastard" I mutter to myself as I walk away.

I want to turn back and give both Screwface and Brody a good hard slap. I can feel my heart beating faster, as though the coppers have caught me on a job of some sort. I enter the main hall and the first person I see is the mouthy cunt standing by his table still throwing hand signals and shouting abuse. If only I knew earlier what I know now. I walk straight over to the table, grab it with both hands and tip it over. The mouthy cunt takes a step towards me and my fist is waiting for him. It connects with his face and he falls back on the floor. His friends are now on their feet wiping down the drinks that have been spilt over their suits. I step towards them and they back up with one of them crouching embarrassingly with his hands in the air in defence. Seconds later, the security has me surrounded. Without placing a hand on me, they walk me towards the back of the hall. When I reach the exit doors, I look back to see Ginge right behind me, followed closely by Brody. Once we are clear outside, the security pull the doors closed behind us. We stand and look at each other for a few seconds, then we hear shouting coming from around the corner.

"That sounds like Hunter's voice."

"Hunter!" Ginge shouts.

Hunter and Larnio come running around the corner breathing heavily.

"The security had grouped together so we couldn't get anywhere near you, we had to run through the reception."

"I was enjoying that as well, they announced that the title fight was up next as we were leaving" Larnio says.

"Do you think they'll let us back in?" I ask.

I look at Ginge and we both start laughing. The others join in and even Brody breaks out a smile.

"Fuck this shit. Let's get back to the Claver" Ginge says.

While walking back to the car, I slow down so that Ginge is slightly ahead of me, as I want to make sure that I am not sitting up front with Brody. I have never been one to keep things in but that situation back at the bar is making me feel uneasy. I will straighten it out soon enough, but I need to speak to Ginge first and make him aware of our little eavesdropper. My head is spinning and I can only assume that it is due to my fucking greed with the free champagne. I feel I am over thinking the situation and it has brought on a bout of anxiety. The banter in the car flows back and forth and I add my worth so as not to arouse suspicion that anything is wrong. Due to some peer pressure, Brody puts the foot down and we make the Claver before closing. The pub is still busy and it is a struggle to get Ginge on his own, as Brody has not left his side since we got back. Each time I catch his eye I want to slap the smug look off his face. What the fuck am I even thinking? He is my little brother. My head is fucking spinning. I need to get out of here, like right now. I manage to manoeuvre myself to the bar door without having to talk to anyone. I step outside and feel the fresh air on my face, I breathe in, filling my lungs and my head starts to clear. Someone else exit's the pub and pulls out a lighter for the cigarette hanging from their lips. I walk a short distance from the pub door still taking deep breaths as I go. My clear head is short lived as the spinning returns. I hear the pub door open again and I look back to see another smoker. I take a few more deep breaths and walk a little further. I know it is coming and as soon as I am out of view of the pub, I go with it and let it happen. The vomit forces my mouth open, and even though I try my best to project it as far from me as possible, I look down through my glazed eyes to see splashes all over my shoes. I see a taxi with the light on but I let it pass. A walk home will probably do me good. This idea lasts about five minutes until I see the next taxi light. I flag it down, time for bed.

Chapter 41

"**R**yan!"
"Ugh."
"RYAN!"

"Wh...What...I'm up, what's wrong?"

"There's someone banging on the front door."

"What time is it?"

"I don't know. It's still dark."

I get out of bed and open the window. When I look down, I see someone slumped on my doorstep.

"Who is it?"

"I'm not sure. I think its Ritchie."

"Ritchie, what's he playing at? He knows not to come around at this time of night."

"I know, he must be stuck, I'll let him sleep on the couch."

I put the light on and go to grab my trousers while Nikki lets out a sigh and pulls the covers over her head. I pull them over one leg and when my foot appears I glance down to see the bottom of the trousers covered in splashes of vomit so I quickly take them off and put on a pair of shorts and a t-shirt and go down the stairs. I open the front door and Ritchie's head slumps forward onto the floor in front of me.

"Ritchie, Ritchie wake up."

I give him a little kick but he does not budge. I crouch over him and give him a shake.

"Ritchie, RITCHIE WAKE UP!"

I turn him over to face me but when I go to move him, my hand feels wet. I stand up and put the hall light on. When I look down, all I see is red.

"Fuck!"

I crouch down again.

"RITCHIE, RITCHIE."

I hear a sound behind me and look around to see Nikki standing with her hand over her mouth.

"Quick. Phone an ambulance he's bleeding."

She rushes off to find a phone and I slide Ritchie inside. Most of the blood is at waist level so I open his jacket and pull up his t-shirt. I can see a wound on his stomach and the blood is seeping out badly. I run to the kitchen and grab a couple of towels. I place one on the wound and press it tight to try to stem the blood flow. The whole time I am shouting Ritchie's name and telling him to wake up. His eyes are open but he has a blank expression. Nikki is still on the phone, the operator is giving her instructions but everything she says I am already doing. The ambulance arrives and the paramedics take over, they keep asking me questions as they work on him but I cannot give them any answers. Moments later, they place him on a stretcher and wheel him out to the ambulance with an oxygen mask on his face. They are in the ambulance for several minutes before one the paramedics come back into the house.

"Listen, this doesn't look good, we're going to have to rush him up to accident and emergency."

I am about to go with them when I look down and realise that I am covered in blood.

"Go and change. I'll phone a taxi" Nikki says.

I run up the stairs and strip off. "Fuck fuck fuck fuck fuck." I keep mumbling. I go to the bathroom and wipe myself down with a wet towel to get most of the blood off. I go back to the bedroom and put on jeans and sweatshirt. I grab my phones and some cash and hurry back down the stairs.

"Taxi will be here any minute."

"Okay."

I go to my phone and the first person I come to is Buster. It rings out. I try again but as it starts ringing, the taxi appears so I shut it down. I get in the taxi and tell him to get me to the hospital as fast as he can. He takes a diversion and I know that on a normal trip, this would be a much longer way but it takes us straight to the dual carriageway, which is quicker. I try Ginge's number and he answers it with the first ring.

"Ginge"

"…" He goes to talk but I cut him off.

"Ginge I'm on the way to the hospital, Ritchie has been stabbed. The paramedic said it is serious. Well, his actual words were 'it doesn't look good.'"

"I'm not too far from there. I'll leave now."

Before he hangs up, I overhear him shouting on Joe in the background. The taxi driver, upon hearing my phone conversation puts the foot down and takes me through two 'no entry' points in the hospital grounds and stops right outside the emergency department doors. I slip him a note, a real one, for his effort. Before walking through the sliding doors to the A and E department, I stand outside and take a few deep breaths. I approach the desk and give them Ritchie's details. She makes a call and then tells me to follow her.

"Can you wait a minute? My other brother is on his way. I'll wait on him."

"Are you sure, I can bring him through when he arrives."

"Yeah it's okay, I'll just wait, thanks."

I walk outside and take in more air. It starts to come back to me how drunk I was last night. I also have a flashback of stumbling out of the Claver to puke up, this, along with the images of Ritchie covered in blood, makes me feel dizzy. I am going to have some serious words with Ritchie when I get him on his own. There will be no more of this fucking smack, no more hanging out with those junkie leeches. I am going to make him stay with me until he gets that shit out of his system. I take out my phone and call Buster but it rings out again, then I see a car approaching in the distance with no headlights on. It stops far back from the entrance and Ginge gets out, he jogs slowly towards me. The car spins around and takes off back into the darkness. Ginge reaches me and I lead the way back through the sliding doors. Upon seeing us entering, the receptionist stands up from behind her desk and walks us through to a small room away from the waiting area.

"The doctor will come and see you soon. Can I get you tea or coffee?"

I think we both have in our head that we will be here a while so we both ask for coffee.

"You know what this room is for don't you?" Ginge looks at me with wide staring eyes.

"No, what is it?"

"This is the room where they give you the bad news?"

"Bad news as in..."

Ginge nods.

"You mean...are you fucking shitting me?"

I grab my phone and call Busters number again. It rings out but when I go to press it again, it starts to ring as he calls me back.

"Buster I'm at the hospital with Ginge. Ritchie's been stabbed."

"What happened?"

"I don't know. He turned up at my door covered in blood. Listen, Buster, it's bad, we're waiting for the doctor coming to talk to us but we've been put in a room out of the way."

"You've been put in a room. Fuck! I'll be as quick as I can." He hangs up.

"Does everyone know what this fucking room is for except me?"

I stand up and attempt to pace the room but it is too small to move anywhere.

"Ryan, watch out"

I turn to see the door opening and the receptionist trying to enter holding a tray with the coffee. I hold the door open while she places the tray on the table in the middle of the room.

"Has anyone been in to talk to you yet?"

"No, not since you put us in here."

"Okay, well someone should be along soon" She says in a quiet voice.

I sit back down and Ginge pours us both a coffee from the little pot. Buster calls again "I'm in a taxi now, is there any news?"

"Nothing yet"

"Okay. I shouldn't be too long."

I take a sip of the coffee and lean back in the chair letting out a sigh.

"Have you called Brody?"

I shake my head.

Ginge pulls out his phone and I suddenly remember the scenario from last night with Brody, I guess it could wait.

"No answer. I know they've never seen eye to eye but I think he would want to be here."

I nod.

We sit in silence, both taking sips of our coffee as though trying to make it last. My mind feels like it is in overdrive and I am happy for the interruption when my phone rings.

"Nikki"

"How is he?"

"We don't know yet. Ginge is here and Buster is on his way. We're waiting to hear from the doctor."

"The police have just left. I don't know who called them."

"It would have been the paramedics, its procedure when it's a stabbing."

"I told them we found him on the doorstep. They want a statement from you, I think they are on their way up, I thought I would pre-warn you."

"Okay thanks, I'll call you when I hear anything."

I finish my coffee and place it on the table in front of me and the second I sit back in the chair the door opens.

Three doctors enter. One male and two female, one of the female doctors starts talking.

"Hi, I'm Doctor Lamb. Are you Ritchie's brothers?"

"Yeah, his father is on his way, he should be here any minute."

"Okay, would you like me to wait?" She says in a very soft quiet voice.

"No, go ahead."

"Ritchie came into us with a deep wound that had penetrated his liver. A large blood vessel was opened internally and this had caused a massive blood loss into the abdominal cavity..."

She blabs on a bit more about the blood loss then I hear the fatal words.

"...I am very sorry to say that we were unable to save him."

Although the Doc did not actually say the words 'Ritchie's dead,' they ring through my head like an echo.

"Ginge, what the fuck" I put my palms out in front of me. "What the fuck?"

I pull out my phone and call Buster.

"I'm nearly there, any news?"

I cannot get the words out to tell him and I burst into tears. I hear him on the other end shouting 'no, no.' I pass the phone to Ginge. He reaches to take the phone from me.

"It's Buster," I mumble.

Ginge puts the phone to his ear but does not say anything. He breaks down and hands the phone back. "He knows."

I call Nikki "He's gone" I say through my tears.

"Oh no, I'm so sorry Ryan."

We both cry for a few seconds and I mumble that I will call her back. I hang up and my phone falls to on the floor as my head drops to my hands.

After a few minutes, I take a deep breath. I pick up my phone and call Brody. It rings for a few seconds before someone answers.

"Is Brody there?"

"Yeah who is it?"

"It's Ryan."

"Ryan, Ryan who"

"It's his brother Ryan. Put him on the fucking phone."

"Hello."

"Brody, Ritchie's gone."

"Ritchie's gone. What do you mean he's gone?"

I try to get the words out but I cannot bring myself to say that he is dead.

"I'm at the hospital. He's gone."

"What? You mean dead. What's happened?"

"I'll phone you back. I can't talk right now."

I hang up.

"Someone will need to phone Emma. I don't have her number anymore."

"I do."

Ginge pulls out his phone and searches for the number and I start to imagine the same situation with someone having to phone Nikki and my kids to tell them. Ginge goes to pass me his phone but I shake my head. As he talks quietly to Emma, I overhear Buster's voice outside the room and he barges in with a nurse by his side. Ginge and I both stand up wiping tears from our faces.

"Where is he? I want to see him?"

"He'll be placed in the viewing room next door shortly for anyone wishing to pay their respects." The nurse says in a soft quiet voice.

"What happened?"

I shrug "I'm sorry Buster, I need some air. I'll be at the front door."

I walk out to the reception and see two officers waiting by the receptionist who is dealing with another patient. I manage to sneak past them easily while they are busy patting down their uniforms talking between themselves. I step outside and the air hits my eyes first, feeling raw from the tears. I stand and take several deep breaths as I come to terms with the news that I have just lost my brother. Ginge follows me outside.

"I think they're here for you" He nods back at the two officers.

"Yeah I know. Fuck them."

Ginge's phone goes and he walks off to answer. Soon after a taxi pulls up and upon seeing Emma inside, I go over to the window and pay the driver. The tears are streaming down her face when she steps out of the car.

"Come on I'll walk you in."

Ginge is halfway towards the car park, still talking into his phone. I walk back into the reception area with my arm around Emma's shoulder. The two officers walk towards me.

"Mr McNaughton. I know this is a difficult time for you but I was wondering if we could take a statement."

"Yeah this is a difficult time, could you come see me another day, unless of course, you are busy arresting someone for Ritchie's murder then I'll understand, but judging by how quickly you lot do your job I guess that's highly unlikely."

I continue walking Emma to the small room but I do not go in. I walk back to the reception area where the officers are heading outside. I hover in the doorway until I see them drive off. I go outside and Ginge is still on the phone.

"I'll have to go. I'll talk to you soon."

"Who was that?"

"Mum."

"She had better not be about to rush up here with her crocodile tears."

"Ryan, don't start" He snaps. "It doesn't matter what she's done or not done, Ritchie is still her son."

"Fuck her" I mumble to myself.

"What did the police say?"

"Nothing, I told them to go and do their fucking job and find Ritchie's killer."

"I think they only wanted a statement."

"Fuck them. I'll find the cunt that did this before they go for their next fucking tea break."

"I already know."

I tilt my head back to gesture for him to tell me "Bring it" I say.

There is no-one in sight, and the closest person to us is the receptionist that is sat at her desk through two sets of sliding doors, but out of habit, I watch his eyes move quickly around him to make sure nobody is within earshot.

"Junkie Jamie" He mumbles.

"Now there's a fucking surprise. That little bastard should have been taken care of years ago" I feel a rage building up in me and my hands begin to shake.

"I'm going to kill him Ginge. I swear on my kids' life, if I get to him first, I am going to strangle him with my bare hands. If he hands himself in to avoid facing me I'm going to get myself banged up in every fucking jail until I get to him."

"He'll be hiding out. He knows we'll be coming for him"

"Put the word out that if I find anybody is keeping his whereabouts from me, they will be getting whatever is coming his way. The only place for that little rat to go will be the dirtiest smelliest junkie hole that you can imagine and I'm going to go through every fucking door until I find him."

"Look, Ryan," Ginge says calmly. "I know this has possibly woken a sleeping Lion in you, but I need you to listen to me carefully. I know you want to go and tear him limb from limb but you need to be smart about this. If you go on the rampage and those coppers catch up with you before you catch up with him, you're going to be stuck in a cell, kicking off, and the whole time he'll be out here taunting you."

I nod my head. "Be like Ginge" I mumble.

He looks at me strange.

"It's something Davie keeps telling me."

Ginge goes to walk back into the hospital but I stay put.

"Are you coming?"

"I don't want to go back in there. I'll need to go home and see Nikki."

"Okay. Well I'm away to check on Buster and talk to Emma."

I nod and turn to walk away but Ginge pulls me back and we both put our arms around each other. We were never the type of brothers for this man-hugging nonsense but I guess at times like this it shows some sense of unity or family bonding. It softens me for a moment. Instead of calling a taxi, I decide to walk until one comes my way. I cannot get the image of

Ritchie covered in blood out of my head. The tears start to roll down my face as I walk. I end up sitting on the kerb by the side of the road with my head in my hands. My whole life has revolved around violence and there has been many people killed in my life but never anyone close enough to have an effect on me. I know Ritchie was no angel and in a strange way, I always thought that if I ever received news that he was dead, it would have been from an overdose due to him hooked on that fucking smack. He did not deserve to die, not like this. I start to get images of Junkie Jamie smiling after stabbing him, running off and laughing as though his life meant nothing to him. I pick myself up off the ground and start walking again. A taxi passes but I let it go, my thoughts are too angry to go home right now. Nikki always said from the day we met, no matter what I do, keep it away from her, leave it at the gate and never bring it home but I need to go home, I need to see her. With my mind occupied and my emotions continually going from sad to anger, the time passes quickly and I am soon walking up my street. All the downstairs lights are on and there is a strong smell of bleach as I approach my front door. I look down and notice all of Ritchie's blood is gone. I put my key in the lock and I feel the door opening from the inside. Nikki is standing with her arms outstretched and tears in her eyes.

"I'm so sorry Ryan."

We step into each other and it softens me once again.

"Ryan you look exhausted, the kids will be up in a couple of hours, why don't you go and have a lie-down? I'll see to them."

She gives me another hug and gently guides me towards the stairs.

I have a quick shower to wash off the remnants of Ritchie's blood and before I even go through to the bedroom, the constant questions have started going through my head once again. I know Junkie Jamie does not need much enticing to pull a blade and Ritchie can be difficult at times but I just want to pick up the phone and ask him what the fuck happened. I wonder where Jamie is right now. I hope those coppers from the hospital do not come back here anytime soon, I know they only want a statement but fuck them. I had better catch Jamie before they do. I turn over in the bed and notice the light peering out from the side of the curtains. I close my eyes tight but when I do, all the different images of Ritchie become sharper in my mind. There is not a chance that I am going to sleep with all this going on. The kids will be up soon. I do not want them to see me like this. I reach over and pick up my phone. I dial Brody's number. I can't be sure what he heard me say last night with Screw-face, but whatever he thinks he heard, I'm going to make him think differently.

"Brody, were you awake?"

"Yeah, I couldn't really sleep after that news."

"Yeah, same"

"Is there any word on who did it or what it was...?"

The noise from outside distracts me. I get out of bed and look out of the window to see that arrogant fucker from across the street sitting in his driveway revving his engine. I take a deep breath and try to think rationally. I am tired, I am a little hungover, and I have just had some terrible news. I take another deep breath.

"Hello, Brody, sorry there was a little distraction there, what were you saying?"

"..." He goes to talk again when I hear a loud bang and the revving is louder. I go to the window again to see him sitting outside my house and looking up while purposefully revving his engine.

"You have got to be fucking kidding me."

I am about to head downstairs and confront him when I hear the car darting away.

"Brody, did you hear that shit?"

"Yeah, what the fuck was that?"

"That wanker from across the street, listen I'm not getting back to sleep anytime soon, can you pick me up? We have some work to do."

"What like, now?"

"Yeah, is that a problem?"

I hear a sigh on the other end and then he mumbles quietly "Okay, I'll come now."

Before I go back down the stairs, I go quietly into the kids' bedroom. I glance over at Davie who is star-shaped with his head facing the wall. I stand over Mollie's bed as she sleeps soundly. I kiss my hand and place it gently on her forehead. I get to the bedroom door and have one more look at them before I head back downstairs. Nikki will be about to wake them up for school and nursery so I need to leave before they see me like this. I know I will look the same to them on the outside but on the inside, I feel like a monster.

"I couldn't sleep."

"I didn't think you would, but you still need to rest."

"Even if I did manage to sleep I would have got woken up anyway. Did you hear his fucking car?"

"Of course I heard it. Someone else did too." She nods towards the living room. I enter to see Biscuit cowering in the corner with his tongue out and breathing heavily. I tap my leg for him to come to me but he stays put. I go over to him and put my hand out. He licks it and attempts to come to me but thinks better of it. I go back to the kitchen for a coffee and when I come back through, I bring his water bowl with me. I place it down a couple of feet in front of him and sit on the couch near the window. Biscuit gradually creeps forward and stretches his tongue to reach into the bowl. He works his way forward with every few sips until he is out from the corner and standing over his bowl. He has a long drink, then slowly walks over and jumps up onto the couch next to me. To an outsider this probably looks like a quiet relaxing moment, sipping coffee, staring out the window with my dog next to me and watching the sun come up. The reality is that I am waiting patiently for a lift to go hunting some filthy rat junkie for killing my brother. I finish my coffee and stand up by the window to keep watch for Brody. Nikki comes through and puts her arms around me.

"Ryan I can't imagine what is going through your head right now and I don't even want to think about what you are away to do. I've never said anything to you about this before because I know you were never put away for that long and I've grown up in that environment with my own family, and you know I've always had the attitude of 'boys will be boys.' However, I know you, and I know what is coming and I am scared. I don't want to see you locked up for fifteen to twenty years."

"You're away to add 'be like Ginge' to this aren't you?"

"Yes. Ryan that is exactly what I am saying. Be like Ginge" She demands.

For how crazy this conversation is, we both manage to smile. Well, under the circumstances, we could consider it as a smile. I pull her tight.

"I'll be like Ginge" I say softly.

"Brody's here." Nikki says releasing her arms from me.

Before walking out of the front door, I pick up the spare dog lead, the one that is unpractical for any species of Dog on the planet.

"Ryan"

I glance back along the hallway to see Nikki standing with her arms folded.
"Be like Ginge" We both say.
I close the door behind me.

Chapter 42

"It was Junkie Jamie before you ask" I say as I get in the car.

Brody nods and is about to talk when I cut him off.

"I don't know what it was about, I don't really give a shit, but I want him found before the police get their hands on him."

"Where do you want to start?"

"Head for Ginge's. I am assuming that it happened at the house that we last saw Ritchie so that area will be swarming with coppers, so avoid there. They will no doubt work their way to mine but they'll be wasting their fucking time."

We both get out of the car and walk into my old home. It's now Ginge's pad as he pays the rent and has been the only permanent lodger in recent years. We walk into the living room to find Ginge, Joe, Hunter and Larnio with various weapons lying around and are dressed up as though they are ready to take on the Taliban. They all stand and as Joe is the closest to me, he turns and gives me a handshake accompanied with a pat on the shoulder.

"Sorry about Ritchie, Ryan."

He then turns to Brody as Larnio and Hunter both lean over the coffee table to shake my hand and offer their condolences.

"So what's the crack here then? Are you boys off to do your National Service?"

"We've made several calls and there's still been no sign of him. I've put out an offer of a fair wad of cash for an address of where this little fucker is hiding and there's still no word, so we're thinking, if there's anybody he'll turn to for help, it will be the Donaldson's, so we're going to do a few raids and take their gear. Someone will talk."

"But what if they're not hiding him?"

Ginge shrugs. "No big deal, it's a good enough excuse to turn them over."

"Fair enough" I nod.

"Are you tailing on with us?" Hunter asks.

"No, Brody and I have a few early morning calls to make ourselves."

On the way out the door, I spot a baseball bat upright against the wall. I pick it up and gently sway it back and forward.

"Can I take this?"

Ginge shrugs "Of course, it's not like we're short on weapons. He nods at the firearms on the coffee table in front of him.

"I take it you two eventually found your stash?"

Ginge winks.

"Keep in touch lads."

With prying eyes everywhere, I put the bat inside my jacket for the walk to the car.

"Brody, head to the Hilltown"

"The same place as before?"

I give him a nod and stare out the window at nothing in particular.

"Brody is it just me, or have you noticed a difference in the amount of traffic and also the number of people going about in general, since going to and from Ginge's?"

"It's rush hour. You know, people going to work, school drop-offs?"

"Uh" I mumble as I watch people going about their business.

"Why, what are you thinking?"

"I might have another idea about flushing out Mr Junkie Jamie"

"...well?"

"Oh it's still a bit early, keep going to Hardy's"

"How are you going to get past the security door?"

"We won't need to. He's going to come out...eventually."

"What do you mean? We can't sit there all day hoping he'll pop his head out the door."

"It's not a hope Brody, it's a definite. You said it was rush hour, what time does rush hour finish?"

"I'm guessing nine when most kids are in school."

"What opens at nine? The fucking chemists, how many chemists are within a mile radius of here? About fifteen and in an hours' time, between the Hilltown, Albert Street and Clepington Road, it will be like the fucking walking dead"

We reach the Hilltown and due to a build-up of traffic going down the Hill, we are at a snail's pace. It comes to a halt and then picks up slowly again. Brody obviously sees me scanning from side to side to see what the hold-up is.

"It's a lollypop lady."

"Uh" I mumble.

She lets a few more cars pass and her sign goes up once again, stopping us. I feel my whole mood drop when I notice a young girl, not much older than Mollie, holding an older siblings hand as they walk to school. Half my mind wants to tell Brody to turn the car around and take me home, then the flashes of Ritchie enter my head and I remember why I am sitting here. Brody parks up outside Hardy's block and although there are plenty of people passing there is no movement in or out. We receive a few glances from passers-by but when I return their stares menacingly, they quickly go on their way.

"Right, fuck this Brody, I'm too impatient for this stakeout shit, that's nearly nine o'clock, I need to get the word out now and get people talking. Drive to Albert Street."

Brody signals and waits patiently on a gap in the traffic on both sides to make a turn on the steep hill. His casually slow speed annoys me a little and I feel that he is doing it on purpose to piss me off, as we make our way along Dura Street, on the approach to the Balmore pub, there is someone across the street with a familiar walk. He is crouched forward with his hood up.

"Quick, take a left."

Brody makes a sharp turn into Balmore Street.

"Pull into the left."

"Who is it?"

We both look back.

"I think it could be Jinxy, one of Jamie's dealers, I can't be sure."

"Brody put your window down."

He walks parallel with the car and I lean over Brody for a better look.

"I'm still not sure. Quick, pull up around the corner. If it's him we'll catch him before he goes to the chemist."

Brody signals again and we slowly pulls out from the space.

"TODAY BRODY, for fuck sake" I snap.

He attempts to go quicker but another slow driver now backs us up.

"Fuck it, stop here."

"But..."

I get out and jog across the road. The person is a few meters in front of me as he turns onto Albert Street. I jog again to catch up with him but when I turn the corner he takes off and runs diagonally across the road without any attention to oncoming traffic, they break and sound their horn at him but he is oblivious as he heads straight for the chemist at the end of Park Avenue. Brody has pulled in to the side, further up the street. I wait for a gap in the traffic and cross over.

"You weren't joking about the walking dead."

We sit in silence as we watch a couple of junkies shouting towards each other from either side of the street. They both end up gathering outside the chemist. A rough familiar female appears from the chemist with a walking stick and starts shouting her odds at one of them. He looks as though he is pleading his case and giving her his patter. The person we are waiting on also appears from the chemist, and the one pleading his case seems to draw him in, to the now, intense argument. He clearly does not want to be involved and walks off while still talking as though in a hurry, he gives them a few hand signals as to where he is going and runs across the road with as little attention to traffic as he did the last time. I am out of the car and crossing the road to cut him off but he manages to get ahead of me. I am half a step behind him and blow a little whistle to get his attention. His head turns slightly and through the gap in his hood, I catch sight of the scar running up his cheek.

"Jinxy"

I reach towards him and grab his throat.

"I want a word with you."

"WH...What, I've haven't done anything, I swear."

I see a few heads turn my way from people in the street so I push him into the doorway of the bookies behind him.

"Where's Junkie Jamie?"

"I don't know. I've not seen him."

He keeps moving his head as though it is on a swivel and he cannot look me in the eye. I grab the top of his hoody tight with both hands and pull his face closer. I ingest a disgusting smell coming from either his clothes or his breath that makes me pull my head back from him.

"You punt smack for him. Where the fuck is he?"

"I don't know I haven't seen him, I swear down."

I have a firm hold to restrict his head movement but his eyes still dart from side to side. I curiously look over my shoulder to see the Junkies from outside the chemist have now gathered on the opposite side of the road. I can vaguely make out them mouthing at me to leave him alone. I ignore them for the moment.

"When was the last time you seen him?"

"Ages ago, honest"

Throughout all my years of dealing with scum like this, I know that the words 'Junkie' and 'Honest' do not go together under any circumstances.

"Where's your phone?"

I release my grip and he goes into his pocket and picks out his phone. The shouting from the across the street gets a little louder and more aggressive, I turn around to see them gesturing towards me.

"I've no credit."

I take the phone from his hand "On your way"

I walk to the edge of the kerb, facing the other junkies on the opposite side.

"You can't take my phone, I need my phone."

"Fuck off, now."

"You fucking bully, give him his phone back" The female junkie with the walking stick shouts at me.

Just as I am about to cross the road I feel a tug on my jacket, I glance around to see him at my side attempting to take the phone back out of my hand. I swing around with my other hand and without too much momentum, the back of my hand connects with the side of his face and he goes down. He stares up at me for a split second before crawling away. I put his phone in my pocket and cross the road. One of the junkies squares up to me and starts to mouth off, I throw a straight punch to his head and he falls back onto the pavement out cold. Curious passing cars and works vans begin slowing down and some even come to halt as they watch the early morning drama. The female junkie is still mouthing and calling me a list of derogatory names. I clock the medicine bag in her hand from the chemist, I know how it works, she has built up a trust with her care worker and the chemist allows her to take her prescription home instead of having to consume it under their supervision. It can only be one of two things in there, Methadone or Valium, or it could possibly even be both, either way, I will get a reaction. I reach forward and grab the bag out of her hand. I tear the bag to reveal her small plastic bottle of Methadone.

"What the fuck are you doing?" She screams.

I open it and force the bottle downwards so that the thick green syrup splashes onto the pavement. She throws her walking stick to the side and dives forward, at first I think she is about to tackle me but she drops to the ground and starts licking the liquid from the pavement. I turn towards Brody's car and can see him at the wheel with his palms facing upwards and mouthing the words 'what the fuck?' The Junkie that I knocked out is still lying with his head back, his eyes are open but he has not come around yet. I lean over him and pat him down until I find his phone. I take it from his pocket and walk back to the car. Brody speeds off.

"It's okay, take your time?"

"What the fuck was that all about? Are we really about to beat up junkies all day until one of them talks?"

"Well that was the plan, but plans can change." I wink as I flick through both of the phones that I have acquired.

"Anyway, before you start judging me, I will clear this up with you right now. That greasy little fucker with the hood was a rapist and as you well know, rapists are the most protected in prison and even have their own wing. If any of the general population manages to get their hands on them, they open up their cheeks from ear to ear so that no matter where that person goes, everyone knows what they are. His prison branding just happened to have come from Junkie Jamie, so after slicing his face open he warned him that if he didn't start taking delivery of parcels and selling his smack, the next time it would be his throat."

"What about the woman that had the walking stick?"

"Don't be fooled by that stick, she's not some poor invalid. She has a hole in her leg the size of a fucking golf ball because the only place left where she can find a vein to jag her needle is in her groin. She's well known for getting young girls hooked on the gear and then putting them on the fucking game."

I flick through one of the phones and come across Jamie in the contacts list. I press to call but there is no credit.

"Head back to the Hilltown, actually no, head up to Brantwood we might catch a few faces up there."

I copy Jamie's number into my own phone but when I press to call, the number is unrecognised. I throw the phone out of the window and go through the next one, there is no contact for Jamie but as I scroll down,

I come across 'Ritchie M.' I show it to Brody and he lifts his head in acknowledgement. I press to call.

"Are you calling it?"

"I'm checking to see if there is credit then I'll message every number asking about Jamie."

With no dialling tone, I launch this phone out of the window as well.

"What is it with junkies, they always having these expensive phones but never any fucking credit?"

Outside Brandwood chemist, is a three-way road junction with bus stops placed all around. Brody finds a space opposite, but the view is not ideal.

"I thought you said plans change, why are we at another chemist?"

"You witnessed that shit on the pavement. If I want information, I'll take their Methadone, they'll soon talk"

"But what if they really don't know where he is, you can't go around pouring everyone's Methadone out in the street."

"You fucking watch me."

We sit for a short while, occasionally turning to look up and down the opposite street, when a taxi pulls up outside the chemist. A young woman gets out and flicks her hair back over her short leather jacket. Brody looks on and turns away. I open the car door.

"Where are you going?"

"I'm away to have a word."

He turns to look at the girl, and then back to me.

"You've got to be kidding?"

"Junkies come in all shapes and sizes Brody. They aren't all smelly thieving housebreakers, although every single one of them will lie through their teeth, or whatever teeth they have left."

I walk slowly over towards the chemist and before I reach the door, she is on her way out.

"Can I have a word?"

"Oh hello Ryan, I need to run, I have a taxi waiting."

"I can see that. It's important."

She gives me the pleading eyes and moves closer to the waiting taxi.

"I'm looking for Jamie."

"I can't help you."

"Do you have a number?"

"My number"

"For Jamie"

"I don't I'm sorry, what's he done this time?"

I am about to blurt it out but I hold back when I see the taxi driver has his window down.

"I just need a word with him."

"I can't help you, Ryan, I've not seen him."

"Could you do me a favour and put the word out that I am looking for him? Actually no, tell him I'm coming for him"

She hurries to get into the taxi.

I start to walk back to the car when I see Spike, another one of Jamie's acquaintances walking towards the chemist from the opposite direction. I wave him over but he signals with his index finger before swaggering towards the chemist door. I continue walking to the car.

"Did the girl have any info?" Brody says from the window.

"No, I couldn't really say much with the taxi driver listening. She was one of many who passed him packages of smack in the jail. I thought about following the taxi until I noticed this slimy fucker."

I lean against the car and wait. He appears moments later and walks into the post office next door, he comes out with a newspaper under his arm and heads straight towards me. As he gets closer to me he lifts his free hand up and pulls it through his long greasy hair, he then reaches out with the same hand for me to shake. He appears offended when I refuse, but his filthy greasy hand is not the only reason, it is more so that he understands this is not a friendly situation.

"I'm looking for Junkie Jamie."

"I've not seen him."

"I need an address."

"I can give you his address."

"I've got his address. I want an address where he is now."

He shrugs "I can't help you, I've not seen him."

"Since...?"

"A week, maybe two"

He moves the newspaper from one hand to the other and I clock the chemist bag folded between it. I lean forward and grab it.

"What the fuck are you doing?" He tries to grab it back but I tear open the bag and take out his bottle of Methadone. I quickly open it and start to tilt the bottle.

"You wouldn't be lying to me would you?"

He takes a step back and smirks at me. "Ryan you can pour that out all you want. I don't take it anymore, I sell it on" He shrugs.

I turn and look at Brody sitting in the car. He gives me a blank stare. I turn back to Spike.

"Here." I hold out the bottle but when he reaches to take it, I turn it upside down and pour it out.

His smug look drops and he throws a punch that connects to the side of my face. I reach forward with both hands and grab him. I pull him towards me and smash my forehead into his nose. I release my grip and he stumbles backwards, I step forward with a punch and he goes down on one knee. He makes a groaning noise while covering his face with his hands. I take a step back and the sly fucker dives upwards throwing both fists. We trade punches for a few seconds and end up in a wrestle on the front of Brody's car. I manage to put him in a headlock and drag his head downwards, hitting it off the bonnet of the car. I release my arm from around his neck and he falls to the ground.

I turn to face Brody "Well, this is clearly not working."

"Clearly" He confirms.

I get back in the car as Spike is getting to his feet. He waits until we drive off before shouting something in our direction.

"I need a new approach."

"I think maybe you're asking the wrong people. These Junkies are probably more scared of being stabbed by Jamie than getting a hiding from you."

"Yeah, you're probably right. I need someone that they'll talk to, someone they'll see as an equal that's not full of shit."

I think for a few seconds.

"Fingers"

"Who"

"Fingers, I wish I'd thought of him earlier. Back to Albert Street Brody, we might catch him."

Brody attempts to turn the car around.

"No keep going, cut down on to Constitution Road, it's quicker."

"By the way Ryan, you fucking stink" Brody says opening his window.

I lift my arm up and sniff where I had been holding Spike in a headlock.

"You're not joking. The smell must have come off his greasy hair."

"So who is this guy we're looking for now, another junkie?"

"Oh no, not at all, he mixes with them though, he sells his painkillers to them and gives them lifts and stuff but he doesn't always take money from them. If you know what I mean"

"So what does he accept for payment?"

"Well, his nickname is Fingers. You work it out."

"What. Really"

"Hey he's in his sixties, he had an accident about twenty years ago and his penis doesn't work, so for obvious reasons, he has gained the nickname Fingers."

"Yeah, but Junkies"

"Cheap thrills, he has to get his kicks somehow."

"Keep a lookout for an old beat up Jaguar car."

"What colour is it?"

"Silver, it's very old with the mascot on the front."

Brody drives slower than he normally does and both our heads turn from side to side on the lookout for Fingers car. Approaching Park Avenue, there is a patrol car parked up on the kerb facing away from us.

"Shit, what do you want me to do?"

"Just keep going. If you do a U-turn in the street it will only draw attention."

"Do you think they're here for you?"

"More than likely"

The traffic lights ahead of us turn red and I quickly turn around to see a car not far behind us.

"Slow down. Let this car catch up."

Through the back window of the police car, I can see the two officers sitting in the front seats. They do not seem too concerned about what is going on around them so we keep our heads facing forward and slowly pass them. The car behind is only feet from us so when we pass there is only a split second for them to clock our registration. The lights turn green and we sail past, the patrol car does not move. We reach the next set of traffic lights and there is still no sign of Fingers.

"Take a left at the bottom onto Arbroath Road and left again up Kemback Street."

"Ryan we can't keep driving about here all day."

"We're not. There's a car park on Kemback Street, stop near the entrance."

On approaching the car park, I clock Fingers car straight away. Brody pulls over to the side of the road.

"Move up a bit further."

"Is that his car?"

"Yeah"

I can see him in the driver's seat but his head is facing away from us. We both stare.

"Are you going over to talk to him or do you want me to drive around?"

"Be patient. Let him finish."

"What do you mean finish. What's he doing?"

"I don't want the word getting out that he's talked to me, he'll lose their trust."

"What do mean. He's on his own."

"No he's not. Just wait."

Moments later, Fingers passenger seat flips up and we both watch closely as a young female gets out of the car. She stands up straight to adjust the tie on her tracksuit bottoms and pulls them tightly around her skinny waist. She closes the car door and smiles at Fingers revealing a row of black rotted teeth before waving and walking off. As soon as she is out of sight, I tell Brody to drive into the car park. We stop in front of Fingers car and Brody flashes his lights at him. He drives forward so that his window is parallel to mine.

"Ryan" He nods. "I don't need to ask what you're after."

"What do you mean?"

"Buster called me earlier. I'm sorry to hear about Ritchie."

I nod.

"I'll find out what I can. If I hear anything I'll let one of you know straight away."

"Thanks, I really appreciate it."

He stretches his arm out of his window for me to shake and I look at his hand and smirk. He realises and tries to explain that he has wipes, even picking up the packet to show me. I wave him off and force a smile as Brody backs slowly out of the car park.

Chapter 43

I glance down at the baseball bat on the floor in front of me then it makes me think. I check the time on the dashboard.

"The Claver will be open now, drive past and I'll pop my head in the door to see if anyone has been in touch."

What I really mean is that I have run out of ideas so I am now going to have to start crashing doors. The baseball bat will do for Brody but I am going to pick up my machete from behind the bar. We are a couple of streets away from the Claver when Brody starts to slow down due to the car in front of us coming to a near stop.

"What's up? What's the problem?"

"It's a tailback. I think someone has maybe broken down."

I roll down the window and reach my neck out to see beyond the cars in front. The tailback goes around the bend towards the Claver.

"Brody turn here, quick as you can."

"What. Why?"

"The Claver is being turned over."

"How do you know?"

"I just do. Hurry up."

Brody swerves into the opposite lane and turns the car around. We drive past the cars that were pulling up behind us and one of them catches my eye. I turn back to check but there is no movement. A few seconds later, I turn back again. This time one of the cars that were behind us also makes a turn in the street.

"We've got a tail."

Brody checks his mirror.

"Are you sure? There are more cars turning now."

"Brody it's a fucking tail. Move it."

Brody picks up speed and after a few sharp corners, I tell him to park up. I check behind but there is no sign of them. I call Buster but it rings out. I call Ginge, straight to answerphone. Seconds later, Ginge calls back.

"Avoid the Claver, Ryan, it's being raided."

"Yeah I know. We could have done with that info ten minutes ago."

"I've only just had the call myself."

"Well it must be you they're after, they can't be going to all that trouble for me pulling up a few junkies."

"I've been informed that they are to detail us on sight, even Buster. Until Jamie's been arrested."

"Detain us under what fucking cause?"

"Intent to pervert the course of justice"

"That's not even a fucking charge. It would never stand."

"It doesn't need to. It's just a made up charge to get us all off the street."

"Listen, we've been through a few of the Donaldson's doors and left word. If we don't hear back by tonight we're going through Mick's door, so I need you to lie low until then."

"I hear you."

I hang up the phone.

"They've to detain us on sight."

"Who, me and you"

"No, all of us, and I'm assuming anybody else that's involved with us. I'm sure they think that with us out of the way they'll have a better chance of catching him."

"But he's going to be in hiding either way, so if they don't catch him, they will use the excuse that we got in the way of their investigation."

"Exactly"

"So what do we do now?"

"We need to lie low for a bit. I need a drink, let's find a quiet pub away from here."

"The West End"

"Sounds good, let's do it"

While Brody is driving, I call Nikki to check in and she tells me that some Crime Squad Officer has been to the door twice looking for me and a patrol car has been sitting outside the house for the last two hours.

"If they are still there when you leave to pick up Mollie, call me and hand the phone to them."

"Don't worry, I'll tell them to move."

"Is everything else okay? Did you mention anything about Ritchie to Davie?"

"No, he rushed off. I'm hoping that nobody at his school mentions anything."

"I'll sit him down tonight and tell him."

"Buster called."

"Looking for me?"

"No, he was asking if everything was okay. He seemed a bit down, I think he only needed someone to talk to."

"Okay, well I might be late tonight."

"Ryan, remember what I said."

"I know, I know, be like Ginge" I mumble.

I hang up and Brody gives me a weird look.

"It means stay out of trouble."

"I kind of got that" He grins.

We drive around by Old Hawkhill and on to South Tay Street. We catch someone vacating a parking space up ahead near the junction with Perth Road, and Brody quickly manoeuvres into it. With plenty of eating places near us, we walk to the end of the street while we decide on where to go. I look down the street to see a patrol car coming in our direction from the Nethergate. As a precaution, we walk quickly into the nearest bar, Medina. While looking around for a suitable table, I discreetly watch the patrol car as it passes the bar. I choose a table that is slightly back from the window but still directly facing out. Brody nips to the toilet and I order a pint and a burger. I order him the same even though he said he was not hungry. I know exactly why he is not hungry, it is because he is down in that cubicle snorting lines of coke. He really thinks I was fucking born yesterday. I am not going to mention it though, not today. Today I need him, at least if he's coked up he can still function, if he was popping those fucking Valium's I would have kicked him in the balls and dragged him up to the morgue to see Ritchie, let him know where those downers can lead him. Sitting on my own staring out of the window at everyone passing, I start to notice little bits of dirt on the outside, then I look along at the rest of the windows and realise they are all dirty. I wonder who cleans them. I wonder how much they charge. I am definitely going to make a go of this window cleaning business, I will not actually clean any windows but I am sure I can drum up some business. It will not be hard to find out the prices and undercut everyone. If I make sure all the boys are well looked after they will want to come work for me. I will take over each round bit by bit.

"I ordered you a burger as well."

"I said I wasn't hungry."

"Well, I've ordered it so you're fucking eating it. You've been up all night putting that shit up your nose so you need to eat."

We both sit in silence staring out the window at the world going by when the waiter interrupts us by bringing our food. I ignore Brody as he picks at his as though it is a plate of fucking dog food. As I tuck into mine, I happen to look up and see a few familiar faces passing the window. They are the original faces of Jamie's mob before he took his downward spiral and latched onto the Donaldson's.

"Wait here, I'm away to check on something."

"What's wrong, where are you going?"

I walk out of the pub and look down the street but I do not see them. I pass the window where Brody is sitting and put my index finger up to signal that I will be back in a minute. I keep walking until I reach the pub next door, the Phoenix. This is an old-school pub with the windows high up and no view of the clientele inside. I stand by the split doors and pull both of them slightly so that I can see inside. The faces are all standing by the bar waiting to be served. I close the doors gently and walk back to the Medina.

"What was it?"

"A few faces from the past, well, Jamie's past. They are in the pub next door."

"Are you going through?"

"Yeah, once I've finished this."

"You can have the rest of mine. He passes his plate with two, maybe three small bites out of his burger and half of his chips. I demolish the lot and down the rest of my pint.

"Right let's go."

We get outside and I tell Brody to go and get the car and meet me outside the Phoenix. I take a deep breath before I pull open the double doors ready to kick off. They are not there. I walk past the bar in case they have taken a seat but there is no sign of them. I walk back out of the pub and look up and down the road. They must have gone into the next pub down, the Nether Inn. I start to walk down the road when I look past the pub to see them crossing the dual carriageway into town. I keep watching them while occasionally turning back to look for Brody. I panic a little that I am going to lose them so I start to cross the road. Brody appears at the traffic lights behind me and sounds the horn. I signal for him to follow me. The lane for crossing straight over is for taxis and buses only and instead of going through it, Brody turns left and has to go all the way up the dual carriageway to come back down and turn right. He eventually catches up with me as I stand on the kerb at the start of the taxi rank near the top of Union Street.

I get in the car and nod across the road "They are over there. Trades Bar"

"Are you going in?"

"Yeah" I pick up the baseball bat from the floor and open my jacket to check it for size. I place it on my shoulder and pull my jacket over it but the barrel sticks out the bottom by a few inches. I look at Brody's jacket.

"What, you're not getting my jacket."

I smirk.

"Swing the car around into Union Street and get as close to the pub as possible. Wait there and keep the car running. I'll go and have a little word with these boys."

When I step back out of the car, I need to keep my hand in my jacket pocket to hold the bat in place. I try to keep a relaxed expression on my face as I casually walk into the pub. The pub is a fair size but it is near empty so it is not too difficult to find them, they are sitting at the far end, opposite the bar. I can hear them talking and laughing loudly. I keep my relaxed expression as I walk through the bar and stand by their table. They do not notice me at first but each of them in-turn appears to go quiet which attracts the attention of one of the barmaids. I slide the baseball bat from my jacket and gently lower it on to the table in front of them. The biggest one among them, Joey, who looks as though he fancies himself a bit, attempts to get up from his seat. I take one hand off the bat and signal with the palm of my hand for him to sit down.

"Do you know who I am?" I say calmly

They all nod.

"Good. I am only going to ask this once, but before I do, I am going to explain something to you. In the early hours of this morning, my brother, Ritchie, was stabbed and killed. Now, the person that did this was a friend of yours, named Jamie, mostly known as Junkie Jamie. Now I do not know if you lot still have some sort of loyalty to him or not, but I will tell you this right now, I am going to find him and when I do, I am going to kill him. So, if any of you have any idea where he's hiding out, I suggest you tell me, because if I find out later that any of you knew and didn't tell me, I will come for you, and when I find you, I'm going to use this bat, and I will smash your skull in with it.

"None of us..."

I release my hand and put my palm in the air.

"Now, it sounds like you are about to talk on behalf of your entire little group here. Are you sure that you want that responsibility?"

He nods confidently "We don't have anything to do with Jamie. None of us does. We were friends with his brother years ago, he moved on, and we went our separate ways."

My stare goes from one to the other around the table. I then lift the bat up and place it back into my jacket. As I turn to walk back out of the pub, I see two of the barmaids staring over, and one of them is talking frantically into the pub landline. I do not need to guess who is on the other end. I exit the pub to see Brody, standing waiting outside of the car.

"What are you doing? I told you to wait in the fucking car."

"I know, it's still running, I thought you might need a hand."

"Get in the car and drive."

Brody floors it down Union Street and takes a right onto the ring road. With each set of traffic lights turning red before us, there is a traffic build-up when we reach our exit route. Brody signals to move over to the correct lane so that we can exit the ring road.

"Stay in this lane."

"What. Why?"

"We've picked up another tail."

"Where" He checks his mirrors

He seems a little panicked and his head turns continuously checking his mirrors "I can't make it out."

"Don't panic. Keep in this lane and follow the ring road back around the town. There are enough traffic lights. It will be easy to lose them."

As we work our way around the ring road there are still several cars in front of us. Each time we approach more traffic lights, Brody pulls back and we are eventually down to one car in front. The tail is still lingering not too far behind. The next set of lights are at green and Brody keeps slowing the pace, I'm thinking, he knows what he's doing, he's done this before. The lights turn amber and the car in front goes for it. I am waiting on Brody putting the foot down to speed through, he hesitates, and when we get closer to the lights, it turns red. I am thinking he is good, he has it timed. Then he stops on the line.

"What the fuck are you doing?"

"What?"

"Fucking go"

"It's a red light."

"That was your chance to lose the tail."

I do not even look over to see his stupid dumb expression. I shout at him to get out.

"What do you mean get out?"

I start to climb out of my seat and shove him towards the door.

"Get to fuck out."

I get behind the wheel while he stands by the door looking at me.

"GET IN THE FUCKING CAR" What the fuck is wrong with him.

The lights turn green and I put my foot down for a split second but it is only out of frustration, I then back up to the slow steady pace. The next lights have not long turned green so I sail through with little pressure on the accelerator. Brody keeps looking behind.

"You still can't see them yet can you?"

"I don't what car I'm meant to be looking for."

"You'll soon see."

The next set of lights in the distance is already at green so I back up more and more. The person driving immediately behind me is ranting and raving at my slow pace, they attempt to move into the inside lane with the intention of undertaking me but I swerve out slightly to stop him, he moves back behind me and starts making rude hand gestures. The lights turn to amber.

"Look for them now."

The lights turn red before we hit the line and I slam my foot on the accelerator.

"This is how you lose a fucking tail."

"Ah, I see them now."

I look in the mirror to see the tail swerving from side to side in a vain attempt to try to squeeze through the cars in front of them. I take the next exit off the ring road and pull over for Brody to switch seats again.

"I never even knew you could drive."

"Brody we can all drive. Not one of us has a license, but we can all drive."

"Why don't you get a license then?"

"That would just give them another reason to keep tabs on us. If they saw any of us driving it would be a free for all to pull us over anytime they felt like it, and you know how that would end."

"We need to park this up somewhere and lie low for a few hours."

"Why don't you phone Ginge and see where he is?"

"We can't hide out at the same place, if they find him, they find me."

"We can go to Tanya's place. She has off road parking at the back of her block."

"The Stripper"

He nods.

"Let's do it."

Chapter 44

Brody called ahead to Tanya and she was happy to let us use her flat to hide out for a bit. She made herself scarce when we turned up at her door and left us to it. I spent the first few hours on the phone, following up numbers or waiting for others to call back with any information. A few addresses had come my way that I wanted to go and check out, but Ginge was insistent that we stay put as Brody's car was now marked and the coppers will stop us on sight. Ginge is determined that he is going through Mick Donaldson's door as he thinks Jamie is hiding out there. Personally, I am not convinced, as I think he is only going through with this to make a point, but who am I to question him, if I had thought of it first, I would have already done it. It has started to get dark outside and time is wearing on. Brody seems content in front of the TV while I am still pacing the floor making enquiries. I keep calling the same numbers repeatedly hoping for new answers. I feel that I am about to climb the walls waiting for some news on Jamie. My phone goes and I answer it without even checking the screen. As soon as I hear Nikki say my name, I know something is wrong.

"I know you have a lot on, but that arsehole from across the street is sitting outside our house again revving his engine."

"What happened to the patrol car?"

"I spoke to them and they were gone by the time I got back from the nursery with Mollie."

"Okay, I'll swing passed and have a word."

"Ryan!"

"Yeah"

"There are other people in the car with him."

"Okay. I'll sort it."

"Come on Brody, let's go."

"I thought Ginge told us to wait for his call."

"That can wait. This is more important."

"What is it?"

"The wanker from across the street from me seems to think it is okay to intimidate my family."

"Really" Brody jumps from his seat and heads straight to the door, I follow on feeling impressed at his sudden loyalty to protect his family.

I call Nikki from the car "Is he still there?"

"Yeah I've told the kids to stay away from the windows."

"How's Biscuit?"

"How do you think he is? He's hiding at the side of the sofa with his tongue hanging out and breathing as though he is having a heart attack."

"Poor thing, I'll call you back in five. We're nearly there."

"Right Brody, don't go into the street, drive passed slowly and see which way they are facing."

We reach my street and Brody edges the nose of the car along until we have a view.

"Ok, they are facing this way. Reverse back and kill the lights."

I call Nikki again.

"Right I need you to go out and start shouting at them but put your phone out in front of you as though you are filming them. He won't give you any cheek and he'll drive off."

She hangs up and a few minutes later, his car speeds up to the junction where we are sitting. He passes us unnoticed and speeds off down the street. I do not have to say a word as Brody spins around and follows them.

"So you do know how to drive."

Brody catches them up but I tell him to pull back.

"Let's see where they go."

My phone starts ringing "It's Ginge."

"Are you ready?"

"No, I've had to go and take care of something."

"Are you out in that car?"

"Yeah"

"I told you it's marked. If they see it, they're going to pull you."

"It was an emergency. I'll call you back shortly."

"Ry..." I hang up.

The car heads for the Kingsway and as soon as he turns at the roundabout, I can hear the roar from his engine, Brody speeds up to catch them but they are gone.

"Do you think they knew we were following them?"

"No, that's the way he drives, he's a fucking idiot. Keep going to the next roundabout, if there's still no sign of him we'll head back."

Brody floors it again after passing the next roundabout, he turns around and as we go to head back, I catch sight of the car pulling into the Pets at Home car park across from the main road. Brody turns at the next slip road and heads back through Longtown road. He creeps slowly around the empty car park and we stop when we see him parked up next to another sporty looking car. We watch as they sit and chat for a bit then he lets his engine rip with a loud bang before reversing out of his space, he wheel spins it around the corner to the adjoining McDonalds car park. Brody follows, there are no other cars near him so Brody pulls up several spaces behind and turns off the engine. I take the dog chain from my jacket pocket and wrap one end around my hand. Brody and I both get out of the car and march towards them. I had already clocked the driver's window open so I head straight for him. I appear at his car door, and in the split second that it takes him to recognise me, I have both hands in the car and the dog chain wrapped around his neck. I cross my hands over so that the chain tightens and I walk backwards dragging him from the car. Two of his friends get out and one of them makes a run for it while one of them stands his ground, Brody floors him. I keep choking the arrogant prick until he is about to pass out. I release the chain from around his neck and give him a few seconds to recover from his coughing and spluttering before reaching down and grabbing his face. I push my fingers tight into his cheeks.

"Now you look at me. I do not normally give warnings but as we are friendly neighbours, I am going to give you one last chance. If you cross me one more time, the only thing you will be driving for the rest of your life is a fucking wheelchair, have you got that. Nod if you understand me."

His head nudges up and down. I release my hands from his cheek, and in the same motion, I throw his head back. He lies flat on the ground looking up at me and I swing my leg back and kick him hard in the balls.

"That's for Biscuit you arrogant prick."

I look up to see several people in their cars watching and the light from their phones tell me that it is time to go.

"Head back to mine."

"What about Ginge?"

"He can wait. I need to see my family."

Brody knows this is important and puts the foot down most of the way. I get him to park across the street from my house

"Wait here. If you see any car stop near my house take off, and I'll meet you over at the back road."

I go into the house and Mollie comes running towards me.

"Daddy daddy, that bad man made Biscuit sad again"

"I know sweetheart but I've talked to him and he's not going to be bad anymore."

I watch as Biscuit comes to me with his tail wagging but still in the down position. I crouch to pet him and he climbs up to me with his front paws to lick my face. The second that I stand up, I see the blue lights flashing from behind the curtains. I pull it to the side and peer through. There are several cars and a meat wagon on the road immediately outside my house. I run up the stairs to the bedroom to get a proper look. I see Brody still in his car, boxed in. They have not arrested him, which means they are only here for me. Several officers come out of the meat wagon in full riot gear. I go into the kids' room and grab one of Davies football socks from a drawer, I pick up one of Mollie's toys that take the large batteries and I remove them and put them into the sock. I walk slowly back down the stairs while wrapping the sock around my hand.

"I told you not to bring this here" Nikki says, shielding Mollie from me.

I hold the hand with the sock behind my back and Nikki leads Mollie and Davie to the kitchen while I make my way to the front door. I walk out towards my front gate and try to count the numbers but the dog handler distracts me. He signals for the dog he is holding to attack, but due to his tight grip of its lead, this forces it onto its back legs. The dog's teeth are showing and along with its fierce snarl, I can tell that it is baying for my blood, along with every officer lined up in front of me. Between the meat wagon and one of the patrol cars, I catch sight of Brody, still sitting in his car, he looks at me and I give him a quick shake of the head for him to stay put. I know what is coming, and even if I catch one of them square on with this sock, it will be worth the beating. One of the officers immediately in front of me steps into my range, I turn my shoulder to get some momentum when I swing the sock and then I notice something move to the side of me. I look down to see Biscuit, wagging his tail and undeterred by the drama in front of him. Fuck. I obviously forgot to close the door properly. I face forward again to see more of them step closer to me including the dog handler, who is itching to release the vicious mutt and let it sink its teeth into me. My first thought is that if I kick off, the first one that goes to strike me, Biscuit will go for him, and they will release that mutt to tear him apart. This is not good. I could not give a shit what they do to me, but Biscuit is my responsibility and I cannot let anything happen to him.

"Look I'll come quietly if you let me put my dog in the house."

"It doesn't work like that Ryan and you know it."

"Just let me knock on the door and my missus will take the dog in, then I'm all yours."

"And you walk into the house and close the door, then we have a standoff like last time, I don't think so. Let us put the cuffs on and ill knock on the door. That's the only way this is going to work."

I glance over at Brody who has his phone in his hand, with a full view, videoing them. The dog handler is shuffling closer to me."

"Biscuit, home!" I shout and point towards the door.

He wags his tail, unaware of the danger he is in.

"NIKKI!" I shout.

I know I am wasting my time, as she will not hear me from the kitchen.

"NIKKI!" I shout louder.

"Ryan let us put the cuffs on and we'll knock on the door."

This is a standoff and I am going to lose either way. I drop the sock and crouch down to pet Biscuit.

"Into the house" I guide him towards my front door.

"Go on, go get Mollie."

The leading officer approaches me and I put my hands out in front of me.

"I don't think so, Ryan. Turn around."

I turn around and he slips the cuffs on. The second they are on, the dog handler extends his mutts lead and it goes straight for me. Its front paws are up and its teeth are inches from my face. I underestimate Biscuit as he turns from a soft cuddly pet into a snarling protective sidekick. He launches himself up and the Dog handler pulls his mutt back while shouting that Biscuit is attacking his dog. Another officer steps forward and smashes Biscuit across his side with his baton. As soon as I hear him yelp, I make a dive towards the officer with the baton but he catches me first and smashes me in the side of the head. I feel the sting but I keep going and fall into him, he misplaces his footing and we both tumble to the ground. I land on top of the officer and his face is only inches from mine. I quickly arch my whole body and use my momentum to smash my forehead into his face. I manage it a second time before the other officers pull me up by the back of my arms before dropping me back down to the ground. The other officers stand over me and let loose with their batons while kicking and stamping on me. I hear a scream and turn my head to see my family in the middle of the garden path watching helplessly as these upstanding officers carry out their brutal assault. The leading officer stands in their way as though trying to block their view while telling them to go back into the house.

"No, I fucking won't go back in the house. I want his kids to see exactly how you treat their father."

They lift me up off the ground and as soon as I am on my feet, I heal kick one of them in the shin and he releases his grip. I turn to make a move on the other officer closest to me, when a heavy blow smashes over the top of my head. With a quick sweep of my feet, I hit the ground and the batons come raining once again. I can hear Nikki screaming at them to stop and when I manage to turn my head to the side, I see Mollie crying and I watch as Davie places a protective arm around her and leads her away inside. I do not remember the last hit but it must have been a hard one, as when I come to, my face is lying in a pool of blood on the floor of the meat wagon. I fight back the tears as I repeatedly say in my head. 'This is the last time.'

PART 4 - BRODY

Chapter 45

It was definitely a good idea that I come back to Edinburgh last night instead of waiting until this morning, as I would never have made it to my meeting today. I was still a bit rough when I woke up in my flat, but after a line of the coke, that Joe had given me yesterday, I soon perked up. He told me it was strong, virtually uncut, but I did not believe him, well, they all say that. I put out a normal sized line and minutes later, I could not feel my fucking face. I had left the flat early as I was to hand Leanna's mail in to her parents' house on the way, but my heart was racing and my mind was working overtime, so I ended up driving straight to my meeting and now I am too fucking early. I guess after handing in my last report I could not wait to find out what they have to say. I told them from the start that Ginge was in charge but Whyte and Drummond would not listen, they were adamant that Ryan was running the show. More importantly is what they have to say about the video I handed in along with the report. They brushed off my beating in the cell but this footage clearly shows those officers taunting Ryan and then beating him in front of his wife and kids. This is not what I signed up for, this is far from their values and training to protect people and my respect for the job I am doing is pretty fucking low. My heart rate is beginning to feel normal, so with a few minutes until my scheduled meeting time, I have one last check in the mirror. I touch my face to make sure all the feeling has returned. I step out of the car and catch a glimpse of the mail that I was to hand into Leanna. I will swing passed after my meeting. Depending on how things turn out here today, I might have some news for her that I am out from undercover, either that, or I could possibly be out of the job altogether. I give my name to the receptionist and when I glance at the clock above her, I am bang on time. As usual, they make me sit in the waiting area. I do not know who organises their schedule because they keep me waiting before every meeting. I would not be surprised if Drummond was doing this on purpose to wind me up, so that when they fire their questions at me, I am agitated and flustered. Well not today, I am feeling sharp and on the ball. I have only been in the building a short time and already I am feeling the heat. I loosen my tie and open the top button on my shirt to let in some air but the release only lasts a few seconds. I want to take my jacket off but I know there will be large sweat patches under my arms. I knew I should not have worn a dark coloured shirt. I clench my hands together and I can feel the clammy sweat running through my fingers. I clocked the toilet sign on the way to the waiting area and I am thinking that maybe I should go and have one last freshen up. If Whyte or Drummond shakes my hand when I enter, they will think that I am nervous when I am not. It is so fucking hot in here. Fuck this. I stand up and wave to get the receptionists attention. I point to the toilet sign and mouth the words as a cautionary measure to make sure she knows where I am going. I run my hands under the cold tap and check myself in the mirror while drying them off. I straighten my tie and push it up higher to hide the open button on my shirt. I stand back from the mirror and pull the tail on my jacket at the bottom, tightening my posture to admire the fit. I turn to the see the side view and slide my hands into my pockets. The tip of my index finger runs along the rim of the sealed bag. Seconds later, I find myself in the cubicle rolling a note. I unseal the bag and place one end of the note towards the powder. I take a deep breath and when I release the air from my lungs, I bow my head and guide the note towards my nose. As the powder is forcing its way up my nose, I hear the toilet door opening.

"Mr Buchanan."

I cough "Yeah"

"Detectives Whyte and Drummond will see you now."

"Okay, I'll just be a minute" I splutter, feeling the dry powder going down the back of my throat

The door closes.

"Fuck" I mutter while I struggle to reseal the bag.

I place it in my pocket with along with the rolled note and exit the cubicle. I tighten up in the mirror once again before walking out of the toilet. The secretary is waiting by her desk and I notice her sneakily look me up and down before leading the way to the interview room where Whyte and Drummond are waiting. The both stay seated and while Whyte gestures for me to take a seat opposite them, Drummond does not even look up to acknowledge me. I know this is all a game to him and when he does look up from his notes, his hard expression does not faze me. He mentions my last report and I confidently begin to explain the situation at the boxing fight in Glasgow, when he rudely buts in, mid-sentence, to ask about my drug taking.

"What about it?"

"Well, if you were under the influence of drugs you might not have heard what you think you might have heard."

"I was hardly under the influence. I may have had the occasional line here and there to fit in but..."

He lifts his hand in a gesture for me to stop talking and I feel my face heating up. My mouth feels tingly and numb. Judging by their expressions and this whole act in front of me, I have a feeling that they are about to undermine my whole report and I need to get my point across before they go any further.

"I was driving that night. I had no alcohol and was with Ryan. He frowns on anybody taking drugs when they are in his company working with him...."

Drummond sniggers "Did you hear that? Ryan frowns on anybody taking drugs" He turns to Whyte and smiles.

Whyte gives him a quick glance and turns to me.

"Brody, can I ask you something?"

"Sure."

"Are you on drugs right now?"

I hesitate before answering and I look from one to the other as they stare at me for an answer. In what feels like a very long awkward silence, my mind has jumped from yes to no several times in the split second that it takes me to open my mouth to talk.

Whyte continues without letting me answer "...You see, it's just that you seem to have some white powder on your jacket and it appears to be dripping from your nose. I glance down to see speckles of powder on the chest of my shirt and jacket. I brush it off and as I breathe harder, more speckles appear. I wipe my nose with my fingers and brush my jacket once again. I look up and feel like a rabbit caught in the headlights. My face suddenly begins to glow with embarrassment and I decide to come clean.

"I can't take it anymore. I am supposed to get involved in this lifestyle to fit in, but when I go home, I cannot switch off. I feel like I have not slept properly in months. I put on this front with them and at the same time I am supposed to gain information, but anytime I ask questions they look at me like I am some sort of leper."

"We are not judging you, we know how hard this is for you, but we need you to be honest with us. We are here to help and assist you in this operation in any way that we can."

"I don't think I can do it anymore. I know the whole operation is to gain their contacts but they never mention them. I have been there when Ginge receives a call on a certain mobile. The numbers do not even have names attached to them. He recognises the number and walks off before answering it."

"How did you manage to overhear the conversation with Ryan and Screw-face?"

"What. By chance"

"Exactly" Whyte confirms. "And that's how you will find out the information we need. By chance, stop trying too hard, don't ask questions, just take a step back from the situation and get involved only when they ask."

"Only get involved when they ask... That night those officer beat Ryan in front of his wife and kids, I was seconds from getting out of the car to get involved. They hit his dog to manipulate him so that they could beat him up. If I was in the same situation I would have done the same, anybody would have."

"Brody you can't let the action of one policeman ruin your whole judgment in this case. You are willing to give up and walk out on a promising career for one incident."

"But it's not only one incident, is it? They are bullies, the lot of them, they held me down in that cell and took turns in beating me, now they have beat my brother in front of his wife and kids. That whole situation could have been diffused in seconds, but I watched them, they wanted him to attack, he wasn't resisting and they knew it."

"Brody those were two completely different incidents and we'll deal with yours as soon as this operation comes to an end. However, with Ryan, okay, the leading officer was possibly out of line, but Ryan confronted those officers, he had a weapon and was intent on using it, he had also spent the whole day beating up defenceless drug addicts, people with severe problems. He was ruthless and a Bully."

With the images of Ryan's wife and daughter screaming, still fresh in my head, it is very hard for Whyte's spin on it to have any effect on the situation for me. The only part of his little speech that has any effect on me is his part about me throwing away a promising career.

"I want out" I hear myself say.

Whyte lets out a sigh and turns to Drummond. He then turns to face me and takes his time before speaking.

"We can do that" Whyte nods "Although, we do have another problem....Jamie is still missing."

I shrug.

"Is it possible that you could stay under until he shows up?"

"What if he doesn't show up?"

"If he doesn't show up in the next week or so, then we would have reason to believe that something may have happened to him," Drummond says.

"And you are our best option to find out exactly what that is" Whyte adds.

Drummond continues "If Ginge or any of his crew have anything to do with his disappearance, this could be the break in the operation that we need."

"Why would this help the case?"

"Think about it, Brody. If we can get something like this on any of them, it may be enough for one of them to talk."

I suddenly sit up straight when I realise where they are going with this.

"I see that we have your full attention once again," Whyte says leaning forward in his chair.

"I guess you do."

"So you'll stay."

I hesitate for a few seconds and my mind is so confused right now, but I feel myself nodding in their direction.

"Glad to hear it" Drummond gives me an encouraging nod.

"Is that all?"

They both look at each other and turn to give me a nod.

"Okay Brody, I'm glad that you have decided to stay on the team and we have every faith in you that you can finally bring a positive result to this operation."

I stand up to leave and the second I walk out the door, the whole 'still on the team' thing is put to the back of my mind as my hand slips in my pocket and I run my finger over the seal of the bag. I reach the receptionist and turn the corner. I pass the toilet and the thought crosses my mind to go back in there but I keep walking. I feel as though they have given me a green light to continue what I was doing. I get in my car and pull out the bag. I pour a little of the powder onto the dashboard to the side of the steering wheel. I use a card to make it into a straight line and pull out the readily rolled note. I tighten the roll until the shape resembles a drinking straw. While letting out some air from my lungs I lean over the steering wheel with the note close to my nose. In one long hard sniff, the powder is gone. I sit back in the seat and look at the large police sign in front of me. I start the engine and make my way out of the car park, ready to continue being 'part of the team.' I glance down at Leanna's mail on the passenger seat. I suppose I had better swing passed her parents' house before I drive back to Dundee, it could be something important. I pull into her street and the first thing I notice is her old man's car in the driveway. I get out of the car and as I walk to the door, a sudden bout of anti-socialness comes over me, so I make an instant decision to put the letters through the door and sneak off.

"I tried to call you."

I hear a voice behind me. I turn to see her old man by the door holding the letters.

"Yeah I eh, had to change my number."

"You seem to do that a lot lately."

"Yeah, it's work" I shrug "Why were you trying to call me?"

He steps out further from his doorway and looks around his neighbour's windows suspiciously as though one of them is listening. "You'd better come in."

I follow him into the living room and he turns to face me.

"Look this has been really hard for me to deal with but I need to tell you, Leanna was raped."

"When"

"A few nights ago, she was out with friends..."

"...is she in?" I ask, cutting him off and walking towards the stairs to her bedroom.

I walk in and the TV is on but she is not watching it. She is lying on her side staring at the wall.

"Leanna"

"Brody, what are you doing here?"

"I came to drop off your mail. Your dad told me what happened."

I sit on the bed and lean down to hug her.

"Did you go to the police?"

She nods "They weren't very helpful though. They said that they will question him but he could say that I consented so then it would be my word against his."

"Who is he? Do you know him?"

"No, he was a friend of a friend. We were all at a house party and you know I am not much of a drinker so during the night I felt a bit tipsy so I went for a lie-down, the next thing I know, I woke up naked and he was on top of me. I froze. I could not even scream for help, it was like a nightmare. I eventually tried to push him off but he was too strong, the more I fought, the more excited he seemed to get. When he finished, he got off me and started laughing as though it was some big joke."

"Who is he?"

"Ross Kirkcaldy"

I lean down and put both my arms around her and I can feel myself shaking with anger. Thoughts are rushing through my head of what I want to do to this guy, it is making my heart beat so fast and with the cocaine in my system, I feel that it is about to explode. I pull myself away from her and we both sit up.

"Are you okay?"

"This is my fault. If I hadn't done what I did we wouldn't have broken up, and you wouldn't have been at that party."

"Brody this is not your fault."

I wrap my arms around her again "I'm sorry" I whisper in her ear.

"You've nothing to be sorry for." She pulls away to look at me "Well you do but it's nothing to do with this" She forces a smile.

I do not return it.

"I am, really sorry Leanna."

"It's okay. I'll deal with it."

She leans in to kiss me and I kiss her back. I do not know what this dirty rapist looks like but I have a random face in my mind of someone on top of her, naked and laughing. I pull away.

"I'm sorry, I need to go"

"Okay."

"I want to stay but this is really important."

"It's okay. I understand."

"I'll leave you my new number. Please call me if you need anything."

"Okay, I will" She forces another smile.

"I'm really sorry" I say as I walk out of her room.

I hurry down the stairs to see her father waiting.

"Brody can I have a word."

"I really am in a hurry" I edge closer towards the front door.

"I'll get straight to the point then. Look, I know this goes against the principles of your job, but I want that bastard to suffer."

I nod in agreement.

"Would it be possible for you to get me an address?"

"And if I did happen to get this address."

He leans towards me gritting his teeth "I'll do fucking time for what he's done."

"I believe you." I nod. "And If I wasn't in the job I was in, I would probably be doing the time alongside you, but I need to explain something. At this moment in time, I am probably more in a position to get that job done than I have ever been, with no questions asked."

"Is that right?"

"You don't know the half of it...Leave it to me."

He nods and pats me on the arm.

I walk out of the house and the fresh air hits me. I feel a little light headed as I walk to my car. I take a few deep breaths and try to take in the conversation that I have just had. I need to talk to Ginge. I pull out my phone. Fuck. What am I doing, this is not a phone conversation? I need to see him urgently, but first...I run my finger over the sealed bag.

Chapter 46

Ten minutes after leaving Leanna, my mind is going crazy with the image of this dirty little rapist on top of her, grinning in the dark with his fucking penis inside of her. I do not think I have ever been in such a rush to get back to Dundee. The cocaine in my system must be at its peak as I am driving like a maniac, flashing people in the fast lane to move over so that I can pass them. When they stubbornly do not move over I quickly drive into the inside lane and undertake them. I look at each one of them as I pass and each face I see is the face of Leanna's rapist. If using a mobile phone while my speed dial touches 100mph to 110mph, or the constant undertaking isn't enough to get me a heavy fine or lengthy ban, I think the high level of cocaine in my system would definitely have me locked up for quite a while. What is worse is the reason why I am in such a hurry. I am about to conspire to have someone tortured. Ginge's phone keeps going straight to answerphone and the only numbers I have are Ryan's, which is clearly no good anymore, Tanya's, and one of Ginge's three numbers, which by the looks of things, he has already changed. I come off the bridge and head for the Claver, if he is not there it is my best chance of someone knowing where he is. When I enter, the place is close to empty. The barman notices me looking around and points me towards the booths up the back.

"I'm looking for Ginge."

He points again.

I walk towards one of the booths where Ginge, Joe and Hunter are sitting.

"Fucking hell Brody, how much of that coke have you taken?" Joe says as all three stare at me.

"What do you mean?"

"Brody your eyes are bulging, you look as though you are about to rip your own face off." Ginge says sounding concerned.

"I need to talk to you."

"I'm listening."

"It's personal."

"Okay, I hear you. Why don't you go ahead to the toilet and throw some water on your face, I'll be right behind you" Ginge nods.

I walk back through the pub towards the toilet and I suddenly feel a little paranoid as though everyone is staring at me. I turn the tap on and run it for a few seconds so that the colder water comes through. I cup my hands and throw it in my face. I lift up my head to see Ginge standing behind me. He wanders along checking that the cubicles are empty.

"Nobody here" He makes a face. "What's up?"

"My girlfriend in Edinburgh, Leanna, she was raped the other night."

"Your girlfriend, I thought that was over."

"Yeah, well, it's complicated."

"Complicated?" Ginge smiles "Have you got a name?"

"Yeah, it was some guy she knew from way back."

Ginge gives me a look. "I need the name."

"Oh, it's Kirkcaldy...Ross Kirkcaldy."

Ginge nods as he searches in his jacket for one of his mobiles. He pulls out two of them and compares the markings he has made to distinguish between them.

"Look Ginge, you know I would do this myself but with me already being questioned about that hit and run, getting involved with this would bring too much attention to me."

"Brody, shh it's okay, I'll take care of it." He says putting one of the mobiles to his ear.

He turns his head and mumbles in a low tone before turning back to me.

"What was the name again Brody?"

"Ross, Kirkcaldy."

"Do you know anything about him? Anything at all"

"I'm sure she said he was a plumber, I think he works offshore."

"That narrows it down." He says raising his eyebrows.

He turns his head away once again and mumbles for a few seconds before hanging up.

"It'll be sorted. Is there anything else?"

"No that was it."

"Okay, go and throw some more water on your face. I'll order you up a drink, you look like you need one...oh and Brody, cool it with that coke."

I nod "Thanks for this" I say as he is halfway out the toilet door.

He turns back. "No need to thank me, it's all favours." He winks before the door shuts behind him.

It is all favours. I say over in my head, repeatedly. If he can pick up the phone and have something like that sorted in less than a minute, here's to the favours he has done...or is owe, or maybe he means I owe the favour, but to whom? Fuck. I throw some more water on my face and the cold water shocks me enough to bring me to my senses a little. What the fuck have I done? Earlier today I was ready to walk away, I told them straight, what the fuck happened? In the space of a few hours I have totally lost sight of why I am here, I am now one of them. What the fuck is happening to me? I bang my fist on the wall. I have a horrible anxiety flowing through me and my head feels as though it is ready to explode. I turn and punch the door. Somehow, I had an image of my fist going through it but the door is solid, it does not even leave a mark, well except the reddish dot on my knuckle. I punch it again with my other hand. The pain in both knuckles has made the anxiety subside. I open the toilet door as someone else is coming in and I can't help but think how awkward that could have been if he was a few seconds earlier, but then again, randomly punching toilet doors isn't out of the ordinary in this pub.

I head over to the booth and slide in next to Joe.

"That one is yours Brody" Hunter points to a full pint amongst the various half-filled ones.

"Oh, cheers" As I reach over for it, I notice my knuckle is now glowing red. I take a sip from the glass and discreetly put both of my hands down by my sides out of view.

"So what's the latest on Junkie Jamie, any sign of him?"

They all shake their heads and I am tempted to ask more questions but there is an eerie moment of silence along with a few strange looks and this brings on a sudden bout of anxiety. I reach over for my glass and take another sip.

"Joe for fuck sake, do me a favour and phone your guy to get some Valium dropped off for Brody here will you?"

I look up to see Hunter smiling and Ginge shaking his head at me.

"Why what's wrong?"

"What's wrong?"

"Brody in the five minutes since you've sat down you've been fidgeting about in that seat and playing with that glass as though it's Tanya's nipple.

We've got a situation here that we're trying to figure out and you being in that state is not fucking helping."

"What situation, wait, what state?"

Ginge raises his eyebrows at me. "Joe, can show him the video once you've made the call?"

"What video?"

Joe finishes his call and flicks through the screen on his phone. He leans towards me and holds out his phone for me to see. It is footage from a house party where someone is ranting about sorting out the McNaughton's for the last time. 'One down two to go' he says with a grin, clearly referring to Ritchie's death. The next time that he sees Ginge, he is going to slice him up while making slashing motions with his hand. Before the video cuts off, he comments that he is going to petrol bomb the Wise Mans house while his kids are sleeping.

"What the fuck?" I glance up at Joe and then back to the phone, which has now stopped playing.

"When was this filmed?"

"It was sent to me an hour ago?"

I want to ask more questions but I stall. I reach for my glass again while I try to think of something to say other than Junkie Jamie.

"So I guess it's going to be a busy night?"

"I guess it is" Ginge says.

I take a long slow drink as I contemplate the night ahead and now understand the silence around the table. I assume they are planning the details of how to remove this person from the house party and have him dragged away to be tortured.

"Joe I think that's your guy" Hunter says.

Joe and I turn to see someone standing by the pub door. I move to let Joe out of his seat and he waves to attract his attention. Joe signals to him and he swaggers across the middle of the pub towards the toilet.

"Just go and see him, Brody. He knows what you need...well, he will once he looks at you." They all laugh.

"Why didn't you just tell him to come over here? With the shit that goes on in this pub, selling a few Valium isn't exactly a big deal"

"Because we are discussing business here, and Joe knows when to respect that" Ginge says sternly.

I trudge across the pub floor with my head bowed having been put in my place, well, what exactly could I say to that. I open the toilet door to see Joe's acquaintance pacing back and forward.

He tilts his head for me to follow him into the cubicle.

"It's cool. You're okay in here mate"

"No, I've been warned before to keep it discreet."

"Yeah, by whom"

"An older fella, big guy"

I am about to say Buster but I let it go and follow him into the cubicle.

"How many you needing?" He says pulling out a small bag full of blue pills.

"I'm not sure. I've only ever taken them to help me sleep but apparently I'm a bit too wired"

He looks up at me "Yeah you do look a bit wired. Tell you what. I will give you four, two for now, to mellow you out, and two for later to get your head down."

"Sounds good"

I watch as he tries to fish the pills out of the small bag with his grubby fingers.

"Actually I'll take a few extra. How many have you got there?"

He holds the bag up to eye level and does a quick count. "There's probably about twenty in there."

"Fuck it, I'll take them all."

Without a hint of hesitation, he holds the bag out in front of me. I take it from him and hand over the money. We exit the cubicle and before the toilet door has even closed behind him, I have two of the blue pills in my mouth. There is a dry taste to them and as I walk back to the booth, they have crumbled to a powder in my mouth. I sit down and reach for my drink, taking several large gulps to wash them down.

"Brody you might want to wipe your mouth" Hunter frowns.

"For fuck sake Brody" Ginge says.

"What. What now?"

"You have blue froth all around your lips" Joe says in a low tone.

I pull my arm across my mouth and the blue remnants transfer to the sleeve of my jacket.

"Oh fuck."

"Most of it has come off, wipe it again" Joe says.

I do it with my other arm and the blue remnant appears on the opposite sleeve.

"That's it, it's all off."

I use my hand to try to rub the blue from my jacket but it only works it further into the material.

"Right, I think I've figured out what to do" Ginge says leaning forward in his seat. "First thing, Joe, get the mate that sent the video to you to send you the guys number and also let us know the minute he leaves that house party."

I glance to Joe as he pulls out his phone and the blue on the sleeve of my jacket catches my eye. I put my finger in my mouth and wipe some saliva to try to help remove the blue but this only seems to make it worse and it now appears even more obvious.

"Brody, this is important, forget the fucking jacket, it'll wash out."

"Sorry." I stare at him to give my full attention.

"We need to pick up another phone. Joe?"

"I can get one."

"Actually I have one in the house, we'll swing passed mine and pick it up. We also need a squeeze bottle filled with petrol."

"Sorted" Joe says.

"Brody give Hunter your car keys."

"Why? I'll drive."

"Sorry but right now, you're a liability. Give Hunter the keys."

I hand over the keys and we all make our way out to the car. I sit in the front and even though Hunter is driving, Ginge is giving out the instructions. His usual laid back attitude and humour is now gone and every word that comes from his mouth is sharp and to the point, sounding more like commands. First stop is Ryan's street, as Ginge needs the house number of the neighbour that has been harassing him with his loud car. Hunter drives slowly up the street and we find his house easily due to his Subaru sitting in his driveway. There are no numbers on some of the doors so Hunter reverses and drives forward while we try to work them out. We lose count, and as he puts the car into reverse once again, Ginge snaps.

"Fuck this. Joe get your arse out there find out what number it is"

"I'm surprised Ryan didn't torch his car the first time it happened," Hunter comments while we all watch Joe run from one house to the other checking the numbers.

"Yeah, I'm sort of wondering that myself. It's worked in our favour though."

"21," Joe says in between breaths when he gets back in the car.

"Ok. Hunter, the lockups...Joe, you know what to do?"

"A Molotov"

"And the squeeze bottle. It doesn't need to be filled, just enough to make a few splashes."

"Do you want the car done as well?"

"No, you better not. That would be too obvious that it was a setup."

We drop Joe at the lockups and drive to Ginge's house. I wait in the car with Hunter while Ginge goes into the house to pick up another phone, he then instructs Hunter to drive towards the dual carriageway.

"What number did Joe say again, 21 was it?"

"21" Hunter confirms.

Ginge sends a text with the house number to the person in the party's phone.

"It's done" He immediately starts to dismantle the phone.

He snaps the sim card in two before throwing all the pieces of the phone out of the window. When we drive back to pick up Joe he is standing by the kerb holding a plastic carrier bag. As soon as he gets in, the smell of petrol fills the car.

"I've just received a text, the guy in the party is well on and has mentioned several times that he is going home."

"Text him back Joe and tell him to try and persuade him to stay for another drink, the drunker he gets, the better. Brody, this where you come in, he doesn't know you, if he sees any of us three, he will click that something's up."

I turn in the seat to face him. "So what is it you need me to do?"

"The guy you saw in the video, he is about to leave the party. I need you to hang around near the house and wait on him. When he leaves, you run towards him, and as you pass him, squirt some petrol down the leg of his trousers. If you can get some on his trainers, even better, but you must do it from the front. Do you think you can manage that?"

"Of course"

Joe hands over a pair of rubber gloves. "Here, you better wear these, keep the squeeze bottle as far from you as you can when you use it."

I take the gloves from him and stretch them over my hands. Hunter pulls into a bus stop by the side of the road.

"Right Brody, he's going to come out of that block of flats across the road, apparently he stays a few streets away from here so don't leave it too late. As soon as you see him, run ahead, cross the road and run towards him, spraying him as you pass. That is it, job done. We have another little job to do, so we'll meet you back at this bus stop."

Joe lifts up the plastic bag and opens it. I reach in and take out the plastic squeeze bottle.

"Keep the gloves, I'll need them later" Joe says.

"Oh and Brody" I turn back to Ginge as I get out of the car. "Don't fuck this up" He says sternly.

I close the door and the car takes off at speed. I stand and watch the lights fade into the distance and then disappear as it turns at the end of the road. I look up and down the street and decide my best position to view the entrance to the block is a small garden wall, several metres from the bus stop. With the block now directly in front of me, I stare up at each window to try to work out which one has the party going on. I rule out two of them that have their lights out and with a few shadow movements going on behind a few curtains, the only way I could really tell is if I was close enough to hear the music. My concentration moves from one window to the other and occasionally up and down the street, I also keep my eye on the blocks at either side. I start to feel a mellow sensation coming over me and I realise the Valium must be kicking in. Ginge's last words of 'Don't fuck this up' keep going through my head and when I check my watch, I start to think that maybe I've been staring at a certain area too long and the guy has come out unnoticed. I decide my best option would be to take a line of coke to keep me more alert. I pull out the small bag and roll a note. A quick sniff into the bag and I am soon perked up and watching every single movement behind every curtain, including the entrance to the block, all at the same time. With still no movement, I start to think that maybe I really have missed him. I check the time again and prepare to call Ginge with the bad news. The second I dial his number I hear voices from across the street. I hang up when I see several people appear at the block entrance. I recognise the person from the video straight away. I overhear them mention taxi. Fuck, what if he is not going home. Should I run over now? I stand up from the wall with the squeeze bottle in one hand and my phone in the other. A taxi pulls up and it is one of those large taxis, which block my view. Fuck, fuck fuck. I am seconds from pressing Ginge's number once again. The taxi drives off leaving the person standing. Relieved, I place my phone back in my pocket while watching him wave to the people in the taxi. I walk parallel with to him as he staggers along the pavement. I wait until he is a fair bit from the block and then I start to walk faster up the street. I break into a light jog and once I am far enough ahead, I cross the road and turn to face him. I jog slowly towards him and place my arm down by my side with the squeeze bottle facing outwards. With only several meters between us, I reach out further and squeeze the bottle hard. I catch a glimpse of it hitting his jeans and trainers as I pass. I speed up once I pass and do not look back. I keep running until I pass the block of flats and then I slow down to a fast walk. I clock a drain by the side of the road and reach down to squirt out the rest of the bottle and place it in a bin outside one of the other blocks. I cross the road and slow my pace down further to a stroll. While walking back I see my car pull into the bus stop up ahead, I wave to get their attention and Hunter drives towards me with Ginge up front.

"All good" Ginge asks.

"All good"

I start to peel off the rubber gloves.

"Just keep them on. You can do the next job as well."

I shrug "What is it?"

"Joe will explain."

He reaches down and lifts the carrier bag from between his feet.

"Careful with this, keep it in the bag for now, in case you spill it. You need this too" He hands me a ski mask.

With the feel of the bag and the smell, I do not need to open it to know that it is a glass bottle filled with petrol.

"Have you done this before?"

"No, but I've had to dodge a few over the years when I was on the front line" I smile to myself in the dark. My humour lost on them.

"Ginge are you sure you don't want me to do it?" Joe says.

"No, I want Brody to do it" Ginge insists.

I feel a little pressure, as though Ginge is testing me, but I brush it off. "I'll be fine, I'll manage."

Hunter pulls in at the end of Ryan's street.

"Okay Joe, this is your forte, show him what to do."

He reaches over and takes the bottle from the bag.

"Okay, when you throw it, hold it here." He demonstrates. "If you hold it here, or here, you will end up with a sleeve covered in petrol and if the flame hits it...it will be goodnight Brody"

He hands me back the bottle and pulls out a lighter.

"Now when you light it, make sure it is well lit, let it burn close to the top of the bottle."

"We're going to drive two streets up, you walk down slowly, do the job and run to the next street, take off the ski-mask and walk to the next one, don't run. Look for the car. We'll be parked with the lights off." Ginge says.

I pull the ski mask over my head before stepping out of the car.

"Do you remember the house?"

"Yeah"

"It has a Subaru in the driveway, you can't miss it."

"I remember" I snap.

"Okay, just checking...Oh and Brody...Don't fuck this up"

They drive off and I stand and stare at the scene in front of me. It reminds me of an old painting, a wide road with large trees and dimmed streetlights up both sides of the pavement. There is an unusual pattern of lights from homes where people are going about their business, relaxing after a long day at work, putting their kids to bed or catching up on their favourite television programs. And then there is me, an undercover policeman, a person in a position of authority, whose job it is to protect them while they go about their business behind those closed doors, but no, I am about to disrupt each one of their cosy lives by bringing an act of extreme violence straight to their doorstep...Why? Well, there are two ways of looking at this, one is that an absolute dickhead of a neighbour has been terrorising a family with young kids and very nervous dog, even after numerous warnings to back off. The other way of looking at it is simply, his car is just too fucking loud. I reach the driveway of the Subaru, and when I look up, I feel a bit relieved that all the lights are out. I am hoping that he is not home. If he is, it is highly likely that he will be in bed and will escape easily. The last thing I need is a dead body on my conscience. I do not think I could cope, the 'I was just doing my job' will not really cover it. I glance down the street and give each house a long hard stare for any movement. I ignite the piece of material hanging from the end of the bottle. The flame starts to work its way up the material quickly so I step over his garden wall and walk towards the living room window. I reach back with the bottle the way Joe instructed me, and without any hesitation, I launch it into the centre of the window. There is a loud smash and before I even get a chance to see the flame take hold, I have stepped back over the garden wall and I am running up the street. Before I turn into the next street, I take a quick look over my shoulder to see the intense blaze. I want to continue running but I keep to Ginge's instructions and slow down to a light jog. I pull the ski mask off and slow to a walking pace. I reach the next street and as I walk towards the car up ahead, an image of the person that I sprayed with petrol enters my mind. He will no doubt wake up from his drunken stupor in a few hours' time, unexpectedly arrested, and shipped straight off to Perth to face an eagerly awaiting Ryan. I attempt to walk faster but my legs are like jelly and my heart is beating so fast I think it is about to pop. I stop at the car door and take a few deep breaths.

"All good" Ginge's asks as I fall heavily into the back of the car.

I struggle to answer with my dry mouth but I manage to splutter a reply "All good."

Hunter casually drives off.

Chapter 47

I open my eyes to see the shape of Tanya's naked slim curves in front of me. I am awake but still in the drowsy in-between stage of actually getting up. I pull the cover up over my shoulder and close my eyes again. I can hear a low beeping noise from my phone but I am too comfortable to reach for it. I also think that if I focus long enough to see the screen it will bring to much reality to my in-between moment, I am not ready for that yet. I pull the covers tight around my head to block out the beeping...some time passes but I cannot tell if I psychologically blocked out the noise or if I dozed off again, either way, the fucking beeping is still going on, hopefully, the battery will go flat and it stops. 'Beep...Beep...Beep' ...Fuck, I pull the covers from my face and open my eyes. The beeping is from beyond Tanya. I rise and see the phone next to her on the chest of drawers. There is a small light flashing each time it beeps. I reach over Tanya and grab the phone. It is only nine o'clock and I have eight missed calls. One from Leanna and the rest from Ginge, there is also a message from Ginge.

'Phone me when you are up'

Glancing at the wonderful view laid out in front me, and knowing that Leanna has called me, has left me feeling somewhat guilty, especially after swearing to myself yesterday that I was not going to come back here. If I remember correctly I couldn't get here quick enough, but the worst thing about it, is that I drove here with one thing on my mind, to take more Valium, actually I didn't even wait until I got here, I didn't even stop the car, I swallowed them while sat at the traffic lights the minute I left Ginge. I suppose I had better call him back. I sit on the edge of the bed as I try to locate my clothes. I find my boxers and t-shirt and go through to the kitchen. I decide to make coffee first but the second I put the kettle on, Ginge is calling again.

"Hello" I groan.

"You just up?"

"Yeah...what's going on, why are you calling so early?"

"Early?"

"Yeah, it says nine on my phone."

I pull the phone from my ear to double check. Yep, nine

"It's nine at night Brody."

I walk over and pull the curtains to see the blur of the streetlights.

"Oh."

"We have another job on. Pick us up at the Claver when you're ready."

I go to reply but the line cuts off.

 I sit down with my coffee and when I reach for the remote to turn on the TV, I have a double take, lying on the table next to the remote are two lines of coke. Tanya must have left them for us to wake up to. I know it was not me as the lines are perfectly straight and lying parallel to a neatly rolled note. I take a sip of my coffee and place it down before picking up the rolled note. I contemplate her train of thought last night that she thought I would be generous to leave her a line when I woke up, and then I lean over the table and sniff up both of them. By the time I have finished my coffee my whole body is tingling. I go to the bathroom and when I look in the mirror the image feels like a stranger staring back at me.. Maybe I should not have been so greedy and taken both lines. I creep quietly into the bedroom and find the rest of my clothes. Before walking out the door, I look back at Tanya sleeping soundly. As much as I tell myself never to come back here, looking at her perfect body it is enough for any man to keep coming back here. I slip into my jeans and search the pockets to find the bag with Valium. Fuck! It is empty. Curiously, I delve deeper into the corner of my pocket and the tip of my finger touches them.

 "Yes" I whisper to myself.

 I fish them out, four little blue pills. I pop two in my mouth and head to the kitchen for a drink. I leave the flat quietly and walk down to the car, I am still trying to convince myself that I will not come back here. Driving off I hear a low thud coming from under the car. It stops for a bit and starts again when I hit a rough part of the road. I vaguely remember the thud on the way to Tanya's last night. I can only assume it was when Hunter was driving it. I wonder what damage he has done, it sounds as though he has maybe hit a speed bump or a pothole too quickly, the cunt. I will need to check it in the daylight. The Claver is busy when I enter and I notice Buster by the bar. I can see that he is well on, so I try discreetly to sneak by him.

"Hey, hey" I feel his arm around me.

He pulls me close and straight away, I can smell the strong stench of stale alcohol. He has clearly been on the drink all day as he slavers some nonsense in my ear. Over his shoulder, I notice Ginge In the corner. He grins and gives me the thumbs up, a sarcastic 'good luck' gesture at having our highly intoxicated father capture me for a talk. He releases his arm and I smile and nod while patting him on the shoulder while trying to pass him without offending him.

"Have a drink son."

"No, I'm fine. I'll get one shortly I just need to have a word with…"

"Have a fucking drink with your old man."

"I will, I just need to have a …

"Fuck them, whoever they are, they can wait, come on, you're having a drink with me." He gestures to the barman by pointing at his pint and putting up two fingers. After surrendering to Busters demands, I turn to face the bar in defeat. While he jibbers in my ear about his family and his boys, he suddenly stops mid-sentence to order us a couple of shots. No sooner have we threw them back but he has ordered two more.

"No Buster, I can't. I'm driving."

"One more, come-on"

I look over at Ginger who is in deep conversation with Joe.

"Okay, fuck it. One more"

"That's my boy."

I clink the shot glass with Busters and knock it back. As soon as I slam it down on the bar, I walk around Buster and make my way over towards Ginge.

"Here, take this seat" Ginge nods at Joe to move.

I wave him off but Ginge insists "Joe has an errand to run" He says patting Joes vacated seat.

"What's the old man been saying?"

I look back at Buster who has now moved onto his next victim by the bar. "Something about being proud of his boys"

Ginge moves in close to my ear "I have a surprise for you tonight."

"I'm not really sure if that's a good thing coming from you."

"Oh, it's good, you'll like it."

"I thought you said we had a job on."

"It's a bit of both" He winks.

"Listen I don't think it's a good idea for me to drive, I've just been caught up doing shots with Buster."

"That's okay, someone else will drive."

"That's fine, as long as it's not Hunter," I raise my voice to gain his attention but he does not acknowledge. "My car has had a dull knocking sound. Did you guys hit a pothole or something?"

"Hunter...HUNTER!" Ginge shouts "Brody says you're not allowed to drive his car again as there's a noise coming from it, did you hit something?"

He shrugs "I don't think so...maybe" He smiles back at Ginge.

I lean back in the chair with a straight face, feeling annoyed. Ginge looks at me sympathetically.

"Brody, trust me, we took great care of your car. What benefit would it be for us if we damaged it?"

I nod "I suppose."

"Listen, Joe will be about twenty minutes, I'll get another drink in and we'll make a move."

I nod and when Ginge goes to go the bar, I head for the toilet. I stand by the urinal and think about the last two pills in my pocket. If I am honest, they have been on my mind since the second Ginge mentioned that someone else would drive. I place one in my mouth with the intention of keeping one for later, by the time I turn to rinse my hands, I have the other one in my mouth and am cupping water from the tap to wash both of them down. I will pull Joe aside after the job to hook me up for more. I am back in my seat before Ginge has returned from the bar. He places a drink in front of me.

"So what is this job tonight?"

"Let's just say it's a bit of retribution and also a test of loyalty."

"You've got me intrigued, I feel a bit hesitant now."

He puts his hand on my shoulder and grips it affectionately "Brody I'm your brother, I'm your blood, trust me."

He leans away from me and we both turn to see Joe back sooner than we expected.

"All good"

Joe twists a little to show a backpack over his shoulder "All good"

"Okay boys, drink up" He says rising to his feet.

I pick up my pint and start taking large gulps.

"Brody I didn't mean that literally. It was a euphemism for 'time to fucking go'"

I place my drink back on the table and use my sleeve to wipe the remnants from my mouth. After handing the car keys over to Hunter, I am the last to leave the table and I feel myself taking bigger steps to catch up with them as they walk through the pub. Hunter and Ginge stand by the nearside doors and I know I am not driving so when Ginge signals for me to get in I know I am about to be wedged between him and Larnio. We drive off and seconds later, I hear the knocking and it seems louder than before.

"Do you guys hear that knocking? It wasn't like that yesterday."

"Are you still blaming me for it, Brody?" Hunter asks.

"I'm not blaming anybody, it's just a bit of a coincidence that it wasn't like that when I gave you it but it's been happening since I got it back."

Hunter turns the stereo up louder.

"I can't hear anything" He shouts while glancing at me in the mirror.

With no instructions from Ginge about this job that we are on, I start to get a little curious when we make our way through the city centre and onto the Tay Road Bridge.

"So where is this job?" I ask.

"It's out of the way a bit. Don't worry, we've done the reconnaissance, it's all checked out."

I still have no idea as to what the job is, but I have learned not to ask too many questions, so I do not say anything further. We travel along a tight country road for several miles and Hunter turns into an open gateway with no signpost. The road is rough and appears more for tractor type vehicles, he has slowed down considerably but the journey is still bumpy and the knocking from the car is much louder as we drive over each bump. Joe unzips his holdall and passes around the ski masks. Ginge puts his on but rolls it up away from his face. I notice Larnio also do this so I adjust mine so it is the same. At a turning point in the road, Hunter turns off the music and stops the car. In the darkness, I can make out a path next to the road that leads to an overgrown field lined with trees. Joe gets out of the car with his backpack and walks around to Ginge's side. He opens the door while rummaging in the backpack. He pulls out a handgun and hands it to Ginge.

"Safety's on."

He rummages again and pulls out another handgun "Safety's on"

"Good work Joe. You know the drill." Ginge closes the door and they wait until Joe is out of sight up the path before driving on. We come to another turning point in the road but we move from the tracks and drive partially into the woodland. Hunter kills the lights and keeps driving forward slowly for another twenty to thirty metres and stops. In the darkness, I can hear a sound that I know too well, the safety release from one of the handguns that Ginge has in his lap. He pulls back the barrel and slides it forward manually. He pulls the magazine down and slams it back in until it clicks. He does the same with the other handgun and then hands one to me. Ginge opens the car door to get out and Hunter and Larnio follow suit. With my head full of questions, I continue sitting in the car while running my hand over the gun. Then I suddenly realise that I can still hear the knocking from the car, even though it is not moving. I step out to see the three of them standing by the boot.

"I take it this is where the knocking was coming from?"

"Surprise" Ginge says enthusiastically.

They all stand firm as I move in closer to the boot. I press the button to open it. The interior light comes on to reveal someone curled up in the foetal position, cable tied and blindfolded. Hunter and Larnio lift him from the boot and he starts to kick out. Hunter lets his feet fall and Ginge steps forward and smacks him in the head with the handle of the gun.

"Stop struggling, you fucking dirty little beast." He shouts at him as he lies in a heap on the ground.

Hunter lifts him to his knees.

"Is this...?"

"This is him" Ginge confirms.

"But I thought your mate was going to take care of him."

"I arranged to have him brought here. I thought you would have preferred to do it yourself."

"I only wanted him beat up bad, I didn't want him killed."

"Yeah well, we found out a bit more about him, he's done this twice before, both cases were dropped, he's also been beaten up before for the same thing and he still went on to do it your Leanna. This filthy scumbag is never going to stop. He will go on and on until someone stops him, permanently."

"So you expect me to shoot him?" I let out a nervous laugh.

"Hunter, Larnio" Ginge states their names.

Hunter shines a torch in his face while Larnio unties the blindfold. His eyes are deep and creepy. They are not what I was expecting. His mouth is still taped shut and he looks as though he has had a severe beating with patches of dried blood all over him.

"I can't do it" I turn away.

"Brody I risked a lot to get him here for you. What's the problem?"

"I just can't do it."

"Brody you were on the front line, you must have shot and killed plenty of people. People that were just like you, innocent people that were brainwashed into fighting for their country, probably never hurt anyone in their entire lives, now you're hesitating to put a bullet through someone that raped your girlfriend, your precious Leanna."

"That was different, those people were about to kill me, this is an unarmed man, this feels more like an execution."

"Untie him" Ginge shouts.

Larnio pulls out a blade and cuts the cable ties from his ankles and wrists. Ginge steps towards him and holds out his handgun. The person takes it from him

"There, now he's armed" He snaps... "Now shoot the fucker and get this over with."

I watch the person get to his feet and turn to make a run for it.

"BRODY" Ginge shouts.

I jolt forward in an attempt to make chase but he stumbles and falls over. He turns on the ground and as Hunter quickly points the torch in his direction, I see the shine of metal from the gun pointing towards me. I hear the light click of him attempting to press the trigger but the safety catch is on. I automatically react by squeezing the trigger from the gun in my hand, and a familiar blast echoes through the air. I keep the gun pointing at him as I wait for the slightest movement. Once the echo starts to fade, there is silence all around me. Hunter moves in closer with the torch and I see the small hole in his cheek where the round entered his face and there is a large pool of blood quickly gathering at the back of his head.

"It's okay Brody, you can lower the gun, he's isn't moving"

Ginge steps towards me and takes the gun from my hand. He leans down and picks up the other handgun from Kirkcaldy.

"You know you've done the right thing, Brody."

"The right thing" I mumble.

Chapter 48

The last time I woke up, I was so cold that even with the covers wrapped tight around me, I was still shivering violently. It did not help that the covers were also damp with sweat from the previous time that I had woken. Now, I can actually feel the drops of sweat rolling over my body. It would maybe be easier to get through this if I did not have the image of Kirkcaldy's face permanently in my mind. If only Larnio had not turned over his body. All I remember is the large whole where the bullet excited the back of his head. A sight that I had seen many times before, only, I was in a country of war, and it had become a standard daily occurrence. We would repeatedly remind ourselves that if it were not them, it would be one of us. If I had not received my exoneration to train to box, I would have still been there, continuing the kill or be killed way of life. I know Kirkcaldy tried to pull that trigger but he had feared for his life. I was the aggressor and he was only defending himself. What I did was cold-blooded murder. Fuck, fuck. I feel so ill. I need to sleep this off. I do not even know where I am, I must be in Tanya's, if I were in Leanna's she would be checking on me every ten minutes. I turn my head and make out a small glass of water glistening in the darkness, seeing this makes my mouth feel dry. I hardly have the energy to sit up but I manage to reach up and touch the glass. With my unsteady hand, I bring the glass to my lips and take a sip. I spill it down my chin and onto my chest, the cold forces me to sit up. I place the glass back on the side and attempt to wipe the remnants from the sheet. I slump my head back onto the damp pillow. I reach up for more Valium in the hope that another sleep will shake this off. I move my fingers around the base of the glass but I cannot find any. I touch my phone and pick it up to use the light to search. Fuck, I must have taken them all. Wait, I am not in Tanya's flat. I shine the phone around the room. I am in a hotel. I get up and go to the window. I know the street below. I am back in Edinburgh. I feel the shivers starting again, and I hurry back to the bed pulling the covers tight. I still have my phone in my hand, I need to check the time but I am shivering so much now I do not want to move and let any cold air under the covers. It would be pointless anyway, as I do not even know what day it is. I hear a creak from outside the room and my mind goes into overdrive, I curl up in a ball, listening intently, trying to make out every noise. My paranoia has me convinced that someone is coming to kill me. I begin to overheat so I throw back the covers, if they are here to kill me, the bed sheets are hardly going to stop them, and with the way that I am feeling right now, they would probably be doing me a favour. I stretch out on the bed and pick up my phone. There are several missed calls from Tanya and Leanna. Both have messaged me asking to get in touch, nothing from Ginge. I shrug myself further up the pillow and pick up the TV remote from the side unit. I channel hop back and forward to find something suitable but I struggle to find the energy to hold the remote mid-air. I pull the covers back over and turn on my side. I feel a rumble in my stomach and the thought of food gives my head a welcome break from the images of Kirkcaldy. If I were at Tanya's she would pick up the phone and order all kinds of tasty junk food. Leanna would probably cook me up something healthy or nip out to the shop at my request. I get up and switch on the tiny kettle in the room to make a coffee. I feel the rumble in my stomach again and I sit on the end of the bed as I contemplate having to leave the room to get some food. By the time the kettle boils, I have already decided to go for food. I reach down and pick up my clothes off the floor, as I pull the t-shirt over my head, I cannot tell what smells worse, the clothes or me. I pick up my phone as I go out the door. I guess this is out of habit, as I do not intend to call anyone. I head straight to the nearest takeaway but the small queue inside is enough to make me continue walking. I go into the mini supermarket next door and scan the isles for something appetizing but the smell from the takeaway is still lingering in my nose. I overcome my fear of contact and head back next door. I look up at the menu and the more I scan each board the more confused I am about what I want. I can tell the person at the counter is becoming impatient, as he stands tapping his pen waiting to write down my order.

"A pizza, a large pizza" I stutter.

"What you want on pizza" He says in his broken English.

"Cheese, a large pizza with cheese"

I pay him and turn towards the others waiting. A couple of them glance at me a little too long before looking away. I locate a vacant spot to stand and wait on my order. Subconsciously, I know the position is further back from anyone else so that I can avoid any more eye contact. The person at the counter is constantly taking orders in between serving the customers and it becomes a comfort when the shop empties and I am the only one left. I get back to the room and make another coffee before going back to bed with the pizza. I slowly devour each slice until there are only a couple left. I throw the box aside and drink the coffee. I curl up on the bed and flick through the TV channels but nothing keeps my attention long enough to stop my mind from the torment of what I have done. What the fuck happened to me? I had a great career in the army. I done my stint on the front line, I boxed for my country, I was unbeaten, I was up for promotion and could have had a cushy job as an instructor. I left it all to follow my childhood dream, and this is where it has led. I curl up and look away from the TV into the darkness. I need to put this right. This is not about the job anymore. It is not about Ryan or Ginge. This is about me. This is my life. Those two pricks Whyte and Drummond have pushed me too far. They knew I was in trouble, I had pleaded with them to pull me out but no, they had to push me that little bit further. I grit my teeth and punch the mattress. I sit up in bed and lean over for my phone. I dial my emergency number from memory. It rings out. I slump back onto the pillow. My mind starts to wander again when my phone startles me.

"Hello" Whyte answers.

"It's Brody."

"Brody is everything okay. You have not checked in for over a week. Where are you?"

"I'm out" I mumble.

"Okay."

"I mean I'm out. I'm off the case" I say firmly.

"Okay."

"I want my transfer. I want it immediately."

"You sound different. Are you sure everything is okay?"

"I'm fine. I just want my transfer."

"Is it okay to call you on this number?"

"Yeah"

"Okay. I'll call you tomorrow with a time and we'll sit down and discuss your options."

"No, no more discussing. As of now, I am off the case and I'm coming in to arrange my transfer."

"Okay. We can do that."

I hang up knowing that when I turn up tomorrow things will not go as smoothly as Whyte has confirmed. There will no doubt be some sort of catch to this whole thing. I need to think this through thoroughly. They have proven to manipulate any situation so I know they will have every angle covered which could fuck me over. I am not going to give them time to discuss it. I will be at their office first thing and demand a meeting on my terms. This will be my best option to catch them off guard. I set an alarm on my phone and place it to the side. I pull the covers over me and curl up on the bed with a more positive mind. My phone sounds several hours later and realising that it is the alarm, I bury my head under the covers hoping that it will stop. When I eventually reach over to turn it off, I notice that it is Leanna calling. I do not answer and minutes later, she sends a text to let me know that there has been a letter de-livered for me. I sit up in bed and call her back.

"Hi Brody, sorry for calling you so early but I thought this could be important, the letter has no stamp so it has been hand delivered."

"Really, what does it say?"

"It is hand written and says FAO D.C. BUCHANAN. I guess its work."

"Yeah it's work."

"But why would they put it through my door?"

"I called them last night to say I was off the case. I never mentioned where I was, so I assume they thought I was at yours."

"Do you want me to drop it off?"

"No I have a meeting with them early this morning. I'll swing passed on the way to their office."

Okay, I'll see you soon."

"Bye."

I wonder what they have sent out to me, I am hoping it will be my transfer forms but it will more than likely be some other document to fuck me over. Whatever it is, I need to be at their office before them and catch them unprepared, I will force them to have an emergency meeting. I leave the hotel and have to search around for my car, I find it parked in a space around the back, I am thankful that I was sane enough not to park it on double yellows, not that it would matter as I might not have it much longer. Once I declare how I acquired it, they will no doubt make me hand it over as evidence. I fucking love this car. I drive to my own flat and have a much needed shower, I dig out some clean clothes, no labels today.

I arrive at Leanna's and she meets me at the front door. She gives me a long hug and I follow her into the kitchen.

"Is your Dad not around?"

"No, he only took time off to be with me, but once I was up and about I told him to go back."

I lift my head in acknowledgment.

"It's okay Brody. He told me what he asked you to do."

The image of Kirkcaldy pointing the gun at me flashes through my head.

"I know it must have been hard for you to go against your principles with your job but I'm glad that bastard suffered."

I look at her a bit shocked that she is so open about having someone murdered. I am guessing rape must bring that out in someone. She places a newspaper in front of me, it lies open on a page with the headline 'Man tortured by thugs.'

"No mention of him being a filthy rapist though."

I read the first few lines about a young man who near bled to death after thugs broke into his flat and nailed his testicles to the floor. I skim quickly down the page to read details of the thugs slicing both sides of his cheeks. Then I read the name as though it has jumped off the page and is glowing in front of me 'Ross Kirkcaldy.'

"He's still alive?"

"Yeah, unfortunately"

"And he wasn't shot?"

"No it doesn't mention that he was shot." She says leaning over my shoulder to see the paper. "Wait, was he supposed to get shot?" She gives me a surprised look.

"No, I eh, I thought I read that somewhere, I must have it mixed up with something else that I had read."

I scan over it from the start, double-checking the details but my eyes keep focusing on his name. A sudden rush of heat comes over me. I take a deep breath and open a button on my shirt.

"Sorry Leanna but I need to go." I pass her the paper.

"Are you okay?"

"Yeah it's just this meeting, it's really important" I walk towards the front door.

"Brody, what's going on?"

I give her a strained look. "I need to go." I plead.

"Okay, please call me later."

"I promise."

"Oh the letter" She rushes off to the living room and comes back with the letter for me. I give it a quick glance.

"Thanks, I promise I'll call you okay." I step towards her and kiss her on the cheek.

I break into a light jog as I hurry to get to my car, I look up before I drive away and she is still by the door waving me off. Once I am out of sight, I pull over and tear open the envelope. A blank DVD disc falls out onto the seat, no note. I look at the envelope again. FAO D.C. BUCHANAN What the fuck is this. I throw it aside and drive out onto the dual carriageway in the direction of the Police Headquarters. I pass a small newsagent and try to read the headlines on the boards outside, I check the time. Fuck it! I make a sharp turn at the next junction and pull into the lay-by near the shop. I pick up several different newspapers and while making my way to the till, I am half expecting the police to swoop in and charge me with murder. I get back into the car and start flicking through every page searching for anything that remotely mentions a murder...nothing. I keep glancing down at the disc and then back to the clock. I turn in the road and head back to mine.

Chapter 49

I walk into my flat and go straight to the DVD player. I place it in the slot and stand back from the TV. The screen is black for a few seconds, then and a date appears in the corner of the screen, footage from a camcorder. I hear a few familiar voices but it is still too dark and out of focus. The camera changes to night vision and zooms in from a distance. It focuses on the back of a car, my car. It then hits me what and where this is. I know what is coming and I want to switch it off but I feel frozen to the spot. I hear someone mumbling and it sounds distorted, as though someone doing a voice over, it is not until the camera zooms in further that I realise the voice is mine.it. As the situation plays out, it is exactly how I remember it. Larnio reaches in to remove the persons blindfold and when I see those deep evil eyes, I know there is only one person that this could be...Junky Jamie. The camera zooms out slightly to take in the scene and I watch as he falls to the ground and turns to point the gun at me. There is a loud blast and a flash of light as his head blows backwards. I stand rooted to the spot until Ginge appears on the screen to take the gun from my hand. Clearly the person who made the disc was not satisfied with the whole set up, that they deliberately make a point of catching my face on screen and freezing it for a few seconds before the disc cuts off. It begins to play from the start again and just as I lean down to take the disc out of the machine, I look up and notice that apart from Jamie, who is still wearing a blindfold at this point, I am the only one with their face showing. Every single detail of this was set up for me. I stand back from the TV and call Ginge.

"Well hello there Mr. Movie Star."

"We need to talk" I demand.

"Well you know where to find me." He says with a hint humour in his voice before hanging up.

"Fuck." I throw my phone across the room. "Fuck"

I grab the disc with both hands and bend it until it snaps and then I step towards my TV and kick it over. "Fuck, Fuck, Fuck, Fuck"

I take a few deep breaths as I try to figure out what to do. Well for one thing, I guess he knows I'm undercover now, and I'm assuming there are other copies of the disc...I have no option, I need to go see him, I need to know what he plans to do with the footage. I pick my phone back up and march out to the car. With all the anger flowing through me, I am surprisingly calm as I make my way back to Dundee. My phone rings while crossing the bridge but I let it ring out, I know it will be Whyte or Drummond confirming a time for me to come in this morning. I head straight for the Claver, a place that I thought I would never have to set foot in ever again. I struggle to find a parking space, even in the surrounding streets. While walking towards the pub entrance there is a large group gathered outside having a smoke. It is not until I am closer that I notice their attire, the clean white shirts accompanied by the black ties. I receive a few nods as I approach the entrance and someone opens the door for me.

"Oh thanks."

"No problem."

I look in to see Buster, as usual, by the bar. He is also suited up and hugging people. Then it hits me. Ritchie's funeral

"Shit"

As I walk towards him, he looks pale and withdrawn and appears to have aged overnight. He turns to see me and stalls. For a split second his delayed reaction makes me think he knows everything and is about to order me out of the pub. He brushes the people near him to the side and leans in pulling me forward and embracing me with his huge arms.

"Grab a seat son." He says releasing me. "I'm getting a round in." He says with a shaky voice and tears in his eyes.

I turn to see a few tables pushed together and a row of faces all suited up staring back at me. Ginge has his back to me and Larnio gives him a nudge to get his attention. He looks over and smiles at me.

"Brody" He stands up and hugs me. "Come on, move up and give him a seat." He ushers me to a seat near him and everyone moves around the tables to accommodate me. I nod in acknowledgement.

Buster comes from behind to place a full tray of pints on the table and starts passing them around.

"Drink up boys."

Ginge passes one to me and holds his pint towards me.

"For Ritchie" He nods.

Our glasses clink together and I take a sip and place the pint in front of me. I do not intend to drink it. I sit quietly as I listen to the funny stories about Ritchie from everyone around the table. Even some of the bad bullying things that he did to people have some added humour to them. I do not see the funny side but I do appreciate the effort of them trying to make him sound more human than the horrible prick that he was.

"Was Ryan allowed out for it?" I ask.

"Yeah he was cuffed to a screw the whole time."

"That must have been really tough having to go straight back to Perth after that."

"He didn't appear to be as upset as I thought he would, but I guess he was putting on a front as he knows a lot of eyes were on him. He did mention that he shouldn't be in long as there is apparently a video of the police beating him, so when that surfaces it will be a bargaining tool for the charges being dropped." Ginge says locking his eyes on me.

Someone from across the table shouts to for his attention and a smug look comes across his face before he turns away from me.

After a while, it starts to look obvious that I am still sipping the same flat pint that Buster had bought me earlier, so after the same monotonous stories about Ritchie are doing the rounds for the second time, I decide it is time to leave. I slide the pint to the middle of the table and stand up from my seat.

"You off" Ginge looks up at me.

"Yeah I have a few things to do."

I keep eye contact with him as I step back from the table.

"Hold on Brody" He stands up and we both take a few steps away, out of earshot from the table.

"Stay for another drink."

"No I can't."

"Come on, I know you two never seen eye to eye, but it is his funeral. Come on, one more drink...Then can talk."

"No I can't. I need to go" I shake my head.

"There's a big game Saturday, you up for it?"

"I shake my head again "It's not for me anymore Rodney, its over."

"What do you mean, it's over?"

"I mean I'm not the person you thought I was."

"You're blood, that's all that matters."

"I'm sorry."

"Never mind sorry, come and have a drink."

I take a few short steps backwards "I need to go."

I turn to face the door and keep walking. When I reach my hand out to open the door, I curiously turn back to see that he is still in the same spot watching me. I head outside and continue towards my car.

"Brody" I turn back to see Ginge outside the pub, walking in my direction. "Hold up." He shouts.

"That was Jamie in those woods wasn't it?" I say as he approaches.

"You know it was."

"You fucking arsehole, that whole set up was for me wasn't it...every little fucking detail"

"Brody, you have no idea. Don't feel bad, the guy was a murderer, he has stabbed and tortured innocent people, he was a horrible human being."

"I'm assuming it was Joe that made the video, is it him that put it through Leanna's letter-box?"

"Does it matter who did it?"

"I guess not. But I would like to know why?"

"Oh I think you know why. You said it yourself. You are not the person I think you are. Well, I know exactly who you are. I have known since that first day you walked back into our lives. Do you remember?

"Of course"

"I asked you to come with me to find the witnesses to Busters assault. I pretended to struggle with them. It was a test to see how far you would go. When you stepped out of your car and knocked out those two idiots, I knew I had you."

"You had me?"

"Oh yeah" He nods confidently

"What about Ritchie, Did you own him too?"

He looks at me confused. "Ritchie lost his way. I spent thousands on him, I paid for him to go to a top rehab clinic three fucking times to sort himself out, do you know how he repaid me?...by walking out of there and stepping straight into the nearest dealers house for a hit."

"Did you know he was an informant?"

"Of course I knew, but he could only inform on the things he knew about, and the things he knew about were the things that I wanted the coppers to know."

"Who else knows about me, does Buster know?"

"Only me, and my close associate, obviously. They informed me the second your name flagged up"

"Why didn't you say anything back then?"

"I wasn't sure what your intentions were, but when you turned up at my door that day, I knew exactly why you were there."

"So why did Buster let you take over and not Ryan, why did he give you his contacts?"

Ginge lets out a laugh "Buster's contacts" He laughs again.

"You really don't have a clue do you? Did you actually think Buster woke up one morning and said, here you go son, I've written down some phone numbers, give them a call, they will lay you on a few keys of coke" Ginge makes a face.

"Think about it Brody, I have been locked up in prisons up and down the country since I was sixteen years old. All those arrests for soccer violence, they had me banged up in a cell with some of the hardest faces in some of the toughest prisons. Back then, when shipments of drugs came into the country, it would go from dealer to dealer and it would be cut it so much, that by the time it reached the streets in Dundee, someone would be lucky if there was ten percent cocaine in it. I started bringing it in from my source and word got around. The bigger the load that I moved, the more customers I could create. You have to understand though. I did not go out and push this. The dealers come to me. It was like the old saying, you don't sell drugs, drugs sell themselves, but you already know all about that don't you Brody?" He grins.

"Whenever someone from outside tried to muscle in, all it took was a little phone call from a certain individual down south and they backed off. All I had to worry about was locals, but with Buster and Ryan fronting for me, they took care of all that. Everybody looks at them with their reputations, in and out of jail for all their stupid shit they find themselves involved in, but no one has ever took a step back and looked at the bigger picture, I mean, come on, how the fuck would they have ever been capable of doing what I do without getting caught? They cannot even walk down the street without having the finger pointed at them for every crime that happens. And as for the notion that Ryan runs it all from his cell, I mean, what the fuck do they think this is, Columbia."

"But I've collected debts for him for what goes on in there."

"Yeah, but you know they are not Ryan's drugs, he's not bringing them in, he's not selling them, they are going to get those drugs in there one way or another, whether he likes it or not. All he is doing is taking a cut. If those fucking screws are taking a cut, why shouldn't Ryan?"

"Yeah he told me all this when I was inside. I always thought there was more to it."

"The screws let Ryan do what he wants, the attention is on him and it looks like he is running the show, it's a smokescreen, just like with me. They think they have me all figured out, the Saturday catwalk thug who won't grow up." Ginge smiles at me. "Oh yeah, I have read the file. I am apparently more interested in the label on my jacket and the spot of blood on my trainers. They see me on my mobile phones sorting out meets with other crews but truthfully, I only show up to those games to keep those fuckers on their toes. Ten years ago, soccer casuals were dead and buried in Scotland. I brought it all back and it was not for the thrill of fighting, or the labels, or the reputation of being top boy or any of that other shit that goes along with it. Everyone I know bought into it, from close friends to rival firms...including you." He smiles.

"I noticed your swagger when you left the pub that day to go to your first game, the crew walking behind you, you were buzzing. Your fellow Uniforms who were nearby in their riot van, I am guessing they were buzzing too. Sitting there tooled up with their batons and C.S. Gas, patiently waiting on something to kick off so they can unleash some of their built up aggression. I have given those sadistic fuckers something to look forward to every week. Do you know most of them specifically put in for the football shift and deep down you know they should be thanking me for the overtime. I brought the scene back from the dead for my own personal interest, a diversion. I gained many acquaintances through the game but it also gave me the opportunity to weed out the untrustworthy ones. From how they handled them-selves in a group, to how they acted in a confrontation, even to what they talked about when they had a few drinks on them. I studied them, I never judged them but if they did not fit, they were out and it helped me keep a tight crew. As you have noticed, I have been more than happy to live in Ryan's shadow and this has worked perfectly to keep the attention from me. If you study a business course, they'll teach you that a business has a front, well Ryan and Buster are my front, their reputation and layout was already there, I just took it to another level."

"So you manipulated them?"

"Don't be so naïve Brody, If you mean, did I encourage their behaviour, of course I fucking did, and standing there giving me that judgmental look is pretty fucking hypocritical if you think about the position you are in right now, anyway you know they would be in and out of prison all from their own doing. I just happen to step up and use them to my advantage."

"Like the Donaldson's."

"Exactly, I could have had them wiped out a long time ago but they are good for business. Letting them run around selling their shit drugs keeps the attention from me. They swagger about informing everyone that they have the top Glasgow firms behind them, they do not know the half of it. I've lost count of the number of times those top firms have asked me to team up with them."

A loud commotion from outside the pub distracts us, but when we turn and look, it is only a few people having a carry on. It gives me a few seconds to think.

"I'm now wondering why you're telling me all of this, well, with you knowing that I am..."

"...Truthfully, it's because of Ryan."

"Ryan?"

"Yeah" He nods. "Well you know, Buster, he will always be Buster, but with Ryan...Well, since Mollie came along I've seen a change in him, he doesn't have it anymore. The last few years I have let him front things, only just, so that he still feels involved."

"What about the armed robbery?"

Ginge laughs "Oh that was all hm. He came out of prison one time and he had this mad idea. Proper old school stuff, he was determined to go through with it, he had it all worked out. I oversaw it and he assured me that he was not going to be taking part but come on, its Ryan. I knew he would not be able resist getting involved. I set up the diversion to make sure they had a clean getaway."

"What about Ritchie, with the phone?"

"Ritchie never knew anything about the robbery, if he had, they would have been arrested before they got anywhere near that building. He thought he was texting the rival firm to let them know we were on the way for the meet. He was supposed to ditch the phone once he sent the text but he could not even do that, I guess he thought he could sell it and make some cash. He did have a habit to feed." Ginge shrugs and sadness comes over his face as he turns away in deep thought.

"I'm assuming I'm the one they want now?" He turns back sharp to face me.

I nod.

"I can live with that, I'll take my chances and figure it out. I just need them to back off Ryan. I do not want him in this life anymore. You have seen how they treat him, if they keep coming for him, he is going to snap one day and take a few of those fuckers out, and I cannot have Davie and Little Mollie growing up without a father. He needs to break that cycle."

"So where do we go from here?"

"Well that's up to you Brody. I understand you have a loyalty to your job but just like my loyalty to Ryan in protecting him, you have a loyalty to your family, your blood. You have wanted to be a copper since you were knee high, I still remember you running around with your toy gun and badge trying to arrest everybody, putting your plastic cuffs on them and saying you were taking them to jail. Well, that is until you did it to Buster and he snapped them in half and threw them away."

We both smile "I remember that" I shake my head.

"Brody I know you've had this image of what it would be like to be in the police but now you've seen the flip side of what they are all about, they are criminals just like me, if any-thing, they are worse... You want to be a copper, be a real copper."

"What do you mean?"

"I've noticed you take a liking to the expensive clothes, that flashy car." He nods at my car parked up ahead "The drugs, Tanya"

"Yeah, it's strange how all the bad things feel good."

"That doesn't have to stop."

"I'm not really sure where this is going."

"What I'm saying is, all that doesn't have to stop just because you're a police officer, it doesn't mean that you can't still work for me...You can be a copper with character." He smiles. "That day at your first game, who do you think I was describing when I picked out those characterless people in the crowd? They were all you Brody. In little under a year, I have manipulated you to become you. I have watched you develop into your own character. It's up to you where you go from here though, back to your cosy quiet life with Leanna, no drugs, no violence, no Tanya at your beck and call, and back to wearing your characterless clothes so that you fit in, oh and your car." He shakes his head..."The only time you will come close to a car like that is when you're pulling one over."

"So you're asking me to be a corrupt officer?"

"Brody, you've had first-hand experience of how they treat people and how they fuck people over, every one of them is corrupt, they are sneaky, conniving and devious and they would stab you in the back any chance they got. There is not an ounce of loyalty between them. Every one of my crew has the label of a crook, but if I asked any one of them, they would kill someone for me without question. Think about this, why have the ones that beat you in the cell that day not been charged?" Ginge puts the palms of his hands out and gestures with a smug look. "...Exactly."

"Buster or Ryan would never accept it, me being a police officer."

"They will if they think I was in on it from the start, I'll explain that it was my idea."

"So how does this work? Do I get paid from you?"

"You know how I work Brody, it is all favours" He winks.

"What about you? You're willing to go to all these lengths to keep living this lifestyle, I've seen the kind of money that you pull in, why don't you put it all into a legitimate business, declare it, go travel the world, something other than this."

"I do have a legitimate business...Why do you think we get away with so much in the Claver? Technically my Mother owns it, but she bought it with my money."

"Your mother, I've never heard any of you mention her, not even once when we were growing up."

"Yeah well, I asked her to front it for me. I thought she owed me that much for walking out on us. I also own part of a few other businesses, not on paper you understand. I'm more of a silent unknown partner."

"Why don't you sell up and move on?"

Ginge laughs "Move on. Move on to where?"

I shrug.

"Seriously, could you actually see me sitting on a beach somewhere watching the world go by? Look at the colour of my hair. I would either melt in the heat or die of boredom."

"Don't you ever think about settling down and having kids?"

"Is that what you see with you and Leanna?...while she's changing nappies you are back here snorting coke out of Tanya's arsehole"

I nod and smile "Fair enough."

"Oh there are a couple of long haired ginger troublemakers running about, but they're well taken care of. I've always said from day one, if they ever need anything, I'm here."

"Don't you think they need a father?"

"Oh they've got fathers, whether they know it's their real father is down to their mothers. I don't have a problem with that, when the kids get older and what to come see me, I'm cool with that, my door will be open."

"That's some attitude. I'm sure Buster will be proud."

"Fuck Buster, and fuck anyone that has a problem with it." Ginge turns serious. "Listen, no-body is ever going to tell me how to live my life, maybe it isn't the way society expects me to live, but that doesn't mean it's not right. I enjoy the dealings that come my way, like when you came along, it was fun, it was a challenge, and it kept me on my toes."

My phone starts to ring. I take it from my pocket and look at the screen. 'Withheld number' Ginge glances at it and looks at me.

"I guess you have a decision to make" He turns and walks slowly back to the pub.

I put the phone back in my pocket and let it ring out. I get back in my car and make a U-turn in the street. As I pass the pub, Ginge is still outside, surrounded by the sympathetic mourners. In his trademark wide stance, he looks at me and we both nod in acknowledgement.

Epilogue

The two young girls giggle with each other as they skip through the park. Watched from every angle, they have no idea that they been set up as bait. The parents of one of them had read messages on her phone some weeks before and there was a cause for concern. After contacting the Police, they forwarded them to The Command Unit for paedophiles. Brody had been in The Unit for nearly six months and had already been proving his worth as a Detective. In most cases, The Unit would have gained outside access to the child's phone and taken over communication with the suspect, but with the parents' permission, they let her resume the chat while they monitored it closely, without her knowledge. Due to the gradual process of the messages, they knew they were dealing with a professional predator.

With the meet confirmed, the Detective Sergeant had placed Brody in charge, his military background had shown through in the specific details of his planning and he had split The Unit into several teams covering the whole area. On the day of the meet, the Detective Sergeant had informed Brody that the Detective Superintendent had decided to oversee the whole set up. The whole operation was now out of his hands. If the operation were a success, the Superintendent would take the credit, if it fell through, it would fall on Brody. Brody did not hold his sergeant accountable for the intrusion though, as he knew exactly where the order had come from, it was Detective Inspector Whyte and Detective Sergeant Drummond. They were trying desperately to sabotage his career. Both had been in line for a promotion on the back of the McNaughton case if it were successful, but after Brody disclosed his final report, it did not go down too well. He had exposed every officer that he encountered during his time undercover; the report also contained video footage of his Brother Ryan, taunted and beat up in from of his children. There were dates and times of his repeated requests to transfer from the case, thus due to his vulnerability after an extensive drug-habit had developed through his time undercover and felt pressured from his superior officers to continue with the case. Brody had cunningly used the report to his advantage to gain his promised fast track to a Detective position on the force. The Paedophile Unit was the obvious choice of department that would have been justified and accepted by his family. Since his return to work, Brody had been regularly gaining a number of acquaintances in several other departments of the force, most of them had been the result of tip offs from Ginge and his contacts.

Moments before the girls reach the fenced off play area they are confronted by a large husky type dog. The dog's owner, a man in his early thirties approaches them, he explains that the dog is harmless and will not hurt them. He commands it to stay and the dog obediently stops and sits down. The owner fixes the lead to the dog's collar and after some reassurance, the owner persuades the girls to pet the dog. The girls then move on to the play area and close the gate behind them. There is another man in the play area, he is in his mid-twenties and is pushing an infant child on the baby swing. The two girls go straight to the climbing frame and one of them takes out their phone and sends a text to confirm that they are 'here.' The Unit also receives the message and they wait intently on a reply. As the girls chat intently between themselves, they occasionally scour the park looking for their new 'friend.' A peculiar old man stares at them and circles the play area but appears to keep his focus on the two girls. They move away from the climbing frame towards a set of swings nearer the young man with the infant. The young man overhears them mention the old man staring at them so he turns to face him and stares him down. At this, the old man continues on his way. None of this goes unnoticed by The Unit, as each team discuss their options of apprehending the old man. With no contact made towards the girls, The Chief Inspector allocates Team B to keep surveillance on the old man. The girls continue playing on the swing and chatting to the young man with the infant. The man with the Husky dog, who had left the vicinity of the play area has now returned and makes eye contact with the girls and smiles to them. The old man has come to rest on a bench, a short distance from the play area and occasionally glances around as though checking out the rest of the park. With Team B specifically observing the old man, the rest of The Unit's attention is moving between the now, suspect with the Husky, and a third person, another young male, in his early twenties, who has appeared up the hill at the top entrance and is hovering between the trees while overlooking the whole park. A group of noisy teenagers who were near the far end of the park, have now made their way closer to the play area. With their animated actions, the distraction could agitate their suspect into avoiding contact, and each member of The Unit is watching anxiously. The suspect with the Husky starts to make his way towards the top exit at the same time the young male in the trees has moved closer to the play area, while still watching all around him. Team C, Brody's team, has the command to detain the suspect with the Husky on exit of the park. The teenagers have become more boisterous and as they come closer to the old man on the bench, he gets up and walks off in the direction of the side entrance to the park. Team B receives the command to detain the old man on exit. The young man on the hill checks his phone and looks over the play area. Brody's Team is to abort the order of detaining the man with the Husky and move in on the young suspect.

"He doesn't fit the profile. He's just waiting on someone."

"That's the fifth time he's checked his phone, he's trying too hard to look like he's waiting on someone" The Chief Inspector says over the receiver.

"Or maybe he really is just waiting on someone."

"Are you undermining me? I gave the order to move in."

Brody can sense this is a fix up to sabotage his operation. He hesitates.

Team B apprehends the old man upon his exit of the side gate. The young man on the hill overlooking the park has witnessed the scene. He about turns and heads towards the top exit.

"He's been spooked. He knows we are onto him. Team C, move in now" The Chief Inspector announces.

Brody hesitates again "Team A. Can you deal with it?" He requests.

"Sorry Brody, our hands are tied.

"Detective Buchanan, I gave you the order."

"Fuck, fuck, fuck." Brody says as he runs from his post.

"Team C what is your position?"

Brody hears him but refuses to answer.

"I repeat. Team C, what is your position."

"The girls are gone. REPEAT!" Brody shouts. "THE GIRLS ARE GONE, IN PURSUIT." Brody says in between breaths as he sprints around the perimeter of the park.

He reaches the main road and slows his pace to a light jog and then to a fast walk so that he can catch his breath.

"All Teams, I have them in sight. They are now on the main road a hundred yards from the East exit. They are accompanied by a young man and infant child."

"Team B is now mobile."

"Team B you are in sight, hold back. They are approaching a side street. It is a no through road." Brody looks up the main road and signals to them. They see him and pull in to await his instructions to block the road. Brody reaches the Side Street and edges around a surrounding wall. He watches the young man place the infant into the car seat. He opens the back door of the car and smiles to the two girls as they get in the car. Brody has a mixed surge of anger and anxious excitement at the thought of arresting the suspect. He can also sense the fear that those girls' parents would have if they could see the scene before him. The car pulls out from the parking space and Brody gives the signal to Team B as he steps out into the middle of the road from behind a parked van. He pulls out his I.D. badge and holds it in front of him. A flashing blue light of Team B's vehicle blocks the entrance to the side street.

Brody arrives back at the station and although a commendation is in order, he takes note of the Chief Inspector standing at the far end of the office scowling at him. He is the epitome of Ginge's characterless description, even down to his dull car that has never touched over thirty miles per hour.

"I'm guessing a high five is out of the question." Brody comments to his team.

He knows that Whyte and Drummond are pulling the Chief Inspectors strings, and it is only a matter of time before they set him up for a massive fail. He looks down at his phone to see a missed call from an unknown number. He knows it will be Ginge. He walks to a secluded part of the building before returning the call.

"How is my numero uno employee?"

"I'm doing fine, settling in well actually."

"That's good. I received a message that you called the Claver looking for me."

"Yeah, I have some information regarding your posh bird."

"Rachel? I'm listening."

"Detective Constable O'Neil."

"You're shitting me? A copper, I wondered why she was so keen on using those handcuffs." Ginge lets out an awkward laugh. He is shocked but secretly gutted.

"There's more."

"I'm still listening."

"Junkie Jamie" The name still haunts Brody whenever it comes up "He has a brother."

"Shane."

"That's right. He's been wanted for questioning in a suspicious death from over ten years ago."

"What about him?"

"His passport has been flagged up on arrival from Spain. Officers weren't quick enough to detain him."

"Very interesting, good work Brody."

Printed in Great
Britain
by Amazon